broken Wings

What Reviewers Say About Bold Strokes Authors

KIM BALDWIN

"'A riveting novel of suspense' seems to be a very overworked phrase. However, it is extremely apt when discussing Kim Baldwin's [*Hunter's Pursuit*]. An exciting page turner [features] Katarzyna Demetrious, a bounty hunter…with a million dollar price on her head. Look for this excellent novel of suspense…" – **R. Lynne Watson**, *MegaScene*

"*Force of Nature* is an exciting and substantial reading experience which will long remain with the reader. Likeable characters with plausible problems and concerns, imaginative settings, engrossing events, and a well-tailored writing style all contribute to an exceptional novel. Baldwin's characterization is acutely and meticulously circumscribed and expansive." – **Arlene Germain**, reviewer for the *Lambda Book Report* and the *Midwest Book Review*

RONICA BLACK

"Black juggles the assorted elements of her first book, [*In Too Deep*], with assured pacing and estimable panache…[including]…the relative depth—for genre fiction—of the central characters: Erin, the married-but-separated detective who comes to her lesbian senses; loner Patricia, the policewoman-mentor who finds herself falling for Erin; and sultry club owner Elizabeth, the sexually predatory suspect who discards women like Kleenex…until she meets Erin." – **Richard Labonte**, *Book Marks, Q Syndicate, 2005*

"Black's characterization is skillful, and the sexual chemistry surrounding the three major characters is palpable and definitely hot-hot-hot. If you're looking for a more traditional murder mystery, *In Too Deep* might not be entirely your cup of Earl. On the other hand, if you're looking for a solid read with ample amounts of eroticism and a red herring or two, you're sure to find *In Too Deep* a satisfying read." – **Lynne Jamneck**, *L-Word.com Literature*

ROSE BEECHAM

"…her characters seem fully capable of walking away from the particulars of whodunit and engaging the reader in other aspects of their lives." – *Lambda Book Report*

Rose Beecham (cont)

"When Jennifer Fulton writes mysteries, she writes them as Rose Beecham. And since Jennifer Fulton is a very fine writer, you might expect that Rose Beecham is a fine writer too. You're right… On the way to a remarkable, and thoroughly convincing climax, Beecham creates believable characters in compelling situations, with enough humor to provide effective counterpoint to the work of detecting." – *Bay Area Reporter*

Gun Brooke

"*Course of Action* is a romance…populated with a host of captivating and amiable characters. The glimpses into the lifestyles of the rich and beautiful people are rather like guilty pleasures... a most satisfying and entertaining reading experience." – **Arlene Germain**, reviewer for the *Lambda Book Report* and the *Midwest Book Review*

"*Protector of the Realm* has it all; sabotage, corruption, erotic love and exhilarating space fights. Gun Brooke's second novel is forceful with a winning combination of solid characters and a brilliant plot." – **Kathi Isserman**, *JustAboutWrite*

Jane Fletcher

"*The Walls of Westernfort* is not only a highly engaging and fast-paced adventure novel, it provides the reader with an interesting framework for examining the same questions of loyalty, faith, family and love that [the characters] must face." – **M. J. Lowe**, *Midwest Book Review*

Lee Lynch

"There's a heady sense of '60s back-to-the-land communal idealism and '70s woman-power feminism (with hints of lesbian separatism) to this spirited novel—even though it's set in contemporary rural Oregon. Partners Donny (she's black and blue-collar) and Chick (she's plus-sized and motherly) are both in their 50s, owners of the dyke-centric Natural Woman Foods store, a homey nexus for *Sweet Creek*'s expansive cast of characters.…Lynch, with a dozen novels to her credit dating back to the early days of Naiad Press, has earned her stripes as a writerly elder. She was contributing stories to the lesbian magazine *The Ladder* four decades ago. But this latest is sublimely in tune with the times." – **Richard Labonte**, *Book Marks, Q Syndicate, 2005*

Radclyffe

"...well-honed storytelling skills...solid prose and sure-handedness of the narrative..." – **Elizabeth Flynn**, *Lambda Book Report*

"...well-plotted...lovely romance...I couldn't turn the pages fast enough!" – **Ann Bannon**, author of *The Beebo Brinker Chronicles*

Ali Vali

"Rich in character portrayal, *The Devil Inside* by Ali Vali is an unusual, unpredictable, and thought-provoking love story that will have the reader questioning the definition of right and wrong long after she finishes the book....*The Devil Inside*'s strength is that it is unlike most romance novels. Nothing about the story and its characters is conventional. We do not know what the future holds for Emma and Cain, but Vali tempts us with every word so we want to find out. I am very much looking forward to the sequel The Devil Unleashed." – **Kathi Isserman**, *JustAboutWrite*

broken Wings

by

L-J Baker

2006

BROKEN WINGS

ISBN 1-933110-55-4
This Trade Paperback Is Published By
Bold Strokes Books, Inc.,
New York, USA

First Edition, September 2006

Credits
Editors: Cindy Cresap and J. Barre Greystone
Production Design: J. Barre Greystone
Cover Graphic: Sheri (graphicartist2020@hotmail.com)

Acknowledgments

This really is a better novel thanks to Cindy. Against my expectations, she proved that editing (or, perhaps more accurately, that working with an editor with a terrific sense of humour) can be enjoyable as well as educational. Good on yer, mate. Dearest B knows how much she has herself to thank for this story becoming a book that she can clip me around the ear with as she says *I told you so*. Many thanks, too, to Radclyffe and the team at Bold Strokes Books (especially Andy) for such a supportive environment. Sheri, mate, your cover for this book is sweet as.

DEDICATION

For B.
Always and all ways.

Chapter One

Rye Woods ignored the angry shouts as she steered her flying broom down into the turning lane. She was going to be late. Holly would not be happy. Rye had made a serious mistake in risking the Rootway in rush hour traffic. Flying carpets and brooms jockeyed for every inch forward in lanes of all heights. She bumped the front of her broom handle as she squeezed in behind a large delivery carpet. Ahead, the traffic inching above the bridge across to the Eastside looked no better.

"Shit."

Her broom spluttered, lost power, and dropped. She sprawled on the ground with the broom tangled between her legs. Scurrying pedestrians barely spared her a look. Low-flying traffic shouted at her to get out of the way. Rye grabbed her broom and dodged to the side of the flyway.

She shook her broom. The bristles quivered. She kicked it. The magic spluttered, coughed, and died.

"Fey."

Rye glanced up at the sundial on the side of the high-rise department store tree. She had fifty minutes before the school art competition started. There was no way she could get back to the apartment to change if she were to get to the school on time. She shouldered her broom and began to walk.

She clumped along in her work boots and dirty, ragged pants. She wished she had the money to spare for a taxi. She could imagine only too well Holly's fury at her for turning up fresh from the building site. Rye broke into a jog and spared a wistful thought for those years before Holly hit adolescence. A big sister who worked as a labourer and had no fashion sense had not been a problem then.

Rye jostled her way through the thick stream of pedestrians on the bridge when the first fat spots of rain fell on her shoulders. That was all she needed.

Firefly green lights highlighted the imposing entrance to the school even though it was not yet dark. Rye was panting when she paused near one of the large gateposts. She wiped the mingled rain and sweat from her face. Late model carpets with their comfortable interiors brightly lit flew past her and into the parking lot. This looked like a big deal not only for Holly. All the trepidation and discomfort Rye felt at entering the upmarket school for parent-teacher conferences returned in full measure.

Rye cast a despairing look down at herself. She was damned if she went in and damned if she went home. She swore to herself and trudged into the school grounds.

A well-dressed sprite couple, with their feathery antennae bent under the protection of a shared umbrella, dashed past Rye to the dryness of the front foyer. Rye glimpsed jewellery and good tailoring.

"Good evening," a young pixie man at the door said. His scalp ridges looked relaxed and non-threatening, and the mobile tip of his long, pointed nose barely twitched, but he ever so politely barred her entry.

"Hi," Rye said. "Lousy night for it, isn't it?"

She dug in her jacket pocket for her invitation. The pixie's fixed smile faltered and the tip of his nose drooped as he accepted the damp piece of cardboard.

"Ms. Woods," he said. "Welcome to Oak Heights High School for Young Ladies. Please go on through. Sorrel will give you a catalogue. Enjoy the exhibition."

"Thanks. Where's the bathroom?"

As Rye opened the door to the ladies' room, a woman of indeterminate species, with the fern-like antennae of a sprite sticking out of a hairless brownie head, exited in a billow of expensive perfume. On seeing Rye, her antennae bristled erect and her white, angular features strained in a look of haughty disapproval. Rye's heart sank further. This was going to be every bit as bad as she had feared.

Every quarter, when she received the bill for Holly's tuition, Rye questioned her decision to send her sister here rather than to the local municipal school. Then she would read about another kid knifed in the playground, an arson attack, or a teacher beaten up, and she would empty out her pitiful savings yet again.

The mirror above the hand basins reflected back a flush-faced Rye with her short blue-black hair plastered to her head. She peeled off her wet jacket and draped it on a basin. Her shirt was damp from rain seeping through her jacket. Beneath it, her tight T-shirt clung uncomfortably to her sweaty skin.

"Crap."

Rye risked removing her baggy shirt to drape it over the heated hand dryer. The contours of her folded wings would show incriminating lumps down her back to anyone who came in. Not that she could imagine any of these snooty women thinking that their daughters shared a class with so undesirable an individual as an illegal alien, let alone a fairy. Although she and Holly were not as hairy as bogles, and Rye's upper body was more powerfully built than any frail little brownie, the sisters could pass as having the mixed blood of those two species as long as Rye hid her wings. It helped that there were so few fairies who lived outside Fairyland. Most people simply didn't expect to see members of that species. Still, Rye kept her back to the wall.

She hit the button to start the hot air blowing through her shirt and grabbed some paper towels. She vigorously rubbed her hair to get the worst of the wet from it.

When Rye paused to check her progress in the mirror, she saw that her spiky-haired reflection was not alone. A woman stood bent toward the mirror touching up her lipstick. Her lithe, curvaceous form belonged to a nymph. Green hair, shoulder-length and glossy, identified her as a tree nymph, though her skin was the pale of fine-grained maple wood rather than the reddish-browns more common to dryads. Too young to be the mother of a teenager, she must be one of the teachers. Her willowy figure showed to magnificent advantage in an elegantly simple, short grey dress. Rye's gaze curved along her back, around her very pat-able bum, and down the most amazing pair of legs. Something that had lain dormant inside Rye for many years stirred.

Rye's gaze flicked up to the mirror. The dryad stared at Rye's reflection with eyes the rich, deep brown of bark. Her beautiful face was a perfect match for her body. She made eye contact with Rye's image and smiled. Rye blushed. She quickly looked away and was surprised to find herself holding damp paper towels.

"It's raining quite heavily now, isn't it?" the woman said.

"Um. Yeah." Rye hastily thrust the paper towels in the rubbish bin and yanked her shirt from the dryer. "I...um, I'm sorry. You can use it."

Rye kept her back to the wall as she tugged on her shirt under the reflected brown gaze. She had never felt more self-conscious in a wet, tight T-shirt.

The dryad returned her cosmetics to her purse.

"Don't worry, you're not late," she said. "The judging hasn't started yet."

"Right. Good. Thanks."

The woman smiled and walked out leaving behind a subtle hint of musky perfume and the memory of gently swaying hips.

Rye blew out a breath and shoved her shirt tail into her pants. If teachers looked like that, she could not see why any kid complained about school. Although, Holly would be looking at the male teachers, not the females.

Holly. Rye grimaced at her image as she hurriedly finger-combed her damp hair. Holly was going to kill her.

"Fey," Rye said to her reflection.

In the foyer, a red sprite woman with perky antennae offered Rye the choice of three different teas, lemon water, or non-alcoholic dew. Rye nursed a cup of manuka tea and wandered into the hall. Conversation hummed. Rows of stands held paintings, sculptures, pots, and bits of cloth. Hundreds of well-dressed people stood around talking to each other or peering at the exhibits. Rye frowned at the catalogue. She couldn't find Holly's name. The kid's thing had to be here somewhere, as, indeed, did Holly herself.

Rye drifted down a row of exhibits. She avoided eye contact by devoting her attention to the works of art. Her gaze slipped across vivid daubs of paint, tortured lumps of glazed clay, and eye-bleedingly bright fabrics. She was arrested by a strange collection of things that looked like small purple toilet brushes and tampons. Rye blinked and stared. For the life of her, she couldn't begin to imagine what it was supposed to be. Offering little help, the catalogue merely listed it as *entropy too* by Borealis Woodbine.

entropy too? What, in the name of the Almighty King and Queen of the Fey, was that supposed to mean? It was times like this that Rye most keenly felt her own lack of education. She was prepared to bet that Borealis Woodbine was some pimply sixteen-year-old who rode a late-model broom and who received more in pocket money than Rye did working eight hours a day with a hammer and chisel.

Rye shook her head and turned her frown from *entropy too*. Her quick glance around the hall failed to locate Holly's mop of curly blue-black hair amongst the crowd of antennae, hats, bald heads, and hair of every colour.

"Excuse us." A sylph, so wispy and ethereal that only a pair of large, limpid dark green eyes set her apart from a shadow cast upon the surface of a pond, smiled at Rye. "I'm terribly sorry to interrupt, but we'd like to judge this piece."

"Oh. Um. Sorry," Rye said.

Rye stepped away. In passing, her gaze snagged on the gorgeous woman from the bathroom standing beside the sylph. She smiled at Rye. Rye couldn't help noticing how attractively she filled the front of her dress. Very nice. Much more pleasant to look at than high school art.

"Rye!" Holly squeezed her slender, broad-shouldered body through the throng. Her eyes widened toward horror and her voice dropped to an angry whisper. "You didn't change. I picked those clothes out specially for you. Everyone is staring. Earth, eat me whole."

"Look, I'm sorry," Rye said. "I didn't have time. My broom packed in again. I had to run most of the way from work."

"This is important."

"Yeah, I know. I'm here, aren't I?"

Holly bristled belligerence. "I'm living death."

"I'll go and stand in a dark corner. No one will have to know that I'm with you. Okay?"

Rye found a row of chairs against the wall. She dropped down beside an elderly pixie man. His long nose drooped with age and his scalp ridges looked flattened and worn as if eroded by a lifetime of having a nervous claw rubbed across them.

"You must be a sculptor," he said. "My grandson is very good at—oh. I suppose, since you're one of the judges, that I'd better not try to influence you, eh?" He smiled.

Rye merely nodded. If people chose to misinterpret her scruffy appearance as being an artist, then she didn't have to disabuse them of the idea. Perhaps a generous interpretation of hollowing out trees to make high-density apartments could sit at the other end of the same scale as whittling away at a lump of wood to make something that no one was quite sure what it was.

After about half an hour or so, Holly flopped in the chair beside Rye.

"Did you win?" Rye asked.

"Dunno. They're going to announce the prizes soon. I'm glad you're here, okay?"

"Okay."

Holly leaped up and disappeared in the crowd. Rye grinned to herself.

A blue-haired sprite man who held his antennae stiffly upright climbed onto the stage at the front of the hall and announced the commencement of the prize-giving. The parents drained from the display rows to crowd the stage. Although she couldn't see past the pack of spectators, Rye remained seated through the inevitable speeches. When they finally got to the prizes, she stood. Dotted amongst the teachers were some weirdly dressed people who must be the professional artist guest judges, including the wispy sylph and the beautiful dryad. Rye got a much better view of the latter when she stood to present one of the prizes. Rye thought she must be a model rather than a flaky artist. Rye had not seen a more attractive, desirable woman, even on power tool calendars.

"Holly Woods," the dryad said.

Rye jolted into applause. Holly climbed up the steps to accept the certificate. Rye had no idea what Holly had won, or what for. To her horror, she'd been engrossed in checking out the pretty woman rather than listening to the announcement. But that didn't stop her from being the proudest person in the hall.

Holly stood out the remainder of the ceremony with the other prize winners. When it ended, she wormed her way back to Rye. It wasn't so long ago that Rye would've hugged and kissed her. She still wanted to, but knew Holly would find it embarrassing. Rye settled for a grin and patting Holly's young, wingless back.

"Congratulations," Rye said. "Can I see?"

Holly handed her the certificate. It said that she won first prize in the fabric section for something called *Dazzle*. Holly offered Rye the envelope containing the prize money of fifty pieces.

"That's yours," Rye said.

Holly shrugged. "Everything you earn goes toward us."

"That's different. Keep it. Then I don't have to spend good money on that smelly stuff you keep in the bathroom."

Holly screwed her face up and looked like she remembered where they were just before she stuck her tongue out. Rye grinned.

Friends drew Holly away. Rye searched the catalogue until she located *Dazzle* by Holly Woods. Row 5, stand 16.

Rye eased her way through the crowd. Holly stood beside her entry deep in animated conversation with a group of her friends and their parents. Rye stopped a discreet distance away. Holly's prize-winning creation looked like a pair of luridly coloured placemats.

Holly looked happy and, judging by the number of her friends, was popular. It was times like this that Rye knew scraping every piece to pay for a good education for Holly was worth it. Holly wasn't going to end up sweating her guts out—come rain, snow, or sweltering sun—at some menial job. Just what she did plan to do for a career, though, she hadn't yet discussed with Rye. That was something they probably needed to talk about soon. If Holly wanted to go to university, Rye would have to start looking for a third job. It had been Rye's plan to have saved enough for that by this time, but it just hadn't worked out that way. Raising a child took every piece she earned. With any luck, Rye would have some qualifications from her night courses in a year or two and be able to take a better paying job.

Seeing that Holly was in no immediate danger of being left alone, Rye wandered out into the foyer. The night looked shiny and wet. It was going to be a cold, damp walk home unless, by some miracle, her broom decided to start working again.

Rye sat on the side of a plant trough and sighed. The last time her broom had broken down, she hadn't been able to fix it herself. Rocky put a part in for her, but he said that it was already long past its use-by date and not worth repairing. She couldn't afford a new one. It would take the better part of an hour to walk to the building site, but walking wouldn't kill her. She never managed to get ahead. Something always came up.

Rye ran a hand through her hair and watched rain spattering on the windows. Outside, reflected light glittered in the wet blackness. Mirrored against the night, Rye could see back into the foyer behind her. Couples and their children came out of the hall, paused to stare at the wet night, then gathered their courage to make a dash for the parking lot.

A loud, braying laugh drew Rye's attention across to near the entry door. A group of people were engaged in a spirited conversation. Near them, Rye saw the reflection of the beautiful woman she had met in the bathroom. She stood looking out at the night. Probably waiting for her husband to pick her up. Women who looked like that did not end their days alone. As if Rye's gaze had been a shout to attract her attention, she turned in Rye's direction. Rye hastily looked away and saw Holly approaching.

"I thought you'd vanished," Holly said.

"You had a hundred people wanting to talk to the winner, so I thought I'd wait out here." Rye stood and shouldered her work bag. "Ready to go?"

"We're going to get soaked. Especially at the speed your crappy broom flies. It'd be faster walking."

"We will be walking."

Holly scowled. "The stupid thing hasn't died again?"

"Yep. I told you that's why I was late. Got your coat to put on?"

"Shit."

"Language."

"This reeks." Holly pouted. "Really, really reeks. Can't you fix it?"

"Not here. Come on. The sooner we start, the faster we get home. Holly?"

Holly stopped a couple of paces away. "I'm going to ask Daisy if we can get a ride with them. They have a carpet that works."

Holly bolted back into the hall. Rye mentally swore, sighed, and leaned back against the window. She had no idea how people coped with raising more than one child.

"If it's any consolation, the rain is easing."

Rye turned her head and saw that the speaker was the gorgeous woman. She had moved a couple of steps closer and was looking at Rye. Rye's nerves jangled as if she'd received a low-level shock from a magical power socket.

"I'm sorry, but I couldn't help overhearing," the woman said. "Do you have far to go?"

"Um. Hollowberry. Lower Eastside. It's only about half an hour. But you could be forgiven for thinking it's on the moon."

The woman looked even more dazzling when she smiled. "Perhaps I could give you a lift?"

"What? Oh. That's...that's kind of you. But…um," Rye couldn't think of a polite way of expressing her doubt that the Lower Eastside was anywhere on this woman's route.

"You must be very proud of Holly."

"Yeah. I am."

"This is the fifth year I've helped judge high school competitions. In the main, we see some very ordinary offerings. But occasionally there are some kids who show real promise. Holly has a lot of talent."

"Yeah? Thanks."

The woman stepped even closer and offered a hand. "Flora Withe."

"Um. Rye Woods." Rye was pleasantly surprised to discover that she had a firm handshake.

"Pardon me if I sound rude, but you look too young to be Holly's mother."

"She's my kid sister."

Rye saw Holly approaching. Just a few feet away, Holly looked up from glaring at the ground. She stopped and stared between Rye and Flora. Her expression underwent a dramatic transformation to settle in a mixture of surprise, horror, and disbelief.

"Hello, Holly," Flora said.

To Rye's astonishment, Holly very politely acknowledged her in a calm, quiet voice.

"I could take you and your sister home if you haven't managed to get a ride with your friends," Flora said.

"Wow," Holly said. "You will? Drop through the floor. Oh, Ms. Withe, that would be astronomical. I'll tell Daisy's dad to go without us."

Rye didn't get a chance to open her mouth before Holly darted away to where the Bark family waited.

"Um. Sorry about that," Rye said.

Flora smiled. "I took it as a compliment. Actually, I suppose I should be apologising to you. You hadn't accepted my offer, had you?"

"I wouldn't dare refuse now. I'm on thin enough ice as it is. My life wouldn't be worth living if I made her walk home with me after turning down a ride. But, um, thanks. I appreciate it."

In the light drizzle, Rye grabbed her broom and trotted after Holly and Ms. Withe. The dryad pressed a button on her mobile phone to unlock the doors of a late model sporty flying carpet of the sort that usually figured in advertisements with a near-naked female draped across the front. Rye felt bad about putting her decrepit old broom in the boot. She hoped the bristles didn't leak. Holly had recovered from her shocked shyness and clearly wanted to take the front passenger seat. Rye folded herself into the back, which did not feel designed for much use. She prayed that her boots and clothes didn't stain the upholstery. The carpet smelled like it was fresh from a showroom or a groomer's hardworking hands. She also grew uncomfortably aware of Ms. Withe's perfume and a tantalising hint of pine sap.

They were moving before Rye realised the magic was running. With barely a purr, the carpet rose swiftly. While Holly chatted animatedly, Rye gripped her seat. Breaking more of Rye's stereotypes about artists, Ms. Withe flew very fast and high. The flight to the apartment took about half the time Rye would have thought possible.

Rye climbed out of the carpet onto the parking pad outside her seventh floor apartment. Half of the space was hidden beneath junk because they never used it to park. Her own broom had not been able to make it up this high even on the day she'd bought it. She retrieved her sorry broom from the boot and bent to peer in the flying carpet's window.

"Thanks a lot," Rye said.

"My pleasure." Flora pulled a small black card from her purse and passed it to Rye. "Call me. Anytime."

Rye frowned at the card. She couldn't read it in the poor light.

"You couldn't tell me how to get back to Dandelion Avenue?"

Rye started to give directions, but Holly stepped in with what she claimed was a quicker way. Rye straightened and noticed faces at the neighbour's window. Not surprising. It wasn't too often a piece of hardware like this carpet made it around here without being stripped and burned.

"Nice meeting you both," Flora said.

"Yeah. Likewise." Rye raised a hand. "Thanks again."

Rye watched the carpet zoom away, then followed Holly inside.

"Astronomical!" Holly flopped into a kitchen chair. "Pinch me. This must be a dream. No, it can't be. You wouldn't look like that in any dream of mine. Which means it must be real! Woo hoo!"

Rye put the kettle on to boil and bent to pull vegetables from the cupboard.

"I'm going to die," Holly said. "Ms. Flora Withe. I've ridden in her carpet. It's exactly what I expected her to fly. Style to the stars! I simply must tell Daisy. She'll shrivel with envy!"

Holly leaped to her feet, grabbed the phone, and disappeared into her bedroom. Rye shrugged to herself. Holly seemed much more excited about the few minutes they'd spent in Flora Withe's carpet than winning a prize at school. There were times when Rye wondered if she and Holly were from the same part of Infinity, let alone species.

Rye pulled the black card from her shirt pocket. The printing shimmered silver. It simply said: Flora Withe (959) 445-292.

For the first time in her life, Rye dished up steamed dock roots while preoccupied with thoughts about a woman sexy enough to star in wet dreams.

When Rye tapped on Holly's bedroom door, Holly lay on her bed with the phone cradled against her ear. She blushed and glared spears at Rye. Pictures of music stars cut from glossy magazines covered the wall above Holly's bed.

"My relic wants the phone," Holly said into the receiver. "Call me again, okay?"

She hung up.

"The relic is really here to tell you that dinner is ready," Rye said.

Holly slouched past Rye and into the kitchen. Rye followed.

"Who was that?" Rye asked.

"Just someone."

Holly interrupted nibbling a grilled sparrow's leg to ask, "Can I really spend my prize money on myself?"

"Yeah. Um." Rye chased a honeysuckle flower around her plate. "Holls?"

"What?"

"Um. About earlier."

"What?"

"Thing is—"

"Rye! Fey, you can be annoying. It was a boy, okay? His name is Moss. He's a friend of Daisy's brother. We talk on the phone sometimes. What else do you want to know?"

Rye blinked. "Actually, I was going to ask you about Ms. Withe."

"Oh. I left my body when I saw you talking with her."

"I already apologised for the clothes."

Holly's fork froze midway to her mouth. She stared incredulously at Rye. "It was Flora Withe. It wouldn't have mattered what you were wearing."

"Really? Why not?"

Holly smacked a hand against her forehead. "Flora Withe! You can't tell me that you're the only person in Infinity who doesn't know who she is."

"Actually, I can. Who is she?"

"Only the best weaver in ShadeForest City. Probably the whole country. Maybe even the world."

"Oh."

During her shift that evening, Rye considered the earlier events as she sweated over the smoky, bubbling fat cauldrons at Pansy's Fried Sandwiches. Shorn of Holly's teenage exaggeration and enthusiasm for everything arty, Flora Withe was probably an artist of local renown. Hence her being a guest judge at the school. If her flying carpet was anything to go by, she was fairly successful.

As Rye dunked sandwiches to sizzle in the fat, she savoured memories of Flora Withe. Rye had never met a truly beautiful woman before, nor one who radiated such sensuality.

Holly was asleep by the time Rye returned home from work. From the cooler, Rye grabbed the last of the four small jars of beer she rationed herself to each week. She carried it into the lounge and made up her bed on the couch. She sat awake, sipping, staring at the little black card. *Flora Withe* (959) 445-292. *Call me. Anytime.*

CHAPTER TWO

Rye wrestled an arm out of the bedding and smacked the alarm into submission. She grunted as she swung her legs over the side of the couch. It was still dark. Five thirty.

"Crap."

Rye groped amongst her pile of clothes. She struggled into a tight T-shirt that kept her wings as flat and inconspicuous as possible. The baggy shirt she'd discarded yesterday didn't smell too bad, so she pulled that on over the T-shirt as she stumbled into the kitchen.

She ate breakfast and made sandwiches for herself and Holly. As Rye stuffed hers into her workbag, Holly appeared rubbing the sleep from her eyes.

"You're up early," Holly said.

"So are you. Sorry if I woke you."

"I have a test today. I couldn't sleep. Rye, it's still dark."

"I have to walk to work this morning. Sandwiches there. Don't forget to eat breakfast. And good luck with the test."

Rye strode to the door and grabbed her jacket. As she reached for the door, she remembered that it was Fourth Day. Night class tonight. Rye dodged back into the lounge to grab her textbook and assignment. Her bedding lay on the couch still. Rye swiftly debated and decided to leave it. If Holly had friends over, they closeted themselves in her room. Besides, if Holly wanted to, she could just stuff the bedding behind the couch.

Rye trotted down the stairs. Few lights showed in the windows she passed on her way to ground level. The odd carpet and broom sped along in the near-deserted flyways. At the end of the street, Mr. Cloudnut yawned as he opened his All-Purpose store.

"Hey, Rye," he said. "You're up early."

"Yeah," Rye said. "I've got to walk. My broom died. Um. Those wouldn't be yesterday's papers, would they?"

"These?" Mr. Cloudnut toed a bundle of newspapers. "Yeah. You want one? Take it. No use to me. I just send them to recycle."

"Great. Thanks."

Rye stuffed the paper in her bag and strode away. The chances were that some of yesterday's ads would still be worth looking at today. It beat paying half a piece for today's paper.

The city didn't seem to wake until Rye crossed the bridge to the Westside. She passed several joggers. When she emerged from the Rootway underpass, Rye noticed the time. She was going to be late.

She jogged through the gates into the worksite as the last echoes of the whistle faded. Grub, the half-goblin overseer, glared at her with his yellow eyes.

"Nice of you to interrupt your busy social life to come to work, Woods," Grub said. "Tenth floor."

Screw you, wanker. Rye stomped past him. She panted as she slogged up ten flights of stairs. She passed men and women already chiselling, hammering, scraping, and swapping insults. She was exhausted before she even got her tools out of her belt.

At the break, Rye scanned the ads in her newspaper for second-hand brooms.

Knot, a pixie man whose scalp ridges were unusually deep and close together, handed Rye a cup of treacly tea. "You gonna come to the pub tomorrow?"

"Oh, yeah." Blackie's antenna jerked upright. "They're gonna have that band. With the singer with the tits."

"It's Spike's bachelor party," Knot said. "What do you reckon, Rye? Or you too busy doing your book learning? Homework, like."

"School is for kids," Blackie said. "They say she's all natural. That singer. Can't be. She's out to here."

"I can't go," Rye said. "My broom is dead."

"Oh. And I was thinking you was looking in them ads for a new job," Knot said. "If'n it's a broom you're after, maybe I can help. Brother-in-law's always tinkering with them. I can ask him if he's got one for sale, if you like."

"Great," Rye said. "But it has to be cheap."

Rye turned to the national news page.

Detention Centre Suicide

The coroner's office will be initiating an enquiry into the death of an inmate of the Bramble Street Detention Centre in HedgeCove City. She has been identified as Abstinence, a thirty-five year old fairy, who went by the name of Fern Moonwort. She had been illegally residing in the United Forestlands for the last twelve years after leaving Fairyland without a travel permit. Warders found her dead in her cell yesterday evening. A full autopsy will be carried out, but a reliable source says she took her own life. She was due to be deported to Fairyland this morning.

Beneath the concealment of her clothes, Rye's wing buds defensively clenched so hard that her chest ached and constricted her breathing.

"Topped herself?" Knot said. He read over Rye's shoulder.

Rye started and dropped the paper.

"Never met a fairy," Knot said. "Reckon they must be strange. Wings. And all that religious rubbish. I heard they ain't got a single bang-ball team in the whole country. Can you imagine that? Not somewhere I'd want to live. Not surprising she'd want to kill herself rather than go back."

"But those fairy freaks beat our team at the International Games last year," Blackie said. "We should've won."

"You stupid seedhead," Knot said. "It was Elfland who did the down trou on us. Fairies don't never send any teams anywhere. Must be too busy praying and all that crap."

"Oh," Blackie said. "Well, it's a bloody good job those flying freaks don't have teams. I've heard they're all fucked in the head. And those pointy-eared elf wankers ain't no better."

Rye stood and walked away.

During the lunch break, Knot, Blackie, and the boys went off to the nearest pub. Rye perched on a pile of wood rubble and read the newspaper as she ate her sandwiches. In the international section, there was a short piece about the arrival of a new ambassador from Fairyland. The woman had been a highly ranked priestess before taking up her diplomatic post. Rye shuddered, folded the paper, and threw it away.

Rye's gaze snagged on the green pay phone pod across the street. *Call me. Anytime.* It would only be polite to call and say thanks for the lift yesterday. Rye was strolling out of the gates before she realised what she was doing. The pod was empty. Rye hesitated before stepping inside. She pulled the little black card from her wallet.

Beep-beep. Beep-beep.

Rye wiped her palm on the backside of her pants. It helped that the screen and camera had been vandalised. The dryad wouldn't see Rye in her scruffy work clothes.

Click. "Hi. Flora here. Well, Flora's machine, actually. I'd love to hear from you, so please leave a message. I'll get back to you as soon as I can." *Bleep.*

Crap. She hadn't expected this.

"Um. Hi. Um, look, I…um. I wanted to say thanks. For last night. The lift. In your carpet. You gave me and Holly. Um. From the school. Um. We really appreciated it. Um. Thanks. Um. Bye."

Rye hung up and let out a long breath. "Why did I do that?"

❖

Conscious of having sweated most of the day, Rye threaded her way to a seat at the rear of the class. Mr. Bulrush handed back assignments. Rye saw her large red A and smiled.

At the end of the two hours, Rye stuffed her notes and book in her bag and smoothed out her homework assignment. She waited until everyone else had gone before approaching Mr. Bulrush's desk.

"I'm sorry that it's a bit crumpled," she said. "I had to finish it at work this afternoon."

He smiled. "That will not affect the quality of the contents, I'm sure."

"Thanks. Bye."

"Ms. Woods? If you have a minute, there's something I'd like to discuss with you."

Rye frowned and stepped back. "Sure. What's wrong? Did I mess something up?"

"Quite the opposite. Ms. Woods, have you given any thought to sitting the national certification exam?"

"What?"

"Your work is very impressive. You're on course for a pass with distinction. In my opinion, you won't have any trouble attaining the necessary standard for the national certification, Grade III Exam."

Rye blinked. "Really? Me? That's the proper exam, isn't it, not just the night class one?"

"Yes. The curriculum covers more ground than this night class does, so it would mean some extra reading for you. I'm prepared to help you if you wish to do it."

Rye chewed her lip. "I could pass the certification?"

He nodded. "Why don't you think about it? We have a few weeks before the final date for lodging your application for examination."

On the walk home, Rye's mind whirred even as her body trudged on empty. She had difficulties finding enough time for the work she did now, but getting a qualification would mean she could start looking for better jobs. She dropped her bag inside the door and went to flop full length on the couch without taking her jacket or boots off. Thank the gods that it was Fifth Day tomorrow. Her body wanted to remain prone for a week. Walking to work would take some getting used to.

Holly darted into the room. She looked excited. "I thought I heard you. You'll never guess who was here."

Rye grunted. "Who?"

Holly perched on the arm of the couch. "You'll never guess in a trillion billion years."

"Okay. I won't. So tell me."

"You're a bag of misery tonight. And you stink. You need a shower."

Rye made the ultimate sacrifice and rolled off the couch onto her feet. Her body complained with aches from every muscle. She didn't bother looking for her pyjamas before staggering toward the bathroom.

"Rye! Don't you want know who was here? It was Flora Withe!"

Rye halted in the doorway. "Flora Withe?"

"Yeah. It was utterly astronomical. I thought I was going to die when I opened the door and saw her there. Fey, how I wished she'd come half an hour earlier when Daisy was here. She would've shrivelled with envy that Flora Withe came to my home."

"Did she—What did she come for?"

"She said you left some incoherent message on her answering

machine. Which is so utterly you. Just when I think there's no other way in Infinity that you can embarrass me, you do. It's a miracle I didn't die young."

"I...um, I thanked her for giving us a lift home last night. She didn't have to come here."

Holly leaped off the couch arm and strode across to put a hand on Rye's shoulder. "She would've phoned, but someone forgot to give her their number. Rye, you're so back-then that you should sell yourself to a museum. Don't worry, I told her for you."

Rye scowled as she watched Holly disappear into her room and shut the door.

Flora Withe here? Rye ran a hand through her hair. The idea made her extremely uncomfortable. She had not expected her phone call to lead to that. It was just good manners to thank her.

In the bathroom, Rye sank onto the side of the bath and turned on the taps. She didn't have enough energy to stand in the shower. She dropped her clothes on the floor. As usual, she struggled to peel off her sweat-dampened tight T-shirt. Her first breath of the day after she removed it was the sweetest. Fairy wings had developed to be folded into compact bundles when not in use, but not to be constricted all day. Her wings only slowly unfolded from their cramped position. Rye groaned with pleasure as she sank into the hot water. She should've remembered to grab a beer. No, she drank the last of her weekly ration last night.

Rye woke from a tangled dream of sitting exams naked and of Ms. Flora Withe. She lay in tepid water. Holly's thumping music had stopped, though one of the neighbours had picked up the slack with loud party noises. Rye dragged herself into the lounge and crawled into her bedding. She remembered to turn the alarm off. No work tomorrow. Well, apart from shopping, housework, laundry, and her class assignment.

❖

Rye set her shopping bags down and peered in the butcher's window. She rubbed the circulation back into her fingers as she frowned at the meat. The things she could do with those possum cutlets. And those bat ribs. Rye sighed and hefted her bags. Her imagination never had to worry about price tags.

Rye paused at the intersection of Dandelion Avenue and Ditch Street. Even at midday on Fifth Day, the flyways teemed. Rye waited for the signal and set her bags down to give her hands a rest.

A horn honked right beside her. Rye jumped. She turned to give a three-fingered gesture of appreciation of the fright, but stopped her hand partway. The sporty little carpet with the top peeled back was driven by a stunningly beautiful dryad woman wearing sunglasses.

"Hi, there," Flora said. "Hop in. I'll take you home."

"Um. Hello."

"Put your bags on the backseat."

"Um." Rye was aware of people looking.

"I don't want to hurry you, but the signal is about to change."

"Oh. Right."

Rye set her bags on the back seat and climbed into the front. She snapped the safety harness into place. The carpet zoomed forward and climbed three lanes. Rye squeezed her eyes shut.

"You'll have to direct me."

"Oh." Rye peeled her eyes open and pointed.

Rye guessed that Holly would admire Ms. Withe's flying technique as self-confident rather than suicidal. For the short duration of the flight to the apartment, Rye tried not to pay too much attention to what was going on outside the carpet. That wasn't hard to do when sitting beside a woman more attractive than any in her fantasies. Her companion wore a smart tailored jacket and skirt. Her well-turned legs were every bit as good as Rye remembered. In fact, the whole package was even more desirable than her memories.

"I take it that your broom is still not working," Flora said.

"If it could speak, it'd be begging to be put out of its misery."

Flora smiled. Ravishing. Rye suddenly felt too warm. She pointedly looked down at her hands clenched in her lap.

"Do...do you come this way often?" Rye asked.

"No. I'm on my way back from the opening of a new gallery down in Onionfield." Flora negotiated the turn into Rye's street. "Sixteen ninety, isn't it?"

"Yeah. That tree there. With the broken branches at the top."

The carpet turned into the ascending lane and lifted fast enough to leave Rye's stomach behind for several seconds. Flora parked with barely a whisker's width between the front of the carpet and Rye's garbage hamper.

"Thanks for the lift," Rye said. "Again."

"I'll come clean with you. This wasn't exactly on my route home. I was coming to see you."

Rye fumbled the release latch on the safety harness. "Oh?"

"I'd kill for a cup of tea. Would you think me too terribly pushy if I invited myself in for a drink?"

"Um. I only have plain stuff."

"Marvellous. They served nothing but exotic non-alcoholic punches at that gallery. My tongue is ready to disown me."

Rye smiled. She felt an air of unreality when she opened the door and led the way along the short hall to the kitchen.

The apartment stifled. The tree's heating system was on the blink again. Rye set her bags on the table and peeled off her jacket. She wished she could remove her shirt, but settled for rolling up her sleeves.

"Can I do anything to help?" Flora removed her sunglasses. She wore only light makeup on her creamy skin. Even in the dingy setting of Rye's kitchen, she looked gorgeous.

"Um. You did. You saved me twenty minutes walk. Sit down. I'll put the kettle on and tidy this stuff away."

"Couldn't you shop somewhere closer?"

"I suppose so." Rye set pots of pollen and honey on a shelf. "But the stuff is fresher at the market. And cheaper. You never get kowhai flowers like this at the hypermart. They put something on them to make them stay yellow longer in the store. This is what they should look like. Taste much better, too."

One of Flora's green eyebrows twitched. Her interested stare sharpened. Uncomfortable, Rye turned away to put her vegetables in the bottom bins.

"Holly not home?"

"She's shopping," Rye said. "She has to decide what to spend her prize money on."

"You don't go together?"

Rye smiled. "She'd rather ask the doorpost about clothes than me. To be fair, she'd get better advice that way."

Flora laughed.

Rye grabbed two mugs from the cupboard. They were thick and mismatched. Still, if Ms. Withe had not baulked at entering an apartment in Hollowberry, she probably wouldn't run screaming at cheap, ugly crockery. Rye gave herself the mug with the chip in the rim. She hesitated over biscuits. Her willowy guest looked more like the body-sculpting-at-the-gym type than the sort to eat junk food. On the other hand, Rye wanted something sweet, and Ms. Withe need not eat if she didn't want to. Rye surprised herself by shaking a few biscuits onto a plate rather than just plonking the jar on the table.

"Holly seems a very nice young woman."

"She was," Rye said. "Before adolescence. I'm hoping she will be again when she comes out of it."

Flora smiled. "Do you two live here alone?"

"Us and the damp patches. There's no room for anyone else."

Flora drank half her tea like she really needed it and then helped herself to one of the biscuits. Rye noticed she didn't wear a ring, bracelet, earring, or tattoo that might indicate she was married. Still, there were so many different species, races, and religious groups that Rye didn't pretend to know all the possible symbols to indicate that someone was in a committed relationship. For all she knew, dryads might marry several husbands at once and have children by planting acorns.

"Do you have any children?" Rye asked.

"Me? Oh, no. But I hope to, eventually. Five or six, perhaps. Or seven."

"Good luck."

Flora smiled. "Maybe I'll change my mind once I realise what's involved. As an only child, I have some rather romantic notions about large families."

"You're welcome to borrow Holly for a few days as a cure."

Flora chuckled. "Have you been looking after her long?"

"Eleven years. Not that I'm counting."

Flora's green eyebrows soared. "You can't have been much older than Holly is now."

"Nineteen. It was the best thing I ever did. No matter how pissed she gets me, I don't ever regret it for a second. More tea?"

"Yes, please." She sat back in her chair. "Look, let me be honest. I was coming to see you for more than just a cup of tea."

"Oh?"

"I could've called, but I got the impression that the phone isn't your best medium of expression."

Rye blushed at the same time she self-consciously grinned. "Um. You noticed. What did you want? If it's about some stain I left on the backseat, I'm sorry."

"Did you? I don't mind. What I wanted to ask is if you'd like to have a few drinks with me."

Rye felt every speck of her body go still.

"I know this place near the bridge," Flora said. "Very low key. Relaxed. The music isn't so loud that you can't hear yourself think. In fact, it's quite comfortable for conversation. We could—Have I said something wrong?"

"Um." Rye found it difficult to breathe. She ran her hand through her hair and scowled at the peeling wallpaper.

"I'm sorry. I didn't mean to make you uncomfortable. You'll probably find this hard to believe, but I'm not normally this pushy."

Rye's mind had gone blank.

"Branch," Flora murmured. "I've done this rather badly, haven't I? I'm so sorry. Look, I think I'd better leave. Please think it over. If you change your mind, you have my number. And thanks for tea."

Rye stood with a scraping of her chair legs. Her limping brain realised that she had better see her visitor out.

The front door slammed.

"Hey, Rye!" Holly strode to the kitchen. "You'll never guess what is parked—Oh. Ms. Withe."

"Hello, Holly," Flora said.

Rye chewed her lip and didn't know where to put herself. Flora behaved as though the awkwardness didn't exist. She looked genuinely interested when Holly dug out her purchases to show her.

Rye sat and watched and tried to think. Flora Withe wanted to have a few drinks with her. Was that so shocking? Rye had been out to the pub with some of the blokes from work on odd occasions. Rye imagined Flora Withe would prove better company than Knot and Blackie. There was the disturbing aspect that she was easily the most attractive woman Rye had ever met. But that was not likely to matter. Rye had been safely celibate for years, and it was highly improbable that Flora Withe was gay. Even if she were, Rye would be deluding herself to think that the successful, stylish, poised, beautiful dryad would want anything to do with a builder's labourer. On the other hand, she was a very nice person. The last hour or so had been enjoyable and easy...and adult.

"I'd better be going." Flora rose and picked up her sunglasses and purse. "Thanks for the tea."

"I'll see you out," Rye said.

Holly leaped to her feet. "I'd better come to give you directions. Rye is hopeless. You'll end up in the river."

"Don't you have to go and show Daisy your new clothes?" Rye said.

Holly's rebellious pout faded in an eye blink. "Oh, yeah. Stupid me. Okay. See you later, Ms. Withe."

Holly grabbed her bags and strode out. Rye frowned. That had been unexpectedly easy.

"She's a good kid," Flora said.

"Yeah. But very strange sometimes," Rye said. "I guess it's the hormones poaching her brain."

Flora smiled. "Look, I'm really sorry about before. Can we forget I said anything?"

"Um. Well. I was sort of thinking that...um. Yeah. I mean to the drinks."

Flora's eyebrows lifted. "Yes?"

"I was a bit, you know, surprised. So, if...if the offer still stands."

"Of course. When? How about Third Day?"

"Um. No, I can't," Rye said. "How about next Fifth Day? Or today?"

Flora blinked. "Sure. Why not? No time like the present. Shall I pick you up at seven?"

"Can...can I meet you at the corner of the street?"

Chapter Three

Rye surveyed the piles of her clothes. She pulled on her tightest of tight T-shirts. Then what? Rye frowned and ended up choosing the shirt and pants that Holly had picked out for her to wear to the school art exhibition.

She pulled out the loose knot in the wall and retrieved a small wad of money. She had just paid Holly's school fees, so her savings only amounted to fifty-five pieces. She took a ten piece note. That would cover the cost of a couple of jars of beer. Although, Flora Withe did not look the beer type. She probably drank wine. Rye reluctantly took a second note and promised herself that she would forgo next week's beer ration.

Rye tapped on Holly's bedroom door. Holly made no attempt to disguise her surprise.

"What are you dressed like a normal person for?" Holly asked.

"I'm...um, I'm going out for an hour or two."

Holly smiled. "Yeah? And here I've been thinking you're dead from the neck down."

Rye tugged nervously at her shirt sleeve. "Um. One of the blokes at work is having a bachelor party. I told you."

"No, you didn't."

"You probably weren't paying attention. It's Spike. He's getting married. So...Um. I won't be gone long. Will you be okay? If you'd rather I stayed, I will."

"Go! I'm not three years old. I can throw a wild party."

Rye stiffened.

"Joking," Holly said. "Shit, you can be hard work. I'll quietly decay here on my own and finish my homework, okay? I'll keep the chain across and not open the door to anyone strange until you come back."

Rye frowned and strode to the front door.

"Wait!" Holly called. "Those pants. You can't go in them."

"What's wrong with them? They don't have holes."

"Gods of fashion, see my martyrdom! Come and put these on."

Rye poked her head into Holly's room and saw a pair of new black pants thrust at her. "Where did you get those?"

"I showed you them earlier. I bought them with my prize money."

To Rye's surprise, the pants were a good fit. They were baggy enough in the back of the legs that her wing membranes didn't show and they were exactly the right length. Rye took a critical look at Holly. Her little sister was as tall as she was. When had that happened?

"Much better," Holly said. "If you get any stains on them, I'll kill you. Slowly. With blunt instruments. And eyebrow tweezers."

❖

Rye should not have been surprised when Flora flew past the grimy bridge district, with its docks, warehouses, and seedy bars. They continued to the trendy north side of the bridge. None of the streetlights had any broken lamps. Rye had no real idea where they were, except that she was out of her natural habitat. The carpet lowered into a parking lot. Rye made out the name Owl's Nest on the wall sign.

They stepped into a world wholly alien to the Ball and Chain Pub. Instead of smoke, a blaring jukebox, and tables sticky with spilled beer, this place was subdued lighting, tasteful music, and chic décor. Rye's attention quickly slid from the booths and bar to her companion. This was the first good look she had of Flora in decent lighting. She wore a slinky little black dress. Rye's wing buds twitched.

"Good evening, Ms. Withe." A well-dressed woman nodded to them. "Can I show you to a place at the bar or a booth?"

Rye trailed them to a booth. She tried not to be so conscious of Flora's body. She didn't realise that she had agreed to a drink until a waitress brought them each one. Before Rye could dig out her wallet, Flora dropped a crisp twenty on the waitress's tray. The size of the bill for two drinks made Rye blink. She sipped her drink, which contained a strong spirit, and made a mental note to eke this one out because she could only afford one round.

"You...you come here often?" Rye asked.

"I used to. When I was younger. I'm slowing down. I must be getting old."

Rye didn't think she looked very old. Although, it was harder to pick the ages of some species than others. She looked sleek and firm, with no hint of brown or autumnal reds or gold in her dark green hair. If Rye had to guess, she would go for early thirties.

"I seem to have lost most of my appetite for loud music and non-stop dancing all night long," Flora said. "I've noticed that when I do come here now, it's usually on nights when they don't have a live band. I'd rather talk and get to know someone. I suppose that's a rather sad admission. How about you? What sort of haunt do you frequent?"

"Um. I don't get out much. When I was younger, I couldn't leave Holly alone." Rye didn't mention that she had worked two jobs back then, too, and couldn't have afforded a busy social life even if she'd wanted one. "I don't have much time."

"I can't begin to imagine how you raised your young sister on your own. I don't think I could have done it. Nor anyone else I know. I do admire you for it."

Rye shifted uncomfortably and sipped her strong drink. She wished she had a beer instead. She wasn't used to spirits.

"Um," Rye said. "So, Ms. Withe, Holly says—"

"Flora. Please."

"Um. Right. Flora." Rye cleared her throat. "Holly says you're a famous artist."

"That's very flattering, but not terribly accurate."

Rye began to relax as their conversation wandered away from her and over every possible topic. This really was much, much better than the grunted conversations she had with her drunken workmates at a pub. When it came to ordering fresh drinks, Rye only sweated for the several minutes between placing the order and when she handed her two ten piece notes to the waitress.

"I'm having a few friends over for dinner on Second Night," Flora said. "You'd be more than welcome."

"Um. Thanks. But I can't. Um. I have night class."

"Night class? What are you studying?"

"I'm aiming to take the longest ever to get a basic business certificate. I've been at it for six years and still have a couple to go."

"That's astonishing. I do admire your perseverance."

"It's not by choice. I can't take more than two classes a year."

"So, you're not only raising your sister and putting her through a good school, but you're also educating yourself?" Flora shook her head. "You're amazing."

Embarrassed, Rye stared down at her remaining drink. She glugged it in one swallow. When Flora smiled, Rye couldn't help smiling back. She also couldn't help flicking a glance down at Flora's bosom. Rye quickly looked away. She felt too warm and light-headed.

"Um. Where is the bathroom?" Rye asked.

While Rye waited in the bathroom for a stall, one of the women at the basins gave her a disturbingly frank appraisal.

By the time Rye emerged, some couples had taken to the dance floor. She gave them a wide berth as she made her way back to the booth. There was something odd about the dancers, though Rye couldn't immediately identify what it was. She frowned around at the other patrons when she sat. In all the time they'd been here, she had been too engrossed in Flora to notice anyone else. With a jolt, she realised that all the couples dancing together were women. Rye's gaze jerked to the booths across the room and to the bar. Banshee, naiad, sylph, leprechaun, and dryad. They were, one and all, female.

"Is something wrong?" Flora asked.

Rye stared at her. Slowly, oh so slowly, her brain drew out the shocking conclusion of what being in a gay bar meant about Flora. Rye reached for her fresh drink and swallowed heavily.

"Rye?" Flora touched Rye's wrist.

"Um." Rye felt horribly conscious of the light press of warm fingertips against her bare skin. She turned her frown away to the dancers.

"Did you want to dance?" Flora asked.

"What? Oh. Um. I can't imagine I'd be any good at it."

"It's not a contest."

Rye followed her. She felt awkward, stiff, and self-conscious. When she concentrated on Flora, though, she relaxed. Flora's smile, her voice, the way she swayed held Rye's attention firmly fixed. Rye noted the shape of her lips, the curve of her throat, and the roundness of her bosom. That long-dormant part of Rye uncurled and grew stronger inside her.

The music changed to a slow number. It seemed the most natural thing in the world that Rye and Flora draw closer together. Flora rested her hands on Rye's sides. Rye didn't pull away and didn't want to. At some point, her own hands found Flora's waist.

She could feel Flora moving to the music. Beneath the mingled aromas of floral perfumes, fruity drinks, and musty whiffs of pheromones from different species, Rye smelled a faint, elusive scent like pine sap. It made her want to press close to Flora, to touch her and to inhale deeply the smell of her skin. Rye felt drunk, and not only from the alcohol she'd swallowed.

Flora ran her hands up Rye's arms. Their bodies almost touched.

"Let's go back to my place," Flora said.

When they stepped out into the parking lot, the cool night air slapped Rye in the face. If anything, it made her head spin worse. She closely followed Flora to the flying carpet.

Flora slotted her mobile into the ignition but turned to Rye without starting the engine. Her hand burned the side of Rye's face. No power in all of Infinity could have stopped Rye from twisting around to kiss her. The first passionate kiss Rye received in years, soft and warm and probing, hit her like a bolt of pure magic.

"Oh, Elm," Flora whispered. "I've needed to do that since I saw you in that bathroom."

Their kisses merged their mouths. Hot, wet, hungry. Their tongues writhed together, deeper, stronger. Beneath Flora's musky perfume, Rye again smelled that tantalising scent like pine sap. It seemed to be the essence of Flora. Rye couldn't inhale it deeply enough. Her hands clutched at Flora, needing to touch all of her. Her flesh felt more than alive where Flora's body pressed against her. Rye shifted to maximise their contact all along her length. She slipped off the seat and ended up kneeling in the foot space.

Flora giggled. Rye felt stupid.

"It had to happen to one of us, didn't it?" Flora said.

Rye wished it hadn't been her. Flora pulled her close and ran her hand through Rye's hair. For that look in her eyes, Rye would've fallen off a hundred seats.

"I was in danger of thinking you too good to be true," Flora said in a husky whisper. "At least now I know that you and this is real."

Rye kissed her and finally touched the warm, smooth skin of her naked thigh. Flora threw her head back to moan. Rye kissed Flora's throat and worked her lips down the salty skin to the bosom lifted close to her mouth. To her astonishment, Flora's breasts had firmed. Rye clasped her wildly erotic discovery. The dryad's chest hardened to the texture of wood. Through the silky fabric of Flora's dress, Rye's lips squeezed and teased nut-hard nipples. Flora moaned and dug her fingers into Rye's hair. Rye's wing buds twitched against the restraint of her tight T-shirt and drew the cloth even tauter against Rye's aching nipples. The insanely sensitive spot below the base of Rye's neck, between the top of her wings, throbbed in counterpoint with the matching one between her legs. Flora's leg slid up to Rye's hip. Rye knelt on the seat with one leg and thrust her hand up Flora's dress. Her fingers found damp panties.

"Oh, fey," Rye whispered.

Flora's hips moved into Rye's touch even as Flora slid down in her seat. Rye's fingers worked beneath the lacy panties. She found pubic hair that felt soft and springy like warm moss. Flora groaned and she clutched at Rye's hair and shoulders as she writhed to the rhythm of Rye's fingers. Rye's wing buds strained against the restraint of her T-shirt as her wings tried to unfold with her arousal.

"Oh, Elm," Flora panted. "Oh, Holy Elm."

Need drove Rye's fingers harder and deeper into slippery flesh. Even though Rye was maddeningly aware of the tangy smell of Flora's arousal, it did not fully swamp out that thin trace of pine sap which seemed to have infused her brain and every excited nerve and fibre. Flora groaned with rising pitch toward her climax. As she jerked with her release, her blindly clutching fingers hit the hotly throbbing lump high on Rye's back. Rye loosed a shuddering groan as her world squeezed with the pleasurable pain of orgasm.

Rye sagged, panting, and nearly slid off the edge of the seat again. She rolled back to slump into her seat. Flora sat with her eyes shut and her head thrown back.

After a few moments, Flora reached across to lay a hand on Rye's thigh.

"Oh, that was good," Flora whispered.

Rye lifted the hand to kiss.

Flora sighed and shifted. She sat up and leaned close to Rye. "Maybe I'm not quite as old as I thought. Torrid sex in a parking lot. Not a usual geriatric activity, I wouldn't have thought."

Rye smiled. She liked the feel of Flora's hand sliding down her chest and twisted closer to give Flora easier access. She put a hand on Flora's hip. Just touching her felt wonderful.

"You're the most beautiful woman I've ever seen," Rye said.

Flora smiled as she kissed Rye. "And you have a truly impressive physique, lover. Real, not manufactured in a gym. You're so real. Everything about you is genuine. And strong. You're so wholly unlike anyone I've met before."

Flora ran a hand down from Rye's hair to her shoulder and then across Rye's back. Her hand stopped. Through Rye's clothes, her fingers rested on the hard lump of the top of Rye's right wing bud. She frowned.

"This isn't going to be the most romantic thing I ever say to you," Flora said. "Which species are you?"

Rye's blood went cold. She stared with horror at Flora. "No."

Rye twisted around, wrenched the door open, and scrambled out of the carpet.

"Rye?" Flora called.

Rye stumbled to her feet and ran.

"Rye!"

Rye's mind blanked. The need to flee took over. She ran and ran.

❖

Rye unlocked the front door. Luckily, Holly had not left the chain on. Rye crept inside and slumped on the couch. Her alarm clock showed that it was after three o'clock. In the dark, she couldn't see her hands. They hurt. She must have hit something. She didn't know what.

Rye clenched her fists against the pain and squeezed her eyes shut. She couldn't remember what she had done between leaving the bar with Flora and coming to her senses an hour ago sitting on a bench in the dark on the river bank. If she had hurt Flora, she would never forgive herself. In fact, it might be the end of her if Flora went to the police. She would deserve it this time. Unlike the last time, she knew that she was capable of doing something destructive in her panic.

Fuck.

Holly would get her wings in a year or two at most. Then she'd be safe. Eleven years, Rye had managed to keep her life together. Why couldn't she have continued for just a little longer?

Her world had unravelled with her willing aid.

She had not been prepared to meet anyone like Flora Withe. Flora had somehow cut through all Rye's protective layers. Rye had very much wanted to have sex with her. Everything else had vanished in a surge of lust. Had they done it? Was that what caused her panic? Had Flora discovered she was a fairy? Or had sex with Flora triggered memories of what had happened after the last time Rye had had sex?

Rye slumped back full length on the sofa and put an arm across her eyes. She didn't want to think about that. She didn't want to think about any of it, but whatever she'd done in that gaping hole in this evening might have put her and Holly in serious danger. What was she going to do?

When the alarm sounded, Rye roused herself. She changed into work clothes and mechanically went through her morning routine. She felt so numb from worry and lack of sleep that her workmate's cheerful reminder that today was a half-holiday failed to make any impact.

The hours before the morning break whistle crawled by. In her worst moments, Rye imagined Flora's broken body and police carpets, sirens wailing, heading for the building site.

The whistle sounded. Rye dropped her tools and raced down ten flights of stairs. She paused to regain her breath at the pay phone pod. Mercifully, the video screen was still inoperative.

Beep-beep.

"Please get the machine to answer," Rye said.

Beep-beep.

"Please be the machine."

"Hello. Flora here."

Rye winced. *Shit.*

"Hello?" Flora said.

Rye stared in anguish at the phone. At least Flora sounded fine. She wasn't dead or in the infirmary.

"Hello?" Flora said. "Is anyone there?"

Rye hung up. She sagged against the wall and squeezed her eyes shut. "Why couldn't I say something to her?"

Miserable and tired, Rye trudged back to work. When the building site closed at lunchtime, Rye began walking home with thoughts of falling onto her couch and catching up on some sleep. After she crossed the bridge to the Eastside, though, she stopped to look upriver. Flora had said that she worked at home most days at her loom.

Rye turned north and kept a lookout for a pay phone pod. At the cost of a quarter of a piece, she entered Flora's phone number and received her address. Newbud was the very trendy north-eastern suburb. Rye had been there once a couple of years ago when Holly had pestered her to take her to the Art Museum.

Rye passed cafés, galleries, rare book shops, boutiques, and gourmet parlours. She felt horribly out of place in her work boots and patched clothes.

She had to ask three times for directions to Whiterow Gardens. At about the time she saw the street sign, she noticed a flower shop. She stopped to frown at the bewildering profusion of blooms. She had not the faintest idea what Flora might like. In reality, she knew very little about Flora. Yet they might have had sex together.

"Hello." A smiling sprite woman with yellow hair waved her feathery antennae in greeting at Rye. "Those orchids are perfectly wonderful, aren't they? So regal."

Rye picked some flowers at random. They cost a lot more than she expected. She carried the small bunch up the street and turned into Whiterow Gardens. Rye stopped and stared at the tall, stately trees. If she had had antennae, they would have drooped. She might work at and live in the cheapest and shoddiest of apartments, but that didn't prevent her from recognising the other end of the scale. Flora had downplayed her success. She lived in the housing equivalent of her expensive, late-model flying carpet. The whole short, exclusive street oozed money. You could practically smell it.

"Crap."

She had no business being here. Someone who couldn't afford the fare on public transit to get here did not belong in this street.

Rye turned around and trudged back toward the main flyway. She dropped her pitiful bunch of flowers in the first rubbish bin that she passed.

❖

When Rye returned home after her evening shift at Pansy's, she had to knock for a couple of minutes to get Holly out of the bathroom.

Holly emerged rubbing her wet hair and wandered off toward her room.

"Ms. Withe phoned," Holly said.

Startled, Rye jerked her head around. "She did? What did she want?"

Holly paused in her doorway to shrug. "You can use a phone, can't you? You talk to her."

"It's too late for me to call anyone. Just tell me what she wanted. Did she leave a message?"

"No. She asked if you were home. That's all."

Rye scowled. She could not have done anything terrible to Flora last night. Flora had not set the police on her. Nor had the immigration officers swooped to apprehend the illegal aliens. Flora could not have guessed that she had wings. Which meant they probably had not had sex. Or, if they had, Flora hadn't told the authorities about Rye.

For some reason, Rye felt even worse. She glanced at the clock. It really was too late to call. She was too tired to think straight. She would get in touch with Flora tomorrow.

❖

Rye slept through the alarm and arrived late for work. Grub, with a malicious glint in his yellow eyes, gave her the filthy job of burning the rubbish. She coughed and her eyes streamed all day from the smoke. She stank before the first break whistle. Still, no one could smell you on the other end of the phone.

Beep-beep. Beep-beep. Click.

"Hi. Flora here. Well, Flora's machine, actually. I'd love to hear from you, so please leave a message. I'll get back to you as soon as I can." *Bleep.*

"Um," Rye said. "Flora? It's me. Rye. Rye Woods. Um. Holly said you called. Um. About Fifth Night."

"Rye?" Flora said. "I'm here."

Rye started and bit her lip. "Um. Hi."

"Do you usually fuck and run? You know, that was the shittiest thing anyone has ever done to me."

Rye grimaced. "I…um. Sorry. I'm sorry. I didn't mean to—"

"It was a casual act of abandonment? Or a thoughtless screw? You have no idea how much better that makes me feel."

Rye winced and banged her forehead against the pod wall. "I'm sorry."

Rye hung up. "Fey!"

She thought she heard the pod phone ringing as she crossed the flyway, but that seemed unlikely.

Rye could not get her head into her lesson at night class. She might have been better skipping it and going to bed early. The stink of smoke from her clothes and hair gave her a splitting headache.

She trudged out into the night and buttoned her jacket against a light drizzle. Just to make her day perfect, it was possible that Holly would be a sulky pain when she got home. Surely life was supposed to be better than this.

A horn honked. Rye looked around and saw Flora's carpet parked on the other side of the flyway. Rye's heart gave an odd thump. She hesitated, chewing her lip, before jamming her fists into her pockets and crossing the street. Flora looked stiff and unhappy. Rye braced herself for another stream of angry abuse. She probably deserved it.

"Do you want to talk?" Flora asked.

Rye got into the passenger seat.

Flora stared at her. Rye thought she looked gorgeous but quickly directed her frown at her own lap.

"I have had two of the worst days thanks to you," Flora said.

"I'm sorry."

"I get so angry when—" Flora wrinkled her nose. "Is the school on fire?"

"You smell smoke? Um. That's me. Sorry."

"Oh. Do you mind if I put the air cleaner on?"

"No, go ahead."

Flora pressed a button on the instrument panel. She really was marvellous to look at.

"Where was I?" Flora asked.

"Um. Angry with me."

"Oh, yes. I get furious every time I think about you running out on me. Then I'll blame myself for causing it. Then I'll get angry with you all over again and cry a little."

Rye scowled at her hands. This was worse than being shouted at. And she still didn't know exactly what she'd done. "I'm sorry."

Flora sighed and leaned back in her seat. "The worst part is that you have done—are doing this to me. I shouldn't be so strongly emotional about a casual fuck and a disastrous date. Elm knows I've had both before."

Rye squirmed.

"When I walked into that bathroom at the school and saw you," Flora said, "my whole body thought sex. But later, when we talked, something else happened. I had to get to know you. I've never chased anyone before. Maybe I'm not cut out for it. But you went out with me. I thought the evening went amazingly well in the bar. We talked. We danced. Elm's sake, we fucked! It doesn't get much better than that, does it?"

"We did? In the bar?"

Flora's head snapped around. She looked livid.

"I can't remember," Rye said. And the Almighty King and Queen of the Fey knew she would have wanted to remember that if she could.

"You can't remember?" Flora said stonily. "I made that little impression on you?"

"No. I mean yes. Shit. I don't know what I mean. I remember leaving the bar with you. And wanting to—wanting you. Then I don't know what happened for the next four or five hours. It's blank."

Flora glared at her.

"It happens to me sometimes." Rye made a hopeless gesture. "It's not your fault. It's me. Um. Oh, fey. I don't know what happens to me. My brain stops working. I wish I could remember. I really do. I'm sorry."

The air was tense enough to walk on.

"I'm sorry," Rye said. "I'm glad I didn't hurt you. Physically, I mean. Um. I think you're wonderful. And sexy. And beautiful. And fun. And I can't believe you looked twice at me. Um. I'm sorry for whatever I did. It was probably the stupidest thing I've ever done. I'll always regret it. And I'll always wish I could remember having sex with you. Bye."

Rye reached for the door handle.

Flora grabbed Rye's jacket sleeve. "Wait."

Rye remained tense as she stared at Flora. Flora didn't look angry anymore.

"Why is it that nothing goes as I expect when I'm with you?" Flora sighed and sank back into her seat. "If a thousand women told me they couldn't remember having sex with me, I'd never forgive any one of them. And think they lied out of spite. But I believe you, Rye Woods. I don't even feel any enthusiasm for finishing the rant I'd practised to deliver to you. Holy Elm, help me. I must have dry rot."

Rye was slow to realise what was happening. It didn't seem real that Flora might be granting her a reprieve. She turned to stare incredulously.

"Do you really think I'm wonderful?" Flora asked.

"Yes."

Flora smiled. "Do you still want to get out?"

"No. And...um. For what it's worth, I can't believe that I really wanted to leave you on Fifth Night either."

"Oh, no. You were most emphatic."

Rye scowled. "What...what did I do?"

"You developed this highly unflattering look on your face and bolted without a backward glance. Is this a medical condition? Is it something I have to look out for in the future?"

"Um. It doesn't happen often," Rye said. "Future? You mean—?"

Flora reached forward to turn on the carpet's magic. "I'm not making any more plans where you're concerned. I've given that up as a waste of time. Let's just see where things take us, yes?"

Rye grinned. "Um. Yeah. Please."

"You'd better strap in."

"Oh. Right. Um. Before I do...Can I kiss you?"

Flora turned to her. "I thought you'd never ask."

Rye leaned across and met Flora's lips halfway. Almighty King and Queen of the Fey, that felt good!

Flora smiled and stroked Rye's face.

"Um," Rye said. "When we had sex did we undress?"

Flora smiled self-consciously. "No. We barely made it into the carpet. We didn't take the time to remove a single piece of clothing."

Rye mentally sighed with relief and patted Flora's hand.

Flora looked thoughtful. "Do you have a problem with—? Never mind. I'd better get you home."

Chapter Four

Holly leaned against the kitchen door post. "That smells good. A zillion times better than your singing sounds. I thought you were putting a weasel through a cheese grater."

Rye stopped singing and reached for the shaker to sprinkle pollen on the grilled sparrow's wings. "Knowing what you consider good music, I'm flattered."

Holly poked her tongue out then dropped into a chair. "Wow. This looks great. You don't usually do your special cooking during the week. What's the occasion? Did you do so well at school that they had to invent a new letter better than A for you?"

"You've got that school trip on Fifth Day morning, haven't you?" Rye asked.

"What a waste of a day off! Staring at stupid ruins. Who cares about them? If the limping old tree is so important, how come they let it rot? And a bunch of boulders. It's not fair that they're making me go and stare at the stupid things for hours."

Rye smiled. Fifth Day. Flora Day.

❖

Rye had never shopped so fast. She set her bags down near the intersection of Dandelion Avenue and the Citrus Flyway. She was a quarter of an hour early. She nervously fidgeted. She wished she could tell if her armpits smelled. Not that they were going to have sex. No. Definitely not. She dare not risk that again. And it seemed highly unlikely that Flora would want to do it again if last time had been so awful. Not that Rye didn't think about sex and Flora about every five seconds. The gods seemed cruel beyond imagining that they'd let her forget having sex with Flora.

Rye turned around to check her appearance in the window of a large broom salesroom. She stepped closer and peered inside. They had all the latest shiny models displayed to excite the greatest envy in potential shoppers. The price of a second-hand broom was going to be difficult enough to find. No point looking at new ones.

Rye sighed and turned back to watching for Flora's carpet. This last week had been exhausting. Still, her body would get used to walking to the building site every day. She wouldn't have minded so much if it didn't take a good two hours out of her already short days. Realistically, she would only be able to see Flora on Fifth Days. How many school trips would Holly be taking this semester?

Rye had not been on a second date before, so she wasn't sure what happened. But it wouldn't be sex. Too much depended on Rye's continued concealment. Holly could not be more than a year or two away from getting her wings. That would signal her transition from child to adult. Had they still been in Fairyland, it would mean the commune council would give Holly her own piece of land to work, she could legally own possessions, and she would take her place on the benches at the front of the temple. Most importantly for her continued residence in the United Forestlands, getting her wings meant, under fairy law, that she became legally responsible for herself. So none of their aunts or cousins back in Fairyland could get her deported by claiming guardianship over her. And since she had been a wingless child when Rye took her out of Fairyland, Holly could not be held accountable for her departure or any laws she had violated in leaving. So they couldn't get her back on those grounds either. Once she developed her wings, she would be safe.

In breaking her strict celibate habit of the last eleven years, Rye courted danger for them both. Flora might guess that she was a fairy. But Rye couldn't help herself. Flora was so good to be with. Rye had not experienced much friendship before. Surely this couldn't hurt?

Flora's carpet pulled up. Rye put her bags in the boot and climbed inside. Flora smiled at her. Rye's return smile was just the outward show of the tingling warmth and pleasure Flora's proximity sparked inside her.

Flora steered her carpet to the end tree in Whiterow Gardens and zoomed up the ascending lane to the very top. She lived in the penthouse. Rye glimpsed a swimming pool in the groin of a branch before the carpet descended into a garage. The deep unease that Rye had felt when she walked to Whiterow Gardens failed to materialise. Whenever she was with Flora, something strange happened to the tiny speck of Infinity around Rye. It bent into a more optimistic shape that centred around Flora Withe and feeling good.

"Do you have anything that needs to be put in the cooler?" Flora asked.

"Um. Yeah. Do you mind?"

Flora grabbed a couple of Rye's shopping bags from the boot before leading the way inside. Rye's first impression was of tidiness, tasteful and pristine hard-to-keep-clean colours, light, and space. Flora's living room alone was larger than Rye's whole apartment. A wall of windows looked out onto a private deck containing the swimming pool. The pale carpet looked like the only foot traffic it received was when someone walked over it behind a vacuum cleaner. Rye grimaced down at her boots.

Flora led Rye through into the kitchen. Rye stopped and stared. It was as if she had walked into her dream: enormous stove with plenty of burners, acres of bench space, a vast table, a chopping block, and shiny rows of pots and pans hanging within convenient reach. You could really cook in this kitchen.

"Cooler's here," Flora said. "I'll make tea."

When they returned to the lounge, Rye slipped her boots off. To her horror, both her socks had holes. She tried to keep her feet tucked out of sight when she sat on one of the sofas. Flora sat on the other end of the same sofa. Close but not dangerously so. She looked very good in a tight top and little skirt. Rye sipped her tea and imagined immigration officials beating down her door to come and arrest Holly and herself. No sex.

"How is Holly?" Flora asked. "Shopping this morning?"

"On a school trip. And hating every moment. Not that I can blame her this time. It sounds very boring. History. It's not Holls' favourite subject."

"What does she like?"

"To hear her, nothing," Rye said. "She's bursting for the day she can leave school. I had hoped she'd go to university, but she doesn't seem at all keen. Maybe she'll change her mind. She does that as often as she changes her clothes."

"You'd like her to take a degree?"

"No one can take your education away from you, no matter what else they do."

Flora frowned and cocked her head.

"I want Holls to get a good job," Rye said. "A degree is her ticket to that. But I'm not sure she hears me over the noise of her crash music."

Flora smiled. "I'm surprised that she doesn't like art. She has natural talent."

"She gets average grades in most subjects, but I know she could do better if she tried. She used to when she was younger. She was more interested in school then. If they had classes on giggling about boys, gossiping with her friends on the phone for hours and hours, and playing loud music, she'd be a straight-A student."

"We all go through that, don't we? It's that dreaded adolescence. There isn't a creature of any species which doesn't suffer it, is there?"

Rye turned away and drank to hide her frown. Her own adolescence had been very different from Holly's. But then, that was what Rye worked hard for.

Rye's gaze snagged on a pair of wall hangings with patterns that almost matched, but didn't quite. They made her feel that they should and that it was her eyes that were wrong, not the symmetry.

"Did you make those?" Rye asked.

Flora turned to look. "Magnificent, aren't they? A friend wove them. They're the best things she has ever done by a wide margin in my opinion, though I don't tell her so in quite that way. But it's nice of you to think they might have been mine."

Rye took another look around the room. She hadn't noticed the paintings and pots before.

"Would you like to see what I do?" Flora asked.

"Yeah, I would."

Flora smiled warmly. Rye's heart gave an odd flutter.

Rye slipped her hand into Flora's and let her lead her through the apartment. They entered a room alive with light and colour. The windows started partway up the walls and curved around to cover half the ceiling. Rye could see green leaves, blue sky, and white clouds. Balls, skeins, and hanks of threads of every material and hue spilled out of baskets on the floor and formed rainbows on the shelves.

"Sad to say," Flora said, "but this is my closest companion."

Rye stared at the loom which dominated the room. It looked large enough to make a good-sized rug on, though it was only partly threaded now.

"If I worked out how many hours I've spent with this," Flora said, "compared to the time I communicate with people, the answer would be thoroughly depressing to any normal being."

Rye looked around at the colourful bits of cloth and rough watercolour sketches tacked to the walls. She stepped across to peer at a circular piece of cloth.

Flora moved closer. She glanced between the cloth and Rye. "Well? Or would I be better not asking?"

"Art and stuff usually makes me feel very stupid," Rye said. "As though my brain is missing the bit that other people have which lets them make sense of shapes and colours."

"This doesn't?"

"Not as much. I don't understand what it's supposed to be. But it feels okay to look at."

Flora smiled. "I'll take that as a compliment."

"I'm sorry. I shouldn't say anything. I don't know what I'm talking about."

"You gave me your honest reaction. I can't ask for better." Flora gently stroked Rye's sleeve. "I don't know many people who are unafraid enough to be as honest as you are. I don't just mean this. I was thinking about in the carpet the other night."

Rye frowned down at the floor. Honest. That was the last thing she could be.

"I've upset you," Flora said. "I'm sorry."

Rye shook her head. She discovered that she was holding Flora's hand. She lifted it to her lips to lightly kiss it. She was suddenly aware of Flora's body so close and the musky smell of Flora's perfume. Flora took a deep breath and her fingers curled around Rye's. Her eyes looked dark and intense. That elusive hint of pine sap diffused up into Rye's brain again. She pulled Flora against her to kiss.

"Oh, Elm," Flora whispered.

Their lips parted and their tongues joined eagerly. Flora pressed warm and pliable all against Rye's front. Her chest rubbed against Rye as her breasts firmed with her arousal. Rye groaned and buried her face in Flora's neck.

Flora stiffened and pulled away. She put her hands against Rye's ribs. Her hardened chest rose and fell rapidly.

"Is this a good idea?" Flora said.

Rye swallowed and tried to get her brain working again. She stumbled back. Her wing buds pressed against the wall. Rye used the discomfort to help bring herself back to sanity.

"Fey," Rye said. "I'm sorry. I didn't mean to—Shit."

"You're not going to run out on me?"

"No."

"Let's go and sit down."

As Rye trailed Flora back into the living room, she wriggled her errant wing buds back into place.

"Look," Flora said, "I'm not telling you anything you don't already know when I say that I am very attracted to you. But I've been burned. I don't want that to happen again. You came on like a falling tree. I wouldn't have minded, but I think I need you to tell me when you're ready."

"I'm sorry."

"I don't mind. If you say today, I'll be more than happy to pick up where we left off. If we have to wait, I shall. There's more to a relationship than sex. Or should be, to make it worthwhile. But you have to tell me."

❖

Even though Holly was not due home for another hour, Rye felt nervous about Flora flying her all the way up to the apartment's parking pad. She should've asked Flora to drop her off at the corner of the street, just to be safe.

"When can I see you again?" Flora said. "Second Night is your night class, isn't it? How about Third Night?"

"Um. I can't. I'll be working."

Flora frowned. "You work nights, too?"

"On First and Third Nights. Second Night and every second Fourth Night is night class."

"You have two jobs?"

"How about next Fifth Day?" Rye said. "I'm sure I can work something out with Holly."

"I'll look forward to it. Call me."

"Of course."

❖

Late on Fourth Day afternoon, Rye stood in the line at the pay hut door.

"You coming to the bar, Rye?" Knot said.

"Nah," Rye said.

"You got a hot date?" Blackie asked.

"Real hot," Rye said. "I've got to fix the bloody table leg."

"If it's stiff legs you want to play with, Rye," Budge called from farther down the line, "reckon we could find someone at the pub for you, eh, Knot?"

Most of the blokes within earshot laughed. Rye made an obscene gesture suggestive of Budge's inability to hold an erection.

"Woods!" Grub called. "Wake up."

Rye stepped inside to stand at the table.

"Full week," Grub said. "No deductions. Sign here."

Rye signed her name beneath all the X's, thumbprints, and claw indentations of her fellow workers. She took the pay packet outside and opened it to count. Three hundred and twenty pieces. One hundred and sixty-five for rent. Ninety for food. Twenty-five for lights and fuel. Eight for water. Twenty for that new pair of shoes Holly needed. Twelve for unexpected stuff that always came up.

Rye tucked the packet in her back pocket, hefted her bag, and strode through the gates. She waved to Knot and the boys, then turned the opposite way for the long walk to the Hollowberry Municipal School for her night class.

A low-flying carpet passed Rye, an old song trailing from its speakers. Rye picked up the tune with a whistle. She was smiling to herself as she trotted down the Rootway underpass. A shower of fat raindrops did nothing to dampen her high spirits. Life wasn't so bad.

Rye strolled through the school gates ten minutes early for her class. She had just stepped inside when the lights died.

"No panic!" A goblin caretaker hurried down the corridor with a torch bobbing in his big grey claw. "Power dead. Go outside."

Rye went to stand out in the parking lot. She nodded to one or two of her classmates. More students arrived and the time for the start of class passed, but the school remained black. After about a quarter of an hour, one of the teachers came out to say that the classes had to be cancelled.

Rye shouldered her bag and headed for the gates. When she hit Lowbranch Street she automatically turned right, but she had not gone more than a dozen paces before she stopped. A large transit carpet flew past, crammed with people going home from work. Rye frowned. She had two hours before she was due home. Holly would be around at the Barks' house. She had her pay in her back pocket.

Rye ran back down the street and stopped at the first public transit node. She quickly scanned the flashing timetables. Newbud. There had to be a route that could get her there. Yes. The brown carpet to the bridge district node and the taupe carpet to Newbud. She felt only a slight twinge for her extravagance as she handed over four pieces for her fare. She would not buy beer this week.

She had changed to the taupe carpet and was whizzing north from the bridge district before it occurred to her to wonder that Flora might not be at home, or might have company.

Rye jogged to Whiterow Gardens. The flutters of unease and sense of not belonging didn't stop her from looking for the call panel on a decorative but also sturdily functional gate around the base of the tree. There were only ten buttons. That meant each apartment occupied a whole level to itself, unlike the sixth of a wedge that Rye lived in. She wiped her hands on the back of her pants before pressing Flora's button.

A jogger in trendy gear shot Rye a disapproving look as he passed. Rye craned her neck to see if she could see any lights in Flora's penthouse.

"Crap," Rye said. "I should've called first."

Click.

"Rye!" Flora said. "What are you doing here?"

Rye grinned and looked up to see where the camera might be. "Um. If it's not a good time, I could—"

The gate clunked open.

"Come up," Flora said.

Rye smiled all the way up ten flights of stairs. She paused on the porch to regain her breath and wipe sweat from her face before knocking.

Flora looked surprised when she opened the door. "Is the elevating carpet not working?"

"Elevating carpet? Oh. I'm so used to the one in our tree being broken that I didn't think to look for one."

Rye set her bag down inside the door and kicked off her work boots. Flora wore baggy casual pants and a snug little top that seemed designed to draw Rye's attention to her chest. After an awkward moment of staring, they exchanged chaste kisses.

"What a great surprise," Flora said.

"I'm not interrupting?"

"No. I'm all alone and thinking about you."

Rye grinned like an idiot as she followed Flora through to the living room.

Flora fetched Rye a cold beer. "I couldn't remember what sort you mentioned that you like. They all look the same to me. The man in the store suggested this brand."

"Wow. This is great. Thanks."

Flora smiled as she sipped her glass of wine. "I thought you had night class?"

"The school had a power cut," Rye said. "So, I thought—Can you smell burning?"

"Branch!" Flora leaped to her feet and dashed into the kitchen.

Rye followed. Smoke hazed the room. Flora stood holding a pot which oozed black smoke.

"I suppose it will have to be Lowood's takeaway for tea again," Flora said. "Or my usual table at the Ravenous Acorn."

Rye took the pot from Flora and ran cold water into it. The charred lump in the bottom hissed.

"What was this?" Rye asked.

"A highly nutritious and appetising meal that any idiot could prepare by simply heating it in water for seven minutes. I suppose that makes me a special kind of idiot."

Rye smiled and set the incinerated remains aside. "Where do you keep your food?"

"That is the pantry. You don't have to heat my dinner for me."

"I have no intention of doing that." Rye pulled open both doors to reveal a vast walk-in pantry. "Wow. You could lose a whole family back here and still have room for the preserves."

Barely a tenth of the storage space was occupied. She found some thrush's eggs that smelled reasonably fresh.

"There's not much in there," Flora said. "You probably guessed that I don't often try to feed myself. For fear of lowering your opinion of me, I'm not only hopeless with food but also extremely careless. If something stays in there long enough to grow legs and crawl out, it's welcome to its freedom."

Rye smiled. "Do you like omelettes?"

Flora watched with undisguised amazement as Rye chopped, grated, and whisked. Her surprise deepened when she tasted the result.

"Hmm," Flora said. "That's really good. Really, really good. You know, Rye Woods, you constantly take me by surprise. Which not many people do."

Rye smiled to herself as she wiped down the counter. This was a great kitchen.

"I feel really guilty about having you cook for me and then making you watch me eat," Flora said. "Won't you have something?"

"I'll make dinner for me and Holls when I get home. But anyone who buys me Midnight Beer has a right to ask for more than an omelette. Where do you keep your detergent?"

"Leave that. You are not doing the dishes. Aloe will do them in the morning."

"Aloe?"

"My housecleaner. I suppose if I had a particle of sense I'd hire a cook as well."

Rye trailed Flora into the lounge. She should not have been surprised that Flora could afford to pay someone to do her household chores for her.

Flora sat close, with her legs drawn up beneath her. "How long can you stay?"

"I usually get home just after eight. I'm not sure what time the transit carpet will get back, so I'd better not leave it too late."

"Don't be silly. I'll take you. When are you going to get a new broom? It must be wildly inconvenient without one."

Rye shrugged. "Tell me what you wove today."

Flora smiled and began talking about her day.

At some point, Rye finished her beer and started a second. Smooth, dark, and malty, it was about the best beer she'd ever tasted. Flora had carried her jar of wine into the lounge and was well on the way to finishing it. Flora's company and the beer softened the Infinity space around Rye in a very pleasant way. Coming here was the smartest idea she'd had in years.

"Oh," Flora said, "if you've come from work, does that mean you have a bangy thing with you?"

"Bangy thing?"

"You know. For hitting things that stop working properly. One of the shelves in my workroom is loose. If I bribed you with another beer, would you save me from having to deal with a tradesman who will call me girlie?"

Rye smiled and went to get her hammer from her work bag.

Flora showed her the offending shelf. Rye immediately saw the problem and fetched a screwdriver. It was the work of half a minute to tighten it.

"There you go," Rye said. "All fixed. Girlie."

Flora's eyes widened in mock outrage. She threw a hank of wool at Rye. Rye threw it back. Flora grabbed two more and hurled them. Rye bent to scoop up as much as she could hold and tossed them.

Flora grabbed a long loom needle and advanced threateningly. "Girlie?"

Rye backed away, laughing, with Flora stalking her. When Rye tripped and landed on her backside, Flora leaped forward to tickle. Rye grabbed for her wrists, all the while laughing. Their wrestling knocked over baskets and spilled more yarns on the floor. Flora began laughing too. Rye rolled her over and pinned her amongst the colourful mess. Flora lay beneath her in glorious disarray. Rye stopped laughing. Flora lost her smile. Rye's breathing grew faster and shallower. Flora's eyes darkened.

"Rye," Flora said. "Should we—"

Rye kissed her. After a moment's hesitation, Flora responded and slid her arms up around Rye. Their kisses grew harder, more insistent. Rye had never wanted anything as passionately as she wanted Flora. Rye's lips couldn't encompass enough of her, and she wanted to feel Flora against her whole body. Flora's hands clutched at Rye as she writhed and strained beneath her. Her moans bucked Rye's arousal up and up. Rye's wing buds jerked on the brink of bursting through her T-shirt. The scent of pine sap swamped every other smell and set the blood roaring through Rye's veins.

Rye peeled Flora's top off her and stared at the dryad's firm breasts before cupping them in her hands and sucking at them with her mouth. Though breasts and nipples were hard against Rye's tongue, Flora's pale skin was still satin smooth. Flora's fingers dug into her hair and shoulder. Rye's wing buds tried to unfold with her soaring excitement. She didn't care. She impatiently tugged at Flora's pants. For a moment, she paused, panting, to savour the sight of the naked dryad lying on a fragmented rainbow. She plunged her face into Flora's groin.

When Rye worked her lips back up to her throat, Flora tugged Rye's belt undone. Rye shoved her pants down and lowered herself onto her. They writhed and strained against each other, moaning, and rising to their climaxes. Flora's every gasp and half-cry stoked Rye's lust. Their groans came faster. Their bodies rubbed harder. Rye grunted and clutched at Flora as her world crashed with pleasure. Not long afterward, Flora spasmed against her.

Rye sagged. Flora took a shuddering breath and sat up to clutch Rye's shirt front in both hands.

"Don't leave me," Flora said. "I couldn't handle it a second time. Do you hear me, Rye?"

Rye grunted.

"Are you still with me?" Flora asked.

Rye nodded. As her crisis passed, she began realising what they'd done. She was naked from the waist down. She could feel a darkness hovering just around her, ready to pounce.

Flora's fists tightened. "Listen to me. I don't care what you are. I don't know what species you are, but I don't care. Do you hear me?"

"Shit."

"It doesn't matter to me. Rye, look at me. Please."

Rye lifted her head. Flora's serious concern showed through the flush of her afterglow. Rye frowned and put her hands over Flora's fists. She looked beyond her. They were in Flora's workroom. Rye sucked in air as if she hadn't breathed for an hour.

"Flora," Rye said.

Flora smiled. "Yes, lover. Branch, you had me frightened."

"I'm sorry."

"Do you remember?"

"Yes."

Flora leaned close to lightly kiss Rye. She loosened her grip on Rye's shirt. "What do we do now?"

Rye sat back on her heels. Her wing buds poked uncomfortably inside her shirt. "I...I don't know."

"Well, why don't you put your pants back on? I won't look."

Flora turned away to gather her clothes. Rye put a gently restraining hand on her arm.

"It doesn't matter," Flora said. "Honestly. What is important is that you don't feel as though you have to run away from me."

"You're wonderful."

Flora smiled. She softly stroked Rye's cheek and rose. Some magic passed from her fingertips to infuse the whole of Rye's body and mind. Flora really was the most incredible person in the whole of Infinity.

"Wait," Rye said.

Rye yanked her shirt off. Flora watched. Rye wrestled her tight T-shirt up over her head. The release of her cramped wings and chest was like a second orgasm. Returning blood flow tingled in several places.

Flora's gaze roved Rye's bare torso with her typically small pair of breasts and the pronounced breastbone and upper body musculature of a winged creature. Flora would not yet be able to see the wing buds on Rye's back, which were the compact bundles formed by the folded sections of each wing support lying hard against each other.

Slowly, fearfully, Rye strained to unfold her wings. The five sections of each of her wing supports sequentially snapped out straight. Rye's wing supports jutted up above her shoulders. Flora did not run screaming in horror. Instead, she looked like she'd been turned to stone.

Rye stood. Might as well let Flora see it all. She lifted her wing supports until they projected at the flying angle, which stretched her thin membranes to their full extent from her shoulders, down her back, the back of her legs, and to her ankles.

"Oh, Holy Elm," Flora said. "You're a fairy."

Rye stood her ground as Flora stepped close. Rye began to feel the enormity of what she'd done. This was the first time since her escape from Fairyland that she had revealed her species to anyone. Her wings twitched. She had to exert herself to prevent them from defensively folding. She did fold her arms across her chest.

Flora rested a warm hand on Rye's arm. "Thank you."

"You...you don't want to throw me out?"

"Throw you out? Because you're an even bigger turn on than I thought? Oh, Elm, I have to touch your wings. May I?"

Rye nodded.

Flora reached out to softly stroke Rye's wing membrane. "It's warm. And pliable. So smooth."

Flora wandered around behind Rye. Rye again had to concentrate not to let her wings snap into a defensive fold hard against her back. Flora's delicate touches made her shiver.

Flora wore a soft smile when she walked back to Rye's front. "Amazing. I'd love to see you fly."

"We don't. Not really. We glide."

"Then I'd love to see you glide."

"I can't," Rye said.

"I suppose it would create something of a sensation for you to hurl yourself between trees naked. Although I'd be more than happy to watch."

Flora slid her arms up Rye's chest and shoulders until she touched wings. Rye held her close so they touched naked body to naked body without even air separating them. Flora kissed her.

"You...you don't mind that I'm a fairy?"

"Of course not. You thought I might?"

"I tell people that Holly and I are of mixed bogle and brownie blood. Because most people don't like fairies. They think we're all freaks and religious nutters who should be shipped back to Fairyland."

Admitting that she was not a legal resident, and the questions that would beg, would involve another giant leap of faith Rye wasn't prepared for. It was scary enough that she'd revealed her species.

"Is that what triggered your bolt after our first time, at the club?" Flora said. "And why you asked if we'd taken our clothes off? Because you thought I'd discovered that you're a fairy? And you feared that I'd have such an adverse, prejudiced reaction that it would cancel out my attraction and liking for you?"

Rye shrugged. "It's easier and safer to hide."

"Well, I'll certainly keep your secret. Of course I will. It's obviously so very important to you. But you don't have to hide from me."

❖

The next Fifth Day morning, Rye found it hard to concentrate even on so mundane a task as making breakfast. She had a date with Flora at ten o'clock. And sex.

"I'm away, Holls," Rye called. "Remember that I'll be late. I'm going to the library after shopping. Okay?"

"Don't forget the borage juice this time," Holly called.

"I won't."

Rye hurtled down the stairs to the base of the apartment tree and ran toward the market. She raced through her shopping. When she carried her bags to the rendezvous, she found Flora waiting for her. As soon as Rye climbed in and snapped the safety harness on, Flora hit the power. She speeded away. At Flora's apartment, they began undressing each other before they got out of the carpet.

Later, Rye sighed and eased herself up onto an elbow. They lay tangled together on the floor in the short hall between the garage and the living room. Their discarded clothes formed an untidy trail back to the carpet. Flora stretched lazily and smiled at Rye.

"I suppose it's too late for me to play hard to get?" Flora said.

"That's okay. Cheap and easy is fine by me."

Flora looked deeply offended, but ruined it by sitting up to loop her arms around Rye's neck and kissing her.

"Hmm. You taste good," Flora said.

"You feel good. And smell nice. That hint of pine sap. It's like bonking a building site."

Flora hit her and rose. She looked gorgeous as she stalked away. She paused halfway across the living room and gave Rye a look that clearly indicated Rye ought to be following her.

They settled on a sofa to feed each other bits of fruit. Rye soon discovered that juice tasted much nicer licked off a dryad's body. Sex on the sofa left colourful stains on the upholstery.

After a long, hot, steamy shower, they reluctantly dressed.

"I'd better get home," Rye said. "Holly will be forgetting what I look like."

"Would I offend you terribly if I said that I hoped your school will have another power cut?"

Rye smiled and pulled Flora close. That she, Rye Woods, could enjoy the privilege of touching so beautiful, so sexy a woman was nothing short of a miracle.

"I don't have class this Fourth Day," Rye said.

"Oh, goody. Can you come over?"

Rye frowned. "I want to. More than anything. But I mustn't leave Holls. The kid sees little enough of me as it is."

Flora looked disappointed. Rye bent so that their foreheads rested together.

"Do you think they'd invent a whole new day of the week for us?" Rye asked. "One that we can have just to enjoy ourselves in?"

"Fuck Day."

"I'm betting it would be very popular."

Flora slid a couple of fingers into Rye's waistband and gently tugged. "Until then, Fifth Day mornings will have to be our fuck days. You can make it next week?"

"Even if I have to tie Holly in a chair and run all the way here carrying my grocery bags."

"We needn't be quite that drastic." Flora lost her smile. "This is going to be the longest week of my life."

"I'll call."

"It's not the same. But please do."

After a long, lingering, regretful kiss, Flora fetched her purse. Rye retrieved her groceries from the cooler.

Rye asked Flora to stop the carpet at the street corner before her tree.

"You don't want Holly to know about us?" Flora said.

Rye frowned out of the side window. Flora wouldn't understand if Rye told her that she didn't want Holly to know she was gay. Rye did not want to explain about Fairyland and her fear of getting sent back.

"She hasn't seen me with anyone before," Rye said. "Um. It's complicated. I mean, it could get complicated. Do you mind?"

"As long as you're not ashamed of me."

"What? No! Of course not. She thinks you're the top of the trees. But I bet she'd think you were a lot less stylish if she knew you were seeing me."

Flora laughed. "I wish I'd had a little sister."

Chapter Five

Rye pulled her jacket collar up against the wind and strode toward the school gates. She wasn't at all sure she really understood this new accounting module as well as she had the economics one. She should read more. There were just not enough hours in the day or days in the week. If she'd been able to take the public transit carpet to work, she could've read on her way to and from the building site. Mr. Bulrush had asked her again about the certification exam. Rye really liked the idea of taking the proper exam, and saving herself some courses, but the preparation would take even more of the time she didn't have. And the exam itself was likely to carry a fee.

A carpet pulled alongside her. She grinned and bent to see Flora.

"What are you doing here?" Rye asked.

"Cruising for some hunky dyke to pick up and grope," Flora said.

Rye climbed in. Flora dimmed the windows and twisted around to get closer to Rye. Their first kisses were like those of parched women slaking thirsts.

"Elm, I needed that," Flora said. "Do you mind? I simply couldn't wait to see you again."

When Flora dropped her off a discreet distance from her tree, Rye watched the carpet lights until they disappeared. She sighed. Fey, it had been wonderful to be with Flora for even just half an hour. It was going to be a long time to Fifth Day. If only they could meet more often. Rye needed to do something about transportation. She crossed the street to Cloudnut's All-Purpose Store for a newspaper.

Holly was in her room when Rye got home.

"It's me, Holls," Rye called as she went to the kitchen.

Evening work at new health bar. Must be friendly and well-presented.

Rye drew a pencil line through that ad.

Casual labour wanted for after hours cleaning. No experience necessary. Evenings and nights. Flexible hours inc. Fifth Day. Good remuneration. Apply T. Rivers, Asst. Personnel Supervisor.

Perfect. Rye drew a dark circle around the advertisement. In fact, it sounded too good to be true. What was wrong with it?

The kettle whistled. Rye rose and went to pour boiling water onto the pan of chestnuts.

"How was school?" Holly flopped into a chair at the table.

"Okay."

"You always say that."

"So do you. How did your day go?"

Holly wrinkled her nose and tugged the newspaper closer. "What's that smell?"

"Probably the bracken," Rye said. "It's not as fresh as I thought."

"No. It's not cooking. It's like perfume. Really nice perfume. That's so twisted. You haven't actually started to use personal hygiene products?"

Rye glanced down at the front of her shirt. Crap. Holly must be smelling Flora's perfume. What could she possibly say? "Um. The only stink in this house is that grunge you keep in the bathroom."

"No, it's not like anything of mine. Why are you looking at Help Wanted ads? You didn't finally tell Pansy where to shove her fried sandwiches?"

"I need another job."

"*Another* job? What were you thinking of doing, letting people do medical experiments on you while you sleep?"

"I can't afford to save for a new broom on what I earn now." Rye stirred the bracken. It really was past its best. She'd not buy from that imp again. "I should be able to find something to do on those Fourth Nights when I don't have classes. Or Fifth Day afternoons."

Chair legs screeched on the floor. Holly stomped out and slammed her bedroom door. Rye frowned. What was that about?

After dishing up dinner, Rye knocked on Holly's door.

"Holls? Dinner's ready."

"I'm not hungry."

"Have you been eating junk at your friend's house again?"

Music blared from behind the door. Rye returned to the kitchen and ate her dinner in unsmiling solitude. She washed up but left Holly's plate on the table. She wished she had a beer, but she had not bought any for this week.

Rye carried a cup of tea and the newspaper into the tiny lounge, made her bed up on the couch, and lay down to look through the job ads. She stared at the one she had circled earlier.

"Shit."

Rye scored a line through the ad. Assistant personnel supervisor. She'd be expected to fill out all the official paperwork, including the citizen identification number which she did not have.

After Rye finished reading through the chapter set in class, she snapped off the light. Holly still hadn't emerged from her room. Rye's thoughts drifted in a much more pleasant direction. Flora.

❖

When Rye arrived home the next night, Holly was not in. Rye couldn't even find a scrawled note.

Rye unhappily set about making soup. After she finished adding the last lumps of fennel root, Rye wiped her hands on her tea towel apron and sat to open her mail. One bore the fancy crest of Holly's school. Rye chewed her lip as she tore the envelope. If the kid was in some kind of trouble—

"Crap."

Holly wasn't in trouble, Rye was. School fees were going up an extra three hundred next semester. How was she supposed to find that? Her work at Pansy's only just covered the current fee.

The door opened.

"You're late," Rye said. "Where have you been?"

Holly slammed her bedroom door shut and turned her music on loud. Rye silently counted to ten before returning to her mail.

When Holly emerged to eat, she still wore her school clothes.

"If you spill food," Rye said, "you'll have to wear the stains to school."

"If I didn't go to that stupid school, you wouldn't have to work all those jobs to pay for it."

"You are not leaving school. When you're my age, you'll be grateful for a decent education. You might even thank me for sending you to that school."

"Easy for you to say. You never went."

Rye winced. That drew blood. "You'd probably enjoy it more if you got better grades."

"That's your answer to everything, isn't it? Well, I hate school. I'm not good at it."

"You used to be. If you tried—"

"I do! I'm stupid. Is that what you want me to say? I'm not smart like you. It doesn't matter how much you force me, you'll never get my brains bulging out of my head. And forcing me to stay at school forever isn't going to make me like it any more. It's a stupid waste of time."

Rye's fists clenched. "You would've liked your life even less if we'd still been in Fairyland."

"I doubt that." Holly shoved her half-empty bowl away and stood. "At least I'd not be a freak who has to lie all the time."

Holly stomped into the bathroom and slammed the door.

Rye dropped her spoon on the table. "Give me the power to endure."

❖

In the haven of Flora's apartment on Fifth Day morning, Rye should have been able, for a few precious hours out of a week, to devote herself wholly to her own pleasure with Flora.

"By the Elm, you're tense, considering what we've just done." Flora knelt behind Rye and kneaded her naked shoulders.

Rye grunted and grimaced at the flickering fire.

"Work?" Flora asked.

"Very hard work. It's Holly. She's being an impossible pain. She only speaks to tell me how much she hates her life and hates me."

"What's her problem?"

"I wish I knew." Rye reached for the mug of beer that she had only taken two sips of before they had flung themselves together on the hearth rug.

"School? Boys?"

"I phoned the school. Her counsellor says that she isn't having any problems. Looks like it's just me. And she's not talking. She slams doors. Just when I thought her adolescence couldn't possibly get any worse, it does."

Flora kissed the back of Rye's neck and slipped around to sit in front of her. She sipped wine.

Rye stroked one of Flora's legs. "I wish fairies were one of those species that shove the young out of the family nest at an early age."

Flora laughed and put her other leg within Rye's reach.

"What worries me," Rye said, "is how angry she gets me. I'd never forgive myself if I laid a hand on her, but it seems like she's goading me to see how far she can push. And sometimes it's a close thing."

Flora looked thoughtful as she stroked the edge of Rye's wing membrane. Rye watched the firelight playing across Flora's body. No sculptor who chiselled and sanded the palest, finest-grained wood could dream of creating anything close to Flora's smooth, curved perfection. For a breathless moment, Rye felt overwhelmed by awe. That she, Rye Woods, should be here with Flora, and be allowed to touch Flora, didn't seem real. Rye forgot Holly and all her other problems as the Almighty King and Queen of the Fey twitched aside the dirty curtains that normally shrouded life and allowed Rye a peek of transcendent joy.

Flora's fingers stilled and she looked up. "I have an idea. You can reject it and you won't ripple my pond. How about I try to talk to Holly?"

"You?"

"I know my credentials from dealing with teenagers aren't extensive, but I do have the advantage of never having to tell her to tidy her room or do her homework. And I have a carpet that is astronomically stylish. Plus the undeniable assets of my personal flair and irresistible charisma."

Rye smiled. "You forgot modesty. I wonder if it would work?"

"How about I invite you two to dinner over here?"

"You can't cook."

"I can take us out to a restaurant for the eating bit."

"No!"

Flora looked taken aback. "What did I say wrong?"

"I'm not letting you put yourself out of pocket because of my problems."

"Out of pocket? I was only planning to buy the three of us dinner, not part ownership in the place."

Rye frowned down into her dark beer. She was sure she could not afford to pay for her and Holly at any restaurant Flora patronised, nor did she own anything of equal value she might give in return. Much as she would like help with Holly, there had to be something else they could do that would not entail her becoming obliged to Flora.

"Why don't you invite me to dinner at your place?" Flora said. "We could—No, wait, I have a brain wave. To get Holly on her own, why don't I take her shopping for the ingredients? Then you can cook the stuff when we get back?"

"That might work." Rye nodded. No fairy could argue the fairness of one providing food and the other the labour to prepare it. They could sit down to share the meal on equal terms. "You wouldn't mind?"

Flora sat up to loop her arms around Rye's neck. "I'd be spending time with you. I'd like to get to know your little sister."

"Not this version of the Holly Hormonal Monster, you won't. But I'd be grateful if you'd try. I'm down to the last pea in my pod with her."

"You could always thank me in advance."

Rye smiled and let Flora take the beer from her hands.

❖

"We really need someone who can work four nights a week," the woman said.

"Oh. Right," Rye said. "Um. Thanks."

Rye hung up and crossed out another ad.

"Fey. You wouldn't think it'd be this hard to find something. Just a few hours a week."

Rye tossed the newspaper in the bin and trudged into the bathroom. She leaned against the shower wall and let warm water stream over her wings and body. She felt so damned tired that she could fall asleep here.

Yet, she had another three-hour shift making fried sandwiches ahead of her tonight. The thought of another job held very little appeal. But then, it wouldn't be forever. She just needed enough for a new broom. Her life would get much easier when she could cut down her travel time.

❖

Rye strolled out of the building site gates. She spied Flora's carpet parked down the street. Rye waved a hasty parting to Knot and the boys before jogging away.

Rye dropped her workbag on the back seat and turned to Flora. "Wow. You look great."

"Why thank you. You're making my hormones tingle, too, lover."

"You didn't dress up like that just to meet me?"

"Why not?" Flora steered the carpet up into the highest lane. "But on this occasion, I'm on my way back from a busy afternoon. I had lunch with my father. Then a meeting with my agent. And finally, I've just come from talking with a gallery owner."

"Don't they expect you arty farty types to dress worse than me?"

Flora flashed Rye a mock threatening smile. "It's a good job I have my hands full. The next time you say arty farty, Rye Woods, I'm liable to throw something at you. And for your information, I've never found that displaying my assets to best advantage hurt my chances of dealing with anyone."

"Works with me. I'm very much taken with your assets."

Flora patted Rye's thigh. "How is Holly?"

Rye grimaced and grunted. "The aggravation monster continues to stomp through my life. You know what I need right now?"

"Sex."

"I was thinking of a large shot of raw bark spirits. Your idea is better."

Flora smiled.

When Flora parked on the pad outside the apartment, Rye took a deep breath before getting out. Would Holly think it strange that Flora had given her a ride?

"Holls," Rye called. "I'm home."

Rye ushered Flora down the few paces to the kitchen. Holly's door was shut and imperfectly muffling the jarring sounds of the latest crash music.

Rye put water on to boil. "I'll fetch her once I've made tea."

Holly emerged on a blast of noise as Rye poured. She shot Rye a petulant look before slouching off toward the bathroom.

"Can you turn that down?" Rye said. "Ms. Withe and I can hardly hear each other."

Holly spun around.

"Hello, Holly," Flora said.

Surprise shattered Holly's sulk. "Ms. Withe? Wow. Is there any tea for me?"

Rye and Flora shared a look as Holly bolted to turn her music off.

"I was on my way from the Lightning Tree gallery," Flora said, "when I spotted Rye walking along. She's very kindly invited me to dinner on Fifth Day."

Holly's eyes widened improbably. "Astronomical. The Lightning Tree gallery is one of the most famous in Noonpine, isn't it?"

"It has something of a high profile," Flora said. "I know the owner. Letty Elmwood. She's showing one or two of my pieces there."

"Astronomical," Holly said. "Rye is an utterly stinging cook. Her maple malt sauce will slay you. You have to come to dinner, Ms. Withe. You'd really like it."

Flora smiled. "Well, perhaps I might then. But only if I'm allowed to make a contribution. How about I bring some food? Although, I must admit that my culinary knowledge and skill stop somewhere around boiling water."

Rye hid her smile behind her mug of tea.

"Maybe you could draw me up a list of ingredients?" Flora said. "Or perhaps you could come with me, Holly? And help me buy what Rye needs."

"Me?" Holly said. "Oh, yes, please! That would be scathing."

Holly accompanied Rye when she escorted Flora out to her carpet. Rye could only exchange looks of amusement and gratitude with Flora. The carpet zoomed away far too fast. Small wonder Flora collected traffic tickets like other people did beer mats.

"Shit," Holly said.

"Language," Rye said.

"I left my body when I saw Ms. Withe sitting in our crappy kitchen. Ms. Flora Withe! And I'm going shopping with her! Me, Holly Woods. I simply have to tell Daisy!"

Holly dashed for her bedroom. Rye shut the door and grinned. Flora's plan was already working.

❖

On Fifth Day, Holly spent all morning repeatedly changing her clothes. Rye did her homework assignment, cleaned the toilet, and sorted the laundry. When Flora picked up Holly, Rye would take the clothes down to the machine. She would make a lightning shopping trip to the hypermart for her weekly groceries before Flora and Holly returned, since there probably wouldn't be time to get to the market and back.

Holly burst in with a magazine.

"I meant to show you this," Holly said. "Daisy gave me it."

Rye took the magazine. It was one of those expensive glossy women's ones.

"It's a couple of months old," Holly said. "But it shows that Ms. Withe is—Oh! That must be her at the door. Page thirty-one."

By the time Rye stepped into the hall, Holly had let Flora into the apartment. Under a tailored casual jacket, Flora wore a lacy top that looked more like underwear to Rye. Rye also had trouble keeping her eyes off Flora's tight pants.

Holly bubbled with enthusiasm as she climbed in the carpet. Flora winked at Rye before flying off. Rye grinned and went back to her piles of dirty clothes. She scooped up the magazine to read while she was down waiting for a machine in the laundry root.

Half the machines were out of order, so Rye had to join a queue. She pulled out the magazine. Cosmetic, diet, perfume, and clothes ads were occasionally interrupted by bursts of text. Page thirty was the start of a section called Needle's Eye. It was a gossip column. Rye didn't recognise any of the names of who was with or without whom. She turned the page. At the bottom of page thirty-one she saw a photograph of Flora in a long evening gown. Flora looked stunning. She looked like she was at a glittery party.

> *ShadeForest City's rising weaving sensation, **Flora Withe**, attends **Gale Purslain**'s birthday ball at Aspen Falls in the company of **Frond Lovage**, fresh from the triumph of her latest play. Are they an item again? We'll keep our Eye on this couple.*

Rye scowled at the woman in the photo beside Flora. Rye hadn't noticed her before. Frond Lovage was a skinny dryad taller than Flora and with a thinner face, reddish-brown skin, and a twiggy look. Her gown was more showy and less attractive than Flora's. *An item again?*

"Hey, wake up." The squat pixie woman behind Rye prodded her in the arm. "If'n you don't want that machine, I do."

Rye stuffed dirty underwear, smelly shirts, and stained pants into the washing machine as she thought about Flora and her sleek dryad companion at a rich party. *An item again?*

Rye frowned all the way around the aisles at the hypermart.

She propped the magazine open on the table where she could see Flora's photograph as she put her groceries away. It made sense that two dryads get together. Frond Lovage looked rich and successful. *Triumph of her latest play.* The skinny stick probably flew an expensive, sporty carpet like Flora's. She wouldn't work two jobs and live in fear of being deported. Rye slammed the pot of honey on the shelf so hard that the wood creaked.

An item again? Flora and that Frond creature had been an item before. Dating. Dancing. Frond Lovage would be able to buy Flora more than one drink in an evening. And wouldn't have holes in her socks when she took her shoes off to have sex with Flora.

Rye stomped back up the stairs with her bag of clean laundry and dumped it on the couch. She would bet every piece she was ever likely to earn that the triumphant Frond Lovage never did her own laundry. *An item again.*

"Crap."

Rye banged the kettle too hard on the stove when she set it to boil. She flung the offending magazine into a cupboard and stomped back to sort her laundry.

The front door opened.

"Rye?" Holly called. "We're back."

Rye glimpsed Flora as she walked past the doorway to the hall on her way to the kitchen. Frond Lovage would not make Flora come to a dismal little one-bedroom apartment in the Lower Eastside.

"Rye?" Flora appeared in the doorway joining the lounge and kitchen.

Rye found herself smiling. Her seething inadequacies and speculations miraculously evaporated to insignificance as she looked at Flora. Flora winked.

"You'll never believe what we got." Holly stood behind Flora. "Come and see. We went to the most astronomical shops."

Rye jolted. She stood in her run-down apartment with her little sister watching her. She ran a hand through her hair.

"Come on." Holly beckoned impatiently.

"Um. Okay." Rye stepped over her laundry bag and almost, but not quite, brushed against Flora in the doorway.

Paper bags crowded the table. Most bore names which included the words emporium or gourmet. A ripple of deepest unease made Rye's wings clench. She should have known that Flora wouldn't shop at the open-air market.

"Look at this one first." Holly thrust a bag at Rye.

Rye unwrapped generous wedges of three different kinds of cheese and released mouth-wateringly sharp scents. Two were splendid for cooking with. The third would make a killer accompaniment to the right dessert. Rye had only ever handled them briefly during her stint working in a restaurant and in her imagination when she prepared dream meals.

"The woman at the shop said that these were fairly versatile," Flora said. "I confessed that I was hopeless and had no idea what you might want to cook. Well? Did we do okay?"

"Wow," Rye said. She couldn't help mentally pricing the three and coming up with an uncomfortably large number.

Bag after bag disgorged expensive, fragrant, and exotic fruit, vegetables, spices, and sauces. Rye's anxiety soared apace with the estimated price. The last bag was from a butcher. She peeled back paper wrapping to reveal three large fillets. They looked fresh, succulent, and with just the right traces of fat through them. It looked suspiciously like ferret meat.

"Holly and I weren't sure what to get," Flora said. "So we picked what looked nicest. It's ferret. According to the butcher, it won't need hours of preparation or marinating."

Rye shook her head and reverently set the package on the table. Her gaze darted across the other raw materials of the dinner. Possum milk cheese. Yellow moss. Lavender honey. Silver fern fronds. Roasted raspberry seeds. Dried white Cabbage Tree berries. Almighty King and Queen of the Fey, she had never had ingredients like this before. This was going to be the best meal she'd ever prepared.

"If there's anything else you need," Flora said, "I can fetch it. It's no trouble."

"Um. Thanks." Rye squeezed around the table and knelt to rummage in her tiny cooler. "Holly, did you eat the last of the kahikatea seed paste?"

"No," Holly said. "You won't get a sensible answer out of her now, Flora, until we sit down to eat. She goes into this trance-like state where her eyes go blank and you expect her to start dribbling at any second. Sometimes it can be hard to spot from normal Rye, but trust me, I'm an expert. She's in cooking frenzy. If we're really out of luck, she'll start singing."

Rye did sing, and hum.

At one point, Rye turned around and saw Flora leaning in the doorway. Flora smiled.

"You really enjoy doing that, don't you?" Flora said.

"Um. Yeah."

Flora sidled around the table and slid a hand into one of Rye's back pockets. "You look very sexy wearing that tea towel tucked into the front of your pants."

Rye's gaze snapped between both doorways as she eased away from Flora. "Not here."

"What's wrong? Oh. Holly's in the bathroom."

Rye peered down the hall. "She'll be out soon, then."

"Rye, I'm missing out on my Fifth Day fuck because of Mission Holly," Flora whispered. "You aren't seriously intending to deprive me of a quick smooch and grope?"

Rye's wing buds tightened. She glanced between Flora and the bathroom door. "It's not that I don't want—Fey. Here she is."

Rye stepped away to pretend to look for something amongst her modest collection of second-hand recipe books on the cooler. She heard Flora sigh. Later, while Flora and Holly talked in the lounge, Rye opened the plate cupboard and rediscovered the glossy magazine. Frond Lovage was out and loud for all to see. She didn't have to worry about what would happen to a gay woman who got deported back to Fairyland. Or the equally nightmarish possibility that she had put her little sister into the position of being the one to provide the testimony that would condemn her to the fairy priestesses as a lesbian. Frond Lovage would not have denied Flora kisses.

An item again? Flora might still be kissing Frond. On those days when Rye worked evenings, attended night classes, or stayed home with her little sister. Rye jammed the magazine at the back of the vegetable bin before she began heating the pan for grilling the ferret fillets.

The greatest shame about dinner was that Rye had to serve it on chipped, cheap, mismatched crockery on a table in the cramped, dingy kitchen. Flora very politely pretended not to notice. Holly was amazingly unlike her recent self, even before Rye allowed her a glass of wine.

"Oh, Holy Elm," Flora said. "This is fantastic. Rye, these acorns are making my tongue want to expire out of pure pleasure."

"I told you," Holly said.

Rye grinned self-consciously.

"To the chef." Flora held up her glass. "My deepest compliments."

Rye blushed. "I think I overcooked the crumbed cheese. And used a pinch too much manuka bark in the sauce. And the texture of the moss didn't quite come out as I expected. A little too gooey."

"Mine's perfect," Flora said.

"She's always like this," Holly said. "Same with her school work. She gets so many A's that they must be running out of them, but Rye just shrugs and says she could have done better."

Flora gave Rye a look which made Rye reach for her wine.

After dessert, Holly voluntarily helped Rye wash the dishes. To Rye's astonishment, Holly then announced that she was going out. Rye would have bet good money that Holly would have wanted to spend every moment she could in Flora's company.

"I told you," Holly said. "I have to speak with Daisy."

"Don't be long," Rye said. "School tomorrow."

"I'll be back by nine," Holly said. "Exactly nine. Not a minute later or a minute sooner. Promise. See you later, Flora. Thanks for taking me with you. I had a crackling time."

"You're welcome, Holly," Flora said. "I'm sure we'll meet again soon."

The door thunked shut behind Holly.

Rye looked at Flora. Flora looked back. Rye's wing buds twitched as if they wanted to attract Flora's attention. Flora smiled and advanced on Rye. Rye hesitated for another look toward the door before succumbing to Flora's nearness. Rye's aching fingers finally got to slide over Flora's tightly encased bottom. Flora's clever fingers deftly deprived Rye of her shirt and undid her pants while they kissed. The couch groaned alarmingly as they dropped together onto it. Rye's last coherent thought before she came was the realisation that this was the first time she had made love with anyone else in her own bed.

"Oh, Elm, I needed that." Flora eased her arm out from beneath Rye.

Rye kissed Flora's shoulder and sat up. She pulled her clothes back on and fetched their glasses of wine. She was relieved to see that Flora took her cue and wriggled back into her pants.

"You don't wear those often, do you?" Rye said.

"Do they make my bum look fat?"

"Your bum is perfect. It's my eyes I'm worried about. They nearly fell out staring at you."

Flora smiled and lightly kissed Rye. "You say the sweetest things. Almost as sweet as that maple dessert."

"It was too sweet?"

"Not a speck. Oh, yum. It's a good job I don't have a supply in the cooler at home or I'd end up as large as a stump." Flora slid a hand up and down Rye's thigh. "That was the nicest meal I've eaten in an oak's age."

"Only because you live on takeaways and boil-and-eat packet meals."

"No. I mean it. Laurel and I tried this new restaurant for lunch the other day. The Red Vole. Dinner tonight was miles better than what I ate there. I'm not saying that only because I want to screw the chef again."

Rye kissed Flora's hand and changed the subject. "Where did

you manage to find a place to trade in the Horrible Holly for a nice model?"

Flora laughed. "She's a good kid. She wasn't in the least horrible. I wish I'd had a little sister like her. Although, I do realise that it might be different if I lived with her."

Rye smiled. "So? Did you learn why I'm the evil bog monster?"

"You really need to talk with her."

"I tried. It's hard to do when she keeps slamming doors in my face." Rye sighed and shook her head at the memories. "But if I ever get the opportunity, what should I be talking about?"

Flora sipped her wine as if considering her words before answering. "I know you have definite ideas about what you want Holly to do with the next few years of her life. Do you know what Holly wants?"

"I haven't a clue. She just tells me that she hates school. But that's just a phase."

"Are you sure?"

"I'm not having her end up in jobs like mine. Once she's got a good education, she can choose a good career."

Flora patted Rye's thigh. "Is this how you discuss it with her?"

Rye bristled. "What are you saying?"

"Nothing. Easy, lover. I'm not criticising you. Or belittling your parenting skills. I'm trying to help. Holly doesn't want to walk out of school and into any old job, if that's what you're worried about. She has given her future a lot of thought. A lot more than I ever had at her age. It's impressive how much talking she's done with people, and not just her careers counsellor at school. She's actually gone to ask people about their jobs. Which I find amazing."

Rye frowned. "What does she want to do?"

"She wants to develop her strong natural talent. She wants to get into fabric and clothes design."

Rye scowled. "She does?"

"You're not really surprised? If you remember, we met the evening I handed her first prize for a fabric creation of hers."

Rye downed the remainder of her wine and rose to pour a refill.

"Holly wants to leave school at the end of this year," Flora said, "and take up an apprenticeship. She's even made a list of people she would like to train with. She's dead serious."

Rye took a long swallow of wine.

"What's wrong?" Flora said.

"I suppose paying apprenticeship fees will be the same as university enrolment."

"Fees? No. You won't have to pay. And I'd have no problem helping her find a placement. I know—"

"No!" Rye's emphatic gesture spilled wine on the floor. "I pay. I don't take anything I don't have to. I don't need charity."

"Charity? No. I'm talking about a scholarship. And I can talk to people I know and introduce Holly to them. It's important she finds the right placement to suit her and her teacher."

"Oh." Rye scowled down at the stains on the floor. Stains on stains. "Scholarship?"

"Yes. Holly is very talented."

Rye set her empty glass down and paced. Holly wanted to become an artist? That wasn't at all what she had planned. "It's not exactly a steady job, is it? Not with proper prospects and security."

Flora smiled and spread her hands. "Some of us manage to make a living."

"I know. But you're good."

"I've been trying to tell you that Holly promises to be very good."

Chapter Six

Rye sat on the roughly finished floor and pulled her free copy of yesterday's newspaper out of her work bag. Blackie handed her a mug of tea. The boys dissected last night's big game while Rye scanned the advertisements for brooms and work available. Finding nothing, she turned to the front page.

Treaty Ratified After Heated Debate.

The controversial trade and amity treaty with Fairyland was approved with a slender majority last night after fierce debate in parliament. The government stressed the financial benefits that might flow from the new treaty. Opponents claimed that no democratic government should deal with closed, totalitarian societies that persecute their own citizens. They concentrated their attack on civil rights abuses allegedly rampant under Fairyland's theocratic regime. The extradition clause came in for fiery argument.

A cold ache tightened Rye's stomach. Her wing buds and the flight muscles across her chest clenched uncomfortably.

"What does extra-thing mean?" Knot asked.

"Extradition," she said. "Um. It's when a country hands someone back to the country where they came from. They do it so that people can be punished in their own country, where they committed their crime."

"Sounds about right, don't it?" Knot said. "Why should we have to put up with dregs coming here? Got enough of our own."

"I reckon they should send all foreigners back where they come from." Blackie's stubby antennae bristled erect. "Especially fucking elves. Whiny wankers. And fucking gnomes. There's nothing worse than a fucking gnome."

Knot grinned. "Ain't your mother-in-law a gnome?"

"I'd shove that fat old bitch on a ship to the Plainlands tomorrow," Blackie said. "Actually, I'd drop her in the sea with a rock tied to her beard. Gnomes. Shit. They're all the fucking same."

Knot turned to Rye. "What's that word for people like him?"

"Bigots," Rye said.

"I ain't!" Blackie said. "I got pure sprite, bogle, and gremlin blood in me. Born and raised here. I'm no fucking foreigner. And I'll tell you another thing. Those fucking fairies have got it about right. Keep all the weird bastards in their own country. I heard they hang crims there. I reckon it'd be no loss if those flying freaks all hung each other! Then none of the bastards could come here."

Rye stood and walked away.

❖

Rye could not imagine how she could be more comfortable. She reclined on one of Flora's sofas with the naked dryad a warm weight lying against her front. Flora idly smoothed part of Rye's wing membrane against her own hip and thigh. Rye could smell Flora's perfume and their sex. Beneath that, and even more compelling than both, she smelled that tantalising aroma like pine sap. Rye bent her nose closer to Flora's hair and closed her eyes. She inhaled deeply. The pine scent invaded her brain and permeated her whole being, as if Flora was what Rye had been missing all her life.

Rye reverently kissed Flora's hair. Her lips pressed a knot. Flora's hair had formed a tight, nasty tangle about the size of the top of Rye's thumb.

"I wish we could be like this forever," Flora said. "It's the strangest phenomenon. Whenever I'm with you, the rest of Infinity fades into nothing. Yet time speeds up."

Rye's smile quickly faded. Her fingers found another tangle in Flora's hair. And another. Her fingers worked their way around the crown of Flora's head to find it ringed with the knots.

"Gently." Flora sat up.

"Sorry. You've got some nasty knots."

Flora twisted around to level a strange look at Rye. "Knots?"

"Tangles in your hair. If you get a comb, I'll tease them out. I used to do Holly's hair for her. I hardly ever made her cry."

"You don't know much about dryad biology, do you?"

"I know a lot more now than I used to. Why?"

"These aren't hair tangles. They're buds."

Rye frowned. "Buds? You're about to flower? Or have I somehow pollinated you?"

Flora laughed. Rye felt stupid. Flora captured one of Rye's hands to kiss.

"They mean that I'm serious about someone," Flora said.

"Oh."

Rye was conscious of a watchfulness beneath Flora's smile. She had no clue how to interpret it and didn't know what she was supposed to say.

The moment passed. Flora rose and padded into the kitchen to fetch the abandoned jar of wine. When she returned, Rye sat up and swung her legs over the side of the sofa so that Flora could sit astride her lap. Flora held the glass to Rye's lips for her to sip then drank from the same spot herself. Being with Flora felt so right and natural. This could not be wrong.

"What are you thinking?" Flora asked.

"That you're the sexiest thing on two legs."

Flora smiled. "You find creatures with more legs sexier?"

Rye tickled Flora until she threatened to dump the contents of the wine glass on her head.

"Can I fly you home from work on Fourth Day?" Flora stroked Rye's neck and shoulders. "In rush hour traffic, that should give us a good three quarters of an hour of hand-holding and quick, steamy kisses. That might just keep me from exploding with sexual frustration until next Fifth Day."

"Yes, please."

Rye ran her hands along Flora's thighs, hips, and around to her buttocks. Warm, fascinating curves. So smooth. So perfect. How was it possible to be awed by Flora and yet, at the same time, feel completely comfortable with her?

"You've got the most adorable look on your face." Flora said. "What are you thinking?"

"How amazing you are. By the way, not this Fourth Night or the next, but the one after, I have it off. The school is closed for some holiday. Holly is going to a birthday party." Rye ran her hands up Flora's back. "So, how about you and me planning a hot evening together?"

"Fourth Night? I can't. I'm hosting a duty dinner." Flora grimaced. "Branch, Trunk, and Root, it would have to be the one engagement I can't cancel or shift. These are people it's important for me to be nice to, but who otherwise might not be within my closest social orbit. My agent. A couple of gallery owners. The curator of a private museum. You could come."

"Um. I don't think I'd have any place with them."

"I don't blame you," Flora said. "I'd rather not do it myself. I think I'm repressing it. I haven't even arranged a caterer yet. We could end up eating takeaway from Lowood's Mushroom House. That would boost my reputation, don't you think?"

"It would get you talked about."

Flora smiled and gently stroked Rye's wing support.

"Oh, Elm, I suppose I—" Flora's fingers stilled. "Rye? If I wanted an enormous favour from you, would I be better reminding you of an incident for which you still owe me an apology, or promising sexual favours?"

"Sex. What do you want?"

"Cook for me. Please."

"Sure. Do you actually have any food in the house?"

"I don't mean now," Flora said. "My dinner party."

Rye stared, aghast. "What?"

Flora set her glass aside and looped her arms around Rye's neck. "You could do that divine ferret dish again. Those acorns! My mouth has wet dreams about them. Although, I think one or two are vegetarian. I'll check. Please, lover. Say you will."

Rye shook her head. "You need a real cook."

"You are a real cook. But no maple malt sauce. I couldn't possibly sit in the same room with Windy Hempweed and have memories of you licking maple malt sauce off my breasts."

Rye grinned.

"Please," Flora said. "It'll be a proper business deal. I'll pay you twelve hundred pieces."

"Fey." That was as much as she earned at the building site in a month.

"It's what I paid the last time. Dinner for six. Four courses and nibbles beforehand."

"Over a thousand pieces?" Rye said. "Just for cooking dinner?"

"You'll have to buy all the food. And pay for someone to help serve. I bet Holly would do it."

"She's going to a birthday party."

"I bet she won't if you tell her that Privet Thunder is one of my guests. He's only the top of her wish list for apprenticeship teachers. It would do her no harm at all to become a name and face to some of my guests."

"That's not fair."

Flora smiled. She wriggled closer, so that their breasts touched, and began stroking Rye's wing support. Flora's other hand stroked Rye's hair, teased the nape of her neck, then ran down toward the sensitive spot between the place where Rye's wings joined her back. Flora kissed her deeply. Rye could barely conceal her rising interest.

"Is that the best you can do?" Rye said. "I doubt I'd fry you a sandwich for that."

"Oh!" Flora's face was a picture of outrage.

"Are you sure you're a dryad and not a leprechaun?"

"You shit!"

The ensuing wrestling bout tumbled them both onto the carpet. They lay in a tangle laughing.

"Do we have time for another fuck?" Rye asked.

"Are you sure you want to with this sexless lump?"

Rye eased herself over Flora and spread her wings. Flora's eyes widened as they usually did and her breasts rose with a sharp, deep breath. Rye could not understand how her broken, ugly wings turned Flora on, but she wasn't complaining. Rye kissed Flora and began slow hip motions.

"You are the most desirable creature in Infinity," Rye said. "And you know it. So, how about that screw?"

"Why not?" Flora reached up to touch Rye's wings. "I had nothing planned for the next twenty-three seconds."

Later, when Rye was tying her boot laces, Flora came to stand close and smooth Rye's hair.

"So?" Flora said. "Will you cook for me? Please, lover."

"Yeah. Okay."

Flora bent to kiss her. "Thank you. I know it'll be terrific."

"What if I screw up? Will it ruin your career?"

"Of course. Rye! I've eaten your cooking. I have every confidence in you. And—"

Ryc stood. "And what?"

Flora ran a hand down Rye's chest and ended by taking hold of her hand. "And I have something to tell you, but I'm not sure this is the right time."

"Is this about the pollination thing?"

Flora smiled. "Buds. It's related, yes."

"You're not going to have my acorns?"

Flora looked astonished and she burst out laughing. "I can see that I really need to teach you some dryad biology."

"If the lessons are anything like I've been getting so far, I might have to fail a few classes so that I need remedial tutoring."

Flora stroked Rye's cheek. "How did you remain celibate for all those years? I can't believe you didn't have women flocking around you. But just make sure you keep fighting them off now."

Rye frowned to herself as she followed Flora through into the garage. "You'd be jealous?"

"Of course. Wickedly. Vindictively. There is not another species breathing who comes close to dryads when it comes to possessiveness. There, I've warned you. No other women."

Rye climbed into the carpet and snapped the safety harness in place. Her memory conjured the photograph of Flora and Frond Lovage. Rye would not ask about them, because she didn't want to know the answer. She was fortunate to get even a part of Flora's life. And, dryad or not, that Frond creature couldn't be so great between the sheets if Flora spent half her life panting for Rye.

❖

One thousand two hundred pieces.

Rye punched her pillow into a more comfortable shape. Sure, she had to buy the food, but the profit should make a nice start to her second-hand broom savings.

Flora had given her a copy of an old dinner menu, so Rye had an idea about what was required. The thought of her food being set in front of all those posh artists gave her more than a ripple of unease. Part of her, though, was thrilled at the challenge. It would certainly be a more enjoyable way of earning some extra cash than cleaning municipal toilets.

Rye slid a hand under the sofa cushion beneath her pillow. She pulled out the magazine with Flora's photo. Rye put her hand on the page to hide Frond Lovage.

"I don't know how much longer you're going to stay interested in me," Rye whispered. "But I intend to savour it. I'll cook all the dinners you want."

Rye drifted off to sleep with menu ideas swirling through her mind.

Rye knelt in soil. She tugged weeds out with her fingers. A shadow fell across her. She looked up. Sunlight momentarily blinded her. She saw the outline of a female body in a loose shift and with folded wings. A face resolved out of the brightness. A homely, round, lovely face. Chastity, the junior priestess. She smiled and held out a hand.

The garden vanished. Rye stood in the temple robing room. Chastity shut the door and smiled at Rye. She had the most beautiful scalloping on the edges of her wing membranes. Chastity kissed her.

Crack! Rye saw the priestess's arm scythe downward. The whip snapped against flesh. Chastity's body jerked. She didn't cry out or make a sound. Blood ran from her wings. Bloody rents in the membranes looked like vampire mouths. Blood ran down the back of her legs and onto the floor. Chastity turned around, but it wasn't her any more. She was Flora.

Rye stood out in the open. Her mother lay at her feet in the mud. It oozed on her mother's wings. Blood seeped from the corner of her mouth. Dead. Holly stood staring at Rye, but she was sixteen, not five years old.

Alarms screamed all around. Rye tried to cover her ears. She ran. The noise followed. They were going to catch her.

Rye jolted awake with a shout dying on her lips. Her alarm clock buzzed. She panted as if she really had been running from all the priestesses in Fairyland.

❖

The building site whistle sounded three long blasts for down-tools.

"You heard," Knot called. "Down we go. Take your things. Assemble near the gates."

Rye trotted down amongst flurries of speculation from her fellow workers. When they gathered, Grub the overseer stomped out to talk to them.

"Due to a safety problem," Grub said, "we have to stop work for the day and close the site."

A loud cheer drowned out his next words.

Knot elbowed Rye. "Smile. The pubs will be open in an hour. A whole day drinking, and not having to tell the wife."

"But it's a day without pay," Rye said.

Knot shrugged and turned to arrange his unexpected holiday with some of the others. Rye frowned. She shoved through the dispersing crowd.

"Mr. Grub! Wait." Rye strode across to the scowling overseer.

"What do you want?" he said.

"Look, if you need someone to help make things safe, I'm willing to work."

"Ain't nothing you can do. Push off. I'm busy."

Rye frowned at his retreating back. "Shit."

It was eleven o'clock in the morning. She couldn't even go to Pansy's to try to work an afternoon shift because the fast-food shop didn't open until three.

Rye jammed her fists in her pockets and strode down the street. She was going to be short this week. Good job she was doing that cooking for Flora soon. Rye stopped. She had most of a day stretching emptily ahead of her. Flora hadn't mentioned anything special she would be doing today.

Rye burst into a run when she emerged from the Rootway underpass. She could be at Flora's in time for lunch.

Rye wiped the sweat from her face and pressed Flora's buzzer. Flora answered promptly.

"Rye! Has something happened? Are you all right?"

"I'm fine. The council shut down the building site for the day. Are you busy?"

The gate clunked open. Rye strode through and waited for the elevating carpet. It whisked her up the ten flights without any sensation of movement. Rye stepped out and put her arms around Flora. Flora moved fluidly into the embrace and returned Rye's kiss. Rye's hand slid down to Flora's backside. Fey, Flora felt good.

Flora broke off for air. When Rye tried to kiss her again, Flora put her fingers against Rye's mouth.

"Hold that thought, lover," Flora whispered. "Laurel won't stay long, I'm sure."

Rye stiffened and jerked her arms from around Flora. They weren't alone?

"Laurel is my closest friend," Flora said. "I'm sure I've mentioned her a hundred times. We often have tea and gossip with each other. I'm glad you two can meet."

Rye's world tightened and darkened with the first tendrils of incipient flight-panic. Flora's warm fingers gripping Rye's hand helped stabilise her. Rye took a deep breath and let Flora lead her along the hall to the living room.

A dryad woman with red and gold highlights in her hair smiled at their entrance. Laurel looked a good ten years older than Flora. She put aside a cup of tea and rose. Rye knew she should not find the situation frightening or intimidating. The woman was Flora's friend. Her smile and curiosity were wholly natural. Rye's wing buds contracted hard all the same.

"Laurel, there's someone I'd like you to meet," Flora said. "Laurel Stone, this is Rye Woods."

"Oh," Laurel said. "Hello, Rye. This is a pleasant surprise."

Laurel held out a hand. Rye wiped her hand on her pants leg before completing the shake.

"Flora has spoken a great deal about you," Laurel said. "So, it's nice to be able to put a face to the name."

"Um. Yeah." Rye said.

"Flora says that you're a builder?" Laurel said.

"Um. Yeah," Rye said.

"Let me get you a drink," Flora said. "Beer?"

"Um. Oh. I'll go."

Rye all but bolted for the kitchen door. Her hands trembled as she popped the top off the beer. She glugged half of it. Flora wouldn't have told her friend that Rye was a fairy, would she?

Shit. Someone else knew about her affair with Flora. She might have guessed, but she hadn't. How much had Flora told? Not only her own, but Holly's, future lay in the balance. Rye was playing with fire for a few fucks. This had to be the stupidest thing she had done in eleven years.

Flora slipped her arms around Rye from behind. "Laurel has tactfully left. I don't remember, but were you quite that inarticulate when we first met?"

Rye lifted her beer and found the jar empty.

"Rye? What's wrong?"

"What have you told her?"

"The usual. Girl talk stuff. How sexy you make me feel. How hot you are on the sofa. What squirmy hardware you have. That—"

"Crap!" Rye broke free of Flora's arms and stomped out.

"Rye!" Flora ran after her. "What's the matter?"

Rye scooped her work bag off the floor and slammed a palm onto the button for the elevating carpet. Flora interposed herself between Rye and the door.

"What's happening? Rye? You're going to have to tell me, because I'm out of my copse here."

"I should never had done this. Fey! Stupid!"

"What is stupid? Branch." Flora grabbed the front of Rye's jacket. "Are you going to run again?"

"Do you have any idea what would happen to me if I got sent back? And Holly? Shit!" Rye tugged free and stormed around the curved hallway to the front door. "I should never have done this. Never. My own fucking fault."

"Rye!" Flora came running. "I didn't tell her that you're a fairy. I didn't."

Rye paused with her hand on the door.

"I didn't tell her that," Flora said. "I promised you, remember? You don't believe me?"

Rye was angry and scared, but that thing was happening again as it always did when she was with Flora. The harshness of the world lost its potency.

"Don't you believe me?" Flora stepped away from the door. "You don't trust me? If you don't, then perhaps you had better leave."

Rye took a deep breath and released the door. She ran her hand through her sweaty hair.

"I would never tell anyone," Flora said. "Believe me?"

Rye nodded. She held out her hand. Flora took it.

"I'm sorry," Rye said. "It's scary. No one has ever known before. It's always been just me and Holly. When she was little, I had to lie to her. I told her we were of mixed bogle and brownie blood. I hated doing that to her, but I couldn't risk her blurting out the truth. When she was older, I told her. I still worry sometimes because I'm not sure she fully realises how dangerous it would be for us to get sent back."

"What would happen to you?"

Rye shook her head. "It's Holly I worry about. The kid has no idea what it's like. After here, she wouldn't take well to life there. Not at all. It's...it's very different."

Flora laid a hand on Rye's chest. "Lover, I won't tell anyone. Please believe me."

Rye nodded and let out a long breath.

"Come back into the lounge," Flora said. "Let's sit down. Tell me how I've managed to win the privilege of your company at this time of day. And how long I have you for."

Rye kicked her boots off and accepted another beer. Flora sat close. As Rye talked, she relaxed. Between beer and Flora, the world mellowed. The phone beeped. Flora excused herself to go and answer it at the wall plate near the door.

Rye took a deep breath and closed her eyes. Almighty King and Queen of the Fey, this was a much better way of spending the day than on the building site. It was such a luxury to be able to stop and do nothing for a few hours.

"Rye?"

Rye opened her eyes. Flora bent over her. She lay on Flora's sofa with a duvet thrown over her.

"It's five o'clock," Flora said. "I thought it was about time we began thinking about getting you home."

"Five? I didn't sleep all afternoon?"

"You looked exhausted. I'm not surprised. You really need to take better care of yourself. If I walked half the distance you do in a week, I'd die."

"We didn't even have sex? A whole afternoon with you, and I slept it away. Fey."

"It didn't go quite as I expected, either. But you obviously had some rest to catch up on."

Rye shook her head. She was too disgusted with herself for words.

Flora stroked Rye's hair and kissed her cheek. "It gave me a bounce to walk in here every half an hour or so and see you there. You looked very cute."

"Asleep," Rye said unhappily. "Shit. I'm sorry."

"Maybe we'll get it right next time."

"There may never be a next time. I can't rely on the council shutting down the site too often."

"Don't say never," Flora said. "There are other ways we can arrange time together."

That night, while frying sandwiches, Rye did some hard thinking. The cold, unpalatable fact was that there was not enough time in a week for her to work two jobs, possibly a third, go to night school, spend the faintest smear of time at home with Holly, and have anything left over for her relationship with Flora. Something had to go. She needed the jobs. She couldn't live on any less than she earned now, and she really needed more. A broom would give her more time, and leave her with a little more energy. To afford the broom, she needed a third job. She spent so little time at home with Holly as it was that she could not reduce it any further. The only possible conclusion was that she must stop going to night school or end it with Flora.

Chapter Seven

Rye stared at the photograph in the magazine. Flora was gorgeous.

Their relationship was never going anywhere. Rye had known that from the start. Perhaps it was best that they ended it sooner rather than later. It might hurt less that way.

Rye sighed.

Flora was a successful artist. *ShadeForest City's rising weaving sensation.* Rye was a builder's labourer and sandwich fryer. Flora lived in a luxurious penthouse apartment in the trendiest suburb in the city. Rye lived in squalor. She couldn't even afford two bedroomed squalor. Flora swirled comfortably through the glittering upper ranks of society. Rye had to hide for fear of discovery. And as an uneducated lump, she would not have anything to say to those people even if she got dumped amongst them. Flora inhabited the tops of trees. Rye grubbed around amongst the roots.

She was Flora's novelty bedmate. When the fizz wore off, Flora could pick up some other lucky woman and whisk her away in her fancy carpet.

Rye gently stroked the photograph with a fingertip. The thought of Flora with anyone else caused a physical pain. Flora was one of the nicest people Rye had ever known. Fun to be with. Not at all as she'd expected from some rich, high-flying artist.

"Oh, fey," Holly said from the doorway. "Are you still moping?"

Rye started. She hastily shoved her notebook on top of the magazine. "What do you want?"

"When is dinner?"

"Um. Soon. I was waiting for you to emerge from all that noise."

Rye watched Holly go into the kitchen, then quickly jammed the magazine under the sofa cushion. She found Holly slouched at the table. Rye handed her some dock roots to peel.

"I hate being poor," Holly said.

"Me, too."

"It's all right for you." Holly grabbed a dock root and hacked the tail off it. "You don't spend all day with kids who have mobiles and the latest clothes and get their hair done and everything. Then there's me."

"If a person likes you for what you own, rather than who you are, then they're not really worth knowing."

"You always say stupid shit like that."

"Language."

Holly slammed the dock root and knife onto the table. "It's true! My life is so miserable. And you don't care."

"You got invited to that girl's birthday party, didn't you? Poppy what's-her-name? Didn't you tell me that she was the most popular girl in your class? She clearly doesn't care that—"

"I never wanted to go to that stupid party anyway!"

Holly jerked to her feet and stormed into her bedroom. Rye had seen tears.

"Holls?" Rye pushed Holly's door further open. Holly lay face down on her bed. Rye went in and sat to stroke her back. "What's the matter?"

"I can't go to the party. I don't have a present to take. We can't afford one."

Rye resisted the temptation to point out that Holly had recently squandered all her fifty piece prize money from the school art competition.

"Daisy is giving her the most scathing pair of earrings," Holly said. "Everyone else will be giving great stuff. And I'd be this giant nothing. I hate my life. Hate it."

"Look, I know this doesn't help with this problem, but if you didn't want to go to the party, maybe you could help me. I've agreed to cater this dinner for Flora."

Holly tensed and twisted her head to direct half a teary frown up at Rye.

"I'll need someone to help serve and stuff," Rye said. "Her guests are these big-wig artists."

Holly wriggled around further. "This is at her house? A proper dinner party, just like you read about? With artists?"

"Yeah. A bunch of important ones by the sound of it. Not that the names mean anything to me. She said there'd be one bloke called Privet Sunder."

"Thunder." Holly sat up. "You're peeling me? Privet Thunder is going to be at Flora's dinner party, and you're going to cook it? And I could go and meet him?"

"Yeah. But you'd—"

"Fucking shit!"

"Language!"

Holly leaped to her feet and bounced on the bed.

Bemused, Rye waited for Holly to jump down to the floor. "Wait! Before you begin the endless conversation with Daisy, this is work. You won't be an honoured guest. You'd have to do all the icky stuff I told you to. Peeling vegetables, stirring pots, and serving the table."

"I heard. Of course I'll do it! A Flora Withe dinner party with Privet Thunder there! That's a squillion times better than Poppy Wildcorn's limping birthday party. Daisy will gnaw her leg off!"

Rye smiled to herself as she followed Holly into the hall. "You hate helping me in the kitchen."

"That's different. Privet Thunder! My mind has just melted."

Rye watched Holly carry the phone into her bedroom. She wandered back into the kitchen to finish preparing dinner. Clearly, she couldn't break up with Flora until after the dinner party. Good. She didn't have to think about it for over a week.

❖

"We got close to the bed," Flora said.

Rye smiled and helped Flora up off the bathroom floor. Flora reached in to turn the shower off. Rye began pulling her underwear on.

"Do you have to wear such tight clothes?" Flora asked. "There are times we can barely peel you out of them."

"I need to keep my wings as flat as possible."

"Doesn't it hurt to have them cramped up like that all day?"

Rye shrugged. “I’m used to it.”

“I’d love to see you walking around with them out. And flying.”

“I can’t fly.”

“Glide, then.”

“That’s not what I meant.”

Rye tucked her loose shirt into her pants as she followed Flora out of the ensuite bathroom and through Flora’s bedroom. Something about Flora’s bedroom made Rye uncomfortable. A huge walk-in closet covered all one wall. It was bigger than Rye’s living room. The carpet was thick and springy enough to make her feet feel like they’d won a lottery. The huge bed looked like something that would be advertised in a glossy magazine. In fact, the whole room looked straight out of an up-market advertisement. The same might be said of the kitchen, but Rye felt less intimidated there. Possibly because it was the one place where Flora did not radiate complete, unthinking self-confidence.

Rye filled the kettle and set it on the stove to heat. Flora sat at the table to munch biscuits.

“I wonder why I always crave something sweet post-coital?” Flora said.

“Take the taste out of your mouth?”

“I like the taste of you. You’re unlike anyone I’ve had sex with before.”

“Is that good or bad?” Rye asked.

“Good. Definitely good. I have buds, don’t I?”

Rye padded over to bite off part of the biscuit that Flora held up for her. Flora playfully lifted her legs around Rye’s thighs and locked her ankles.

“So, why couldn’t you glide?” Flora asked.

That magic of togetherness was working at full blast, because Rye felt merely a faint tendril of unease about the topic of her wings. The only person she’d ever discussed it with was Holly. That had been a difficult conversation.

“My wings won’t hold me,” Rye said. “The supports were broken. And not set properly. That’s why they don’t look straight.”

“That must have been a nasty accident.”

“Yeah,” Rye lied.

“Couldn’t you get them re-set?”

Rye shrugged. She kissed Flora and changed the subject. "Did you get a chance to look at that menu?"

"Yes. Let me fetch it."

Rye made tea and joined Flora at the table. Flora had written some annotations on the menu Rye had made up.

"This sounds terrific," Flora said. "I've made just a couple of suggestions. And by the way, I love the sound of those fruit and wine jellies."

Rye nodded. "Okay. That looks good. Did you find out how many vegetarians there are?"

"Two. And there's one partial insectivore. I hope that's not too much of a nuisance?"

"Nope."

Flora stroked Rye's arm. "I'm really looking forward to this. I know you're going to do a splendid job."

"I'm so nervous that I can hardly spit."

"I thought you might be. But I have every confidence in you. Did Holly agree to help?"

"Oh, yeah," Rye said. "The kid who hates washing up begged me to let her peel veggies and sweep floors. She found this article in one of her friend's mum's magazines about napkin folding. Would it be a problem to have cloth rabbits and butterflies all over the table?"

Flora laughed. "Just make sure she doesn't put the rabbits in front of the vegetarians."

When Flora went to dress, Rye had a moment of wondering how she could possibly contemplate not seeing Flora any more. It seemed like the stupidest idea in all of Infinity.

Rye took a last look at the menu before folding it and stuffing it in her pocket. She could get most of what she wanted at her normal market, but she would need to find a source for the more exotic ingredients. There were some boutique gourmet food shops she passed on her way home from the building site. In the Noonpine area, of course.

"Crap," Rye whispered. How was she going to pay for any of this?

Flora breezed back in. She picked up her purse and lightly kissed Rye. "Much as I'd like to keep you here forever, I suppose I'd better take you home."

"Um. Yeah."

"What's wrong?"

Rye squirmed. She loathed having to do this.

"Rye? Is it something between us? About this morning? The dinner? Holly? Please talk to me, or I'll begin imagining the worst."

"Um."

Rye wanted to curl up in a hole and pull a rock in on top of her. But she didn't have a choice. There was no way in Infinity that she could afford to buy the ingredients herself. Her wings pulled tight against her back. Her chest muscles were taut enough to hinder easy breathing.

"Um. About dinner," Rye said. "I...um. Is there any way you could advance me some of the money?"

"Oh. Of course. I should've thought. Here." Flora pulled several banknotes out of her purse. "Is this enough? I can get you more if you need it. Actually, why don't I write you a credit note for the rest right now?"

"No! This is good. Really."

Rye shoved the cash into her pocket. She didn't want to have to admit that she didn't have a bank account into which she might deposit a credit note.

❖

On Third Night when Rye returned home from her shift at Pansy's Fried Sandwiches, she saw the light on in the kitchen. Holly knelt beside the cooler.

"Touch those and you're dead," Rye said.

"I was just making sure they were safe."

"Uh huh." Rye peered over Holly's shoulder to count the fruit cups.

"All there. See?" Holly poked her tongue out.

Rye pulled her shirt off as she strode to the bathroom. "Did you manage to borrow a plain black dress?"

"Yeah. Ivy Samphire's sister had one. You want to see it?"

"I trust you."

"When did that happen?"

Rye ignored that and shut the bathroom door. She trusted Holly not to want to look like an idiot in front of Flora and her posh guests. One less thing to worry about. She stepped into the warm shower and fretted about a hundred other things that might go wrong.

The next morning, Rye left Holly transit fare to get from school to Flora's house.

Rye had dropped her tools and grabbed her bag before the blast of the lunch whistle died away. She hurtled down the steps and across the site. Less than quarter of an hour later she jogged into a street of poncy boutique shops in Noonpine.

Flashily-dressed people sauntered to their lunch appointments or sat around the outdoor tables at restaurants and cafés. Rye clomped along in her boots. She picked up her box of specialty vegetables and spices at the Mulberry Shoot. They were wickedly expensive, but she couldn't prepare the dishes she planned without them. At Grain and Sons Fine Meats, she purchased ferret fillets and their selection of insects even included the big smoked wetas she wanted. The bill there ate up the last of the cash Flora had given her.

Rye carried her box down past the awnings, benches, and display boards. She noticed the name Lightning Tree Gallery. Wasn't that the place Holly raved over when Flora said she had some of her work on display in it?

Rye strode over to the window. A large chunk of bent blue glass sat on a pedestal on the other side of the window. Rye shook her head. She supposed it meant something to someone. Beyond the glass lump, the gallery interior looked intimidatingly posh. Paintings and hangings littered the walls. Which ones were Flora's?

"Oh, look!"

Rye turned to see a pair of young female sylphs dressed in diaphanous robes in matching shades of faded orange. They were holding hands as they stepped close to the gallery window.

"It's still here," the taller one said. "Oh, darling, wouldn't it be perfect for the lounge? I'm sure I can convince auntie to buy it for us for a wedding present. It's only seven thousand. Even she can't complain about that."

Rye thought her eyeballs might drop out. *Seven thousand?*

Rye walked off, taking her burden of groceries and astonishment. Seven thousand pieces for a lump of glass? No wonder Flora could think nothing of paying twelve hundred for a dinner party, or casually pulling over three hundred pieces from her purse. It was a different world.

Flora didn't answer her buzzer, but the gates clunked open. Rye felt very strange letting herself into Flora's apartment.

"Flora? Babe? Are you here? It's me. Rye."

Rye wandered around the curved corridor to the kitchen. It was empty, pristine, and just waiting to be cooked in. Rye put her fruit cups in the cooler. She found a note stuck to the pantry door.

> *Gone to the salon to get myself made beautiful. Back by 3:00 or 3:30 at the latest. Fingers crossed. Do whatever you need to. The wine I told you about is in the bottom rack. BTW, the florist will be delivering at 4:00. If, by some nightmare, I'm not back, please leave the flowers on the table. I'll take care of them when I get home. If you need me for anything (Except sex. Alas!) press the blue button on the phone screen. It'll automatically connect to my mobile.*
> *Love, F.*

Rye smiled. She folded the note and slipped it into the back pocket of her pants. After lighting the ovens, she set the chestnuts to steep in the rosemary water.

Rye hummed as she alternated between stirring pots and shaping little acorns to look like stars. This was the most incredible kitchen. The knifes were sharper than sin. Flora probably never used them.

Rye was so absorbed in her cooking that she didn't notice that Flora had returned until she spoke.

"Rye? You like?" Flora paused halfway across the kitchen to strike a pose. "It took long enough to do. It's got enough spray on that it's brittle enough to break."

"You look terrific."

Flora quickly closed the gap to give Rye a long kiss. "Hmm. I've been looking forward to this all day. Everything going okay?"

"Great. I'm only panicking about twenty things."

Flora smiled. "Something smells good already."

"You feel good."

Rye kissed Flora. The temperature of the kiss rose. Rye's hands explored Flora's body. Flora pressed against Rye in all the right places.

The buzzer sounded.

"Branch," Flora said. "That'll be the florist."

Flora had the delivery people set the flowers on the end of the table, well out of Rye's way.

"I'd better show you where everything goes." Flora led Rye through into the dining room.

"Holly is bursting to do this," Rye said.

"I'm bursting to do you," Flora said.

"We'd better not mess your hair."

Flora sighed. "I suppose you're right. But it won't be easy knowing that you're just through there. Especially not when Windy starts prosing on about some esoteric subject. I just know I'll be thinking about sex the whole time and have nothing intelligent to contribute."

Rye grinned.

Flora set about arranging flowers in vases. Rye hummed to herself as she moved between the stove and the preparation counters. She only had to glance across to see Flora. It would be very easy to get used to doing that.

After taking the last vase out into the living room, Flora returned to stand close to the stove.

"Something smells really yummy," Flora said. "May I taste?"

"No." Rye shooed her away.

"What can I do?"

"Nothing. You're the boss, remember?"

"What time do you expect Holly?"

Rye glanced at the clock. It was nearly four-thirty. "Soonish."

"Then I'll set the gates to automatically open again."

Flora pulled up the screen on the main communications unit and fiddled with several on-screen menus before sinking into a chair at the table. She idly toyed with the baby carrots. Rye took the chair beside her and moved the carrots out of Flora's reach. Rye began peeling and trimming them. Flora wriggled around and laid her legs across Rye's lap.

"So, who are these people tonight?" Rye asked.

"Well, Leaf Longdale is my agent. He's a cutthroat, but I'd willingly pay him twice as much as long as I don't have to do all that hateful wheeling and dealing."

"He seems to have done pretty well for you."

"Yes, he has," Flora said. "He's not someone whose company I enjoy socially, but I have complete faith in his business acumen. Leaf can get very argumentative. The least pretty event in the whole history of Infinity is Leaf Longdale and my mother in the same room."

"Your mother is argumentative?"

"Mother is always right."

"Oh."

"Exactly." Flora stole a carrot and nibbled the end off before Rye could wrestle it back. "Then there's Letty Elmwood. She's a middle-aged lesbian sylph. I'm guessing that you'd not like her one little speck. She's terribly gifted and terribly aware of it. She owns the two most important galleries in the Three Forest area, including the Lightning Tree in Noonpine. For some reason I've never been able to fathom, she likes me."

"Perhaps she finds you attractive."

"I'm not her type," Flora said. "She prefers strong, muscular women. Letty is a divinely opinionated control freak, but, I've heard, is very much a 'throw me on the bed' type. I should make sure she doesn't see you. I'd have a hard time keeping sweet with Letty if she stole you from me."

Rye shifted uncomfortably, though she knew that Flora was only teasing.

Flora listed the other guests. "And, lastly, Ginger Grangegrass. Founder of the Newbud Collective. He's the one I'm going to ask about taking Holly. He's not the top of her list, or exactly at the forefront of innovation and daring, but he's an excellent teacher and has a knack of knowing where someone's strengths lie."

Flora sat forward to kiss Rye. Rye took the precaution of clamping a hand around Flora's wrist to prevent her from stealing more carrots. Flora slumped back with an exaggerated pout which made Rye want to kiss her even more.

"And then the sixth one is that Flora Withe woman," Rye said.

"What's she like?"

"All right, I suppose."

"All right?" Flora said. "I'd heard that she's fabulously talented, terrific in bed, a great hostess, and wildly fun to be with."

"Dunno where you heard that."

Flora's eyes narrowed dangerously. "And just what have you heard?"

"That she's a year or two past her best, and—"

Flora gasped. She grabbed a handful of peelings. "You wretch!"

Rye lunged to clamp her hands around Flora's wrists. "But she has okay legs."

"Okay!" Outraged, Flora twisted and writhed in Rye's grip. "Okay? Just okay?"

Their tussle shoved the table back a couple of inches. Flora eventually freed a hand and jammed a fistful of carrot peelings down the front of Rye's shirt.

"Can I do that, too?" Holly asked.

Rye shot out of her chair so fast that she came close to dumping Flora on the floor. "Holls! How long have you been—I didn't hear you."

"Hi, kiddo," Flora said. "How was school?"

Holly dropped her bag, slumped in a chair, and helped herself to a carrot. "Boring."

Rye's blood roared through her ears. Flora looked up at her with a very matter-of-fact expression as if she had no idea why Rye was so distressed—as if she and Rye had not just been caught in a highly compromising position.

"Hey, your hair is astronomical," Holly said.

"It should be," Flora said. "I was at the salon so long that I could've grown an extra head by the time they'd finished."

Rye shoved around the table and stomped into the hall. Her hands shook so badly that she couldn't get the carrot peelings from her shirt without dropping them on the floor.

"Rye?" Flora said.

Rye jumped.

"It's okay," Flora said. "It's not a problem."

Rye glared but held her tongue because Holly appeared in the doorway behind Flora.

"She's been in a stupid mood for over a week," Holly said. "Moping around as if the world was about to end. And she goes on at me for teenage moodiness."

"Perhaps cooking will help," Flora said. "I'd better leave you two to it. I have some things to do before I dress. Yell if you need anything. Okay?"

Rye nodded stiffly. She walked back into the kitchen and tried to remember what she'd been doing.

"Isn't this the most astronomical place you've ever seen?" Holly asked.

"Um." Rye looked around. Everything seemed unfamiliar. Then she heard the soup pot bubbling. She dashed across to remove it from the heat. "Finish those carrots for me. And wash the chamomile in cold water. Shake it well. Give the floor back here a quick sweep. Then go and ask Flora to tell you about setting the table."

"Slave driver," Holly said.

"You begged me to let you do this," Rye said.

Rye knew that Holly poked her tongue out at her back but bent her attention on the soup.

About half an hour before the first guests were due to arrive, Rye sent Holly off to change into the black dress she'd wear for serving. She didn't return for nearly twenty minutes.

"Where have you been?" Rye asked. She swung around from the stove and stopped.

"Flora helped me get ready," Holly said.

Rye blinked. The young woman in front of her, with the makeup and budding figure, wasn't the skinny little kid sister she was used to seeing. When Rye hadn't been looking, Holly had grown up.

"Flora said I could pass for eighteen or nineteen," Holly said. "Wow, those little pastry things look really good. Do they have that fish paste and blackbird's egg stuff in them?"

"Um. Yes. No scoffing them."

Rye frowned as she fetched a jug of wine from the pantry and began stirring some into the sauce mixture. She kept glancing at Holly. The kid looked old enough to have her wings.

"Flora said that I've got great skin," Holly said. "And Flora said—"

"Go and double-check that the table is set properly," Rye said. "Did you remember to put water jugs in the dining room?"

"Yes, she did." Flora walked in through the doorway from the dining room.

Rye turned. Her eyes bulged. She hadn't thought Flora could get more beautiful than when totally undressed, or in that glitzy magazine photo, but Flora looked stunning in a long, slinky dark green dress and a few diamonds.

"The table looks fabulous," Flora said. "I love the napkins. Holly, could you please check that I put water in the vase near the patio door?"

Holly bolted.

"Well?" Flora said. "Will I do?"

"Um."

"Did you mean to pour wine down your trouser leg?"

"Fey!"

"Relax. Holly is fine. Dinner will be great."

Rye dabbed at her leg with a dish cloth. "Relax? When you look like that? I'd have to be dead not to notice."

"That's the nicest compliment you've ever paid me."

"What did you do to Holly?"

"She's going to be a pretty woman."

"Not as pretty as you."

"You're getting better at that. That just might make amends for the disparagement of my legs."

Holly poked her head around the door. "Flora, there's someone at the door. Shall I let them in?"

"Yes, please."

As soon as Holly stepped out of the kitchen, Flora blew Rye a kiss. The strength of the temptation to return it for real, with Holly so close, surprised Rye.

The hours of the evening whizzed by in a heated blur of steam, carving knives, serving spoons, sauces, plates, and dirty dishes. Once, Rye peeked through the living room door to see Flora laughing with some of her guests. When Holly returned to refill a tray, she alerted Rye to the fact that one of the men had a habit of resting his hand on Flora's back. Rye knew an almost overwhelming urge to stomp out there and break his fingers.

Later, Rye sneaked a look at the dinner table. The main course seemed to be going down well with Flora's wine choice. Her brief glimpse of the heavily powdered sylph, Letty Elmwood, convinced Rye that Flora was correct in believing Rye wouldn't like her. Rye couldn't imagine the woman who wouldn't be utterly overshadowed by Flora Withe.

CHAPTER EIGHT

Rye pulled the plug and let the dirty water gurgle down the sink hole. She wiped her hands on her dishtowel apron and removed it. She dropped down onto a chair at the table. Holly sat slumped asleep using Rye's rolled up jacket for a pillow on the table. Rye ate one of the leftover desserts. Not bad. Perhaps a shade too sweet. Maybe she should use a few black currants to give it a little more breadth of taste and a dash of tartness.

The door from the hall swung open. Flora smiled as she came in.

"Rye, you're a genius!"

"Ssh." Rye put a finger to her lips and nodded at the sleeping Holly.

Flora took Rye's hand and tugged her through into the dining room. She clicked the door shut behind them. She slid her hands up Rye's chest and around her neck. Her kiss was like a goddess breathing life into Rye. Rye slipped her hands around Flora's waist and held her close.

"I've been dying to do that all evening," Flora whispered. "You've no idea how many times I was tempted to come in there to you."

Rye smiled and started another long, exploratory kiss.

"Your dinner was the best I've ever given," Flora said. "Truly, Rye. Everyone raved. If anything, I think the vegetarians loved that mushroom and chestnut dish even more than the rest of us did the ferret. Three of them wanted to know how they could hire you."

"What?"

"Really. Rye, you're very good. Superb. As a cook, too."

Rye grinned.

They kissed again. This time more probing. Flora slid a hand down Rye's back.

"That's strange," Flora said. "It feels like you're wearing a bandage."

"I am." Rye turned her head toward the door.

"She's asleep," Flora said.

"I thought I heard something. She worked her heart out tonight. The poor kid's exhausted."

"Why don't you put her to bed in the guest room? It'd save you having to wake her up and drag her home. And I bet anything you like that she won't mind waking up here in the morning."

Rye coaxed a still half-asleep Holly to rise and mostly carried her to the bedroom. She lowered Holly onto the bed and eased off her dress before letting her sink onto the bed. Rye pulled the sheets up around Holly and gave her a kiss on the forehead. Holly was asleep again before Rye softly closed the door.

Rye followed Flora through to the living room and dropped onto the sofa. Flora extinguished most of the lights before joining her.

"How much do you think she saw?" Rye said.

"She saw me stuffing peel down your shirt. We were acting like a pair of children. If she gave it a second thought, she didn't mention it to me. That really is a bandage, isn't it? What did you do to yourself?"

"Nothing." Rye took the glass from Flora's hand for a sip of wine. "I bound my wings this morning."

"That must be very constricting. And hot."

"A bit. But they move around and twitch a lot when I'm near you. It's safer to keep them bound."

Flora's fingers already worked the buttons down Rye's shirt. She soon had the shirt off and began unwinding the bandage.

"Great Branch, your wings look terrible. All pale and scrunched up."

Rye grunted when she tried to unfold her wings. She had to ask Flora to help. Flora was very gentle in easing them out straight, but Rye had to bite her lip. Parts of them were numb and the blood rushing back made them tingle and ache.

"You're going to have to stop doing this to yourself," Flora said. "It's like a tourniquet. One day the poor things will drop off."

Flora ran her fingers firmly along Rye's wing supports as if massaging life back into them. Rye sighed and sagged.

"You should be very pleased with yourself," Flora said.

Rye grunted. "That feels really good."

"Come into the bedroom," Flora said. "You can lie down and I can do this more easily. And I have got to take a shower. However lovely this hair looks, I could not sleep on it."

Passing into Flora's bedroom triggered Rye's unease. Her wings drooped. She fumbled the buttons on the back of Flora's dress.

"Coming?" Flora stepped out of her dress and kicked off her high-heel shoes. "I bet some warm water will do those wings a power of good. And we can do some serious foreplay with the shower gel and a sponge."

"Um. I can't."

"Why not?"

Rye chewed her lip and glanced at the door. "I can't have sex with you. Not with Holly here."

"She's asleep three rooms away," Flora said. "You could skin a live hedgehog in here and not wake her."

"I'm sorry. I can't."

Flora looked unhappy. "What is the worst thing that could possibly happen if Holly learned that you and I are having an affair?"

Rye scowled. The worst? If she and Holly were deported, the priestesses would question Holly and get her to say that Rye was gay. Then Holly would blame herself for the rest of her life for what they'd do to Rye. Even if Rye confessed and warned her never to say anything, they'd get it out of her. If questions didn't work, they'd use whips and clubs. No, it was far safer for them both if Holly knew nothing. Safer still if Rye went back to hiding until Holly developed her wings.

Rye turned away from Flora. She and Holly would both be safer if she returned to the single life that had served so well for eleven years. She knew that her relationship with Flora was never going anywhere. How could it? Rye couldn't compete with Flora's rich dryad girlfriend. The novelty of bonking a builder's labourer was going to wear off for Flora sooner or later. And Rye needed to stop stealing the hours to be with Flora, and having sex, from time she should be spending with Holly. With her Fifth Day mornings again free for the kid, Rye could continue her night classes without feeling guilty about Holly never seeing her. Rye needed those classes, and the qualifications she could get, to get ahead for herself and Holly.

Rye clenched her fists at her sides. All those good, strong reasons didn't stop part of her from screaming out that she didn't want to break up with Flora. But she had to. And she couldn't keep putting it off.

"Rye?" Flora put a hand on Rye's arm. "Is this something connected with Fairyland?"

Rye flinched, but not from the physical contact. Flora's unexpected question hit dead centre at the fear underlying the problems in Rye's life.

"I bought some books on it," Flora said. "I wanted to learn as much as I could about fairies. Seeing that you're the first one I've knowingly met. Your past is something you never talk about, but I've had enough hints that it's not pleasant. And, to be honest, I sometimes feel like I'm treading a high wire in the dark where you being a fairy is concerned."

Rye's wings defensively folded against her back.

"I knew Fairyland was a tightly closed society and very religious," Flora said, "but I had no idea how restrictive life must be there if you're not one of the upper levels of the priestly hierarchy. I was horrified to read that most people live in rural poverty and with no proper machinery. And they have capital punishment. It seems unreal that anywhere in the world in this day and age could be so backwards and barbaric. I can't imagine growing up in a place like that would be much fun. And I'm guessing that being gay wasn't looked on kindly."

Rye looked around for her shirt. She felt very vulnerable.

"I'm not at all surprised you left there," Flora said. "I can't understand why more don't."

"Um. Most don't know there's anywhere to go. We don't get much schooling. No reading or writing. No geography." Rye's thoughts slowed and congealed, just like her brain shut down before she ran away. "But...but our commune was in the south. Near the mountains. I figured there had to be somewhere on the other side of them. And even if it was full of evil monsters, like the priestesses said, it couldn't be any worse than...than where I was."

"I can completely understand your leaving the place," Flora said. "It's not hard to guess that being a lesbian didn't make your life there easy. And however much I deplore the necessity, and what it says about our society, I think I can see why you feel you'd rather hide your fairyness than face prejudice. But what I don't understand is how Holly knowing that you and I are seeing each other is a problem. For you or Holly. You're not likely to go back, are you?"

Rye walked away and was confused to realise that she was in Flora's bedroom.

"Is the way your wings are all folded up part of your withdrawal from me?" Flora asked.

Rye ran a hand through her hair. She was naked to the waist. It was very hard to think. "Um. I think...maybe I'd better leave. It'll be better that way."

"I'm not sure I follow you. What do you mean?"

"Um. That...that we had a good time. But it would be better if we didn't see each other again."

"*What?*" Flora strode around to stand in front of Rye. She looked as though Rye had struck her. "Not see each other? What do you mean?"

Rye had to look away. "Um. We—It's best if we end it now."

"End it now," Flora repeated hollowly. "You're dumping me? Is that what I just heard? I...I don't believe it. Is this because I wanted sex and you didn't?"

"No!" Rye rubbed her face and tried to get her brain working again.

"Then why? Because I talked about Fairyland? Or is there someone else?"

"No."

"But—" Flora shook her head and put a hand to her face. "This can't be happening. I thought we were doing great. We didn't spend as much time together as I'd like, but I thought that was because you couldn't, not that you didn't want to."

"Um. Maybe you should find someone who can spend more time with you."

"You're the person I want to spend time with."

Rye looked away to the doors. "You could have your pick of women like me."

Flora hissed in breath. "Holy Elm. Is that what you think? That I cruise around picking up women for casual sex for a while, then toss them aside? Rye? Is that how you think of me?"

Rye's wings tightened even harder against her back.

"Have I given you that impression?" Flora demanded. "Or is this a conclusion you've reached all on your own? Branch! Answer me!"

"Flora, I—"

Flora cracked a stinging slap on the side of Rye's face. "I hate what you do to me. That you can do it so easily. I should really be hating you."

Rye wanted to be a million miles away. It didn't help that she didn't want to be doing this.

"All this while," Flora said, "I've been thinking we were fine. Branch, Trunk, and Root! Trust the buds. My arse! This is the shittiest end to a great day. Did you set me up for this? Give me such a wonderful dinner so that you could break my heart afterward?"

Rye squirmed.

Flora stalked to the doors and yanked one open. "Get out."

Rye wandered to the door but stopped near Flora. Rye could hear Flora's angry breathing. She could feel Flora stabbing a glare at her, but couldn't look at her.

"I'm sorry," Rye said.

"By your logic, I was just a casual screw to you, wasn't I?"

Rye bit her lip and scowled down at the carpet. This hurt.

"What are you waiting for?" Flora said. "You want to watch me cry? Rub salt into the wound?"

"Oh, fey." Rye turned to see Flora with tears already rolling down her cheeks. Something snapped inside. "No. Oh, gods, no. You're the most wonderful person I've ever met."

"Then why in the name of the Holy Elm and All the Trees of the Sacred Grove are you dumping me?"

"I—"

"How can I be so wonderful and...and at the same time be someone who just casually picks women up and casts them aside when I've worn them out? How? Come with me." Flora grabbed Rye's wrist. "I've got something to show you."

Rye let Flora tow her around the hall. Flora shoved open the door to her workroom and flicked the lights on. Rye blinked in the sudden brightness.

"See." Flora pointed to the unfinished weaving on the loom.

Rye frowned at vivid colours in an abstract design.

"I've been working on it for barely a week," Flora said. "My fingers ache to complete it. It's as though the pattern is pouring out of me ready-made. It's as though every part of me resonates with it, and it's part of me. My fingers are moving of their own accord. This thing is happening independent of my brain. It's like I'm pouring pure emotion out, but that it's leaving me fuller, not emptied. I feel a little drunk when I rip myself away from a weaving session. Vitalised. More alive.

As if I've tapped into the essence of Infinity. This hasn't happened to me quite like this before. Not to this extent. Not so raw. So intense. So amazing. It's how I wish all my creations would come to me."

Rye didn't know what to say.

"You want to know what it is?" Flora said. "It's how I feel about you."

Rye looked up from the cloth to Flora's face. Flora's expression made Rye hurt. She felt as lousy as it was possible to get without the mercy of dying of it.

"Here." Flora plonked a pair of scissors in Rye's hand. More tears spilled from her eyes. "Your turn. Show me what you think of me."

Shit.

"Go ahead. Cut it up. Hack it apart."

Rye threw the scissors away. They clattered on the floor. Rye clasped Flora's face in both hands and kissed her on the lips. After a momentary stiffness, Flora kissed back. Angry. Hungry. Rye tore Flora's underwear as she pulled them off. Flora's grip on Rye's hair and wings blurred pleasure and pain. Rye ground Flora into the wooden floor as she drove her to a climax. Flora's ungentle fingers hit the spot between Rye's wings to push her over the edge in a jagged orgasm.

Panting, Rye rolled onto her back. She stared up at the ceiling half-dazed. Beyond the bright lights, the glass part of the roof showed unrelieved blackness. What was she doing? Her life had become this thing out of her control. It slipped and writhed away from her, and carried her along. Dangerous. Wonderful. Scary. Amazing.

Flora's fingers found Rye's hand. Rye spread her fingers so they interleaved with Flora's. Flora smiled and wept at the same time. Rye sat up and gently lifted Flora to hold her. Flora sobbed against Rye's shoulder.

"You are wonderful," Rye said. "And sexy. And beautiful. I've never known a woman like you."

"Then why are you leaving me?"

"I'm not. If you'll forgive me. Please forgive me."

Flora lifted her head to study Rye's face. "I love you. I've been scared to tell you. I didn't know how you'd react. I'm thinking that I should've risked it."

"You love me?"

"Why is that so surprising? You don't really think that I just wanted a casual bonk before throwing you out for another? Do you?"

Rye wiped a tear from Flora's cheek. "I don't know what I was thinking. I'm sorry. Really sorry."

Flora stroked Rye's face. "We have a lot of things to work out, don't we?"

Rye stood and helped Flora to her feet. Flora scooped up her discarded underwear. Rye grabbed her pants. They didn't let go of their joined hands.

"Will you promise me one thing?" Flora asked.

"Considering what a shit I've been tonight, you can ask whatever you like."

"One day, will you tell me what is really happening with you? Why you feel you have to hide us from Holly? About your past and your fairyness? And why you want to bolt whenever we get close to the subjects?"

Rye sighed. She did owe Flora some explanation.

"I don't mean now," Flora said. "I don't think I could cope with any more drama tonight. Let's go to bed. Separate beds, if you like. And sleep knowing that we'll still be lovers when we wake."

Rye nodded and kissed Flora.

Rye padded across the darkened living room and scooped her discarded shirt and bandage off the floor. At the door, she turned back to see Flora silhouetted in the doorway on the far side of the room. Rye blew a kiss. Flora blew one back.

❖

Rye woke alone in a bed large enough for three. The sheets and crumpled pillow showed where Holly had slept. Sunlight poured in through the window. They had forgotten to close the curtains last night.

I love you.

No one had ever said that to Rye before. Flora didn't seem the sort who would just say that, and certainly not under last night's circumstances. And there was the weaving. Rye wasn't just a casual fuck. She had got everything wrong. So very wrong.

Rye scrambled out of bed and tugged on her pants and shirt.

One of the living room glass doors to the patio was open. Flora stood on the edge of the pool wearing a wet sexy bikini. Holly broke the surface of the pool. She was wearing her bra and panties. Rye hoped they didn't have holes.

"That was really good," Flora said. "You had a great angle as you broke the water."

"I wish I could dive as well as you," Holly said.

"You just need some practice," Flora said.

Rye grinned and walked away. She found the kitchen as she'd left it last night.

Rye carried a tray of tea and toast out to the patio.

"Woo hoo! I'm starving." Holly splashed to the side of the pool.

Flora wrapped a robe around herself before joining them at one of the tables. She reached for a cup of tea and shot Rye the warmest look. Rye felt as tall as a tree.

"Hey, Rye," Holly said, "Flora is judging at the Oaklee Art Fair next Fifth Day. We can go with her, can't we?"

"I know it's short notice," Flora said. "So I won't be in the least offended if you have something else planned. I only found out last night myself. Chervil twisted my arm over dinner. So, technically, it's your fault, Rye. If I hadn't been feeling so good because of that fabulous meal, I might have resisted."

"I told you that she could cook," Holly said. "Everyone really liked it, didn't they, Flora?"

"Utterly," Flora said. "Letty Elmwood wants to know how she can hire you for a dinner she's arranging."

"Blow!" Holly said. "Letty Elmwood. You know who she is, right?"

"The sylph with all the makeup plastered on her face," Rye said.

Holly grimaced. "She owns the Lightning Tree Gallery. Fey, Rye. How can you be so smart and know so little?"

"I wonder that myself sometimes." Rye cast a glance at Flora. "Life keeps throwing the wildest surprises at me."

"So, can we go next week?" Holly said. "To the art fair?"

"If you do, don't spend all your wages there." Flora pulled an envelope from her robe pocket and put it on the table.

Rye frowned at the envelope. It must contain the residue of the twelve hundred that Flora had promised her. Rye felt very reluctant to take it. She lifted her empty hands from the table, leaned back in her chair, and shook her head.

"Uh oh," Holly said. "I know that look. When Rye gets all knotted about money, you're not going to make her see sense."

"Would you do me a favour?" Flora said. "There's a jar of sorrel massage oil in the bathroom off my bedroom. Can you fetch it for me, please?"

Holly leaped to her feet and dashed away.

"Take it," Flora said. "You earned it."

"Um. It doesn't feel right. It's too much. And I was so shitty to you last night."

"That has nothing to do with this. You did a terrific job. You earned every piece. And you really should give Holly some payment."

"Look, I kept track of how much I spent, if you cover—"

"No. We had a deal. You can't go changing it on me, just because you know that I'm in love with you. Take it. And I think coming to the art fair would be a great opportunity for you to talk with Holly about her career, don't you? I sounded the waters with Ginger about Holly's apprenticeship. He's open to the idea."

"I don't know what to say. Thanks."

Flora winked.

Holly returned. "Is this the stuff?"

"Yes." Flora rose. "I have to take a shower and dress before I drop you two back home. Why don't you rub some of that on Rye's back for her?"

"Ew." Holly faked gagging.

Flora put a hand on her shoulder. "If I wanted my sister to take me to an art fair, I'd do this small thing for her."

Holly absently worked the massage oil into Rye's wings as she sat on the bed in the guest room. Rye wondered if Holly thought it was strange that Flora would make such an odd request. Holly, though, was completely rapt with Flora's home and lifestyle.

"My mind melted when she showed me her studio," Holly said. "I got to see what she's working on. Wow! And her sketches. Her loom! Daisy will gnaw her arms off with envy when I tell her! We can go to the Oaklee Art Fair, can't we?"

"Yeah. Sure."

"Woo hoo!" Holly leaped up and bounced on the bed.

"Stop that!" Rye grabbed one of Holly's calves. "Don't break the bed."

Rye packed away her gear from the kitchen and left Holly to look for anything she missed. She found Flora in her bedroom. Rye glanced behind before taking the two swift paces closer to her and kissing her.

"Can I keep seeing you?" Rye whispered. "Please?"

"Yes. Please."

Rye grinned, but stepped back out of reach and glanced again at the doorway. "And we'd love to come with you to the art fair next week. Thanks. For everything."

Flora smiled.

Rye thanked her again after she and Holly climbed out of Flora's carpet onto the parking pad outside their apartment.

"Thank you," Flora said. "Dinner was great. Oh. You'd better take this. It's Letty Elmwood's card."

Rye accepted it and frowned.

"She wants to talk to you about catering a dinner for her," Flora said. "I told you."

"I didn't think you were serious," Rye said.

"Give her a call. You'll see how serious she is. If you have any questions, feel free to contact me. You have my number."

"Um. Okay. I will."

Rye waved until the carpet zoomed out of sight.

"She's the pinnacle," Holly said. "The utter pinnacle. You'd better not get all knotted and stupid and drive her away. I couldn't forgive you for that."

Rye frowned as she followed Holly into the apartment. "What was that supposed to mean?"

"Do I get any wages? Still, I suppose you'd better keep it for food and stuff."

"No. Here you go." Rye slipped a fifty from the envelope.

"Woo hoo! I bet there are going to be so many scathing things at the art fair next week."

"You've not been invited to any more birthday parties, have you?"

Holly frowned. "Why?"

Rye thought better of what she was going to say. "No reason."

Holly disappeared into her bedroom trailing the telephone cord. How had Rye failed to instil any money sense in her? In what other areas had her parenting skills let the kid down?

Chapter Nine

Rye tried to pay attention to the class, but her heart wasn't in it. She dreaded the talk she'd have to have with Mr. Bulrush at the end of the lesson.

Rye lingered until everyone else had left the class. Mr. Bulrush packed papers into his case.

"I was hoping to talk with you, Ms. Woods," he said. "The deadline for entry for the certification exam is coming up. You should really be starting your extra work."

"Um. Yeah. Well, the thing is that I can't sit it."

"There's no need for you to feel intimidated."

"Um. No. It's not that." Rye bit her lip. "I don't have time to do the extra work. In fact, I'm going to have to quit class."

"Quit? Well. This is a surprise. Is there something I can help with?"

"Um. No, thanks." Rye shrugged. "Home stuff. I'll take this class again next year. Look, thanks for teaching me. I appreciate it. Maybe we'll catch up next year."

"I understand when domestic circumstances interfere," he said. "But it seems such a waste. Look, why don't I wait to cancel your registration? If you find things change in a few weeks, you can pick it up again. You'll have no problem passing even with a few missed assignments."

Rye didn't think she would be able to return any time soon, but she smiled. "Thanks. That's nice of you."

He offered her his hand. "Good luck. I hope to see you again."

Rye shook his hand.

Her work boots clumped and echoed on the hard floor of the school corridor. The sound was hollow. Rye tried not to think of the chance she'd just passed up. She never got ahead. Her key to a better paying job and a more comfortable future lay in learning and getting qualifications. But she couldn't keep up with her classes unless she earned more, so that she could buy a broom, which meant she had to put her learning in abeyance while she took a third minimum wage job.

Rye jammed her fists into her pockets. "Fey."

❖

On Fourth Night, Rye went straight home from work instead of going to the school. Holly's music blasted from her bedroom.

"Holls! Turn that down or I'll go deaf."

The music stopped as if by magic—or as if the magic powering the speakers suddenly died. Holly darted out of her room.

"Rye? What are you doing here?"

"I live here occasionally, remember? This kitchen is a mess. What have you been doing?"

"I was going to clear it up before you got home. Isn't this Fourth Night? Don't you have class?"

Rye rolled up her sleeves. "I'll be working at Pansy's tonight. She's letting me pick up a couple of extra nights while one of the girls is off having a baby. You know, it takes as little effort to put the stoppers back in these jars as it does to pull them out."

"Extra nights? Did the week suddenly get longer without anyone telling me? And that still doesn't explain—Rye, you're not actually peeling out of class? Not you? Not Miss Education Is the Beginning and End of Life as We Know It?"

Rye plonked the jar of hazelnut flakes back in the cupboard with too much force. "Give it a rest."

"You *are* peeling! You'd skin me alive if I did that."

"I'm not skipping class. Because I don't have classes any more."

"But it's only the middle of the term. How can—"

Rye banged a pan on the stove and rounded on Holly. "I've quit. Okay? Now give it a rest."

"Quit?" Holly lost all her flippancy. She frowned across the table. "Rye, how could you quit? You were—"

"I need the money!" Rye's fists clenched. "Now, leave it alone. I mean it."

Holly threw her hands up as if to ward off Rye's scowl. "Okay.

Okay."

Rye continued glaring at the doorway after Holly left it. "Fey."

That night, after showering away the fumes from the cauldrons of bubbling fat, Rye slumped on her sofa bed. Her textbook and notebooks sat on the packing crates and old door that she'd converted into a desk.

"I need the money. I need a broom. That will give me more time. I'll be able to see Flora more. And spend more time with Holly. I didn't have a choice. Next year, I'll be able to fly between classes and home and work and Flora's place."

Rye climbed into bed and lay staring at the ceiling. There was a new patch of mould forming. The people upstairs must've spilled something again.

It would've been nice to be with Flora right then. Still, Flora would be coming by in the morning to take them to the art fair.

❖

"How do I look?" Holly struck a pose.

Rye turned around from setting the knot back into place in the wall over her money stash. How much money would it cost for their admittance to the fair? "Um. Fine."

"Not that I know why I'm asking you. You're not really going to wear that? On my tombstone, they'll put: Here lie the tortured remains of Holly Woods, her young life was cut short by an agonising attack of bad taste."

"What's wrong with my clothes? The holes are all patched."

Holly rolled her eyes. Her parting shot was, "It's a good job you're a fabulous cook."

Rye frowned.

Someone tapped on the door.

"I'll get it!" Holly shouted. "It'll be Flora."

Rye folded herself into the rear seat of Flora's carpet to allow Holly to sit in the front. Flora kept peering over the top of her sunglasses to make eye contact with Rye via the rear-vision mirror while Holly craned her neck to look up, across, and down for anyone she knew. Holly's estimation of Flora's utmost stylishness suffered a dent when she fiddled with the carpet's sound system.

"That's the sort of cobwebby stuff Rye listens to," Holly said. "You ought to hear Funguz. And Slash the Chrysalis."

"You think so?" Flora sounded amused. "Would that be safe at my age?"

"They're so scathing and this minute," Holly said. "Oh! That's Orpine Madder. In that carpet there. She's the snottiest girl in the whole school. And we're going to pass them! Astronomical. Don't look. Pretend you don't see them. I'm going to wait until we're passing before I look surprised and give her a little wave. I'd hate for her not to realise that I'm in the stylish carpet that is passing her family's dusty old thing."

Rye smiled. She shared a look with Flora's image in the mirror. Flora fully restored her idol status by speeding up to whiz past the Madder family carpet in the lane above them.

At the entrance to the park, Flora flew past the queues waiting to cram into the parking lots and parked in the VIP area.

Rye followed Flora and Holly into the big red VIP tent. Volunteer workers greeted them. Rye found herself handed a sticky tag with "Guest" printed on it and a glossy brochure.

"Ms. Withe?" A pixie woman beamed up at Flora and held out her brochure and a pen. "Could I get you to autograph my brochure, please?"

"Sure." Flora took the pen and signed her name across one of the pages.

"I really, really liked *Adventures in Four Panels,*" the pixie said. "I went to the gallery, like, every day in my lunch to see it."

"I'm glad you enjoyed it." Flora smiled and handed the pen back. "Now, if you'll excuse me."

Flora went off to check her judging duties. Holly made a beeline for one of the hospitality hostesses. Rye jammed her hands in her pockets and frowned back at the little pixie woman, who was now wiping tables. People wanted Flora's autograph?

"This cup of tea is yummy," Holly said. "Raspberry leaf and hazelnut. And free. You should get one."

"What was that woman talking about?" Rye asked.

"*Adventures in Four Panels*?" Holly said. "My eyes dropped out when I saw it. Only a copy in art class, of course. Not the original. Flora was still an apprentice when she wove it. Haven't you ever seen it?"

Rye shook her head.

"A really, really fabulous cook," Holly said.

Rye scowled.

Rye trailed Holly and Flora through a sea of people and colourful alleys of stalls displaying oddly-shaped pots, lumps of glass, paintings, lurid clothing, tortured bits of metal, and supplies for making them all. Wind chimes tinkled behind the noise of chattering and laughter. Music thumped somewhere. Jugglers and tumblers moved through it all attracting knots of spectators.

Later, Rye's bored gaze snagged on a stall displaying cooking pots and pans. She left Flora and Holly discussing some knitted rags to saunter across. She lifted the lid on a double boiler.

"That's one of my best sellers," the elderly pixie man said.

"Yeah?" Rye caught sight of the price tag and nearly dropped the lid.

"You look like you're in the trade," the pixie said.

"What? Oh. No. I work on a building site. You make these yourself?"

"I used to have an apprentice. My son, Hop. But I work alone now. Between us, it's getting a bit much. I really need someone to come in and help me with the heavy work. But no one wants to work just a few hours a week."

Rye looked up from enviously studying a frying pan. "What sort of work?"

Ten minutes later, Rye strolled away from Nuttal's Pot stall whistling. A hundred pieces for two nights' work. Okay, it sounded like heavy, dirty stuff, but it paid well. Mr. Nuttal seemed to be a nice bloke. Not the sort to work her to death.

Rye stopped to frown around at the seething crowds. Where were Flora and Holly?

After wandering fruitlessly for more than an hour, Rye bought herself a hideously expensive jar of beer and found a spot to sit on a grassy knoll near the dancing stages.

"There you are!" Holly slumped down beside Rye and started eating from a paper plate.

Flora lowered herself on Rye's other side and handed her a plate of food. "We've been looking for you."

"How much is it for the food and entry?" Rye said.

Flora waved that away with her fork. "Tell me what you think of the lavender shoots."

Rye dug her wallet out. "Will twenty cover it?"

"It's my treat," Flora said. "I'm not inviting you two out and expecting you to pay."

Rye frowned. Holly glared at her as if she were contemplating throttling her.

"Look," Rye said, "I owe you."

Flora shook her head. "No, you don't. Your food is getting cold. Try the lavender shoots. Oh, Holly, look. That's Chicory Field. The sculptor I was telling you about."

Rye's frown deepened as she shoved her wallet back in her pocket. She hadn't realised that by accepting Flora's invitation to come with her, she had tacitly agreed to let Flora pay for them all. She would have to be more careful in the future.

While Rye brooded on how she might discharge this unintended obligation, she happened to glance aside and see Flora giving her a scorchingly saucy look. Despite sitting in the middle of a crowded park and Holly close on her other side, Rye's wing buds twitched in response. She lost her thread and had trouble thinking about anything other than sex.

Holly finished her food, leaped to her feet, and strode away to find a bathroom.

"I could have sex with you right now," Flora said.

Rye nearly choked on a lump of boiled dock root. "Here?"

"Doesn't the idea of public sex turn you on?" Flora said.

"It scares me to death."

"Oh. Then I suppose I'll just have to keep seducing you in my lair," Flora said. "Hmm. I have to go and do my official thing shortly. Why don't you take the opportunity to talk with Holly about her career? Which reminds me, Holly said you've given up night classes. Is that true?"

Rye shrugged and reached for her beer. "Just until next year."

"But why? I thought you loved doing it? And were a straight-A student?"

"I can pick it up again next year."

Flora frowned. "Does your decision have anything to do with us?"

"Here comes Holls."

Flora glanced across to where Holly wove her way through the crowds. "Did you arrange something with Letty Elmwood?"

"Um. No."

"Why not?"

Rye shrugged. "It doesn't feel right. I'm not a proper cook or caterer."

"Branch, you can be hard work sometimes. I have to go. We'll talk about this later."

Flora and Holly exchanged a few words before Flora strode away. Holly dropped down beside Rye and helped herself to Rye's beer.

"I hate you," Holly said. "I wanted the earth to eat me when you started getting all knotted about paying for the food. Why can't you be normal? Flora doesn't care about a few pieces."

"That's because Flora has a lot more of them than I have."

Holly angrily plucked at the grass. "You always say stupid stuff like that. It's not the end of the world if Flora wants to buy us lunch, is it?"

"It's not Flora's place to feed us. That's my job."

Holly scowled. "I'm going to earn so much money that my kids are never going to be embarrassed about me paying for anything. And I'll be able to afford mobiles for them. And give them good clothes from a real shop, not the second-hand. And not live in some mouldy apartment."

"I hope you do."

"And I'm going to give you thousands and thousands. And I bet you'll keep it all tucked away somewhere and patch your shirts anyway even though you could afford to buy new."

"I'll be interested to see how you cope with teenaged children just like you."

"I'm going to be with Flora." Holly leaped to her feet.

"Holls! Wait. Sit down. There's something I want to talk with you about."

Holly glowered.

"Flora is judging," Rye said. "We'll go and find her just as soon as she's finished, okay? Please sit down."

Holly subsided unhappily and played with Rye's beer jar. "I wish I was Flora's sister."

"She was telling me that it takes a lot of hard work doing what she does."

Holly looked wary.

"But if I really liked doing it," Rye said, "and if I were really good at it, then I'd give it my best shot. Flora told me that it's what you want to do."

"You're not pissed?"

"Why should I be angry?"

"Because it's not a proper eight to five job. And I wouldn't go to university."

"I know that."

"It'd take me years and years to go solo like Flora," Holly said. "But I'd work in shops and boutiques. Get an apprenticeship with some top artist. I'd work really hard. Not like school. This would be real work. It's what I really, really want to do. And have for ages. I won't change my mind."

Holly bristled defiance, as if expecting Rye to fight her on this. Rye considered that. What did it say about their relationship if she intimidated her?

"Holls, if this is what you really want to do, then I'm behind you all the way."

"Shit. You are?"

"Language." Rye glanced around to make sure no one sat within earshot. "How much do you remember about Fairyland?"

"Not much." Holly shrugged. "What you told me. Why? We're not going back?"

"Never! I got us out of there so that we could do what we wanted, not what someone told us we had to do. You're...you're someone different from me. What I've been wanting for you...well, maybe it's really what I'd want for myself. I should've asked you a long time ago what it is you want for yourself."

"Wow."

"You're nearly old enough to get your wings. You're nearly an adult. It's time I started bearing that in mind."

"Yeah?"

"But that also means that you have to start taking more responsibility for yourself," Rye said.

"Does that mean I can stay out late at night? And drink?"

Rye frowned. "It means that if you want to drink, you pay for it yourself."

"Oh."

"Come on, let's go and find Flora."

Holly leaped up and fell in beside Rye. "You're not so bad. When you're not getting all knotted."

Rye grinned.

"I'll have to thank Flora," Holly said. "I owe her half of Infinity for this. Who'd have thought anyone could talk you into being reasonable and letting me do an apprenticeship?"

Rye lost her grin.

They found Flora in a massive tent crammed with people. She was sitting at a bench with some other people signing autographs. Rye and Holly found a place on the grass to wait where they could watch the tent entrance. Over an hour passed before Flora emerged.

"Sorry it took so long," Flora said.

"You really do have fans, don't you?" Rye said.

"She's one of the best," Holly said. "I told you that."

Flora peeled off her name tag. "I'm not going to be Flora Withe for the rest of the day. How's that?"

The way Flora smiled made Rye go all warm and forget everything else. So much so that Rye halfway reached to hold Flora's hand before she remembered. It occurred to her that, no matter how many autographs Flora signed for all those people, only Rye Woods got to kiss Flora and give her orgasms on her living room floor.

"Florrie!"

Flora stopped and turned. An older dryad woman, with red and yellow highlights in her hair, leaped up from a chair beneath an awning.

"Aunt Ramble," Flora said.

"Little Florrie." Ramble stepped across to envelop Flora in a hug. "It's been an oak's age. I was just saying to Wind that we hadn't seen you. I bumped into Hazel three or four days ago."

"My mother was Upriver?" Flora said.

"One of her charities," Ramble said. "She didn't mention anything about you having buds."

"Oh." Flora lost her smile and stiffened.

Ramble directed a sharply interested stare at Rye. "Perhaps you'd like to introducc me to your budmate, Florrie?"

"Oh," Flora said. "Um. Ramble Vine, these are my friends Rye and Holly. Perhaps I could call you, Auntie? We really must be going."

Rye felt Ramble's stare on her back as they walked away.

"What did she mean about buds?" Holly said.

"It's a dryad thing," Flora said. "Aunt Ramble is actually my mother's cousin. She's the district coordinator of the Community Art Fund."

Rye frowned. She had not seen Flora disconcerted before. Ramble had stared to the point of rudeness. Had Flora told her about them?

By late afternoon, the crowds had grown even larger. Rye drew a breath of relief when they passed into the calm of the VIP parking lot. Flora flew her carpet up and out. Lines of waiting carpets and brooms still clogged the floating parking beacons.

"How about we end the day together?" Flora said. "I'm hungry enough to eat an early dinner."

"Me, too," Holly said.

Rye frowned and frantically tried to remember what food she had in the house. She had delayed her weekly grocery shopping until tomorrow.

"I've been told about this new restaurant in Oak Heights," Flora said. "They specialise in imp food. Their interior decoration is supposed to be like a grotto. What do you think?"

"Astronomical!" Holly said.

"No," Rye said. "No, thanks."

Holly's back set rigid. Rye could imagine her murderous expression. But, then, Holly didn't have only twenty pieces in her pocket. When Flora parked, Holly stormed into the apartment and slammed the door. Rye sighed.

"What did I say wrong?" Flora asked.

"Not you. Sorry about that."

"Call me?"

Rye nodded.

Inside the apartment, Holly's music was loud enough to hurt. Rye pounded on the door. When she received no answer, she shoved the door open.

"Turn it down!" Rye shouted. "Or I will."

Holly hit the switch. "You don't want me to have any fun, do you?

I hate you so much."

"Very mature."

Holly picked up her pencil holder and hurled it at the wall near Rye.

"You keep this up," Rye said, "and I'll spank you like I used to when you were a little kid."

"I hate you. Hate you!" Holly screamed. "How could you embarrass me like that in front of Flora?"

"You'd rather I was embarrassed in the restaurant when I couldn't afford to pay for anything?"

"Flora would've paid!"

"It's not Flora's place to pay."

"She has so much money that she wouldn't care."

"I care. We're not charity cases."

"I'm the only kid in my whole school who has never eaten at a restaurant. Do you know that? Do you know how that makes me feel?"

"You have eaten at a restaurant."

"When I was seven and you washed dishes in one. Big fat fucking deal."

Rye's wings and fists clenched. She forced herself to bite back her retort and take a couple of deep, calming breaths. "Considering your present behaviour, it's a good thing we didn't eat out with Flora. Maybe I was too hasty in thinking you were becoming an adult. This doesn't convince me that you're ready to leave school and start an apprenticeship."

Rye walked out. She thought she heard Holly mutter "bitch", but chose to ignore it. What she wouldn't give to be with Flora and forget the rest of Infinity.

CHAPTER TEN

On First Day after work, Rye hung her jacket on the peg inside the front door and braced herself for a resumption of combat.

"I'm home, Holly."

Rye carried her groceries through into the kitchen. Holly appeared when Rye put away the last bag of dandelion roots. She looked sullen.

"How was school?" Rye asked.

"Stupid." Holly slumped into a chair. "I want to get a job."

"You're not leaving school. What happened to the idea of wanting an apprenticeship?"

Holly gave her a filthy look. "You quit school."

"I had no choice. I have to pay for you to keep going."

"You needn't. I never wanted to go to that limping school. And the job is at Mr. Cloudnut's store across the street. Filling shelves and stuff. After stupid school. So there."

"Oh. Okay. As long as it doesn't interfere with your homework."

"You won't even know that I'm gone. You're never here!"

Holly stomped out and slammed her bedroom door.

Rye took a deep breath. This was a good development. If Holly worked, maybe she'd have more feel for the value of money.

Rye filled the kettle to start dinner. Tonight was going to be her first night working at Mr. Nuttal's pot boutique. If things worked out, and it became a long term job, she'd have saved enough for a second-hand broom in two or three months. Then she'd quit working at Pansy's. That would give her two nights free a week and she'd still be earning more than she did before. One night a week with Flora.

Holly barely grunted two words to Rye over dinner.

Someone tapped on the door.

Holly leaped to her feet. "I'll get it."

Rye stood to gather the dishes.

"Flora!" Holly said. "Wow."

Rye peered around the door to see Flora walking toward her. Had she forgotten a meeting? Although, Flora looked dressed for a date rather than just steamy sex with Rye.

"You've just eaten?" Flora said. "Good. Take a shower."

"What?" Rye said.

"Can you find her something to wear?" Flora said to Holly.

"What is this?" Rye said. "I've got a job to go to."

"I'll drop you off there afterward," Flora said. "Oh, Holly, stuff some of Rye's work-clothes in a bag that she can change into."

"Afterward?" Rye said.

"We have an appointment with Letty Elmwood," Flora said. "You're going to talk to her about cooking her dinner. I'm taking you. Moral support. Holly, clothes, please."

"I'm on it!" Holly said.

"But—" Rye said.

"I know I should have warned you, but you might've wriggled out of it," Flora said. "I talked with Letty. She needs to have something in place in the next day or two. You need to take a shower."

Rye frowned in the direction of the living room where Holly was making disparaging comments about Rye's clothes.

"Look," Rye said, "I appreciate your effort, but I can't do this. I'm not a real cook. I haven't spent years at chef school or in training kitchens or working in restaurants."

"You don't like cooking?" Flora asked.

"Of course, I do. But what—"

"And you're extremely good at it," Flora said. "And didn't you say that you earned more doing it than your usual evening job? Which, you have also told me, you hate. So, why not do something you like doing and will pay you well?"

Rye couldn't immediately counter that. Holly burst out of the living room and thrust a clean tight T-shirt at her. Flora checked her watch.

"We really don't want to be late," Flora said. "Letty can be funny about punctuality."

Rye snatched the T-shirt off Holly and stomped down to the bathroom. When she stood drying herself, Holly shoved some clothes into the bathroom. Despite her continuing misgivings, Rye took them.

A few minutes later, Rye sat frowning in the passenger seat of Flora's carpet as they sped toward the Upper Westside. Flora put a hand on Rye's thigh.

"Am I being too pushy?" Flora said.

"Yeah."

"I cannot understand why you're so resistant to this. It amazes me that you don't cook as your full time profession. I've brought a copy of the menu that you did for me. You need to think up some alternatives. Letty won't want exactly the same as I did. What other mains could you do?"

"Um."

"How about possum?" Flora flicked on the light so that Rye could see to write. "I had some very succulent possum the last time I ate with Daddy at his club. Slices off a roast, I think it was."

"Um. Yeah. I guess I could always try a haunch."

"Terrific. Write that down. Now, what would you serve with it?"

By the time Flora stopped her carpet outside a fancy big house in Overhill, Rye had three complete menus planned.

"You can do this," Flora said. "I have faith in you."

"Um." Rye saw the tall, skinny silhouette of the sylph at a glass door.

Flora patted Rye's thigh. "You're my girlfriend, remember? Letty can keep her hands off."

"As if," Rye said.

Rye took a deep breath and climbed out of the carpet. She would not have had the courage to walk inside if Flora hadn't been beside her.

Forty minutes later, Rye dropped back into the passenger seat and stared half-dazed at the notebook in her hands. Flora started the carpet and flew them away.

"Safety harness," Flora said. "Well? That wasn't so bad, was it, lover? Mind you, from the way Letty was looking at you, I'm so glad I'll be at this dinner."

"Shit." Rye ran a hand through her hair. "Sixteen hundred. Did she really agree to pay me one thousand six hundred pieces? Why...why did you say so much? I was only going to say twelve hundred. And I thought that was a lot. Too much."

"Letty can afford it. In fact, she'll respect you more for charging more rather than less." Flora squeezed Rye's thigh. "Panic not, lover. You give her the dinner you discussed, and she'll be getting her money's worth and more. Plus, you'll need to pay someone to help. I'm sure Holly will want to do it, but for eight people, you really need someone else as well. Have a look in my purse. There should be a green card with a number on the back."

Rye felt uneasy about rummaging inside Flora's purse. Amongst an eclectic collection of loose change, banknotes, lipstick, tissues, breath mints, and a tampon, she found several cards. One was green.

"Yes, that's it." Flora said. "Briony Butterflower is a sister of my housekeeper, Aloe. She's an apprentice, so she's always looking for ways to make some extra money. I've met her several times. Very pleasant and capable. Give her a call."

Rye felt more dazed than ever. "You've thought of everything. I had no idea you were so aggressively organised."

"Only when it comes to other people. Now, don't you have to put your work clothes on? Where am I supposed to be taking you?"

Rye remained in a haze of disbelief as she contorted herself through changing her clothes. Part of her mind was already planning what ingredients she'd need, how they should be prepared, and the best way to present the dishes.

"Sixteen hundred!" Rye said. "That's five times more than I earn in a week."

"Really?" Flora flicked a frown at Rye. "Oh, Elm. I'm glad Letty didn't see you like that."

Rye zipped up her pants. "The strangest thing is, I'm already working out what I'm going to do."

Flora smiled. "Am I forgiven, then?"

"Yeah." Rye kissed Flora's hand. "You're wonderful. Even when you're being pushy."

Flora parked outside the darkened pot boutique. "I wish I were taking you home."

"Me, too."

Rye waved until the carpet's rear lights vanished around a corner. She trudged around the back of the row of shops and thumped on Nuttal's back door.

While Rye hauled load after heavy load of metal waste out to a dumpster, her mind swirled with cooking, one thousand six hundred pieces, and Flora. After an hour, Rye sweated and ached. Her hands hurt and her clothes were filthy. Maybe this wasn't such a good job.

"Hey, there." Mr. Nuttal, the elderly pixie, shuffled into the workroom. He carried a tray holding a plate of biscuits and a pot of tea. "That looks great. Come and sit down."

"Um. Thanks. But I'd rather get finished."

"That looks like more than enough for tonight." Mr. Nuttal poured the tea into two large mugs. "Mrs. Nuttal brewed this special. And she made the biscuits."

Rye bit into a biscuit and found it dry and too sweet.

"Here." He put fifty pieces on the table.

"Um," Rye said. "I've only done an hour."

"You've done the work I wanted done. All that junk cleared out of there. That's what's important to me. Not how long you take."

Rye pocketed the cash. "Thanks."

"You still want to come back on Fourth Night?"

"Yeah. I'd like to."

"Good. Maybe we should settle on Second Night and Fourth Night," he said. "Oh, and you can take your shirt off if you get too hot. I know how sweaty it can be working in here with the burners going. You've not got anything this old man hasn't seen before."

Rye didn't contradict him.

❖

On Third Night, Rye put aside her meal planning and went to tap on Holly's bedroom door. Holly sat at her desk chewing a pencil end.

"I'm off early tonight," Rye said. "I'm going to the library before I go to Pansy's."

"Uh huh."

"Um. If I wanted a book to teach me something about art, where would be a good place to look?"

Holly smiled and scribbled on a scrap of paper. "I think this has what you're looking for."

The Hollowberry branch of the municipal library contained thin pickings in the cooking section apart from budget meal planning, economic cooking for large families, and wholesome, inexpensive meals. Rye dug out the scrap of paper Holly had given her. *Contemporary*

Artists was a slim paperback with glossy pages. She had been thinking more along the lines of some textbook explaining weaving for idiots. Before Rye put the book back, she turned to the contents page. She saw Flora's name.

Rye flicked to page forty-two. A very nice picture of Flora, which looked fairly recent, filled a third of the page. The section started with a brief biography. The book must have been written two years ago, because it gave her age as thirty-one. Most of the section was devoted to pictures of her works along with stuff written about each piece. So that was what *Adventures in Four Panels* looked like. Rye didn't understand what it was supposed to be, but it was nice to look at.

That night, Rye lay in bed frowning at *Contemporary Artists*. She would have to borrow the dictionary out of Holly's room tomorrow, because most of the technical terms left her for dead. Rye stared at the photograph of Flora as she phoned Flora for their late night talk. Even after all these weeks, it still astonished Rye that anyone as sexy, beautiful, wonderful, and successful as Flora Withe would look twice at Rye Woods.

❖

On Fifth Day morning, Rye ran from the transit node to Whiterow Gardens but still got soaked in the driving rain.

"You're dripping," Flora said. "Take this towel. Strip. I'll fetch you a robe."

Rye grabbed Flora's arm. "I'd rather you warmed me up."

"How about I run a hot bath for us?"

"Oh. Okay."

Rye frowned as she peeled off her wet clothes. Flora usually couldn't wait for sex. She looked only marginally happier when she returned.

"Something wrong, babe?" Rye asked.

"You should've waited. I'd have fetched you."

"I know. But Holly went out early. And I couldn't wait."

Flora's smile seemed forced. When Rye kissed her, she didn't feel physically in tune.

Flora insisted on stuffing Rye's clothes in the dryer herself. The new robe that Flora had given Rye was thick and warm, and Flora had made slits in the back to comfortably accommodate Rye's wings. It was much nicer than anything Rye could have afforded to buy herself, which made her uneasy. When she had tried to decline it, Flora had pointed out that she could not return it now that she'd altered it even had she wanted to. It was something else she owed Flora.

Rye wandered into the living room. The glass doors framed grey rain pounding the deck and swimming pool. A fire burned in the hearth. Rye warmed herself in front of it and smiled as she remembered last week's sex on the rug.

A magazine and some papers lay scattered on the closest sofa. Rye couldn't help noticing the fancy invitation card sitting open beside the magazine. Ms. Flora Withe and partner were invited to some glitzy-sounding event.

Flora came in and took Rye's hand and led her to the ensuite. The huge tub, which was easily large enough to accommodate six, filled fast with steamy water. Flora poured in some green liquid which bubbled and released a gentle scent of chamomile.

Rye climbed in and watched Flora strip. Unusually, Flora didn't make a provocative show out of it. She merely dropped her clothes and stepped into the water. When Rye pulled Flora onto her lap, Flora's head sagged onto Rye's shoulder.

"What's the matter?" Rye said.

Flora sighed. "I'm sorry. It's hormones."

"Anything I can do to make it better?"

"Stay here with me, like this, for the rest of our lives."

Rye smiled and kissed Flora's temple. "I thought you were a tree nymph not a water nymph. Want to talk?"

Flora listlessly played with a mound of bubbles against Rye's arm. "Tell me something nice that has happened to you."

"Okay. I'm in a bath of hot water with the most wonderful woman in the world. It doesn't get any nicer than that. Unless it was last week, when I was lying on the rug in front of a fire with the most wonderful woman in the world after we'd had sex."

Flora smiled fleetingly. "We live for Fifth Days, don't we?"

"I know it's my fault that we don't see much of each other. Can you bear with me for another few weeks? I'm going to quit my sandwich frying job."

"Really?"

"Yeah. Mr. Nuttal pays much better than Pansy, and he's a nicer bloke to work for. He's like I imagine an uncle would be. Or grandfather."

"You didn't know your grandfather?"

"I didn't know my who father was." Rye kissed Flora's cheek. "So, I'm going to have two evenings free. That means more time for us."

"You want to?"

"Of course." *I gave up night classes for this.*

"I woke up this morning halfway convinced that you were a dream. Like a ghost or imaginary friend that no one else could see."

"If I were a dream, surely I wouldn't make you sad?" Rye stroked Flora's arm. "Hey, listen. Thanks to you setting me up with Ms. Elmwood, I've nearly got the money for my broom. That means I'll soon be able to whiz over here for fast sex in my lunch breaks."

Flora smiled, but cocked her head to one side. "I'm not sure I understand. You've been working yourself to death just so that you can buy a broom?"

"Not to death." Rye kissed Flora's wet throat. "Hmm. Definitely not dead yet."

Rye kissed Flora's shoulders and let her hands explore Flora's body. Flora put both hands against Rye's shoulders to hold her away.

"You're not going to turn out to be one of those women who thinks sex is the answer to every problem?" Flora asked.

Rye sagged back against the side of the bath. "I'm sorry."

Flora shook her head and slid away. "No. I'm sorry. This is not how I wanted to spend my time with you."

"You look like you're going to cry."

"I am."

"Hey. Come here." Rye gathered Flora and held her. "I'm sorry, babe. Does this have anything to do with that invitation? I couldn't help seeing it on the couch. Is this a big deal?"

"That's the oddest thing. It's not. It's a fundraiser for a local charity. Quite small. It's on a Third Night. I know you can't make it."

Rye gently wiped a tear from Flora's cheek. "But?"

Flora sighed. "But imagining going without you felt so desolate. I burst into tears. I know it doesn't make any sense. I've been out since we started seeing each other. It's not as though I've become a hermit. It hasn't killed me to go anywhere alone."

Flora's tears were like acid inside Rye. She frowned down at the part of Flora's thigh she could see through the floating bubbles. "This is a small party?"

"Why?"

"Well," Rye said. "If this is important to you, I could go."

Flora's expression swiftly passed through surprise and delight to settle into a soft, teary smile. "Oh, I do love you. Thank you. But I can't let you do that. I know you're not really comfortable with us as a public entity."

"I've said I'll go, babe. I mean it."

Flora lightly kissed her. "I know. And now I feel like shit for having manipulated you into offering."

"What?"

"I did. I got all weepy on you and you were nice to me. "

"I want to be nice to you," Rye said. "I don't feel manipulated. You were sad. You told me why. I saw a way to make it better. I know I'm new to relationships, but isn't that the way it's supposed to work?"

Flora gave her a despairing look, covered her face with her hands, and sank under the water. Rye reached down to lift her back up. With Flora's hair sloughing water, Rye saw how prominent her buds looked.

"Oh, Holy Elm." Flora looped her arms around Rye's neck. "I think I'm going to explode with contrary and irrational emotions. Do you think there's a chance that sex might help?"

Rye grinned. "No harm trying, is there?"

Flora was sitting on the side of the tub and Rye had lowered her head between Flora's legs when she heard a woman's voice.

"Flora!"

Rye jerked upright.

Flora snapped her head around to stare at the door. "Branch."

"Flora?" The woman sounded closer. As if she were just next door in the bedroom. "Where are you?"

Rye bristled. "Who—?"

Flora clamped a hand on Rye's mouth. "I'm in the bath, Mother! I'll be right out."

Rye's eyes widened.

Flora slid off the tub and grabbed her robe. She whispered, "I'll get rid of her. Wait in here."

Rye looked for her clothes. Fey. Where had she left them? Not all over the bedroom floor? No. They were in the dryer. Rye sighed with relief.

Flora slipped out the door and clicked it closed behind her. "Mother. This is a surprise. I didn't realise you still had a key."

Mrs. Withe's reply was muffled, as if she'd turned away.

Rye wrapped her robe around herself and crept to the door.

"Perhaps I could make you a cup of tea." Flora sounded like she was standing with her back to the bathroom door. "In the kitchen. We—"

"Oh! It's true," Mrs. Withe said. "My baby girl has buds."

"Mother, this really isn't a good time to—"

"Do you have any inkling how devastatingly humiliating it is to learn from a stranger that one's own daughter has buds?"

"Hardly," Flora said, "since I don't have a daughter, do I?"

"Well, I don't know," Mrs. Withe said. "There is so much about your life that you find necessary to conceal from me and your father."

Rye heard Flora's sigh through the door.

"I shall never forget," Mrs. Withe said, "the indescribable joy I felt at holding my baby girl for the first time. It even momentarily eclipsed the unspeakable indignity of the process of giving birth. I don't believe my maternal rapture would have been any the less even had I known the heartache to come."

"Mother—"

"A stranger, Flora. How could you be so thoughtless as to let me find out through a stranger?"

"Aunt Ramble is not a stranger."

"So, you know who told me," Mrs. Withe said. "Well, you would, wouldn't you? Since you confided in her and I don't know how many others, but not your own mother. Well, my little girl has a budmate. I won't say that it's not a teeny bit overdue, darling. You're hardly a spring twig anymore. And the Holy Elm knows you've had enough casual girlfriends to last anyone for a lifetime. Next Third Day. Will that suit?"

"Third Day?" Flora said. "Suit what?"

"I'll make sure your father doesn't have any appointments. He wishes to meet your budmate as much as I do."

Rye scowled. Her wet wings folded defensively.

"No," Flora said. "Third Day is not convenient. I—"

"The Second Day after?" Mrs. Withe said. "It can't be First Day, because I have one of my charity meetings."

"No, Mother, I can't make it," Flora said. "We can't make it. Please don't bother looking through your diary. When the day comes that I want to introduce you all, I'll give you plenty of warning."

"Oh," Mrs. Withe said. "Oh, I see. You don't want us to meet your budmate. It can only be because you are ashamed of her."

"I am *not* ashamed of her!" Flora said.

"She has a name, does she?" Mrs. Withe said. "This very special person in your life whom your parents will never meet?"

"Her name is Rye." Flora sounded like she spoke through gritted teeth. "Rye Woods."

Rye bit her lip.

"Oh," Mrs. Withe said. "One of the Rosevale Woods? That's not nearly as bad as I feared. One of your father's cousins married—"

"No," Flora said. "You don't know her family. She comes from—from up north."

"Not Upriver? Though that's becoming a little more respectable now."

"Not Upriver," Flora said. "Farther north. Much farther."

Rye scowled and rested a hand on the door as if Flora might feel her warning touch.

"Oh," Mrs. Withe said. "Then I suppose she's from one of those big farming families in the hills?"

"Does it matter who her family is?" Flora asked. "Or where she comes from? Why don't you ask me if I'm happy?"

"Don't be absurd, darling. Have lunch with me tomorrow. We can make the arrangements for meeting your budmate then."

"All right. Fine. Tomorrow. We'll talk."

Rye didn't hear them leave the room, but she did hear voices muffled as though they came from beyond the bedroom. A door slammed.

Rye chewed her lip. She had not given any serious thought to the possibility of meeting Flora's parents. Mrs. Withe was not going to be pleased to learn that her daughter was seeing a poor builder's labourer. And from what Rye had heard, Mrs. Withe was not the sort to be tactful about it.

Flora yanked the door open. "I need a drink."

Rye followed Flora into the lounge. Flora flopped full-length on a couch with her hands over her face. Rye poured a shot of bark spirits with a dill twist. Flora gulped down half.

"Steady," Rye said.

"Well, you've just witnessed the perfect portrait of Hazel Withe. Panic not, lover, I'll put her off. You won't have to have dinner with them. The Holy Elm knows I'd rather stick forks into my eyes than do that to you. To either of us."

Rye smiled and stroked Flora's arm. Flora looked fragile and her mood brittle enough to shatter. "This wasn't exactly what you needed right now, was it?"

"I suppose you'll want to flee. You know what they say about daughters turning into their mothers."

"I don't know what your mother looks like. I didn't see her."

"She looks exactly as she sounds, only with more hairspray."

Rye smiled. Flora knocked back the remainder of her drink.

"Branch, Trunk, and Root," Flora said. "I bet your mother is nothing like that."

Rye frowned down at her fingers stroking Flora's hand. "No. No, she was different. But not in a nice way."

"I can't believe that she just walked in. Oh." Flora pulled a key card from her robe pocket. "This is for you. I took it off Mother. I've been meaning to get you one made."

Rye lifted her frown to Flora's face. "Your house key? Are you sure?"

"Of course." Flora put the card in Rye's hand and kissed her. "I'd have keyed your mobile into the security codes weeks ago if you had one."

Rye frowned at the key card. She had not expected that.

Flora slipped her arms around Rye and sagged against her. "Oh, Elm. If only I'd worn a hat."

Rye held Flora and stroked her back. "This bud thing is pretty important, isn't it?"

"This is the first time I've had them. I had no idea how bad it was going to be."

"But I didn't think I was your first."

"You're not my first girlfriend. But you are my first buds. They're part of changes my body is undergoing. Not having had them before, I had a brain blank on keeping them hidden. Other dryads notice them. Avidly. And they leap to a whole forest-full of conclusions."

"Like what?"

"That I'm serious about someone." Flora sniffed. "Which means you need to cover them if you want to keep your relationship secret."

"Oh." Rye stroked Flora's back and frowned at Flora's hair. "But what are they? What does getting them mean?"

Flora's fingers gripped the front of Rye's robe. "I've been dreading you asking that."

"Why?"

"Because I don't want to scare you off."

Rye pulled her arms tight around Flora and kissed the top of her head. "Tell me."

"My hormones are running rampant." Flora's fingers mangled more of Rye's robe. Her shaky voice was tight with tears. "I want to live in the same tree with you. I want to have your babies. But it will pass. I promise. I went to a doctor yesterday. She gave me a course of sap. It hasn't kicked in yet. But me being so miserable is going to be enough to drive you away and that...that will be an end to it all."

Rye felt telltale wetness against her neck. "Not a chance. Oh, babe. I'm sorry."

Flora sobbed. "I love you."

"I love you, too," Rye said.

Flora's head snapped up. Her brown eyes, glistening with tears, were wide with surprise. "You do?"

"Yeah. I do."

Flora's tears spilled out and she clung to Rye. She wept, noisily and jerkily, as if sadness were tearing her body apart. It was like Holly used to cry when she was a little girl. Rye held Flora, rocked her, and kissed her hair.

I love you, too. Rye hadn't consciously formed the thought before. But she did love Flora. She was more to Rye than just great sex. Rye was rearranging her life to accommodate her relationship with Flora. She really would have gone to that charity event with Flora.

When Flora calmed, Rye fetched tissues. She brushed the hair out of Flora's face and kissed her temple.

"Look, it's nearly lunch time," Rye said. "Why don't I fix you something to eat? You've probably been living on junk all week, haven't you?"

While Flora ate, Rye dressed. When she returned to the kitchen, Flora looked calm but pale and heart-breakingly lost. Flora put on a brave smile.

"Will you call me tonight?" Flora asked.

"I wish I could stay with you. I hate leaving you like this."

"I'll be fine. It'll pass as soon as the sap starts to work. It helps that you were here. And what you said. Now, go home. Holly will be missing you."

Rye returned Flora's kiss and did not want to let go. "Come with me."

"What?"

"Come home with me. You can have dinner with us. It won't be anything fancy. Just our normal dinner."

"I'd love to. But what about Holly? Are you ready to tell her about us?"

"Didn't you say that you'd been talking to people about apprenticeships and scholarships? You could discuss that with her. That'd be a good reason for you to come over."

"I shouldn't," Flora said. "I know you're doing this to be nice to me. But I shall anyway. Oh, Elm, I don't want to be without you today."

CHAPTER ELEVEN

"You haven't finished that already?" Mr. Nuttal said.

Rye leaned the brush against the wall and wiped sweat from her forehead with the back of a grimy hand. "I'm hoping to get away early tonight, if you don't mind. There's a transit carpet I'd like to catch in fifteen minutes."

"Of course I don't mind. That looks spanking. You got a date?"

"Um."

"I always knew when Hop was keen to be off to see his girls," he said. "The boy took after me. Quite the ladies' man in my youth. Before I met Mrs. Nuttal, of course."

Rye smiled.

"You can wash up in the bathroom through there, you know. Get yourself a little more presentable."

"Um. Thanks."

Rye went to wash her arms and face. She could always shower at Flora's, but it would be nice not to show up looking like something scraped from the bottom of a rubbish dump.

Mr. Nuttal followed her to the rear door and let her out.

"Good night," Rye said. "Give my regards to Mrs. Nuttal."

"I shall. And good luck with your lady friend."

Rye froze. The door clanged shut, leaving her frowning in the early twilight. Lady friend? How had he guessed she was gay? She wasn't that obvious, was she? If he guessed, would Holly?

At the security gate at the base of Flora's tree, Rye dug out her key card. Even though Flora knew she was coming, Rye felt uncomfortable unlocking the gate, riding the elevating carpet up, and stepping into Flora's apartment.

"Flora? It's just me."

Rye set her bag of groceries on the kitchen table. She saw a couple of packages wrapped in shiny paper sitting on the table. Flora hadn't said anything about going to a party. Flora's own birthday was a few weeks away.

"Flora? Babe?"

Rye hung her jacket on the back of a chair and kicked off her work boots. She wanted to experiment with one of the dishes she intended preparing for Ms. Elmwood's dinner. Holly going to her friend's house to do a homework project and having dinner there was the perfect opportunity for Rye to use Flora's kitchen.

Rye began scrubbing mint roots.

Flora breezed in, dropped the sheaf of papers she was carrying on the table, and wrapped her arms around Rye for a kiss. "Hmm. Mint?"

"Mint roots. With a willow bark and fennel sauce."

"Yummy." Flora grabbed one of the washed roots before Rye could stop her. She nibbled. "I could eat these things all day."

"Not these, you won't." Rye picked Flora up and carried her around the counter to deposit her on a chair at the table. "Be good."

Flora held Rye to a long, smoochy kiss before releasing her. "Elm, do you know how wonderful it is just to walk in here and see you cooking? Almost like a normal couple. I couldn't stop thinking about you all day. I found it impossible to concentrate, so I dedicated my afternoon to doing things for you. You wouldn't believe the bounce I got out of scouring every place I know for these."

Flora slid the stack of coloured papers closer to Rye. The top sheet looked official with a fancy design in the top corner.

"They're information and application forms," Flora said. "I think they cover every art scholarship and prize offered at the high school and apprentice level in the country. I haven't looked through them all, but I know there are several that Holly stands a very good chance of getting."

"Wow. Thanks. She'll be thrilled to get these."

Flora beamed. Rye leafed through a couple of the forms, and was more than happy to sit and supply the kiss of thanks that Flora suggested. Flora trailed her fingers over Rye's face as if committing her expression to the memory of touch.

"I'm so pleased with myself for pleasing you," Flora said.

Rye smiled, kissed her again, and rose to return to her mint roots. Flora grabbed her sleeve.

"I haven't finished yet. I told you I've been a busy girl." Flora pushed the two shiny packages close to Rye. "These are for you."

Rye frowned. "Me? What are they?"

"The usual method of discovery is to tear the wrapping off."

Rye's frown deepened. Flora smiled at her in such a way that, despite deep misgivings, Rye reached for the flatter package.

"I had to guess the size," Flora said.

Rye tugged the ribbon loose and peeled the wrapping paper apart. She exposed pristine white cloth.

"Try it on," Flora said.

Rye scowled as she lifted the cloth. She held a chef's kitchen top.

"For you to wear when you go to Letty Elmwood's," Flora said. "I'm sure she'll find that much more impressive than the dish cloth tucked into your pants. Sexy though that is. And I did have rather wicked thoughts about you making love to me while wearing it."

"Um." Rye set the jacket back on the table.

"What's wrong? Too small? I tried to get a big one so that it's loose across your back and doesn't show your wings."

"I can't take this."

"Can't? Why not? It's not just the look of the thing, though you shouldn't underestimate that where people like Letty are concerned. I'm sure it's very practical."

Rye jammed her fists into her pockets. "Um. Thanks. I appreciate the thought. But I can't take it. I...I can't afford it."

"What? No. It's a gift." Flora rose and put her arms around Rye's neck. "Because I'm proud of you. And because I want to see you make a huge success of this dinner." Flora pointed to the second present. "Now, this one really is practical. I know you need these. You've said so."

Rye eyed the package with apprehension rising toward dread.

"Don't worry," Flora said, "I didn't pick them myself. I asked someone who knows what they're talking about. If they're wrong, we can exchange them. Well? Aren't you going to look?"

"Um."

Rye didn't want to touch it, but Flora's excitement urged her. She reluctantly reached for the package and ripped the paper to reveal a set of knives in a wooden block. The block had a fancy E burned into the wood. Rye sucked in breath. Her hand moved as if drawn by irresistible magic. Her fingers curved around a handle. The boning knife felt like it had been made for her hand. The brand name Eveningmoor was etched along the top of the blade.

"Fey," Rye whispered. "Almighty King and Queen of the Fey."

The block held a dozen more knives of different sizes, a pair of poultry shears, and a sharpening steel. Rye slid the boning knife back and pulled out the others in turn.

"Carver. Utility. Paring knife. Wow."

"Are they okay?" Flora said.

"Shit. Eveningmoor. Look at it. Feel it. This is incredible. These will slice and cut anything. And take an edge sharper than sin."

"From the look on your face, I think I did okay."

"These are amazing." Rye slid the knife she held back into the block. "Not that the ones you have are bad. But these are Eveningmoor."

"You wouldn't expect me to know the difference? They're all just cutty things to me. But these aren't mine. They're for you, lover. You don't have any good ones at home. Well, now you do."

Rye stared at her. Flora beamed and slid her arms around Rye's waist to give her a hug.

"You have no idea how pleased I'm feeling with myself right now," Flora said.

"Um." Rye glanced at the knife block. She could not deny an envious pull. "Look. I really can't—"

Flora clamped a hand over Rye's mouth. "Don't say it. Please. Rye, don't spoil it."

Rye kissed Flora's fingers and gently but firmly pulled them from her lips. "I don't know how much these cost, but I do know that they were extremely expensive."

"It's a gift. The cost is my problem. If I don't mind, why should you?"

Rye chewed her lip and scowled at the knife set.

"I want to make you happy," Flora said. "I want to please you. I want to do things to make your life easier and more fun. Can't I do that for the woman I love?"

"You don't have to buy me things to make me love you."

Flora spread her hands. "Rye! You can't really believe that's what I'm trying to do?"

Rye shook her head. Flora slipped her arms around her.

"You are the most difficult person I've ever given anything to," Flora said. "I love you. I was so happy to be able to please you. I'm trying not to feel hurt that you've suggested I'm buying your affections. That doesn't reflect to either of our credit, does it?"

Rye sighed and couldn't look her in the eye. "I'm sorry."

"Do you not want them? Would they not make your life easier? Would they not please you to have, almost as much as it would please me to give them to you?"

"Um." Rye lifted her arms around Flora's waist. "The knives are amazing. As Holly would say, they melted my mind."

"Yeah? You'd like to use them? Try them out?"

Rye squirmed. "Yeah."

Flora smiled. "Why don't you do it?"

"Look, I always pay my way. If Holly or I want something, I provide it. It's always been that way. It's the way I am."

Flora laid a hand on Rye's chest. "Lover, I bought these to please you. As gifts. It's another way I'm telling you that I love you. Is that so bad?"

"I don't get into debt to anyone. I won't owe anything to anyone. I can't take those because I can't give you things back."

"But you do. You come here and feed me. You're doing it this evening."

"That's different. It's not enough."

Flora shook her head. "Are you in the habit of cooking dinner for random women? Or do you only do this for me because I'm a little bit special? That you want to be with me and make me happy?"

"Maybe."

Flora kissed her. "I love you. Now, make me happy by letting me give you something that will please you. And make my tongue and tummy happy by giving me the most delicious mint roots."

Rye did not want to take the top and knives. Cooking dinner was not even close to a balanced exchange, no matter what Flora said. But Flora was so happy, and this was a big deal for her. Rye didn't want to upset her. Being loved and in love had some really tough bits in amongst all the great stuff.

❖

Flora settled with her head pillowed more comfortably against Rye's naked shoulder. "That dinner was yummy. I'd never thought of food as foreplay before you. What time do you have to be back?"

"Holly said that her friend's mum would drop her home at ten-thirty," Rye said.

Flora smiled and clamped a possessive hand on Rye's ribs. "Another two whole hours with you. I could get used to you being here."

"You seem much better. That course of sap is really working, isn't it?"

"Oh, yes. Hormones dampened to manageable levels. I've been able to concentrate on work again. I've almost completed my weaving about us. This is going to sound immodest, but I'm astonished at the way it's coming out."

"Can I see?"

Flora led Rye into her workroom. Rye frowned at the abstract pattern of colours and shapes.

"You're going to think this is weird," Flora said, "but sometimes when I look at this, I'm surprised that I created it. I think it's part of that white fire creativity. It comes out without my conscious input. So, when I take a step back to look at it, it's as if I'm seeing it for the first time. What do you think?"

"What's that green bit?"

Flora looked like she was going to say something pithy but changed her mind. "I told you that this is about my feelings for you? Well, this is your wing."

"Oh. Right. And that blobby purple thing?"

"Your bum."

Rye grinned. "I asked for that, didn't I?"

"Walked right into it."

Rye put her arms around Flora. "I like it. Really. I can't pretend that I understand it. And I couldn't tell you why I like it. I just do. I'm only a builder's labourer. Not some high-flying arty farty type. But I love you. And admire what you do."

"And it's a good job I love you, or I'd have to jab you with a loom needle every time you said 'arty farty'."

"Yeah?"

"Yes!"

Flora lunged for her loom, but Rye grabbed her before she grasped the wooden needle. Flora struggled. Rye hoisted her up on her shoulder and carried her to the lounge. She dropped Flora onto one of the sofas and lay down on top of her. Flora's continuing wriggles had nothing to do with trying to free herself.

After sex, Rye fetched wine. She eased herself down beside Flora on the sofa. They shared a glass. Rye gently stroked Flora's hair. She wished that Flora had not bought her those expensive gifts. No matter what Flora said, Rye knew that she owed her. She had been unable to repay a debt once before, and she wasn't going to let herself fall into that position ever again. No one was ever going to own her. She didn't earn much and those knives were wickedly expensive, but one day she would pay Flora back.

"What are you thinking?" Flora asked.

"How beautiful you are."

Flora smiled and eased around so that she half-lay on Rye's side. Her fingertips lazily traced abstract doodles across Rye's skin. "Who was your first girlfriend?"

"What do you mean? To have sex with?"

"No. The first girl you fell in love with. You see, I'm feeling secure enough in our relationship to pry into your past."

"You're my first love."

Flora lifted her head to stare incredulously at Rye. "You're joking?"

"No. What about you? Your mother said you had lots of girlfriends."

"My mother has a tendency to exaggerate for dramatic effect. You might have heard that, too." Flora kissed between Rye's breasts. "How about crushes, then? You must've had crushes before me."

"Um." Rye stroked Flora's arm. She felt so comfortable, so safe. "Temperance. She was how I realised that I liked girls. She was a cousin. We all lived together, you see. My mother, my aunts, cousins, and their kids. Well, not all the kids. The boys got sent to the men's compound when they were seven. But the girls grew up together with the women. All of us on the commune farm."

Flora frowned but didn't interrupt.

"The women got pregnant and had babies, of course," Rye said. "But I didn't know anything about sex. I don't think any of us girls did.

It was never talked about. The priestesses said it was what the gods made us women for. And women who had lots of children became the matriarchs. But I had no clue how they got pregnant."

Rye put both her hands on Flora's solid warmth as if to anchor herself against the past.

"Temperance was just a little older than me. Which meant we ended up doing lots of chores and stuff together. All of a sudden, it seemed, she became very pretty. I wanted to be with her. I started doing stupid stuff like spending all my free time helping her weed and dig her mother's garden, which didn't please my mother. But I so wanted to be with Temperance that it was worth having my mother mad at me."

"How old were you?"

"Um. It was three years before I got my wings. I suppose that would've made me about fourteen or fifteen. Temperance got her wings young. She persuaded one of the blokes to get permission to leave the commune, and they went together to live in a city. I doubt she gave me another thought."

"I'm sorry."

Rye shrugged. "It was probably better that she left, or the priestess might've put her on penance, too."

Flora frowned. "Penance?"

Rye reached for the glass of wine and drained it.

"I didn't know what was happening with me and Temperance," Rye said. "My mother guessed. One day I was taken off normal chores and put with the kitchen women. None of them were young and pretty. I think the idea was that I'd be safe away from the temptation of girls my own age. Not that I knew that the feelings I had for Temperance might apply to some other girl. Or that they were evil."

"Evil?" Flora said.

"Oh, yeah. The gods made us to have babies. Sex is for having babies, not for fun. So, two girls are acting against the will of the gods by tinkering with each other. Two blokes, too, I suppose, but I never had much to do with the men's compound."

"Oh, Holy Elm. I knew it was bad, but that's...that's incredible."

Rye shrugged. "You ought to have seen the priestess when I told her that I'd seen two women touching each other and that's what I'd wanted to do with Temperance."

"Did they hurt you?"

"I was ignorant, not guilty. I had to be cured before I did more than just think about it. I was given extra chores and prayers to recite as I worked. Most days I'd be so tired that I'd fall asleep. Which would earn me a few strokes of the stick. And I'd have to fast for days, to help purge the evil out of me. Not that it worked. Obviously."

Flora clasped Rye's hand. "Oh, Holy Elm. That's barbaric."

Rye shrugged. "Did you really like the way I did those mint roots? You didn't think they were too salty?"

Flora opened her mouth and closed it again. She took a deep breath before accepting the change of topic. Rye loved her all the more for it and felt justified in risking telling Flora what she had not divulged to anyone else.

❖

Rye tapped on Holly's bedroom door. "Holls?"

Holly did not answer. Rye frowned. Holly had said that her friend's mother would drop her home by ten thirty.

Rye pushed open the door. Holly's room was a chaos of clothes and magazines. Rye picked her way to the desk. She set down the stack of booklets and forms that Flora had given her. Holly should be pleased to get them. If she could get a scholarship, that would not only save Rye a lot of money, but it would make for a fantastic start to her career.

Rye surveyed the mess and sighed. If this was how Holly wished to live, that was her business. Rye sniffed and frowned. That oddly sweet smell could not be what she thought it was. It must be something lingering on one of the bits of clothing from the Goodcause Charity Shop. Some of that second-hand stuff smelled very funny.

Rye stepped over the discarded clothes and shoes. She paused at the door. The smell was stronger here. Not the second-hand shop.

Rye stood chewing her lip. If she rummaged through Holly's things, that would be a violation of Holly's privacy. But if Holly was smoking dreamweed, then she had shattered their trust anyway. And violated a lot more than her right to privacy.

"Crap."

If Holly got caught with drugs, that would involve the police. That wouldn't be just a minor misdemeanour and slap on the hands. The police would find out that Holly Woods was not a legal citizen. And neither was her sister. The next step would be deportation.

Rye knelt and found a top which reeked of dreamweed smoke. She slumped on the floor. "Shit. What did I do wrong?"

How long had it been going on? Right under her nose. And how could the kid afford it? Dreamweed was easily available around here—you could probably buy the stuff in every second apartment in this tree—but it would cost.

"No, she wouldn't."

Rye scrambled to her feet and strode into the lounge. She tugged out the loose knot and pulled out her savings. Rye counted it. Every piece was there. Holly must be spending her wages from Cloudnut's on it.

"What am I going to do?"

❖

When Holly came home at ten fifty, she didn't exude the telltale smell of dreamweed nor act out of the ordinary. Rye decided not to act hastily, much as she'd like to grab her and shake some sense into her.

"Fey!" Holly ran out of her bedroom. She brandished the stack of papers Rye had left on her desk. "Did you put these in my room?"

"Flora got them for you."

Holly dropped onto a chair at the kitchen table and started leafing through the forms and brochures. "This is utterly, completely, totally, and wholly astronomical. Mind melting. Brain bruising."

Rye smiled. Okay, Holly had definitely not lost interest in her career plans. That was a good sign.

"Oh, look." Holly's eyes widened as she lifted out a set of pink forms. "The Borage-Twilight Scholarship. Not in this lifetime!"

"Something wrong?" Rye asked.

"Me? Holly Woods, applying for a Borage-Twilight? They only give one a year in the whole country. And then they don't award one every year unless they find someone who's so astronomically good that they leave a trail of brilliance behind them wherever they walk."

"There's no harm in applying is there?"

"Do you want to see me rejected?"

"You won't get it if you don't apply," Rye said. "Does it cost anything to send the forms in?"

Holly levelled a disgusted look at Rye over some blue papers.

"You have no idea, do you?"

"No," Rye conceded.

Rye watched Holly avidly reading.

"Holls? If there were something wrong," Rye said, "something at school or anything. You could talk to me about it, you know."

Holly grunted. "Photographs or copies, not original artwork. How am I going to arrange that?"

"Holls? Did you hear me?"

"Yeah. Talk to you, blah, blah. Urgh. Write an essay on what I would do with the scholarship if I won it? That reeks! It's not as though I want them to give me money because I think I'm wonderful at writing."

Rye decided not to press the matter of her discovery. The last thing she wanted to do was handle this wrongly.

At work the next day, Rye found herself eyeing the blokes and wondering how many of their kids were playing around with booze and drugs. She'd heard Blackie tell how his missus sent their children to the pub to fetch him back. He boasted how his son was strong enough to help him home when he got legless. So, he wasn't her best source of parental advice.

Through the haze of bubbling fat at Pansy's Fried Sandwiches, Rye watched the customers waiting at the counter. Some looked as young as Holly. The girls wore a lot of makeup and tried to look much older than they were. Some were clearly drunk. Some looked brain fried from smoking, snorting, slurping, or scamming. Rye wondered if any of their parents knew, or cared.

❖

"Here we go." Mr. Nuttal set a tray of cake and tea on the workbench.

Rye accepted a mug of tea and a slice of cake with alarming blue-green icing. "Thanks."

"Now, I'm not the sort of fellow to pry," Mr. Nuttal said, "but you don't seem your usual self today. Trouble in love?"

"What? Oh. No. Nothing like that." Rye broke off a bit of cake and frowned at the crumbs. "Your son ever get a bit wild when he was a teenager?"

"Hop? He crashed his new broom once. And got arrested for being drunk at a music concert." Mr. Nuttal smiled as he shrugged. "Usual stuff. Boys being boys, you know. You having problems with that sister of yours?"

Rye forced herself to eat another bite of dry, sweet cake. "It's not too bad. Experimenting with drugs. Just soft stuff. Dreamweed."

Mr. Nuttal nodded. "I caught our Hop with some of that once. Kept it with his girlie magazines at the bottom of his wardrobe. Luckily, Mrs. Nuttal didn't know what it was. She was more distressed about the magazines."

Rye frowned at him. "What did you do about it?"

"Had a word with him. When Mrs. Nuttal wasn't around, of course. Man to man."

"What did you say?"

Mr. Nuttal stroked his scalp ridges. "I think I asked him what he thought he was doing. If he'd considered the long-term effects. What it might do to the rest of his life. The risks involved, with the police and whatnot. It seemed to work with him. Not that I'm sure it's the best way. These days they have all sorts of school advisors you can ask to help you out, don't they? And community counselling where you can get advice."

Rye chewed her lip as she strode away from the back door of the pot boutique and into the night. Perhaps she should check the library. They carried community information.

She paused to look both ways before crossing the street. Back near the root strip of shops, a distinctively shaped sporty carpet was parked under a street light. Rye strode back and bent to peer in the window. Flora looked pensive and started when Rye tapped on the glass, but she smiled when Rye climbed in and claimed a kiss.

"I nearly walked home," Rye said. "I came out the back. I didn't expect you to be here. I'd have washed more thoroughly if I'd known."

"A little grime won't kill me. I was on my way home. I needed to see you."

Rye smiled. She shoved her work bag in the back and snapped the safety harness into place. "You look fabulous. Been out?"

"Uh huh." Flora steered up into the high, fast lane.

"With someone nice?"

Flora frowned. "My parents. Remember that I had to have lunch with Mother?"

"About us? The bud thing?"

"It mutated into dinner with both of them. Mother getting all diva on me about this is wholly unsurprising. But it's disconcerting that Daddy isn't reining her in. If only I'd worn a wretched hat."

Rye felt acutely conscious of her dirty pants and the stink of sweat she must be giving off. The contrast with Flora all dressed-up and perfectly groomed could not have been greater.

"They're not going to like me, are they?" Rye said.

Flora patted Rye's thigh. "Panic not, lover. I would not subject us to a cosy foursome with them for anything in Infinity. Especially not with the way Mother is jabbing on about it all. Sometimes I can scarcely believe that I survived my childhood without needing intensive therapy."

Rye flicked her frown from Flora's profile to the way street lamps raced past the carpet. "I think you're speeding, babe."

"A traffic ticket would be the perfect end to my night." Flora throttled back the magic. "I'm nearly thirty-four years old! I have my own life. I've lived it quite happily and successfully without their interference for many years. You know, when I was a girl, I used to pray for a sister or brother. Now I thank the Holy Elm and All the Trees of the Sacred Grove that no other child had to suffer my parents."

Rye frowned down at her calloused hands in her patched lap. Flora's rich, snooty parents were going to hate her.

"It was all highly unpleasant," Flora said, "but I did get my own way in the end."

"Oh? Good for you. About what?"

"My birthday party. My parents throw a big one every year. It's not just for me. It's more like the annual Withe family bash. I won't know half the people there. They'll be Daddy's business friends and people from Mother's charity committees. It's normally held at their house. But I didn't think you'd be the least speck comfortable with that."

Rye scowled at Flora's profile. Her, at some big party thrown by Flora's parents? Shit. Flora couldn't be serious?

"I suggested that thirty-four was too old for me to still be having my parents throw me a party," Flora said. "That proved to be as incendiary as I expected. Anyway, to cut a long and ugly story short, they've agreed to hold it at the Top of the Poplar restaurant. And I insisted on a buffet. That way Mother can't make seating plans that will put you right in her firing line."

Rye scowled out at the night whizzing past. "Oh."

Flora loosed a grunt of frustration from the back of her throat. She squeezed Rye's thigh. "I needed to see you. Needed it. Elm. How was your day? How is Holly?"

"Um." Rye ran a hand through her hair and tried to crawl out of her mental abyss of doom. "She...she was bounced about those scholarship forms. Except she hates having to write essays for them."

Flora smiled. "I'm sure she'll do fine. Are you ready for Letty's dinner?"

"Um. Yeah. No. Maybe. As much as I can be. One of the blokes at work has a brother in the carpet hire business. I can get one cheap for the day. To take the stuff over to Ms. Elmwood's place."

"Isn't it about time you had your own transportation?"

"I'm working on it. Hey! That's my turning, babe."

Flora swerved the carpet down into the parking lane and stopped well short of Rye's tree. She dimmed the interior lights, snapped her safety harness loose, and turned to cling to Rye.

"I wish I could take you home with me," Flora said. "You, bed, and a big jar of wine."

"Tomorrow, babe. Oh, I might be a bit late. I have to visit the library first."

Flora looked unhappy.

Rye stroked Flora's cheek. "I'll be there if I have to run all the way. I promise."

"I know. I'm just being selfish. I'll take as much, or as little, of you as I can get. I just wish it was more."

CHAPTER TWELVE

Rye stuffed her shopping list in her pocket and wandered into the hall. Holly knelt on the floor in her room sorting through clothes.

"I'm off shopping," Rye said.

"Okay. I'm going over to Daisy's after I've done the laundry. Dunno when I'll be back."

"Um. Did you want to do something?"

Holly jumped to her feet to stand at the mirror with a T-shirt held against herself. "Like what? Clean the toilet? No thanks!"

"No. I meant—" Rye shrugged. "I dunno. Me and you. Doing something together. I could put the shopping off until tomorrow. It's a nice day. We could go for a walk to the river or something."

Holly looked disgusted. "The river?"

"We used to go there all the time on Fifth Days. Or to the park."

"When I was eight years old!" Holly threw the T-shirt aside and grabbed another from the end of the bed. "Wake up, Rye."

"Okay. Maybe that's not very exciting. But there must be something we could do together."

"What brought this on?" Holly turned her back to peel off her top. "Not some stupid idea you read about in a limping book? Or something that stupid school put into your head?"

Before Holly pulled on her new top, Rye noticed that her back still looked smooth. No sign yet of the lumps beneath the skin of developing wings.

"It's just that we don't seem to spend any time together," Rye said. "Not like we used to."

Holly turned to stare at Rye with an unpromising expression. "How can we spend time together if you're never here?"

"I have to work. You know that. But I'll soon be giving up Pansy's."

"I'm not a little kid any more. I have friends. You don't seriously expect me to hang around with you? You're an embarrassment. I want the earth to eat me whole whenever any of my friends see you dressed like that. Daisy complains about her mother's frocks, but I'd take a few floral prints over that any day of the year."

Holly pushed past Rye on her way to the living room. Rye sighed and followed. Holly grabbed the rubbish sack with Rye's dirty laundry in it.

"Holls, wait."

"No way," Holly said. "This is disgusting enough. I refuse to sort through your clothes to find dirty ones. If they're not in here, I'm not putting them into the machine."

"I didn't mean that. Maybe we could go to a movie?"

"Can you afford it?"

Rye sighed. "You really don't want to do this, do you?"

"I'm not a little kid, Rye. I'm sixteen. I have a life of my own."

Holly stuffed some of her own clothes into the bag and strode out.

Rye leaned against the wall. "Crap."

❖

Rye stepped on board the transit carpet and paid her four piece fare. She walked back to find a seat. Someone stank of stale booze. She saw a seedy looking man with sprite-like antennae curled up asleep on one of the seats. She could understand the temptation to swill yourself into oblivion. What she didn't know was how people afforded it. He didn't look like he held down a regular job. She worked three jobs and didn't have room in her budget for more than four small jars of beer a week.

Hollowberry whizzed by the carpet windows in short, dingy bursts between node stops. Tired, harassed people got in and out. Rye kept glancing at the drunk's shoes sticking out into the aisle. Holly must not end up like that.

Rye turned away to frown out at the passing forest as she wrestled the unpalatable fact that it was her fault that she'd let things slide with Holly to the point where she was using drugs. She had let Holly down. But she had to find some way of salvaging the situation before Holly's experimenting took her too close to a brush with the police. Maybe if Holly knew more about Fairyland she might be more careful about risking them getting sent back. Perhaps Holly was old enough to understand some of that stuff. Rye scowled. She had spent most of her adult life protecting Holly and trying to make sure that she need never know about Fairyland. And it wasn't only Holly she was shielding by never thinking about her life before she ran away.

Rye left the transit carpet at the Gentian Street node. She strolled past the trendy shops and fashionably dressed shoppers. Even though she'd come this way plenty of times now, she was still aware of sharp glances. It felt uncomfortably like those first anxious, watchful years after she'd escaped from Fairyland, when she'd expected everyone to shout an alarm about the illegal alien.

Rye turned into Whiterow Gardens. She swiped her key card to open the security gates. She had to wait for the elevating carpet to come to the ground. The door opened to reveal a blue-skinned naiad. She levelled the most transparent stare of disgust at Rye.

"These are private premises," the naiad said.

"Yeah, I know." Rye's wings tightened against her back. She lifted the key card for the naiad to see. "If you'll excuse me, I need to use that."

"And who might you be visiting? How am I to know that card has not been stolen?"

"You could check with Ms. Withe," Rye said. "Penthouse."

"This really isn't good enough. Trades people must use the service lift. It's around that way."

Rye glanced in the direction the naiad pointed. The naiad continued to block her way. Rye could push past, but that would probably get very ugly. The woman seemed the sort who would scream for the police. Rye sighed and walked around the tree. When she looked back, the naiad stood on the inside of the security gate watching her.

Rye's key card worked with the service elevating carpet. She rode it up to the penthouse. The key would not open the inside door. She had to push the buzzer and wait.

A picture panel burst into life to show Flora's face. "Hello? Rye! What are you doing in there?"

The door slid open.

"Is the elevating carpet out of order?" Flora said.

"Not exactly." Rye stepped out into a small service room between the carpet garage and the laundry room.

Flora put her arms around Rye and kissed her. "What's wrong?"

Rye shrugged. "Everything. Crappy morning. Sorry."

"Want a drink?"

Rye remembered the drunk on the transit carpet. "No, thanks."

Flora ran her hands up Rye's back. "You're as tense as I was last night. Is it Holly? Have you two argued?"

Rye sighed and bent her neck to rest her forehead on Flora's shoulder. Flora stroked her hair.

"Talk to me, lover," Flora said.

"Oh, fey."

Rye slipped her arms around Flora and hugged her close. Flora felt really good. She was the only good thing in Rye's crumbling, crummy life.

"Do you realise that there are people out there who don't even know us who don't think I should be allowed to be with you?" Rye said.

"What has happened? Are you talking about my parents?"

"No. But it applies, doesn't it?" Rye sighed. "I thought I got away from being told what I should do, who I should be, and how I should live my life."

"What's wrong?"

"I'm sorry." Rye released Flora and straightened. "I don't know why I'm letting everything bruise me today. It's been a long week. I shouldn't be dumping it on you."

"I think I'm just about strong enough to bear the weight of you leaning emotionally on me this once."

"You shouldn't have to. We have little enough time together as it is."

"Life doesn't always cooperate with the plans of us mere mortals." Flora clasped Rye's hands. "Which is why we have to give it a helping hand whenever we can. I did something this morning which I should have done weeks ago. For you. No, for us. To make our lives easier. So that we can spend more time together. And so that you don't have to wear yourself out with all the walking and working that you're doing."

Rye frowned. Flora smoothed Rye's forehead with gentle fingers.

"Don't look like that," Flora said. "I know you can be difficult about letting people help you, but this is for us. Both of us. You'll be able to quit that terrible job at the fast food joint tomorrow. And I'd really like it if you'd reconsider and go back to night school. I'm hoping this will help you do that. And it will help me because I'm going to get to see more of you. I won't just be squeezed in between three jobs and all your travelling time."

Rye accepted Flora's kiss, but retained her frown. "What are you talking about?"

"I need more of you. This isn't just my hormones. This is me wanting you around to share my happy times, and me needing you to curl up next to when I'm sad. At first, snatching time with you was exciting. It added an illicit air to the affair. But now—" Flora sighed and ran her hands over Rye's shoulders and arms. "Now, lover, I want more than anything in the world for us to be normal. I have to see more of you."

"Look, I know that—"

"I know it's not your doing. And I understand how things stand with you. Your obligations to Holly. Which is why I've done the only thing I could think of to help the situation. For both of us."

"Babe, now is not a good time for this. I've got some stuff going on that I'm having trouble coping with."

"Rye! You've not been listening to me." Flora grabbed Rye's collar and gave it a gentle tug. "I'm trying to make our lives easier, not harder. Let me show you. Close your eyes."

Rye shut her eyes and let Flora lead her out of the room. The last thing she needed right now was more pressure to reallocate her time, or to feel even more guilty that it was her fault she and Flora didn't spend much time together. Much as she loved Flora, and wanted to be with her, Holly needed Rye more. When Rye had picked Holly up and run away from Fairyland, she had assumed complete responsibility for the kid. She worked to feed them and house them and do her best by Holly. Sometimes, like now, that made her feel like she could barely cope. But it wasn't something she could just shove aside. Rye didn't really expect

Flora to understand. Flora was an only child and never had kids of her own. She certainly never had any money problems. Why did Flora have to do this to her now? Rye needed Flora to be her island of support and escape, not another source of discord. Especially today.

They didn't go far. They walked off carpet onto hard flooring. The air smelled sharp as if an engine had been running on magic in an enclosed space. The garage?

"Open your hand," Flora said.

Eyes still closed, Rye let Flora take her hand and wrap it around something smooth, hard, and cold. A soft, tingling warmth ran from her fingertips to her wrist. Rye frowned. It felt like she'd been scanned.

"I hope I did that right," Flora said. "You can look now."

Rye opened her eyes. They were in the garage. She stood with her right hand curled around the activation plate on the handle of a shiny new broom.

"I was tempted to buy a sporty model," Flora said. "You'd look very sexy on one. But then I remembered you. And, on second thought, I probably wouldn't want you looking too desirable to other women. Well?"

Rye flicked her frown from Flora to the broom. "I don't understand."

"It's for you. The end of your transport problems. So you don't have to work three jobs to save to buy one. And how you can spend more time with me rather than getting here. It hit me last night, when I was feeling so miserable and lonely after I dropped you home. I went to the showroom first thing this morning. This model has extra wide bristles for maximum carrying capacity. You'll probably need that when you do your catering jobs."

Rye scowled at the broom. "Shit. It must've cost thousands."

"Don't think about that. Think about what it means to us. I'd pay ten times as much if it meant a few extra hours a week with you. I know that you have problems with—"

Rye slipped her hand free and backed up a couple of paces. "You... you just went out and bought this? And expect it to make everything okay?"

"What? No! Didn't you hear a word I've been saying? I want to solve—"

"That will not solve my problems," Rye said. "Maybe riding that will make me more acceptable to people like that bitch downstairs. Or your parents. Is that what you think?"

Flora frowned and shook her head. "Rye?"

"You think throwing money at me will make everything okay?"

"No! Elm. I—"

"Well, it won't! Look at me. I'm a poor slob from a slum. I wear cheap, crappy second-hand clothes. That's all I can afford. But I owe no one nothing. What I have, I've earned. No one buys me. No one dresses me up as something I'm not."

"Branch." Flora looked pale and stunned. "You don't seriously think—"

"No one tells me what I should be. No one owns me. I've been there. Never again."

"That's not what—"

"I'm never going to be some successful actress dripping money who goes to glitzy parties with you."

Flora shook her head. "What are you talking about?"

"I've done everything I could for that kid." Rye's hands clenched tight. She turned away from the wall before she put a fist into it. "I don't know what I did wrong."

"Holly? Rye, what is going on here? What has that got to do with this broom? I don't—"

"I can't handle this." Rye stomped to the hall.

"Rye!"

Flora ran after Rye. She grabbed Rye's arm and tugged her to a halt in the hall near the kitchen door. "Don't just run out on me. Don't you think I deserve some explanation for—"

"I can't do this any more. I'm not the sort of person who should have the key to your apartment. I'm not—"

"Don't I have some say in that?"

"Your parents won't think—"

"My parents have nothing to do with this!" Flora made an emphatic, angry gesture with a fist.

"Open your eyes! You and I live in different worlds. Your parents are hiring the most exclusive restaurant in the forest for a day! I couldn't get a job there washing dishes. You're a famous artist. You're in books. Complete strangers want your autograph. I'm a nobody from a third-rate building site. You can buy the fucking moon. I can barely afford the transit fare to get here! You live in a world of flash parties and fine wine. I live in a mouldy slum!"

Flora shook her head. "I've never looked at us like that. Never!"

"It's taken me months working three jobs to be able to save up for a cheap, second-hand broom. You just went out on a whim and got a new one."

"Branch! Forget the stupid broom. We—"

"Forget it? I can't forget it! You—"

"Don't shout at me!" Flora shouted.

Rye stood panting with her heart pounding. Flora put a hand to her forehead.

"You're making me angry," Flora said. "You make it sound like I'm trying to buy you."

"I can't be what you want me to be. I can't be the sort of person who doesn't notice their stares. Or ignore that bitch down there. I work hard. I don't have to take that shit. And I'm not going to let your parents laugh at me."

Flora drew in a sharp breath. "Is that what you think I'd do to you?"

"I can't go to that party. Look at me! This is me. This is all I'll ever be! No amount of stuff you buy me will change that!"

"Why would I want to change you? I love you. Do you think so little of me that—"

"I work my guts out! And still it's not good enough. Do you know how that feels? She's doing drugs because her life is so crappy. Because I got it wrong!"

"Holly?" Flora frowned. "What—"

"I can't cope with all this." Rye dug the key card out of her pocket and offered it to Flora. "You don't need me. Maybe I can still help her."

Flora frowned at the key. She made no move to take it. "Rye? You can't mean—"

"I can't do this any more. I can't. I have to go back to what I can do."

Rye dropped the card at Flora's feet and strode to the front door.

"No," Flora said. "Rye! You can't just—"

Rye slammed the door behind her and hurtled down the ten flights of stairs two and three at a time.

"Rye!" Flora's shout carried from high above.

Rye slapped her hand to the security panel and yanked open the gates.

"Rye!"

Rye ran. Darkness tightened around her. Panic snapped into place and drove her body. Blindly.

A carpet slammed into Rye's side and knocked her off her feet. Pain erupted in her ribs. Horns screamed. Rye hit the ground.

"Hey!" A strange sprite knelt beside her. "You okay?"

Rye blinked up at him. Her ribs and her face hurt.

"She ran right in front of me!" a pixie woman shouted. "You saw it! It wasn't my fault."

"Be quiet, lady," a gremlin man said.

Rye looked around. She was lying in the road with traffic stopped around her. People were staring. She had no idea where she was.

"Take it easy," the sprite man said. "I'll call for an ambulance."

"It wasn't my fault!" the pixie woman shouted. "You're my witness. She ran in front of me. I tried to stop."

"All right, lady," the gremlin man said. "Calm down. The police will sort it out. Okay?"

Rye stared at him. Police? She scrambled to her feet, staggered through a ring of spectators, and ran.

When Rye stumbled past the massive roots of the busy Oak Heights Mall, she knew where she was. She felt the stares as she waited for a transit carpet, but she didn't think she could walk all the way home. In her own neighbourhood, nobody blinked at her lurching along with blood on her face and her hand clamped to her side.

Rye dragged herself up the seven flights of stairs. She fumbled her key and limped inside. Holly's room was open and empty. Rye collapsed on the sofa.

❖

"Rye? Rye, wake up. Please don't be dead."

Rye peeled open her eyes to see Holly leaning over her.

"Fey," Holly said. "You had me worried. You look like shit. Who beat you up?"

"I fell over." Rye winced as she sat up.

"Fell from the fourth floor, more like. Do you want me to fetch an apothecary?"

"No." Rye eased her legs over the side of the sofa. Her ribs screamed in protest. "I'll be all right."

Holly scowled. "If you die, I'll be an orphan. Is that what you want?"

"I'm not going to die. And I don't want any apothecary seeing my wings."

"But you look really crappy."

"It'll pass."

Holly looked unhappy as she strode out of the living room.

Rye leaned back and closed her eyes. She couldn't remember the accident. She'd panicked again. At least she had hurt herself, this time, and no one else.

Rye!

She'd been fleeing from breaking up with Flora. She hadn't planned that. It had just boiled up from nowhere. That naiad bitch. The brand new broom. Flora had looked so shocked and disbelieving. But it was better this way. Rye would have more time at home with Holly. These last few months, she'd been too busy with her own pleasure. She'd forgotten Holly.

I have to see more of you.

It was never going anywhere. The sex had been great, but their relationship only existed within the walls of Flora's apartment. None of Flora's friends or family would regard Rye as a suitable partner for her.

I've never looked at us like that.

Well, it was probably time that Flora did see them for what they really were. Rye could never meet Flora on equal terms. She had spent as many years as she was ever going to as a piece of property. She wasn't going there again.

"Here, let me stick this on you." Holly held a roll of sticking plaster and a pair of scissors. "That cut looks obscene."

Holly's ministrations were well meant but not gentle. Rye didn't mind. A little extra pain made no difference.

Holly made tea. She put honey in Rye's.

"Hot and sweet is what they said in First Aid class," Holly said. "And some other stuff I can't remember. I only got a C. Still, a pass should be good enough to keep you alive."

"Thanks."

"I think you should sit there and not do too much. Are you sure you're okay? You look weird."

"I'll be fine."

Holly shrugged and retreated to her bedroom. Unusually, she left her door open and kept her music volume well below the pain threshold.

Rye finished her tea and eased herself down on her back. She felt empty enough to echo.

Rye jolted awake. The phone rang.

"Hello?" Holly said. "This is Holly Woods. Oh, Ms. Elmwood. Yes. I'm Rye's sister. Rye isn't in right now. May I take a message? Sure. Yes. I'll tell her. Thank you."

Holly poked her head around the door. "You're awake. That was Ms. Elmwood wanting to make sure you hadn't forgotten her. I said you weren't here. She'd like you to call her some time this evening."

"Okay. Thanks."

Rye had wanted it to be Flora, but Flora wasn't going to call. Not after what Rye had said.

"Can you come to the table?" Holly said. "Or should I bring you a tray?"

"What?"

"I made dinner. It's just some soup. I don't think it's very good. It turned out greener than I expected, but we should be able to gag it down. There's nothing poisonous in it."

"You made dinner?" Rye asked.

"You needn't sound so shocked. If you did leave me an orphan, I could feed myself. I'm not completely useless, you know."

"I've never thought you were useless, Holls."

The soup tasted pretty good. Rye said so. Holly shrugged it off, but seemed pleased with the compliment. She wasn't a bad kid. Certainly not irretrievable, like some around this neighbourhood. Rye just needed to put in a little more effort. That was the right decision.

"How are you getting on with those scholarship forms?" Rye asked.

"Stupid essays. Still, I figure I can write one and just change it a bit for each form. I'm going to ask my art teacher and my lit teacher to have a look at it before I send it in."

"Good idea."

"I need to get my art teacher to write some stuff. You know, saying how brilliant I am and how much they should shower cash on me."

Rye smiled and mopped up soup with a hunk of bread.

"I have to get my principal to endorse most of them, too." Holly grunted unhappily. "And some of them ask for any other supporting endorsements. I was thinking of asking Flora. What do you think?"

Rye froze with her mouth full of soggy bread.

"Everyone who is anyone knows Flora," Holly said. "I'm sure these scholarship people will believe her if she says I swing from the top branches. That would really help, don't you think?"

Rye swallowed with difficulty. "Um. I dunno."

"I know that if I were some relic at the Funding Council, I'd put more importance on what Flora said than some stupid, limping essay that some kid wrote."

Holly leaped to her feet, whipped the empty bowls into the sink, and raced into her bedroom. Rye sat staring at the chipped table top. Shit. Her timing could not be any worse, could it? How was she going to explain to Holly that Flora might not be very approachable right now?

Holly bounced back in carrying a sheaf of papers, a pad, and pencil. "There's some stuff that you have to fill in for me."

"Me?"

"Yeah. Legal guardian's approval and all that snail slime. Oh, and I need my citizen ident number. What is it?"

The gash in Rye's face hurt when she frowned. "You need that?"

"Yeah." Holly pulled out a form and unfolded it. "There. See? Section B. Amongst all that obscenely personal stuff I have to fill in. It's a wonder they don't ask my shoe size and how often I go to the toilet."

Rye went cold as she read. Mother's name. Father's name. Date of birth. Place of birth. Citizen identification number.

"What's Flora's phone number?" Holly asked.

"Um. Look, I don't think calling her now is a good idea."

"Why not?"

"I can't remember the number. Okay? Now, leave it alone."

"Wow. Who bit your tit? No need to get knotted! Go back to being half dead."

Holly swept back into her bedroom and shut the door.

Rye ran her fingers across her scalp and swore. She retrieved a beer from the cooler and sank onto the sofa. This was not how today was supposed to have ended.

After her beer, she called Ms. Elmwood and confirmed everything for Third Night. Rye stared at the phone. She could call Flora and apologise.

Rye crawled into her bedding. Flora appeared behind her lids when she closed her eyes.

Don't shout at me!

Flora had looked so distraught. And Rye had just banged on.

I'd pay ten times as much if it meant a few extra hours a week with you.

That was it, wasn't it? Flora thought she could buy Rye. That brand new broom. Rye should never have accepted those other presents.

"Crap."

Rye grunted with discomfort as she wriggled to find a position which didn't hurt. She had to concentrate on Holly. The drug thing. And now this citizen ident number. Could she ask her not to apply for a scholarship? Rye had supported Holly through school, so she should be able to manage for the duration of an apprenticeship.

Rye groped beneath the sofa and found a slim book. She opened *Contemporary Artists* to page forty-two. Flora stood against a wall on which one of her weavings hung. She was smiling.

Rye let the book drop to the floor and blinked back tears.

Chapter Thirteen

Don't just leave that there." Rye snatched up Holly's used breakfast bowl and dumped it in the sink with a crash. "It won't break your arm to be tidy. And you needn't leave that on the table, either."

Holly scooped up her jacket. "What is wrong with you?"

"I'm trying to earn some money so that we can keep eating," Rye said. "I need this kitchen clean for cooking in. If you're not at the school gates by three thirty, I'm not waiting for you."

"I'll be there."

"I have to be at Ms. Elmwood's by four. Do you hear me, Holly?"

Holly emerged from her bedroom carrying her schoolbag. "Half the forest heard. You've been in the crappiest mood since Fifth Day. Terminal grumpiness. No, much worse. The shitties."

"Language! If you talk like that at Ms. Elmwood's, I'll—"

"Unknot!" Holly shouted. "And that black dress is hanging on the back of my bedroom door. Okay? When you fell, you must've broken your teeny tiny little good humour bone. Fey, it's not often it's a pleasure to leave for school."

Rye glared at Holly's retreating back.

Holly pulled the front door open. "You need to get laid."

"What!" Rye shouted. "What did you say?"

Holly slammed the door.

Rye stormed out of the kitchen and along the hall. She grabbed the door handle, but stopped herself. Having a shouting match with Holly for all the neighbours to hear was probably not her best move.

Rye sighed and leaned against the door. She had too much to do today to fall apart now. First stop, Blackie's brother's place to hire the carpet. Second, the library for books on dealing with teenagers and drugs. Then she needed to go to the market, the butcher, and the specialty shops.

Rye felt nervous taking five hundred pieces from her stash. That was a large portion of her savings. Nor did she feel entirely comfortable with having called in sick today, though all her workmates knew she'd been stiff and sore from her accident. It went against the grain to miss a day's work, and so a day's wages, even though she was going to earn more doing the dinner than she did in a month at the building site.

She felt strange flying around in a small rented delivery carpet during the day when she should be at work.

In the library, there were so many elderly folk that it looked like the anteroom at a funeral parlour. In the section ominously called Social Dysfunctions, she discovered a whole shelf full of advice books and information on drugs, alcohol, sex, truancy, gambling, and suicide. She idly flipped through one of the sex books for parents. This would've been handy a couple of years ago. It might have saved her and Holly considerable embarrassment.

Rye carried half a dozen books out to the flying carpet and flew off to the market.

"Hey, Rye, what you doing here this morning?"

Rye looked up from examining tussock roots in a box to see Chive, the long-nosed imp, walking around his stall to her. He wiped two of his hands on the grubby apron that covered most of his shiny brown carapace.

"Ain't Fifth Day already, is it?" Chive said.

"I'm doing some special shopping," Rye said. "Are these fresh?"

Chive spread his four hands. "When does Honest Chive ever sell anything that ain't fresh? How many you after today?"

"That tray should do."

Chive's long, looping antennae quivered. "The whole tray?"

"Yeah." Rye checked her list. "And these dandelion heads. Hmm. They don't smell as fresh as they could."

"You're a sticky customer. Okay, they're left over from yesterday. Just for you, I'll knock twenty percent off the price."

"No thanks. I need fresh." Rye broke off a piece of cress to taste. "Not much zing."

Chive's antennae drooped. "Stickier than a stick insect. Too many customers like you and my larvae will starve. Half price for the dandelion heads and the cress."

Rye shook her head. "The price isn't the issue. I really do need them as fresh as I can get. How is your rimu bark?"

"Peeled from the top of the tree this morning. I swear on my mother's carapace. Try a piece."

Rye nibbled some. "Yeah. That's nice. Good texture. Plenty of taste. Give me one of those big bags full of it."

Chive's antennae jerked erect. "What's the occasion? You throwing a pupating party?"

"I'm cooking a dinner. For eight posh people. I have to get everything right." She looked across to another stall. "Looks like I can get cress there."

Chive wrote the price on the bag of bark. "Gravel's? You don't want to go there. He's the sort who buys the cheap stuff off the bottom pallets at the wholesaler."

"Wholesaler?"

"Farmers, orchardists, and market gardeners take their stuff there. Blokes like me and shops all buy there. Auction or by ballot lots. Look, I'm cutting my own throat, but you ought to go there if'n you're going to do this again. On Bog Street. Past the insect market. I'm sure you could get away with amounts like this. But you have to be early. Business gets done in the first hour after dawn."

"Oh. Right. Thanks. I'll bear it in mind."

Rye loaded her purchases in the back of the rented carpet. She made a note about the address and hours of the wholesaler beside the costs she recorded on her list. If she could buy produce fresher and cheaper, that would make future cooking ventures even more profitable. She flew off toward the Westside.

Rye patronised the butcher in Noonpine where she'd bought the meat for Flora's dinner. It was uncomfortably expensive, but the meat and beetles were the highest quality. The butcher cut exactly the joint she wanted and packed it all in a fancy little cooler bag of moss for her at no extra charge. If she were to ever do this again, though, she would have to take the time to discover another, cheaper meat source. Perhaps there was some form of meat wholesaler in the forest, just like for produce.

Rye carried her bags past the boutiques toward her carpet. She knew the Lightning Tree Gallery was close. She walked past her carpet to look in the window. She didn't see anyone inside. Had she really expected Flora to be here? And if she were, would Rye want to say anything to her? Tonight was going to be awkward enough, even though Rye would be in the kitchen and Flora out mingling with the other guests.

Almighty King and Queen of the Fey, it would have been nice just to see Flora again. Even if they didn't speak. Rye missed her. Badly. When it had just been them, together, she had never felt more comfortable and happy. But that was a bubble of unreality. Flora was the sort of person whose work figured in poncy galleries like this one, and Rye was the grunt who couldn't afford to step through the door.

Rye sighed and strode back to her hired carpet. She had too much to do today to waste time in regrets and fanciful daydreams.

A traffic accident on the flyway slowed her to a hover in several places. The carpet's air blowers didn't work, so Rye lowered the window and leaned her elbow on the ledge. She saw a billboard of a dryad woman advertising the latest play to open at the theatre. The thin face looked vaguely familiar. Rye scowled. Frond Lovage. Yeah, she was the twiggy woman in the magazine photo with Flora. Bigger, her face didn't look any prettier. Flora clearly did not have an eye for conventional beauty. Perhaps that skinny dryad was good in bed. Flora had enjoyed sex with Rye. Did that stick-insect of a dryad toss Flora on a bed and go down on her?

Rye banged her fist down on the horn. "Get a move on!"

The sprite in front used his antennae to give her an obscene gesture.

❖

Rye's kitchen burst to the seams. Her cooler could not hold everything she really should keep chilled. Nor did she have enough containers and bench space to do all the preparative work she would like to have completed in advance.

At midday, Rye forced herself to take a break. She took a sandwich and beer outside to sit on the landing. What great weather. The warm sunlight even made her view of Hollowberry look a little brighter and more pleasant than it really was. Down past the gnarled tree roots, a few parents sat on benches talking while their children played in the tiny grass area. Happy squeals and chirps carried up to where Rye sat. She smiled. It seemed only yesterday that she used to take Holly to play on climbing webs and in burrowing tunnels. She had always had the idea that she would return to those sort of places one day with her own kids. Kids who called "Mum!" to attract her attention to how high they had climbed or who wailed out to her when they fell and skinned a knee. Kids who would grow up free and happy, and who would not know that life could be any other way.

Rye sighed and drank a long swallow of beer. Not that she could even begin to think of starting a family before Holly grew up. And with Rye's record, she wouldn't bet any good money on her chances of finding someone to be her children's other mother. Eleven years of celibacy followed by dropping swiftly and completely in love with the wrong woman did not bode well for a stable, partnered future.

Flora.

Rye lost her appetite. She hurled the uneaten half of her sandwich away and stomped back into her apartment.

Rye packed all the containers and food into the hired carpet. She fetched Holly's borrowed black dress and carefully laid it where it would not get stained or leaked on. In the kitchen, she made a final check of the cooler and cupboards. She picked up the knife block with a sense of guilt and shame. She should not use these. By rights, she should have returned them to Flora. After all, it was hypocritical of her to keep and use gifts after she had slammed Flora for buying her things.

Rye agonised even longer over the pristine, unused chef's white top. She changed into clean clothes and put on one of her normal shirts. Even so, she stood fingering the white top. Flora was probably correct in believing that wearing it would make the right impression. But what would Flora say if she saw Rye wearing it?

Rye strode to the door without picking up the chef's top.

❖

Rye didn't have much time to brood about Flora once she arrived at Letty Elmwood's house. There was just too much to do. Any doubts she had about hiring a second helper vanished quickly. Briony threw herself into every dirty job and her previous experience proved invaluable. She got on with things without Rye needing to tell her every little detail. Briony managed Holly very nicely and endeared herself to Holly by lending her some cosmetics when they changed into their serving dresses.

Rye was putting the finishing touches on trays of pre-dinner nibbles when Salvia, Letty's personal assistant, came into the kitchen.

"Ms. Woods?" Salvia said. "There's been a cancellation. One of the guests can't make it."

"Um. Okay." Rye put her piping bag aside and picked up a pollen shaker. "One of the vegetarians or the insectivore?"

"No. Not one of the special dietary needs guests."

"Okay. Thanks for telling me."

Rye should not have been surprised when, about an hour later, Holly returned for a fresh tray and announced that Flora wasn't there.

"I was hoping to ask her about my scholarship forms," Holly said. "Why wouldn't she be here? You don't think she's sick? Or had an accident?"

No, Rye did not think that was why Flora kept away.

"My sister Aloe works for Ms. Withe," Briony said. "She said she's not been herself this week."

"Is something wrong with her?" Holly said.

"Don't just stand there!" Rye said. "You're not here to gossip! Take that food out."

Rye saw the look between Holly and Briony but chose to ignore it. She had enough trouble fighting against her own disappointment to worry about what other people thought.

❖

Rye hurled the last shovel load of scrap metal into the dumpster. The crash suited her mood. She trudged back inside the pot boutique workshop and clanged the door closed. Mr. Nuttal had come back downstairs. He beckoned her over to the workbench. Rye didn't feel much like a chat tonight, but her problems weren't his doing. She shouldn't take it out on him.

"I've got tea," Mr. Nuttal said. "But I'm thinking this might be an evening for a wee tipple of dew. Your little sister still giving you grief?"

Rye frowned as she popped the stopper from the jar and drank a long pull of fermented dew. "I got some books out of the library. About kids and drugs. They have a lot of ideas about what I can do. She's not a bad kid. I just need to handle it carefully."

"Well, I wish you luck." Mr. Nuttal shoved a muffin closer to Rye. "Mrs. Nuttal sometimes gets these ideas in her head. She's quite the expert on affairs of the heart, as she would say. She thought you might have other things on your mind, apart from your sister. And need an older person to talk to."

"Look—"

Mr. Nuttal held up his claws. "Say no more. I'll keep my lips together and my scalp ridges as smooth as can be."

Rye ran a hand through her sweaty hair. "Um. I appreciate the thought. But—Look, there is something I wanted to ask you."

Rye dug out of her pocket the shiny credit note that Letty Elmwood had given her last night. "I need this cashed. Is there any chance you could do it?"

Mr. Nuttal accepted the card. His scalp ridges drew close together. "Sixteen hundred? I'm sorry, Rye, I don't have that much cash on the premises even before afternoon banking. You can deposit that in your bank, you know."

"Yeah."

When Rye strode around the back of the root strip of shops, she stopped to look along the darkened fronts. No carpet waited under the street lamp.

"I miss you," Rye whispered.

She jammed her fists into her pockets and strode away.

❖

Rye opened the apartment door to a burst of female laughter above Holly's crash music. She kicked off her boots and ducked into the bathroom. When she emerged, Holly stood in the hall.

"I thought you were over at your friend's house," Rye said. "Have you been here alone since after school?"

"Not exactly."

Daisy Bark appeared in Holly's bedroom doorway. "Hello, Ms. Woods."

"Hi, Daisy," Rye said.

Holly followed Rye into the kitchen. "Can Daisy stay for tea? She's a political refugee. She wants asylum."

"Escaping from the explosion zone, more like," Daisy said.

Rye resigned herself to not being able to take off her shirt and settled for rolling up her sleeves. "Sure, you can stay, Daisy."

"Thank you so much," Daisy said. "You're such a better cook than my mother."

"Not that your mother will be cooking much tonight," Holly said with a smirk.

Daisy grimaced. "The only thing the poor relic will be grabbing from the kitchen will be the cooking wine. Or a sharp knife for her wrist."

Holly and Daisy giggled.

Rye straightened from grabbing some thistle roots from her vegetable bin. "Do your parents know where you are? Give them a call. Holly, you can wash and peel these."

Daisy pulled out a garishly coloured mobile phone that looked like a beetle. Rye saw the flash of envy on Holly's face.

"There." Daisy plonked her mobile on the table. "Dad is slick about me being here, Ms. Woods. I heard my mother in the background. She was crying."

"No shame?" Holly said.

"Hey, is that how Verbena Caraway likes her nettles prepared?" Daisy said. "I still shrivel when I think of you at Ms. Elmwood's dinner. So scathing!"

As she prepared dinner, Rye listened to Holly recounting snippets about the people she'd served at Letty Elmwood's dinner. Rye didn't understand all Daisy's comments, but she did recognise a trace of awe.

Daisy Bark's family lived a couple of streets over, closer to the river. Daisy was probably the only other girl in this neighbourhood who went to the same upmarket school as Holly. As friends went, Holly could have done a lot worse. There wouldn't be many of her classmates who would be comfortable in this dump of an apartment. Their shared interest in art proved a bonus. Clearly, the balance there lay in Holly's favour. Holly made considerable mileage out of their past acquaintance with Flora. Every mention was like a knife prick in Rye.

"Do you think you'll need any help when you cook another of your dinners?" Daisy asked. "I'm sure my relics would be slick with me doing it."

"Yeah," Holly said. "Daisy would be astronomical at it. You will hire her, won't you?"

"I'll keep you in mind," Rye said. "But I don't think it's likely I'll be cooking again like that."

"Why not?" Holly said. "You're so good at it. Everyone raved. I bet Flora will tell all her friends about you and get more people to hire you."

Rye shrugged and stood to gather the empty plates. "Do you need me to walk you home, Daisy?"

Daisy and Holly exchanged a look.

"Daisy can stay the night, can't she?" Holly asked.

"We don't really have room," Rye said.

"I don't mind sleeping on the couch," Daisy said.

"She could sleep on my bed and I'll sleep on the floor," Holly said.

Rye turned the taps on in the sink. "Why don't you want to go home?"

"It's ghastly," Daisy said.

"Her brother Campion got caught at school with some dreamweed," Holly said. "Her relics exploded."

"It was Moss who bought the stuff," Daisy said. "He's Campion's—"

Rye, standing at the sink with her back to the table, heard Daisy's sharp intake of breath. She guessed Holly had kicked her. Moss?

"Dreamweed?" Rye said.

"Yeah," Daisy said. "If you'd heard my parents, you wouldn't think it was just something limping like that. You'd think it was slake crystals. Trust Campion to do something so inadequate and get caught. He is such a seedhead."

Rye frowned to herself. Moss? Wasn't that the boy Holly said she talked to on the phone? So, he was familiar with dreamweed, was he?

❖

In the morning, Rye made breakfast for three. She found herself grilling buttercup petals and pollen on honey and oat bread slices.

"Crunchy sunshine!" Holly dropped into a chair and grabbed a hot piece of the toast. "This is so scathing. Try some. Rye used to make this all the time when I was a little kid."

Daisy looked tentative at the idea of children's comfort food, but her first bite converted her. "Nummy."

Rye poured three mugs of tea. Halfway through her first piece of crunchy sunshine, she realised that she'd made the special treat for herself. Fifth Day used to be Flora day.

"What are your plans for today?" Rye asked.

"We can go to my place to see the blood patterns on the walls," Daisy said.

"Look, I think your parents will want you back," Rye said, "but not too many spare bodies around. Why don't you come with me, Holls?"

Holly's lip curled with disdain. "Grocery shopping? Limping."

"Actually, I'm going to Noonpine. To Ms. Elmwood's gallery."

Holly sat up straight. "No shame?"

"I have to visit Ms. Elmwood about that credit note. Then I'm going to buy a broom. I've got enough for one that Knot's brother-in-law has in my price range. I'm going to go over there and give it a test fly. Want to come?"

"Yeah. Okay."

Rye and Holly walked Daisy back to her street. At the nearest transit node, they scoured the timetables for a route to Noonpine. Rye would have walked had she been on her own, but she could afford the fare. Holly bubbled at the prospect of visiting the Lightning Tree Gallery.

"Flora has some pieces there, doesn't she?" Holly said.

"Um. I think so."

On the transit carpet, Holly sat beside the window. She commented on shops they passed, flying carpets, and what people were wearing. Rye let it flow past her. They had not done this sort of thing together for too long.

"Oh, astronomical," Holly said in an oddly hushed voice.

Rye peered past her. The carpet was stopped at an intersection. She didn't see anything outside to warrant the awe. "What?"

"Him."

Holly stared at a young bogle man standing outside a shop talking on his mobile. He had slicked down the dark hair that covered his face and neck with some oil that made it look shiny and very odd. Rye failed utterly to see any attraction, but it was clear that Holly was captivated. Her tastes and Holly's were so vastly different. Flora.

This time last week—just five days ago—Rye was anticipating spending her morning with Flora. It was supposed to have been a warm, enjoyable, sexually active few hours. Instead, it had turned into blackest disaster which left Rye with more wounds than a cut on the face and a few bruises.

"Are your ribs still hurting you?" Holly said. "You're looking like misery on legs again. You should've at least let Mother Puddle examine you, if you didn't want to go to an apothecary or doctor."

"The old gremlin woman from the third floor? The one who used to tell you why you're sick from the way thyme seeds stuck in the creases of your hand? I haven't seen her around for ages."

"You took me to her when I was a little kid and I had a really bad earache," Holly said. "I'll never forget it. It's burned into my brain. She smelled of beer and made these horrible snuffling noises. She made you stuff a bit of boiled radish in my ear. Which only made it worse. You had to take me to the apothecary in the middle of the night and pay twice as much as a regular consultation because I was hurting so much and crying all the time. I bet Mother Puddle would have given you sparrow's feet to wear on your head to heal your ribs."

Rye smiled. "Probably. Or made me suck a goblin's toenail."

"Ew! Puke."

Rye laughed, which did make her ribs ache.

At Noonpine, Holly led the way down through the root mall. Rye followed Holly's flitting from shop window to boutique door.

"I'm going to own a place like this," Holly said of a very poncy clothes shop. "Actually, I'm going to own a string of them. Here in Noonpine. One in Newbud, and one in Onionfield. And in other forests, of course."

Rye frowned at the ultra-fashionable dresses and skirts on display inside. "I hope you do. What would you call it? Holly's?"

Holly grimaced. "Fey, no. That sounds like a little kid's shop. I'm going to call them Imagic."

Rye looked at Holly's profile. That name had not been scraped out of nowhere. The kid had given this some thought.

"I'm serious," Holly said. "I know you still think I'm some limping little brat. But I know what I'm doing. I've written that stupid essay for the scholarship applications. My teachers made some corrections. Which is slick. I'll write anything if it means I get out of school. I need you to fill in those bits about our family and stuff. Then I can send them in."

"Um. Right."

"Once I have a scholarship, I can virtually pick where I want to do my apprenticeship. Flora said so."

"Yeah?"

"Flora said she would help me approach teachers. I'm so glad. Even if I do get to be Holly Woods Scathing Scholarship Girl, it would be a zillion times better with Flora helping."

"Oh." Rye turned away to scowl along the mall. "I'm not sure... um...Flora is a busy lady."

"There it is!" Holly pointed. "The gallery. Come on."

Rye frowned and followed.

Holly opened the door and strode inside. Rye trailed with less certainty. The gallery was a cocoon of hushed calm and a comfortable temperature. The air smelled faintly of sandalwood and money.

"Wow," Holly said in an awed whisper. She walked over as if drawn by magic to a tortured lump of glass. "My mind is melting. This is a Flax Burdock."

Rye glanced at it. "Yeah?"

Holly shot her a disgusted look.

Rye looked around. She wondered where Ms. Elmwood might be. There was a tiny little desk at the back and a set of stairs leading up to a mezzanine level. Rye's gaze snagged on a wall-hanging near the stairs. She frowned. Improbably, the hanging seemed familiar. Rye wandered across to stand staring at it. She recognised parts of the abstract design.

"What's that green bit?"

"That?" Flora said. "I told you that this is about my feelings for you? Well, this is your wing."

"Oh. Right. And that blobby purple thing?"

"Your bum."

"I asked for that, didn't I?"

"Walked right into it."

Rye grinned. Flora had tried to jab her with a loom needle. They then had sex.

"Mesmerising, isn't it?" a female voice said in a husky whisper.

Rye jumped. The speaker was a dangerously thin, older sylph woman with long, wispy white hair, translucent grey skin, and huge, liquid green-black eyes. She stood too close.

"Mesmerising," the woman whispered. "It draws me to it. And draws me from myself. Do you feel that?"

"Um." Rye inched away. "It's Flora's, isn't it?"

"A Withe. Yes. It's called *You In Me*. You *in* me. And now you feel it, don't you? In you."

Rye frowned at the faded, shadowy face still too close to her own.

"Sex," the sylph whispered. "It vibrates with sexual verve. You can feel the erotic energy in every fibre. The sensual power. Intoxicating."

Rye scowled.

"Doesn't it make you want to rip your clothes off?" The sylph's eyelids drooped and her nasal breathing grew unnervingly audible. "Can't you feel the tiniest, squirmy thrill of an incipient orgasm?"

Rye backed up a pace. "Look—"

"Is that Flora's?" Holly said.

Rye spun around. Crap! How could she keep Holly away from the weird woman?

"I thought I recognised those deliciously brusque tones." Letty Elmwood descended from the mezzanine. "Rye Woods. Flora's handsome chef."

"Ms. Elmwood," Rye said. "Good morning."

"That will be all, Celadine," Letty said to the sylph.

"Hello, Ms. Elmwood," Holly said. "Is that one of Flora's hangings?"

"Yes, dear child, it is." Letty turned to look at the weaving. "I have always had the highest regard for our Flora's talent. But the divine little creature has surpassed even my expectations with this. Can you believe that she was going to destroy it?"

Rye scowled. "She was?"

"Couldn't bear the sight of it," Letty said. "Didn't want it in her home a moment longer. Fortunately, I was on the spot. Just yesterday morning. I went over to see why the poor creature cancelled on our dinner. She does look under the weather, doesn't she? Pale beyond the merely interesting."

Rye flicked her frown back to the hanging. Flora unwell? "She... she's going to sell it?"

"If you could persuade her to, I'd be in your debt, darling," Letty said. "It belongs on a bedroom wall. Between us, that wall would be mine if she'd sell."

"What's it called?" Holly asked.

"*You In Me*," Letty said. "Most heterosexuals, I expect, will think it alludes to a man. To the penetrative act. I suppose the frankly sexual nature encourages that egotistical misconception. But it's clearly about lesbian love."

Rye jerked her head around to stare at Letty and Holly. Both studied the hanging. Rye didn't want Holly to hear this—even though she had no idea that it was about Rye and Flora. There was no telling what Ms. Elmwood had guessed about her and Flora—and what she might say in front of the kid.

"It's so searingly honest," Letty said. "You wouldn't expect a sophisticated woman like Flora to be able to produce such a powerful representation of so fresh—almost naïve—love. There's the feeling of falling in love for the first time, and yet it's treated with an experienced passion. A maturity that an innocent does not possess."

"What do you mean?" Holly asked.

Letty smiled. "I mean, darling child, that when you fall in love for the first time, you will not produce something like this. You will not have the experience of sexual knowledge, desire, loss, sadness, ambivalence, disappointment, and joy that love brings. Maturity allows Flora objectivity in self-examination. And, yet, at the same time, you get the feeling of a loss of control. That she tumbled deeply in love—rushed headlong—flung herself into that loved other whom you wish to be one with. As you do that first time. She has captured that euphoric desire for oneness that an older, wiser person often dares not risk. It's perfectly astounding."

Rye stared at the hanging. She was speechless that Flora could take bits of coloured wool and thread and translate her emotions into a form which others could understand. But if Letty was even halfway right in the things she saw in Flora's weaving, that made Rye feel like shit. Small wonder Flora couldn't bear looking at it.

"Yes, dear child," Letty said to Holly. "Definitely her best. I wouldn't be at all surprised if our Flora finds herself amongst the Spindle nominees for this."

"Wow!" Holly said. "A Golden Spindle? Astronomical."

Letty turned a smile on Rye. "Hadn't you seen it before, darling?"

Rye ripped her gaze from the hanging. "How...how much would it cost?"

"She's not selling," Letty said. "But if she were, I'd expect twenty or thirty for it. Double that if she gets a Spindle."

Rye had a wild idea. "Twenty pieces?"

Letty smiled. "Thousands, darling. Thousands."

Rye's idea shattered into inadequate, impoverished, way-out-of-her-class fragments. She should have known. That had been the pattern of her whole relationship with Flora Withe.

"Pleasant as it is to discuss this," Letty said, "especially with you, darling, I suspect this was not the reason you had for serendipitously arresting my tragic slide into ennui this morning."

Rye was still reeling with sticker shock. "Um. Yeah. I came about the credit note you gave me."

"Was it incorrect? Salvia takes care of these things for me."

"Um. No." Rye dug the credit note out of her pocket. "I was wondering if I could have cash instead."

Letty looked surprised, but crooked a finger for Rye to follow her. Rye's heavy shoes clumped on the wooden stairs.

Letty produced a sheaf of banknotes from a wall safe. "There you go, darling. You really must do something to cheer our Flora. I was shocked when I saw her. The divine creature looked haggard."

"Oh." Rye stuffed the notes into her pocket. She checked that Holly had not followed them up. "I...I haven't seen Flora for a long time."

"Oh? Perhaps you should, darling. Perhaps you should."

Rye's shoes beat a rapid tattoo down the steps.

CHAPTER FOURTEEN

Holly and Rye walked toward the low-rise stump where Berry, Knot Knapweed's brother-in-law, lived. A group of people sat smoking and drinking on a broken sofa in the middle of their front lawn. Music blared from houses, carpets, and portable sound systems. Acrid smoke hazed the air from burning rubbish. Guard beetles swarmed to a fence and clicked their claws at the pedestrians. Holly and Rye walked faster.

"You know," Holly said, "I didn't think any neighbourhood could make ours look good. This does."

"Yeah," Rye said. "No matter how crappy you think your life is, there are plenty of people worse off."

Rye pounded on Berry's door. His wife answered, with a smoke hanging from the corner of her mouth.

"Berry!" his wife called. "It's a skirt about the broom."

After she disappeared into the house, Holly smirked at Rye.

"Skirt?" Holly said. "You?"

Rye shrugged. "She might not be sober."

"Blind, more like."

Rye lifted a hand in mock threat. Holly giggled.

Berry tugged the door wider and scratched his paunch. "Dye, ain't it? Knot's buddy."

"Rye. Yeah, that's me."

Rye and Holly picked their way across a littered lawn and around to Berry's shed. Holly looked less than impressed. Rye reserved judgement until she saw the broom. From the clutter, Berry produced a solid-looking model. Not new by any means, but not battered to bits.

"Five years old," Berry said. "Needed some major bristle work. Runs pretty good. Want a beer?"

"No, thanks," Rye said. "Can I take it for a test flight?"

"Sure." Berry offered the jar of beer to Holly. "You want?"

"No, thank you," Holly said. "It's a little early in the day for me."

Rye gave her a sharp look. Holly smiled. Rye grinned. She ought to give the kid more credit.

The magic made a soft rumbling noise that was a shade too loud to be called a hum, but the bristles gave off no worrying vibrations and the engine proved much more responsive in flight than Rye guessed. The broom ascended smoothly and quickly, and descended without a nasty jolt. Mindful of Holly waiting, Rye took only a short test flight.

"Little beauty, ain't it?" Berry said. "Not flash, like, but there's some real nice work in it."

"Yeah." Rye gave the bristles a shake for show. "Hmm. How old did you say?"

"Five years. But there ain't too much of it original parts now. Since you're a buddy of Knot's, I'll be straight with you. Twenty-five hundred."

Holly's eyes widened in disbelief.

Rye grunted and rested the broom against the shed wall. "That's a lot more than I was looking to pay. Eighteen?"

"Eighteen! You shouldn't be working with Knot on no building site. You should be behind bars for robbing honest tradesmen."

Rye grinned at him. Berry had the grace to laugh at his own hyperbole.

"All right," he said. "Twenty-two hundred. And you and me knows you're getting a good deal."

"You want me to write a credit note that you can honestly pay tax on?" Rye said.

Berry shoved a beer at her. "You wouldn't do that to Uncle Berry."

"No," Rye agreed. "But I only have two thou. Honest. Look, let me leave you my number. If you have anything for that price, I'll come and look."

Berry lifted his beer jar and glugged the whole jar down. He belched loudly. "Two thou. Done."

Rye smiled and counted out the banknotes. Berry gave her the paperwork and transferred the ignition activation to her handprint for her.

Rye climbed on. "Coming?"

Holly clambered behind her. "This is one ugly broom."

Rye waved to Berry and flew off. Two-up, the engine lost some of its power, but it still pulled nicely. She felt confident enough to take it along the Rootway.

"Hey!" Holly called. "This isn't bad."

"Beats walking," Rye said. "Anywhere you want to go? How about an ice cream at the Box Street Mall?"

"Yeah!"

Rye threaded through the traffic to the busy mall. She bought them both a bowl of ice cream. They sat outside on a bench and watched the shoppers go by.

"I didn't think you had any more money on you," Holly said. "Didn't you say that you only had two thousand?"

"You're not going to try to get me to believe that you still think people have to tell the absolute truth always?" Rye said. "I could've sworn you'd outgrown that idea years ago."

Holly grinned. "This is yummy. You know, that was pretty slick, the way you beat his price down. And that broom is not nearly as crappy as it looks."

Rye smiled and dug up another spoonful of eucalyptus and bark chip ice cream.

"On my birthday, I'll be old enough to fly," Holly said. "Will you teach me?"

Rye's immediate reaction was to refuse. But why not? If Holly was old enough, she should be able to get around on her own. One day she'd be able to afford her own broom.

"Sure," Rye said. "On the—"

"Fey! You will?"

"On the day you pass the theoretical flying test."

Holly grunted. "I knew you'd say something limping like that. Still, it won't matter. Because I'll study hard and pass that stupid test just like that."

Rye smiled.

"Hey, isn't that Flora?" Holly pointed with her spoon.

Rye nearly dropped her bowl. Her heart hammered as she peered through the crowds. She did and did not want to see Flora. Haggard and pale, Ms. Elmwood had said.

"Oh, no," Holly said. "It's not her."

Rye set aside her half-eaten ice cream. "You about ready to go shopping?"

"No, thanks. I've just remembered that I've got something I have to do."

"Where are you going?"

"Not far. I'll be home after lunch. Okay?"

Rye watched Holly thread her way through the crowds. Rye shrugged, dumped the bowls in the receptacle, and wandered back out to where her new broom was parked. This was definitely going to make life easier.

The new broom laden with shopping bags made it up to the parking pad outside their apartment. It wasn't a swift ascent, but it did get there. Rye had to swipe the key to the outside broom closet a dozen times before the long neglected lock bleeped into operation. The rusty door hinges squealed. Something scuttled out of the light. Rye patted her broom and set it in the closet.

After putting the groceries away and taking the laundry down to a machine in the roof, Rye drifted around the apartment. She idly flicked through her night class textbook. Mr. Bulrush must have terminated her enrolment by now. She had quit working at Pansy's Fried Sandwiches, and she was sure Mr. Nuttal could be persuaded to let her change days to First and Third Nights. That way she could resume classes. But that would put her back to where she'd started from, with no free time for Holly.

Rye sat on the sofa and opened the magazine and the book *Contemporary Artists.* Two pictures of Flora smiling.

"I love you," Rye said. "I miss you so much. It doesn't feel like it's getting any easier to bear. When am I going to fall out of love with you?"

❖

Rye double-checked that she had everything ready. Book about teens and drugs. Pen. Notepaper. She and Holly would share a beer while they ate dinner and then, all relaxed and receptive, they'd talk. Just like the book said. Except the book didn't mention beer. Understandable, perhaps, considering it was all about substance abuse. Rye, on the other hand, felt she needed a drop of something. This wasn't going to be easy. She had several fine lines to walk, according to the book. She didn't want to screw it up.

Holly was chatty and happy while they ate. She just didn't seem to fit the profile of a teen drug user. But Rye had smelled dreamweed smoke on Holly's top. She owed it to them both not to ignore the issue.

"Daisy's brother is such a seedhead," Holly said.

"Um." Rye cleared her throat. "Don't you like his friend? Moss, isn't it?"

Holly shrugged and stabbed a lump of dock root with her fork. "He's okay, I guess. But not very mature."

"Yeah? But don't you talk with him on the phone?"

"Sometimes. Not much. He keeps saying he's gonna get his own broom, but he hasn't. He doesn't own his own mobile. And he rubs with some burrowers. As if that would impress anyone."

"Burrowers?"

"Yeah, you know. Kids who have left home and live on their own in the burrows over by Danklee Park. Near the riverbank."

Rye frowned. "You think that's a good way to go?"

"They don't go to any limping school." Holly stood and stacked the dirty plates in the sink. "And they ride around in their own carpets and do whatever they like."

"Stolen. Those sort of delinquent packs don't work. They steal to get money and stuff."

"Save your breath! You needn't give me the big social responsibility lecture. I'm not planning on becoming a burrower. Fey, you can be so back-then sometimes. You're worse than Daisy's relics, which is saying something."

"If you know those kids steal and get into shit like booze and drugs, why do you think they're slick?"

"I don't! Fey." Holly sighed and leaned back against the sink. "Moss thinks that telling people he rubs with burrowers will make them think he's so slick. But it's stupid."

"You've been pretty adamant about wanting to leave school. You don't—"

"Rye!" Holly threw her hands in the air. "I want to leave school to do something important! I'm going to be famous and fabulously wealthy. Just like Flora. I don't want to end up in a stupid muddy hole in the ground with some losers. You are such hard work. Parents couldn't be this bad."

Holly stalked away to her bedroom and turned on her music. Rye sat at the table fiddling with a pollen shaker. The book hadn't prepared her for this development. Okay, Holly wasn't planning on dropping out for a life of crime. But she hadn't denied her connection to this Moss boy, either.

Rye took a minute or two, and the last of her beer, to fortify herself before approaching Holly's room. Holly lay on her bed reading a glossy magazine.

"Holls?"

Holly sighed audibly but didn't lower her magazine. "What? Want to accuse me of selling small children to giants for snack food? And for your information, I did not steal this magazine. Mr. Cloudnut sometimes lets me have the ones with ripped pages for free."

"I'm not accusing you of anything."

"Good. Shut the door on your way out."

Rye sighed. "I'm sorry if I came on a bit strong. It's just that—Um. You know. Sometimes, I worry about you. About both of us."

Holly dropped her magazine onto her chest to reveal a deep scowl. "What?"

"Well." Rye ran a hand through her hair. "You know that we have to—You and me, that is. Both of us. Not just you. We have to keep a low profile in life. Because—"

"Because we're fairy freaks. Yeah. What has that got to do with my life of crime and loserhood?"

Rye steadfastly refused that bait. Keep calm, the book said. "Look, do you know what would happen if you got in trouble with the police? We'd be—"

"I am not in trouble!"

Rye held up her hands. "I'm not saying you are! I just want you to bear in mind that you and I could end up back in Fairyland if anything happened. If either of us got into trouble. Both of us."

"I know that. You've told me a zillion times since I was old enough to have ears." Holly picked up her magazine. "I don't know why you're wasting breath on this. I haven't done anything stupid. Have you? Well, apart from whatever fight you've had with Flora."

"What?"

"I ought to have known that you'd get stupid and annoy the slickest person in Infinity."

Rye's fists clenched. "You have no idea what—"

"And you did it now!" Holly dropped her magazine and sat up. "How limping can you be? Just when I need Flora to write a letter supporting my scholarship applications! Maybe you do want me to drop out and become a nothing?"

Rye's heart beat too hard and fast. She was not calm. What had Holly guessed? How had Rye betrayed herself? The kid couldn't know how she stuck the knife in with every mention of Flora. Rye took a deep breath and struggled for self-control.

"Holly, my friendship with—"

"It's such a good thing that Flora is so slick and stylish," Holly said. "She was utterly okay with writing a letter for me. And she gave me the most astronomical cup of tea. Wild Grape Leaf, it was. I bet we couldn't afford it. But I will, one day. Fey, I wish I could've been Flora's sister. My life would have been so scathing. Like in a magazine. Not this dump."

Rye was gripping the edge of the door so tightly that her hand hurt. "You've talked with Flora behind my back?"

"Last I heard, you aren't her social secretary. I went to her place today. I told you I was going to talk with her."

"No, you didn't. Holly, I don't want you—"

"She was slick with it. Unknot! Anyone would think I committed mass murder, the way you're going on. Didn't you start this by giving me some big boring lecture on being Miss Goody Goody? A bit hypocritical, don't you think? To slice into me for getting my scholarship applications together. Sometimes, I wish you'd drop into a coma then wake up twenty years from now, when I'm old enough that you won't treat me like a baby!"

"Maybe I'll stop treating you like a little kid the day you stop acting like one!" Rye shouted. "I know what dreamweed smells like."

"Dreamweed? What—"

"It was on your clothes, so spare me the excuses!"

"You were snooping! Sniffing my clothes!"

"I'm the drudge who does laundry most weeks, remember? You fuck up with drugs, and we both get busted. Do you hear me? You're not going to get a slap on the wrist and community service. You're going back to Fairyland! We both are. You know what that means? Do you have any idea?"

Rye put her hands on Holly's shoulders and prevented her rising from the side of the bed. "You're going to sit and listen to me. You think your life is crappy now? That why you want to play around with drugs? Well, let me tell you, you get caught with that and you won't know what's hit you. You don't really remember Fairyland, do you?"

"You going to try to scare me? This is shit."

Rye shook her. "I've spent my whole life working for us! So that we can stay here. So that we can be free. So that you never have to know what it's like back there. Maybe I did wrong not to tell you."

"You're hurting me. Rye—"

"You think you'd have liked not going to school? You wouldn't have gone. They don't have one on the commune farm. You do chores. You weed. You wash the floors. You fetch water. From a well. No taps. You get filthy. Anyone can tell you what to do. Your own mother would beat you with a stick. Anyone could beat you. You think you'd like that?"

"Rye, please—"

"You like going out? No going out. There wasn't anywhere to go. You think you don't get nice clothes? How would you like to wear a tunic all day every day? The same one, until it dropped into holes? You'd have to make yourself a new one. Would you like that, Holly? Would you?"

"Rye—"

"And boys. You'd get no chance to mix with some stupid kid who messes with drugs and dropouts. You wouldn't live with any boys. Do you remember that?"

"No, I—"

"The men lived in a different compound," Rye said. "On the other side of the river. You know how you'd meet them?"

"You're hurting me."

"When you get sent back, you'll be shoved onto a commune. You'll work all day, every day, doing stupid, mindless, heavy chores. You'll have no clothes. No fast brooms. No art. No friends. No boys. No magazines. No dreamweed. No dreams, even. Just mud and sweat and prayers and the stick. That sound good to you?"

"Let me go!"

"You've got to know! You've got to understand what you're risking! One day, you'll get your wings. You know what will happen then? Do you?"

"Don't shout at me! Don't fucking shout—"

Rye shook her. "They'll take you. The matriarchs. Your mother and aunts. They'll take you across the river. To the men."

Holly tried to break free. Rye's fingers dug into her shoulders.

"They'll take you to the men," Rye said. "Whether you want to go or not. They'll put you in a room. You and a bed. You can't get out. You'll wait. Scared. Maybe one of your aunts will have cried before she left and given you a kind look. You—"

"Stop it! I don't want to—"

"A man will come for you. If you're lucky, it'll be just one."

Holly went very still. She lost all the blood from her face and whispered, "Oh, fuck."

Maybe it was the whisper, or Holly's horrified expression, but something triggered Rye's awareness of how taut she was, how hard her breathing, and how tightly her fingers dug into Holly. Rye took a shuddering breath. She released Holly and stepped back. Holly stared.

Rye looked around. She was dazed to find herself in Holly's bedroom. What had she done?

"Rye?" Holly whispered.

"Um. Fey."

Rye blindly walked out and into the living room. She stood staring at nothing. What had she done? She hadn't meant to say any of that.

❖

The next morning, Rye shovelled wood shavings into the barrow. She ignored the banter between Blackie, Knot, and Budge. Maybe she should have stayed at home today with Holly. Holly had barely spoken two words over breakfast.

She had fucked up good and proper last night. All her good intentions had snapped to nothing. If Holly hadn't mentioned Flora, maybe Rye could have kept it together. What Rye wouldn't give to be lying on Flora's sofa with her, comfortable, sipping a cold beer, and just enjoy being with her. If only the rest of the world did not exist. Just for an hour. But Flora was haggard. Perhaps not nearly as pale and horrified as Holly had looked last night.

Rye worked hard to make her body ache and hurt. To force her brain to stop thinking about what an utter mess she had made of everything she came into contact with lately. She wouldn't have been surprised if her new broom stopped on her way to work this morning.

At lunchtime, Rye chewed her sandwiches and brooded. If she had found Holly visiting Flora unexpected, then Flora must've been floored by Holly suddenly turning up at her tree.

Rye scowled and strode across the street. The pay phone pod had a new picture plate. The next pod was vandalised. She dug a coin out of her pocket, jammed it into the slot, and dialled before she could lose her nerve.

Beep-beep. "Flora's mobile messages. Talk to me."

"Um. Flora? Babe? It's me. Rye. Um. I know you probably don't want to hear from me, but—Look, about Holly. I didn't know she was going to bother you. I'm sorry. Okay?"

Rye rammed her fists in her pockets and trudged back to the site. She had not really looked forward to talking with Flora, and yet she felt disappointed at not having heard her again.

"What you looking so dumpy about?" Knot said. "That broom Berry sell you a dunger?"

"Nah," Rye said. "It's pretty good."

"Then you should come to the Ball and Chain on Third Day," Knot said. "Bunch of us getting together in the afternoon to have a few drinks and watch the game."

"Third Day?"

"Yeah. It's a holiday. You didn't forget? Even this worm meat company can't make us work on Leaf Fall Day. What do you say? If anyone looks like they need a drink, it would be you."

"You're not wrong," Rye said.

"That's the idea. Everyone will be there."

When Rye arrived home, Holly was in the bathroom. The strongest floral perfume leaked from under the door.

"I'm home, Holls."

Rye strode to the kitchen. She hadn't expected a reply.

Perhaps she could do something with Holly on Leaf Fall Day.

Perhaps one of those fairs, like they went to with Flora. Holly had enjoyed that. Although, Flora had probably been a greater contribution to that than the fair itself.

Rye cooked to take her mind off everything. Holly emerged from the bathroom and went into her bedroom without saying a word. Rye plunged nettle stalks into boiling water and burned her hand.

"Holly? Dinner's ready."

No answer.

Rye banged on Holly's bedroom door. "Holls?"

"I'm not hungry."

"It's your favourite. Sparrow's legs and willow sauce."

"I'm not hungry."

Rye sighed. "I'm sorry. I shouldn't have said what I did last night. I didn't mean it. Okay?"

"Leave me alone."

"Don't you think we should talk about it?"

"Leave me alone."

Rye ran herself a hot bath and briefly toyed with the idea of holding her head under the water long enough to solve all of her own and everyone else's problems.

When Rye emerged, Holly's plate sat on the table with the food half-eaten. Good enough. Rye washed the dishes and drifted into the lounge. She used to be frying sandwiches at this time on First Nights. Now she sat alone in the living room, an unwilling listener to Holly's sound system through two closed doors. Quality time with her kid sister.

Rye fetched herself a beer. She made her bed on the couch and climbed in with her night class text. She might as well keep up with her reading. It would come in handy when she took the course again next year. By then, Holly would have started her apprenticeship. Would that make her more or less easy to live with? She wouldn't have school to whine about. On the other hand, she would probably have a much more active social life—including sex. Rye grimaced.

Rye finished her beer and lay back to read about accounting. The numbers blurred and her eyes sagged closed.

Rye ran. Her tunic flapped about her knees. She could not run fast enough. She was being chased. She waded across the river. She couldn't look back, but they were chasing her.

Her mother stood in front of her brandishing a stick. Her wings trembled. Afraid or angry? She shouted at Rye. Unnatural. Evil. Should have beaten it out of you when you were young. Should have left you to die when you were born.

Her mother lay dead in the mud at Rye's feet. Holly sat crying. Rye bent to pick her up, but then she stood in the robing room at the temple. They had Chastity tied up. Only it wasn't Chastity. It was Flora. The priestess lifted the whip. Crack!

Rye jerked awake. It was after ten. Holly was still playing music and the phone rang. Rye stumbled out of bed and grabbed the phone.

"Hello? Yes?"

"Rye?"

"Flora?" Rye felt a rush of wild relief at the sound of her voice. "Oh, babe, are you all right? Um. Fey. I'm sorry. I was having a bad dream."

"Dream? You were in bed? Are you unwell?"

Rye closed the hall door and carried the phone to the couch. "No. I'm fine."

"I got your message. I would've called earlier, but I thought you worked."

"Um. Yeah. I did. But I've quit." *Oh, you sound so good.* "Um. Are you okay?"

"You don't have to apologise for Holly coming to see me," Flora said. "I didn't mind."

"What? Oh. That." *I love you. I miss you. It's killing me to hear you and not be with you.* "I heard that you weren't...um. Oh, shit. Can I see you?"

"I think we both need some closure. Don't you agree?"

"Um. Yeah," Rye said. "We need to talk. But not like this. I'm crap on the phone."

"I know."

Flora sounded like she smiled. Rye wanted to cry.

"My timetable is more flexible than yours," Flora said. "When would suit you?"

"Um. How about Third Day? That's a holiday. I'm not working. I'm sure Holls won't miss me for a couple of hours."

"Fine. My place or neutral ground?"

Rye winced. "Um. There's this eating house at the Conifer Street Park. Do you think you could find it?"

"I'm sure I could."

Rye ransacked her empty mind for something to say to prolong the conversation "I—"

"I'll—"

Rye beat her forehead with the heel of her hand. "I'm sorry. You go first."

"I'll see you on Third Day morning, then."

"Um. Yeah. Okay."

Click. The line went dead.

"I love you."

Rye replaced the handset and slumped. That wasn't how she'd wanted that conversation to have gone. Why did she always lose her brains at the most important times?

❖

The next morning, Rye made breakfast and prepared sandwiches for her and Holly for their lunches. When she heard Holly's alarm go off, Rye poured two mugs of tea. Holly slouched in, dropped in a chair, and pointedly didn't look at Rye.

"Do you have any plans for tomorrow?" Rye asked. "Leaf Fall Day must be a school holiday if my crappy company is giving us the day off."

Holly grunted and spooned more honey in her tea.

Rye had wanted a broom, hadn't she, so that she could spend less time travelling and more time at home? The joys of family breakfasts.

"Are you still fuming over the other night?" Rye said. "Look, forget it. We're never going back."

"I don't care about that crap."

"Good," Rye said. "Then why are you so—"

"Can't you just leave me alone?" Holly stood in a scraping of chair legs. She stomped into the bathroom.

Rye sighed and slumped low enough to bang her forehead gently against the edge of the table several times.

"Women," Rye whispered.

That was her problem. All the crud in her life stemmed from women. If she hadn't been gay, she wouldn't have broken that prick's arm when they took her over to the men's compound, and then she wouldn't have been sent to the temple for punishment. If she hadn't been at the temple, she wouldn't have had sex with Chastity in the robing room. They wouldn't have been caught. Rye wouldn't have run away and had her wings broken. Then Rye wouldn't have bided her time, made her plans, and fled for good. And taken Holly out with her.

Rye frowned. No, that wasn't true. She probably would have broken that prick's arm even if she'd been straight. How could any eighteen year old virgin who was completely sober, ignorant, and afraid, want sex with three men she had never met before?

Rye shook herself and grabbed her work bag. She had more than enough problems in the present without dredging up the past. She must concentrate her efforts and energies on things she could do something about.

Chapter Fifteen

Rye slid her tray along in front of the cubby holes full of food. They had muffins. Flora liked muffins. These looked pretty nasty. Rye had not baked muffins for Flora. She should have.

"Mum! Mum! I want that, Mum!"

A small pixie child bumped against Rye's legs as he strained to point to a sticky cake. Rye shoved her empty tray around to the cashier.

"Pot of puriri leaf tea," Rye said. "And milk, please. For two."

Rye put her tray aside and found a booth. The jar on the table contained artificial honey. Flora would probably cringe. But this was Rye's world. It was the kind of place she could afford.

Rye stared out the window. It was an overcast day with not much wind. Grey and still. Kids played in the park. Excited shouts and squeals carried to the eatery. A couple walked their millipedes on matching red leads. Joggers ran along the walking paths. On the far fields spectators watched ball games. She couldn't see Flora.

Someone approached the table. Rye's heart leaped. And sank. It was just the woman with her tea order.

Rye arranged the cups. One for her and one for Flora. It didn't seem real that Flora would be sitting there, across the table, within arm's reach, in just a few minutes. Rye did so desperately want to see her again, even though she knew they would be leaving as separately as they arrived. Closure. Rye wasn't exactly sure what Flora meant by that, but it sounded final. That was probably what they needed to do. Perhaps then the hurt might ease.

A large, boisterous family of sprites entered in a noisy wave. Rye's glance began to slide away from the doorway when she saw Flora behind the sprites. Flora made eye contact with Rye. Rye felt like someone had smacked her in the chest with a chair.

Flora wore casual pants and top and a narrow-brimmed hat. She did look pale. Rye wanted to kiss her so much that she ached. After an awkward moment, Flora slid into the booth.

"You...you found it okay?" Rye said.

"Yes. There are a couple of games on in the park today, apparently. Something sponsored by the local newspaper. It would have been hard to miss the large signs."

"Right. Um. I got tea. Only puriri leaf, I'm afraid."

"I'd like that, thank you."

Rye poured. "You...you look great."

"So do you. How did you hurt yourself?" Flora indicated the fresh scar on Rye's face.

"Um. An accident." When she'd been knocked down by the carpet as she fled from Flora's apartment. "It's nothing."

Their fingers touched as Rye slid the cup close to Flora. Rye looked up. For a painful moment they stared at each other. Longing. Need. Loss. Hurt. Flora looked away.

"Um." Rye fiddled with her cup. "I'm sorry about Holly. I had no idea she was going to pester you. She never said anything until she got back. I...I wouldn't have let her bother you."

"You don't want me to write the letter for her?"

"I don't want her to put you in an awkward situation."

"I'm happy to support her applications. I was one of the judges who gave her first prize in her school competition, remember?"

How could Rye forget? That was when they first saw each other. Rye had been floored by Flora's beauty. She had even missed Holly's big moment, thanks to being distracted by Flora. Perhaps that had been an omen she should've paid more attention to.

"I remember," Rye said. "But I meant because of us."

"Holly doesn't know anything about us, does she? Except what she has guessed. Which, I know you won't want to hear, is probably a lot more than you choose to believe."

Rye frowned across the table. "You didn't tell her?"

"I told her that I wouldn't do anything if you weren't comfortable with it. I did not tell her that you had recently terminated our love affair. You really don't have a very high opinion of my regard for the feelings of others, do you?"

Rye lowered her frown to the table top. "You couldn't have said anything, or she'd have flayed me with it. I'm sorry. Look, babe, I'm sorry. I didn't want her to bother you. But I'm very grateful that you can write the letter she wants. I know it will mean a lot to her and do wonders for her application. Thanks. And thanks for not saying anything about us."

Flora sipped her tea and stared out the window. Rye gulped half of hers and willed herself not to be so stupid and brain numb. This might be the last chance she ever had to talk with Flora. She was making a right mess of it.

"Look." Rye put her cup down and reached across to brush the back of Flora's fingers. "I really wanted to tell you that I'm sorry. For what I did. And what I said. The other day. You know. I didn't—"

Flora looked like she was searching Rye's face for the end of the sentence. Rye bit her lip and stared down. Somehow their fingers had intertwined. Rye made no move to extricate herself.

"I need you to finish that," Flora said. "You see, I haven't been able to think about much else since you ran out on me."

"Um. I didn't mean to say what I did. I...I didn't mean to hurt you. And I feel shitty that I did."

"I didn't see it coming," Flora said. "Didn't have any shadow of a hint. Like the stereotyped spouse. I thought we were fine. I thought I'd found the love of my life."

"Babe—"

"What did you mean to say?" Flora said. "If you didn't mean what you did say?"

Rye bit her lip and stroked the back of Flora's fingers. "That you're wonderful. And that I love—"

"Excuse me, dears." A waitress stood at the end of the table. "Did you want more tea?"

Flora slid her hand free. "No, thank you."

"I'll take this then, shall I?" The woman dumped the empty pot on her trolley.

Rye sighed and ran a hand across her scalp. The noisy sprite family sat in the next booth laughing, whistling, and calling to each other.

"Can we go outside?" Rye said.

"I think that would be best," Flora said.

Rye followed Flora. Almighty King and Queen of the Fey, she looked good. Outside, Rye fell in step with Flora as they wandered along one of the paths through the park.

"I've been thinking it over and over," Flora said. "What you said. What I did wrong. Trying to make sense out of it. To understand what mistakes I made."

"It wasn't all your fault. It was mine. Mostly mine."

Flora shook her head. "You were so adamant. So angry. I thought I was helping, but it was the last axe stroke in the trunk, wasn't it?"

"It wasn't like that. Not that...that simple."

Flora stopped and turned to face Rye. "Be honest with me. Did I really make you feel like I wanted to buy you?"

Rye frowned and tried to think of the right words so that she wouldn't make it worse.

"That was never my intention," Flora said. "I never thought of us like—Clearly, I never looked at us in the same way you did. I know you were uncomfortable with those presents. But I was trying to help. I wanted to make you happy. I hadn't the faintest idea that I was making you feel bought."

"Babe—"

"I had been labouring under the illusion that we were in love. Two people in love with each other. It never entered my head that we should be keeping a financial balance sheet."

Rye scowled down at her shoes. "It wasn't like that."

"But you clearly kept some count about money? It's so bizarre. I've had plenty of relationships splinter, but never because of my bank balance and investment portfolio."

Flora walked away. Rye caught up to her.

"How many poor people have you dated before?" Rye asked.

Flora stopped and stabbed an angry glare at Rye. "I never thought of you as a poor person! You're Rye. The woman I love. The woman I got buds for. The woman who made me laugh. And made me feel good about myself. And made me feel sexy and loved. For the first time in my life I wanted to live with someone. Share my life with her. The good times and bad. Have her children. Money was never an issue for me. I never once thought of you and thought, Oh, good, Rye makes me feel rich!"

Flora stalked off leaving Rye to swear under her breath.

Rye jogged and caught Flora near a deserted bench. She put her hand on Flora's arm to tug her to a halt.

"Babe, please," Rye said. "Can we sit and talk? Please."

Flora stood blinking, not looking at Rye. She sniffed and nodded. When they sat, Rye glanced around. They were in a lightly populated part of the park, though the cheers from the ball game spectators carried across the flower beds and grass. She saw the occasional light of a photographer's flash. The newspapers must be covering the game. Flora wiped her eyes.

"You are sexy," Rye said. "And wonderful. And you should feel good about yourself."

"You made sure I felt very good about myself, didn't you?"

Rye winced. "Look, I'm so sorry that it happened the way it did. I didn't plan it. It just came out. Everything had been building up inside me. And that naiad bitch. I shouldn't have let it all boil over like that, but it did. I regret it. And feel like a shit for doing it."

"But you're not sorry it happened? You did want to end our relationship?"

Rye chewed her lip. She could feel Flora bristling with anger and hurt. "Babe, I don't think I'm meant to be with anyone."

"Anyone? Not just someone with a little more money than you?"

Rye winced. "I couldn't meet you halfway. As equals."

"Do you seriously imagine there would be a single married couple in the whole world if the criteria for partnership was absolute equality of the value of their material assets?"

Rye sighed and risked a glance at Flora. It ripped her heart to see Flora so unhappy. She wanted to wrap her arms around Flora and hold her.

"I know you haven't had many relationships," Flora said. "Did they all break up because of this? Because of your incredible hypersensitivity to money?"

"It's not just money. I don't have anything to offer you."

Flora looked surprised. "You don't really think that?"

"You have everything. I have nothing."

"I don't have everything. But this sounds suspiciously like money, still. Rye, all the time we were together, the times we made love, the times we laughed and played silly games—were you just mentally adding up the value of what I own?"

"No! Of course not."

"The glue between two people is not solely, nor even importantly, money. Love, Rye. Weren't you even a little in love with me?"

"Yes. But—"

"I love you. I respect you. I like you. You give me what no one before ever has." Flora slid closer on the bench and took hold of one of Rye's hands. "You interest me on so many different levels. You are someone who is so unlike me in a multitude of ways. And, yet, we meshed so well. You have so much strength. I don't just mean physically."

Rye shook her head. "We come from different worlds. We live in different worlds. Your parents would have hated me. Your friends would think you'd lost your mind. No one would think I should be with you. You're this beautiful, successful artist and I'm a nobody who works two and three jobs to keep food on the table and pay the rent."

"You think I'm a success," Flora said, "but look at you. You've raised Holly. She's a great young woman. Nothing I have ever done can remotely compare with that achievement. And you did it all on your own. Rye, I admire you. I can't think how I haven't made that clear enough to you."

Rye stroked Flora's hand as she frowned across the flower beds.

"I'm not a success," Rye said. "I'm barely coping."

"Hasn't it occurred to you that I might be able to help?" Flora said. "That I might want to? If your jobs don't give you enough self-esteem—or pay—why don't you do something else? You were working toward that business certificate, weren't you? Before you quit night school. And catering. Branch, you're terrific in the kitchen. I cannot understand why you don't do that as a profession. Do you know that Letty Elmwood told me that she loved your dinner? Trust me, Letty is not an easy person to please. Why don't you set yourself up in a catering business?"

Rye frowned down at Flora's hand between hers. On impulse, she lifted it to lightly kiss Flora's fingers.

"I wish I'd met you ten years from now," Rye said.

"Why? What would be different?"

Rye clung to Flora's hand as she leaned back and stared up at the dirty grey clouds. The hard wooden bench back pressed uncomfortably against her wing buds. Part of her wanted it to hurt more. The game spectators loosed a loud cheer. Rye felt very tired, alone, and defeated.

"Rye? Is it Holly?"

Rye sighed. "Yeah. Partly."

"Trouble at school?"

"No. She's been smoking dreamweed."

"Oh."

"Yeah," Rye said. "Kicked me in the guts. We talked. I messed it up. She hasn't spoken to me in days. She doesn't even want to be in the same room as me."

"Look, I'm sure Holly would just have been experimenting. We all do. Especially at that age. It's not your fault."

"Yes, it is. I've been neglecting her. I was too busy working to be around when she needed me. Too busy doing other stuff to notice what was going on with her. I can't let that happen again."

"Oh," Flora said.

"She has to come first. When I picked her up and took her out of there, she became my responsibility. I can't put the kid aside because I'd rather be doing something else. She didn't ask me to take her. It was my idea. I did it willingly. I have to see it through."

Flora interleaved her fingers with Rye's. "That's one of the reasons I admire you. But you don't have to do it all alone."

Rye slipped her hand free and stood. She took half a dozen paces from the bench before she realised what she was doing. She stopped. She hadn't come here to run away from Flora again. Flora sat looking hurt. Rye walked back.

"I'm sorry," Rye said. "I didn't mean to do that. I...I'm finding this difficult to talk about."

"It's not very easy for me, either."

"I know. I'm sorry."

Flora stood and slipped a hand through Rye's arm. They strolled together along deserted paths. Shrubs and saplings occasionally screened them from everyone, though the roar of the sports fans followed their meandering progress.

"Being one of a couple doesn't mean you have to forget the rest of your life," Flora said. "I can help you. I don't mean money. I mean you and me talking about things. Holly and I get along. I'll never have the relationship with her that you do, and I would never try to, but she and I have a lot in common. Things you and she don't. I don't know much about raising teenagers, but I could learn."

"I wish...I wish there were two of me. Between them, I might have time to do everything I wanted."

"Would you think differently about us having a relationship if I were a man? If you were straight?"

Rye scowled down at the muddy path.

"I think you still owe me that answer," Flora said. "About why you feel you have to hide our relationship from Holly. Does it have something to do with being a lesbian? And how that was regarded when you were growing up?"

Rye stopped and looked around. The closest person was an old green gremlin lady with her beetle on a leash half the park away.

"Don't you think I deserve a little more honesty?" Flora said.

"I...I can't risk Holly knowing I'm gay. If we got sent back, they'd get it out of her. I don't want her to live the rest of her life taking the blame for that."

Flora frowned. "Blame? For what? What would happen if you were known to be gay? Not that it's likely you'll ever go back to Fairyland, is it? Not after all these years. What did they do to you that you still live in fear?"

Rye remembered Holly's deathly pallor after she'd blurted out that stuff about Fairyland. Holly still needed those family details. Details which Rye could not supply without revealing their illegal residence status.

"Rye?" Flora touched Rye's cheek.

Rye drew in a shuddering breath. Why did it feel like her life was disintegrating?

"They tied her up," Rye said. "And whipped her. The blood ran down the back of her legs. They opened cuts in her wings. She didn't make a sound. She just went all limp when she fainted. And still they whipped her."

"Who?"

"Chastity. They caught us in the robing room having sex." Rye heard a cheering roar and flinched.

"Oh, Holy Elm," Flora said. "That's barbaric. Did they do that to—"

Rye grabbed Flora's wrist and tugged her behind a sapling.

"It was going to be my turn the next day," Rye whispered. "They left me on my knees to pray all night. And think about what I'd seen. And imagine how that was going to feel when they did it to me. I escaped. But I didn't get far. They caught me and took me back to the temple. It was the second time I tried to flee, so they broke my wings and made sure they didn't set right. So I could never use them again."

Flora swore under her breath. She had gone as pale as Holly. "Rye—"

"I couldn't afford the fine. My commune took back the land I'd been given when I got my wings, but they didn't give me enough money for it to pay the temple. My mother wouldn't give me anything. She didn't want me back. I was evil and she wished she'd never had me. With my wings broken, no one on another farm or in the city would have given me work because they'd know I was trouble. Not that the temple would let me leave the valley. So, I had nothing and no way to earn anything, but I still owed them. That meant I had to become a temple bond servant. The temple owned me."

"Owned?"

"The only thing I had to pay them with was myself. That made me temple property. I did whatever I was told. They gave me food and somewhere to sleep."

"That's...that's slavery," Flora said. "Holy Elm. It's too horrific to believe. Oh, Rye—"

"I bided my time. I learned from what I did wrong the last time, and I escaped properly. They never expected me to go back for Holly. We got across the river and through the hills. She was a good kid. Better than you'd expect. I could have made better time on my own, but she kept me going. I had to get her away from that. And she hardly ever got homesick or cried, even when we went hungry and cold. Still, being cold and hungry wasn't nothing new. We made it."

Flora clasped Rye's hands. "I had no idea."

"I earn whatever Holly and I need. I always have. I provide for us. We've gone short sometimes, but I've never owed anyone anything. I've never fallen into that trap. No one is going to tell me what to do or own me. Never again. Nor Holly. Not while there's breath in me."

Flora shook her head. She looked between shock and tears. "Oh,

Holy Elm. I never imagined—I wish I'd known. I think I begin to understand."

"I can't risk being sent back," Rye said. "I can't let them take Holly. That's why I have to wait for her to get her wings. She's an adult then. They can't claim her back, even if they found her."

Flora frowned. "But, surely, they can't force naturalised citizens out of this country? Especially not to an inhumane regime?"

"Good morning!"

Rye and Flora started. A pixie jogger raised his hand as he passed.

Rye jerked her hands free and strode away. Fey. She hadn't meant to say all that. It had just blurted out. Like it had on Fifth Night with Holly. Rye raked trembling fingers across her scalp. How many passing people had heard?

The cheer of the ball game spectators sounded ominously loud.

Rye felt Flora's hand on her back.

"I'm sorry," Rye said. "I...I didn't mean to say all that. This wasn't at all what I planned. I'm so fucking useless at this talking stuff."

"I don't think you are," Flora said. "I could wish you'd confided in me earlier. But I can understand why it's not something you find easy to say."

Rye captured Flora's hand and held it firmly between hers. "I can't do everything. Right now, I don't feel like I'm coping with anything."

"You could let me help. You needn't be alone."

"I love you." Rye kissed Flora's fingers. "I wish I'd met you ten or five years from now."

"My budmate." Flora sighed and looked unhappy. "You know, don't you, that I want to be with you? That no matter how hurt and angry I've been with you, I still came here hoping that we could make it work."

Rye's world trembled as if it were about to split apart—or she was. When she really wanted to say yes, she said, "I can't. Not now."

"I'm not so foolish as to ask you to choose between me and Holly. You could have us both, you know."

"I can't."

Flora looked away for a long time.

"I wish…" Rye said, "I wish it could've been different."

Flora slowly nodded. "I think I'm beginning to understand. I might not agree, but I think I'm beginning to see."

Quiet acceptance was harder to bear than Flora shouting at her. Rye made a futile gesture. Flora brushed away a tear. Rye couldn't help herself, she reached out to put her arms around Flora. Flora moved into the embrace. Almighty King and Queen of the Fey, she felt good to hold. Flora gently disengaged.

"I'm not that strong," Flora whispered. "I'll never be able to retain any dignity if you do that again. This is hard enough."

"I'm sorry."

"So am I." Flora reached up to gently lay her hand against Rye's cheek. "So am I. I can't promise to wait forever, but if you change your mind, if ever you need me—"

Rye kissed her. Softly, chastely. "I shall always love you."

Flora turned away quickly and strode off along the path. Rye's eyes stung and her throat tightened.

Flora broke into a run. She cut across the field toward the eatery parking lot. Rye put a fist to her chest as if that might keep her heart from tearing in two.

"I had no choice," Rye said. "I had no fucking choice."

Chapter Sixteen

Rye turned the alarm off, rolled out of bed, and reached for her clothes. Another day to get through. What day was it? Second Day? Third Day? A whole week since...No, it was First Day.

Rye sighed and pulled her pants on.

"I need you to fill this in." Holly dropped a green form on the kitchen table.

Rye forced herself to show some interest. Holly grabbed a round of toast but remained standing. Rye felt a spurt of resentment and anger. She wasn't even good enough to sit beside and share breakfast with? She had given up Flora for this? But it wasn't Holly's fault.

Rye sighed and pulled the form closer. Section B. Family details. Citizen identification number. *Fey.*

"Now that I've got Flora's letter," Holly said, "I want to send them in."

"Yeah. Okay."

Holly disappeared into the bathroom.

Mother's name. Penance. Father's name. Unknown. Date of Birth. Not known precisely. One day in spring sixteen years ago. Place of Birth. Birdwood Valley Commune Farm Number Two, Fairyland.

No, Rye would use the details she had made up for Holly when she had first registered her for school. The one thing she could not lie her way around, though, was the citizen identification number. What, in the name of the Almighty King and Queen of the Fey, was she going to do?

❖

When the lunch break whistle blew, Rye trotted down from the top levels of the under construction apartment tree. She hopped on her broom and flew out the site gates. She stopped at the RainbowSpring branch of the municipal library that she passed every day on her way to work.

Immigration Service. ShadeForest City Branch. 352 Upper Plantain Way. General enquiries (303) 990-032.

Rye scribbled the details down and went to find a street map.

Rye parked her broom. The totara tree containing number 352 was set back in a plaza. The large roots were busy with shops and cafés. Rye stood staring at the tree. Immigration were the people who hunted down illegal immigrants and shipped them back to where they came from. Rye's wings tightened uncomfortably against her back and her heart beat faster. She bit her lip and clenched her fists. She must not panic. She could not run away. She had to walk in there and find out if there was any way Holly could become a citizen before she was an adult with her wings. Rye had to do this for Holly.

Rye forced her legs to move. She passed happy, chatty people. Her breathing grew more rapid. When she saw the big brightly coloured sign for the Immigration Service, her legs stopped. She could see lines of people. Dwarves. Gnomes. Brownies. Fauns. And a half-goblin at the door in a uniform.

Rye could feel the air pressing in on her. Squeezing her lungs. Turning the edges of the world black.

Rye backed up, bumped into someone, and ran.

No! Stop!

When Rye halted herself, she stood in Upper Plantain Street outside a real estate agency. Her heart beat so fast and hard that she thought it might be in danger of bursting. She pretended to look at apartments for sale. She heard no shouts. The uniformed half-goblin hadn't come running to catch her.

"Fuck," she said.

Rye wiped perspiration from her face with a trembling hand. Stupid! What was she thinking? That sort of behaviour might attract exactly the attention she wished to avoid.

Rye climbed back on her broom. She flew back to the building site. That afternoon, she wielded a hammer and chisel as if her life depended on hollowing out a whole room single-handed.

That evening, Holly asked again about her form.

"Tomorrow," Rye said. "Okay?"

Holly looked angry. "I need it. It's important."

"I know. Do you want to talk about what's bothering you?"

Holly shrugged. "No."

Rye watched Holly walk into her bedroom and shut the door. Holly's music blared. Rye felt so acutely alone. She wanted to get very, very drunk. But that wouldn't solve anything and it was the last example she should be setting Holly.

❖

Beep-beep. Beep-beep.

"Come on," Rye said.

Beep-beep. "You have reached the Immigration Service. If you know the extension number of the person or service you wish to contact, please dial now. If you wish to contact General Enquiries, please press one. Press two for visa services. Three for passports. Four for residency and citizenship."

Rye pressed four.

"Hello. My name is Myrtle Smallage. How may I help you today?"

"Um." Rye cleared her throat, which was tightening too much. "Um. Yeah. Look, I was just wondering...um."

"Yes, ma'am?"

"Well, the thing is...I have this friend. Um. She's sixteen years old. She needs an ident number. Is there any way she can get the number before she's an adult?"

"I'm sorry, ma'am," Myrtle Smallage said. "I'm not sure I completely understand your enquiry. At sixteen years of age, your friend is a minor, yes. But she should have a C.I.N. She would have been assigned one at the time her birth was registered. Perhaps we're talking about an individual who was not born in this country?"

"Yeah. That's it."

"I see. What is her current residency status? Is she a visitor? A permanent resident? Because if she is a resident, then she should have a resident identification number."

Rye gripped the vandalised screen and struggled against the pressing dark and rising panic. "No, she's not a resident."

"Only citizens, by naturalisation or birth, can hold a C.I.N., ma'am."

"How...how can she become a citizen?"

"Foreign born individuals can apply to become naturalised citizens after a period of three years residency. Marriage to a citizen would also confer naturalisation. However, since your young friend is not a resident, she would have to apply to become one. And since she's still a minor, a parent or legal guardian would have to make the application on her behalf. Which also means she's underage to marry."

"Okay. How do I apply for her?"

"The exact procedures depend on her current place of abode. Is she in her native country?"

"No," Rye said. "She's...she's here."

"I see. Then her legal guardian needs to make an application for an interim residency permit for her before the expiration of the tourist or visitor's visa on which she is named."

Rye's chest was so tight she feared she would not be able to continue to suck in air. "What...what if she doesn't have a visa or permit?"

Pause. "Are we talking about someone who is living in the country after the expiry of her visa or permit?"

"No. Um. She never had one."

"Oh."

Rye groped to loosen the top buttons on her shirt. She could barely breathe. Her heart pounded so fast and hard that she thought she might be heading for cardiac arrest. She had to do this. For Holly.

"I see," Myrtle said. "Did this minor enter—"

"She was taken away from Fairyland. She hasn't got her wings yet. But she needs her ident. How can I get one for her? Please."

"Fairyland? Oh, I see. Yes. It's common for fairies to apply as refugees. If there are substantive grounds for believing that she would suffer harm were she to be repatriated."

"Yeah?"

"Oh, and a minor could gain citizenship by adoption. If she were to be adopted by a citizen."

"No," Rye said. "That refugee thing."

"Well, it's normal to make an application through a lawyer. It's a complex process."

Rye's heart sank as she listened to the woman explain a load of bureaucratic details. She could not afford a lawyer.

"Fairyland residents generally have a high proportion of

successful applications," Myrtle said. "Usually, the only impediment is if the applicant has a criminal record, either here or in their country of origin."

Rye's wings scrunched up even harder. Still, Holly had done nothing wrong. She had been a wingless child when Rye took her out of the country. Rye had fled Fairyland without permission, but Holly couldn't be held responsible for being kidnapped. Nor could they taint her with anything else Rye had done on her way out of there.

Rye trudged back to work. What was she going to do now?

❖

Someone rapped on the front door. Holly darted from her room and cut in front of Rye to reach the door first. Holly was dressed up. As was Daisy Bark, the person who had knocked.

"You ready?" Daisy said.

"Let's get out of here," Holly said.

"Wait!" Rye walked the three paces down the hall to the door. "Where do you think you're going?"

"Out," Holly said.

"Onionfield," Daisy said. "We've got tickets to the latest Frond Lovage play. *Second Time Loss*. It's going to be astronomical! All the papers give it rave reviews, Ms. Woods."

Rye frowned at Holly. Holly scowled at Daisy.

"You didn't say anything about this to me," Rye said.

"I bought the ticket myself," Holly said. "Out of my wages. Okay? No need to get knotted."

"That wasn't my only concern," Rye said. "You have school tomorrow. And aren't you underage for that play?"

"Don't worry, Ms. Woods," Daisy said. "My mum is taking us. She's wearing the most embarrassing dress, but the theatre is going to be dark most of the time, so no one should be able to see her much. We can run ahead of her from the parking lot to the auditorium and pretend like we don't know who she is."

Rye leaned to see past Daisy. A carpet waited on the parking pad. Mrs. Bark waved by wiggling her fingers. Rye raised a hand. When Holly tried to slip out, Rye grabbed her arm.

"We're going to be late," Holly said belligerently.

"You could've told me," Rye said.

Holly shrugged. "Why? What difference would it make?"

"Don't you think it would've been polite to let me know you were going out?"

"You don't own me."

Rye mentally recoiled. "No, I don't."

"So, let me go. You're embarrassing me."

"Holly—"

Holly jerked free and darted out the door. Daisy Bark paused, looking uncomfortable, before she strode to the carpet. Rye fleetingly considered stalking out there and demanding that Holly return to the apartment. Was it time she reasserted herself? Or would that make it worse?

The carpet lifted and flew away.

"No, I don't own you," Rye said. "But it's my job to take care of you. It still is."

Rye closed the door and slumped to the floor. "It still is. Crap. What am I doing so wrong?"

Rye slid her fingers into her hair and clenched her fists so that the hairs pulled painfully at her scalp.

"Flora."

Rye wanted to be back then. Back at the start of their affair. Before the gifts and crap. When it was just them having sex and being together. Lying naked on the couch and having Flora stroke her wing membrane. Smelling Flora's hair. Forgetting that the rest of Infinity existed. Having someone love her. Having someone want her.

"Fey!"

Rye scrambled to her feet. This was not the way to solve anything. Why did she only remember the good stuff? They'd had insurmountable issues. It would never have worked. She'd better spend her time trying to solve real problems rather than daydreaming.

She had no idea what she was going to do about Holly. The problem was that matters were likely to get worse. Telling Holly that she did not have, nor could she get, an ident number wasn't going to be pretty. Holly would just have to send in the forms without it. Or not send in the forms at all.

If Holly hadn't been likely to get a scholarship, that would have been easier. But Flora was confident that she would succeed. Holly having a good career was exactly what Rye had been working for. The kid was counting on it.

Rye needed an ident number for her. The government way wasn't going to work. Where did that leave her?

Rye grabbed her jacket and went outside. She climbed on her broom and flew off toward the bridge.

Rye pushed into the smoke, stink, and noise of the Ball and Chain tavern. Music from a tinny sound system blared over the talking, laughing, and coughing. She threaded her way through the crowd of mostly men to get to the bar. She didn't see Knot.

"Beer." Rye shouted her order to the pixie behind the bar. "Knot Knapweed in?"

The bartender shoved a jar toward her, took her money, and nodded. Rye turned. She spied some of her workmates at one of the stand up tables.

"Hey, Rye!" Blackie said. "You finally got off the leash?"

Rye smiled fleetingly and eased in beside Knot. She waited for a lull in the disjointed conversation about some team before leaning closer to Knot.

"You know people who can get things, don't you?" she asked.

Knot's scalp ridges pulled closer together. "Depends on what sort of thing you're after."

"Some paperwork," Rye said.

"Official, like?"

"Yeah."

"Knot!" Budge called. "You tell Blackie he's talking shit!"

"Yeah, you're full of it," Knot said. He nodded to Rye to follow him.

Outside, Knot led her to a quiet, dark spot in the parking lot.

"What you after?" Knot said.

"I need a new ident number."

Knot's scalp ridges tightened. "You done time inside?"

"Something like that. You know where I can get one?"

"Maybe. It'll cost."

❖

Rye's wings couldn't get any flatter against her back as she steered her broom into Lichen Street. Most of the streetlamps were broken. Trees showed burned holes for windows. Stripped and burned out carpets littered the sidewalks. A drunk lay asleep near an overflowing dumpster. The shadows seemed watchful. The air smelled of poorly tuned engines and vibrated with lightly leashed violence.

Rye halted in front of the Magic Mushroom. The gambling bar's two tiny windows were barred and shuttered. She really didn't like the idea of leaving her broom out in the street, so she slung it on her shoulder and approached the door.

A tiny metal window snapped open. "What you want?"

"I've come to see Knife," Rye said.

"You a member?"

"I've got business with Knife," Rye said. "Knot Knapweed sent me. He knows Knife. Yeah?"

A shout carried down the street. Rye turned. She heard a scuffle, a crash, then nothing.

The door opened. Rye blinked in the sudden wash of light. She stumbled forward. A claw pressed her chest.

"Not that." The claw belonged to a bulky goblin with close-set yellow eyes and razor-blades piercing his huge, pointed grey ears. "Not inside."

Rye reluctantly set her broom down just outside the door. "It won't get stolen, will it?"

The goblin slammed the door shut.

"Right," Rye said.

She stood in a luridly decorated corridor with fake gilt on the wallpaper, but, oddly, a bare wooden floor. A tawdry, over-decorated door led off to the right. That was where the voices, laughter, and music came from. The place reeked of dreamweed smoke. Rye felt the doorkeeper's malevolent gaze on her.

"Um. Is Knife in there?" Rye asked.

"Back room."

"Right. Thanks."

Rye's wings ached from their defensive tightness. She could feel the goblin watching her. She climbed up a short set of steps and walked around a bend. She stood in a nearly dark dead end. Something scuttled across her foot. She knocked on the only door.

"If that's you, Slug, you can fuck off," a deep female voice called.

"No, I'm not Slug," Rye said.

"Who the fuck are you? Come in. Don't make me shout through the fucking door, you fucking idiot."

The thick smoke congealing the air made Rye cough and her eyes water. She blinked at the huge goblin woman in an improbable mauve negligee reclining on a sofa.

"I'm looking for Knife," Rye said.

"Shut that fucking door," Knife said. "Who the fuck are you?"

"Rye. A friend of Knot Knapweed's."

"That gap-tooth fucking toad owes me money. You got it?"

"I don't know about that. Sorry."

Knife's moist nostrils twitched. "What the fuck do you want, then?"

"Um. Knot said you could get me a new ident number."

Knife's ear tips rose and her eyelids lowered. "Did he?"

"Said you were the person to see."

Knife took a long bubbling pull from a hookah. When she exhaled, she shifted. Her negligee drew tight across her ample front. Rye had no idea that goblin women had so many nipples. The effect was not erotic.

"It'll cost," Knife said.

"Yeah. I figured. I need two. How much?"

"Seven hundred. Each."

Rye tried not to look dismayed. Knife didn't strike her as the sort to haggle. Well, she could do without one herself for now. She'd just get one for Holly. "Okay. When could I get the number?"

"After you give me the fucking money. I ain't no fucking charity. No money, no numbers. You got that?"

"Yeah. I got it. Okay. I'll...I'll get it and be back."

Rye turned. Her head was beginning to spin from the sickly sweet smoke. The door burst open and knocked her backward. She tripped on the carpet and landed on her backside.

"Hey, Knife! What the fuck?" A fat young goblin female with her pointed ears painted toxic green stared down in surprise at Rye.

"Get her off my fucking floor," Knife said. "What do you fucking want? Can't you see I'm busy?"

Rye was already rising when the young goblin grabbed her with strong claws and hauled her up. She gave Rye a hearty slap on the back. The blow caught Rye painfully on the top of her right wing bud and made her grunt.

"Hey!" The young goblin scowled at Rye. "What's on your back? You ain't hiding no weapons, are you?"

"Weapons?" Knife said.

The young female grabbed Rye before she could deny it, shoved her face-first against the wall, and roughly patted a claw over her back. "Fuck! This is just like that whiny fairy that was here. Them's wings, ain't they?"

"So, you're a fairy freak," Knife said.

Rye wanted to bolt. But the young female barred her way, and it was unlikely that the sleazy queen of the underworld would turn her over to the Immigration Service.

"They gonna send you back?" Knife said. "That why you need a new number? Your fucking lot don't like thems that get away, do they? Do some bad shit to the poor fuckers they get back, don't they? This makes it different. A big fat fucking difference. Numbers for fairies are two thou each."

"*What?*" Rye said. "Two thousand? But you just said seven hundred."

"Two thou," Knife said. "Or do you want to fucking argue and pay more, flying freak girl? Or maybe you want to go back home? To the prayers and whips."

Fey. "Two thousand. Okay."

As Rye closed the door behind her, she heard Knife chuckling.

❖

Rye lifted the jug to swallow some more beer. She still had a couple of hundred in savings, so she could afford to sell her broom for a bit less than she paid for it. She'd ask around at work tomorrow. She'd get Berry's number off Knot and ask him if he knew of anyone who was looking for a broom.

The door opened. Rye shot to her feet and strode to the hall. Holly glared at her.

"We need to talk," Rye said.

"I'm tired."

Holly strode to her bedroom. Rye stepped into the doorway to prevent Holly from slamming the door.

"I'm pretty tired, too," Rye said. "I'm tired of you pulling this shit. Don't you think you should have told me that you were going out?"

"Why?" Holly turned her back and began undressing. She threw her shoes at the wall.

"Because I'm your sister. Because I care about you. Because I'd worry myself stupid if you just walked out and I had no idea where you'd gone. Because I'd never forgive myself if anything happened to you. Because I'm getting tired of feeling like shit in my own home."

Holly rounded on her. "I never asked to be your sister! I never asked to live in this dump! I never asked to be a fucking fairy!"

"Oh, grow up! Life is shit! You deal with it. You don't whine about it! And you don't play stupid games!"

Rye slammed the door, stomped across to the living room and slammed that door, too. She sagged onto the couch. She had come that close to hitting Holly.

❖

Rye woke before her alarm. She dressed and trotted down to Cloudnut's All-Purpose Store. He let her have a couple of old newspapers free. She sat poring over the broom wanted ads while she drank her breakfast tea and ate a bowl of budget beech nut flakes. She heard Holly's alarm and continued with her reading. Holly's bedroom door opened. She paused before approaching the table and sitting.

"The play was scathing," Holly said.

"Yeah?"

"Frond Lovage is an astronomical actress. I bet the reviews will be white hot. Can I look?"

"This is yesterday's paper."

"Oh," Holly said. "You can see why everyone says that she's the best new shooting star. Daisy's mum was crying in the last act. It wouldn't have been so bad if she didn't keep blowing her nose really loud. Daisy and me wanted the earth to eat us whole."

"Sounds like you had a good time."

"I did."

"Good."

Rye stood and carried her bowl and empty mug to the sink. She grabbed her sandwiches for lunch and carried them into the hall.

Holly appeared in the kitchen doorway. "Rye?"

"What?"

"I guess I should've told you. About going to the play."

Rye stared at her. She looked sincere. "I would've appreciated that."

Holly folded her arms across her chest and frowned down at the floor.

Rye put her jacket back on the peg and walked toward Holly. "What's been going on?"

"That stuff you said about Fairyland. Is it true? Is that what would happen? Or did you make it up to scare me?"

Rye wanted to hug her. "It's not going to happen. You're not going back. I promise you."

"It's true, isn't it? I've been reading books about Fairyland. I never have before, because I thought someone would guess I was a fairy. But I've read every book about it in the school library now. And they do some horrible shit. But...but that stuff. Like you said. With...with the men. That isn't in any books."

Rye gently brushed an errant curl from Holly's face. "We're not there any more. Sure some of what happens is ugly. We wouldn't have run away from a terrific place to live, would we? But don't let it get to you, Holls. Yeah?"

Holly nodded. "Okay."

"Good. I've got to fly. You be good, yeah?"

"Yeah."

Rye pulled her jacket on, shouldered her work bag, and reached for the door.

"Rye? I saw Flora at the play."

Rye twisted around before she could stop herself. "Yeah?"

"She wasn't anywhere near us. She was in a VIP box. I don't think she saw me. She was wearing the most scathing gown. And this astronomical headdress."

Rye could imagine Flora looking gorgeous. Just like in that magazine article. With Frond Lovage, the star of the play. But Flora couldn't have lost her buds yet if she was still wearing stuff to partly cover her hair. Buds that she got for Rye.

Rye shut the front door with more force than she intended. It should not bother her that Flora was going out, or that she was dating other women. Rye had refused to keep seeing her. It was only natural that Flora continue her life. Hadn't she been seeing that Frond creature before?

Rye yanked the broom closet door open with a shriek of rusty hinges. She grabbed her broom and slammed the door.

"Rye?" Holly stood in the front doorway. "You haven't forgotten that I need that stuff filled in for my applications?"

"No. I haven't forgotten. It'll take me a couple of days, okay?"

"I have to send them in soon."

❖

"I'll keep my antennae tuned," Leek the sprite said. "If anyone asks about a broom, I'll tell them about you. Okay?"

"Yeah," Rye said. "Sure. Thanks."

She trudged back up two flights of unfinished stairs. Knot straightened from taking a measurement on the floor.

"Leek want your broom?" he asked.

"Nah." Rye shrugged and grabbed the shovel. "I'll keep looking. Someone is bound to want one."

Where could she find two thousand pieces? Perhaps Letty Elmwood might know of someone who needed a dinner cooking. That might be worth a shot. Holly would just have to wait a while. She hadn't said when the deadlines for the applications were. Perhaps they had a few weeks. It was worth a try.

At lunch, Rye ate a sandwich as she flew to Noonpine.

The Lightning Tree Gallery was quiet and calm. Rye wiped her hands on the back of her ragged work pants before she wandered inside. Celandine the unnerving sylph was nowhere to be seen. Rye heard voices from the mezzanine. One was Letty Elmwood's. Better not interrupt. Rye walked over to Flora's weaving. They had a fancy little plaque on the wall beside it now. *Flora Withe "You In Me."* There was no price.

Rye stared at the hanging. The pattern reminded her of the chaotic rainbow of coloured skeins beneath Flora as she lay naked on the mess on the floor of her workroom. Rye had never seen anyone as beautiful or as desirable. They had made love. Awed, amazed, and already deeply in love, Rye had peeled off her clothes to reveal herself as a fairy. Flora had not recoiled. Flora had reached out to touch her. Rye could feel the ghost of warm fingers on her wing membranes. She could feel Flora's breath just before they kissed. The press of Flora's lips. She could feel Flora's warm body in her arms. She could hear Flora's laugh. She smiled, because the echo of Flora's happiness made her happy. She had wiped away Flora's tears. She had shared Flora's laughter. She felt again that thrill, which was part surprise and part awe and part disbelief, that shook her every time she saw Flora again after a few days apart. It was as though Flora was still inside her: *You In Me*. Rye had thought most of it ripped out as she had watched Flora run across the park. But, as she stared at Flora's weaving, Rye felt it as strong as ever.

"Flora?"

Rye started. She jerked her head up to stare at the mezzanine. Her heart stopped. Flora stood at the railing looking down at her. Pale. Unsmiling. Watching her stare at the weaving inspired by their love.

"We should be going." Another dryad woman stepped close to Flora. "Flora?"

Flora kept staring down at Rye. Rye stared back. There was not another woman in Infinity like her. Would she read in Rye's gaze how Rye still yearned for her and loved her?

The strange dryad woman wandered out of sight. Letty Elmwood spoke. Flora reluctantly turned.

Rye watched. Everything else in Infinity ceased to exist. Flora was just up there. How long had she been standing there? Had she stood at the railing when Rye walked in and Rye had not noticed? Impossible. Rye would have seen her.

Flora walked away from the railing, but shortly reappeared at the top of the stairs. The other dryad walked behind her. With an unpleasant jolt, Rye recognised Frond Lovage. After a shocked moment, Rye's attention fixed back on Flora. Rye watched her walk down every step. Getting closer. Step by step. Apart from a couple of glances where she was treading, Flora returned Rye's stare. Flora looked like she was searching Rye's face for something.

At the bottom of the steps, Flora halted. Rye watched her. It was all she could do. There was only four paces between them. Infinity became just that short space keeping them apart. Flora glanced at her hanging then back at Rye. She looked like she was waiting for Rye to answer a question.

Every particle of Rye yearned across the gap. She imagined her soul tearing out of her body. It would stride those four paces. It would softly touch Flora's face. It would feel the warmth of her. It would smell that hint of pine sap. It would lightly and reverentially kiss her lips. Then it would fall to its knees and wrap its arms around Flora's waist and hold on as if it would never let her go.

"We really ought to be moving," Frond Lovage said. "You know how I loathe being late. Flora?"

Flora blinked and looked around, surprised, as if she'd completely forgotten the other dryad.

"I booked your favourite table." Frond walked to the door.

Flora glanced back at Rye. Rye hardly dared breathe. *I love you. I want you. I need you. I adore you. I don't care about all that other shit. I want to spend the rest of my life in your arms. Nothing in my life is right without you. Is there anything I can say or do that will persuade you to—*

"Your mother was very kind to send those flowers before last night's performance." Frond held the door open. "Flora? Is something wrong?"

She takes you to lunch at a restaurant and knows which is your favourite table? Your mother sends her flowers? A rising theatre star. Famous. Rich. Of course your parents approve of her. Magazine columnists want you two to be a couple. You deserve someone who can treat you right. Like she can. It's for the best. For both of us.

Flora cast a look at Rye. So sad. Rye's throat tightened with impending tears. *I love you!*

Flora strode to the door.

Rye watched her walk away. Again. Her heart ripped. Again.

Chapter Seventeen

Rye frowned at the packet in her hand. Her mind was blank. She had no idea what she had been intending to make for tea. She had better get herself thinking again before she called those two people Letty Elmwood had recommended that she contact about possible catering jobs. For a pretentious, over-dressed, overly made up sylph, Letty had been really nice to her at lunchtime. Not that Rye's recollection of their conversation was anywhere near complete. Her day had shattered shortly after she walked into the gallery.

"Want me to help?" Holly said.

"Um," Rye said. "Look, I'm not hungry. Can you get yourself something?"

"Yeah. You really don't look good. I could make you something."

"No. I'll be fine."

An hour later, Rye hung up the phone. Okay. Neither Mrs. Henbane-Wheat nor Mr. Mandrake had offered her a job, but both wanted to talk to discuss menus. If only one of them offered her a job, that would be decent money.

"You going to do some more cooking?" Holly asked.

"Yeah. Maybe. I have to go and discuss menus and stuff."

"You should ask Flora to help you," Holly said.

Rye scowled.

"She helped you with Ms. Elmwood's dinner, didn't she?" Holly said.

Rye fiddled with her pencil. "Ms. Withe is a busy lady. She's got more important things to do than waste her time talking to me." The pencil snapped.

"Waste? When did Flora become Ms. Withe? What are you talking about?"

Rye dropped the pencil halves and stood. "I need a shower. Did you leave me a towel?"

Holly frowned at Rye and trailed her out into the hall. "Are you acting like the last dreg in the bottom of a bucket because you and Flora have argued? Did you do something stupid to—"

"Holly!" Rye shoved the door open. "Ms. Withe was very friendly and kind and generous to us both for a while. For which we are both grateful. I am not going to bother her about this dinner thing or anything else, okay?"

For a dangerous moment, Holly looked like she intended to retort. But she gave Rye a filthy look then strode into her bedroom with an exaggerated shrug of her shoulders.

Rye chewed her lip as she stripped. Did Holly have any idea that she and Flora had been lovers? Surely not. Rye had been so careful. Flora had said that she hadn't betrayed them. Rye peeled off her tight T-shirt and drew an unrestricted breath. She stepped into the warm shower and eased her wings out from their daylong tight fold.

Holly probably wanted her to be friends with Flora because Flora was a famous weaver. Holly derived a lot of kudos with her friends from her connection with Flora. And Flora had been kind and encouraging to Holly. Of course Holly liked her. It made sense that she would want Rye and Flora to be friends. No need to panic. There was no reason to think that Holly suspected anything. Not that there was now.

"No. Don't think about that." Rye scrubbed shampoo into her hair. "Think about food. Cooking. Menus. Money. And how you're actually going to get that fucking goblin two thousand pieces. You're going to do it. The kid is going to get an ident number and be safe. Just like you promised her."

❖

The next evening, Rye let herself into the apartment and flicked on the lights. She found a note on the kitchen table.

Rye! Flora called. She wants you to call her back tonight. Holly.

Rye frowned as she fingered the note. What could Flora possibly want to talk to her about? Surely they had said it all? This wouldn't be some stupid trick of Holly's to get her to phone Flora, would it?

"Fey."

Rye strode into the hall and quickly dialled Flora's mobile number.

"Rye!" Flora said. "Thank you for calling."

Rye felt that familiar exhilarated rush at the sound of Flora's voice which was so inappropriate now. "Um. Sure. I got a note from Holly. You called?"

"Yes." Pause. "I'm not sure how to tell you this."

Rye frowned. That was not a good way to start a conversation. "Tell me what? Is this about the gallery? Look, I wouldn't have been there if I'd known."

"No, it's not about that," Flora said. "I know you're going to be hurt. And I hate to do it to you. But I can't not tell you."

Rye's frown deepened to a scowl. What could possibly be this bad? Flora was getting married to Frond Lovage? Oh, no. Not that. Please. "What...what's wrong?"

"I'm guessing that you don't read many women's magazines."

"Magazines? No. Why?"

"This week's copy of *Hedgerow*," Flora said. "Page thirty. You ought to take a look."

"Why?"

"This sort of nuisance happens occasionally. No one really pays any attention to it. Teenage girls do not read *Hedgerow*. Holly will not have seen it. I would bet large sums on that."

"Seen what? Babe, what are you talking about?"

"Oh, branch," Flora said. "There's a picture of us in the gossip section. Listen, Holly won't have seen it and they don't name you."

"Picture?"

"Yes. A photograph. Of us kissing."

"What?"

Rye dropped the phone and bolted for the front door. She scrambled down seven flights of stairs two and three at a time. She hurtled across the street to Cloudnut's All-Purpose Store, but skidded to a stop in time. She couldn't go in there to buy a magazine. Holly was working in there.

Rye ran down the street to the hypermart. She stood sweating and panting in front of the magazine rack. *Hedgerow*? She grabbed a copy of the glossy magazine. Page what? Rye flicked past advertisements, a story about a famous woman and her pet moths, the latest diet, cosmetic tips, more and more advertisements.

"Oh, fuck."

Rye stared. Page thirty. Top centre, under the heading Needle's Eye. The photograph showed her and Flora kissing.

"That's my favourite magazine."

Rye started, jerked the magazine closed, and stared at a squat gnome woman who smiled at her through a wispy white beard.

"They have the nicest stories, don't they?" The gnome grabbed the last copy of *Hedgerow* and dropped it into her shopping trolley.

Rye strode away to the cashiers. She was so stunned that she didn't even blink at handing over five pieces.

Outside, Rye opened *Hedgerow* to page thirty.

> *A hot favourite to be one of this year's* ***Golden Spindle*** *nominees, it looks like* ***Flora Withe*** *is engaged in another successful project. The whisper about ShadeForest City was that* ***Frond Lovage*** *was the inspiration for sexy Flora's sizzling new weaving. The stage sensation currently wowing fans and critics alike in her latest role in the* ***Cumin Bugloss*** *play* ***Second Time Loss*** *was also tipped to be responsible for* ***Flora*** *suddenly sporting a stylish range of hats. Yes, ladies, a reliable source confirms that the dryad weaving star has something to hide:* ***Buds****! True love is in the hair for the thirty-three year old only child of banking magnate* ***Bark Withe*** *and his society hostess wife,* ***Hazel****. But move over,* ***Frond****! Our ever sharp Eye has snapped this romantic moment. Who is* ***Flora Withe's Mystery Budmate****? The Eye will keep searching for the answer to this exciting secret.*

"Crap."

Rye trudged back to her apartment in a daze. She set *Hedgerow* on the kitchen table and opened it to the offending page. The photograph was crisp and clear and unmistakably them. But how? How could anyone have seen them kiss?

They stood in front of a sapling. Flora had worn that hat the time they had met in the park to finally and irrevocably break off their relationship. The irony! The stupid magazine called that a romantic moment. If that sneaky photographer had waited just a little longer, he might have had a very different picture. Flora fleeing in tears and Rye standing heartbroken.

Where had the bastard been? Lurking in some bush?

Rye put a hand to her forehead. "The bloody ball game."

There had been photographers covering the games. One had only to turn around and zoom in. Rye slumped.

Eventually, she heard a strange buzzing hum. The phone hung off the hook. She carried the phone into the kitchen, set it beside *Hedgerow*, and dialled.

"Rye?" Flora said. "Have you seen it?"

"Yeah."

"I'm sorry. But it may not be as bad as you fear. *Hedgerow* doesn't have a huge circulation. And it's only a gossip column snippet. Rye?"

Rye sighed. "Fey."

"Holly will not read *Hedgerow*. Do you hear me? Their audience is middle-aged women with a reasonable discretionary spending capacity, insecurities about their age, increasing waistlines, and an intense interest in other people's intimate relationships. Rye? You're not panicking?"

"No. I'm—Shit!"

Rye dropped the handset and darted into the lounge. She tugged the old magazine out from under the sofa cushion. Daisy Bark's mother had given Holly this. Rye flicked hurriedly back to the front page. *Hedgerow*.

"Crap."

Rye dragged herself back to the kitchen and dropped into a chair.

"Rye? Are you still there?"

"Yeah. She'll see it."

Pause. "Okay. Even if she does, it might not be a disaster. Holly has probably already guessed about us. This may not be any surprise to her. Have you considered that possibility?"

The front door handle lifted.

"Fey," Rye whispered. "She's home. I have to go."

Rye hung up. She grabbed *Hedgerow* and shoved it in the oven.

"It's me," Holly called.

"Um. In here. I'm just going to start dinner."

While Rye cooked, Holly chatted about something that happened at school and a very strange customer in the store. Rye's fear that Holly had leafed through *Hedgerow* magazine in the store failed to blossom into reality.

"Are you planning on seeing Daisy tomorrow?" Rye asked.

"No. One of her cousins is getting married. Her whole family has gone to CopseLake City for it."

Rye mentally let out a sigh of relief. Mrs. Bark would be too busy to read her *Hedgerow* for a day or two.

"I'm going to crash," Holly said. "Oh, did you finish those forms yet?"

"Um. Getting your ident number will take a little while longer. These government things take time."

Holly frowned. "Can't you do something? It's been weeks."

"I'm trying my hardest. Trust me."

"I have three deadlines at the end of next week."

"Oh. Really?"

"Yeah," Holly said. "Two of them are the scholarships I'm most likely to get. Flora said so. I really, really don't want to miss out. I finished all the other stuff and that stupid essay eons ago."

"I know. I'm sorry. I'm doing my best."

Rye waited until Holly was safely in her room before retrieving *Hedgerow* from the stove. She shut the living room door and sat at her desk. She glanced at her scribbling for menu plans. Getting a cooking job or two had looked so promising, but there was no way she was going to get both jobs paid in advance by the end of next week.

Much as she hated to do it, Rye was going to have to tell Holly that she couldn't put in any applications yet. Holly was not going to like that. Just when they'd returned to talking to each other. Rye let her head fall into her hands. Life was shit. Just as she'd told Holly.

Rye sighed, shut her notebooks, undressed, and climbed into bed. She opened *Hedgerow*. The photograph jarred her nerves at first. The more she stared at it, though, the more it grew on her. So that's what Flora looked like when she was being kissed. If only Rye didn't know how miserable they both were at the moment the camera had captured them. Why didn't that show?

Rye lay awake unable to sleep. Holly was going to learn that she was gay and had had an affair with Flora. The magazine reading world had a photograph of Rye Woods to study. What if someone recognised her as a fairy? With her wings hidden most people couldn't tell, but what if they had specialist illegal immigrant hunters in the Immigration Service who were trained to spot disguised fairies? One of them idly flicking through her *Hedgerow* could see the picture. Or, perhaps, that new ambassador from Fairyland, the one who'd been a priestess; maybe she read *Hedgerow*. Glossy magazines were probably some form of evil, but anyone who was sent outside Fairyland to live as a representative must be regarded as holy enough to resist the lures of consumerism, frivolity, and vanity. Maybe they even had people at the embassy whose job it was to scour papers and magazines looking for escaped fairies.

That final kiss had sealed the end of her affair with Flora. It might be the end of Rye Woods.

❖

Late on Fifth Day morning, Rye steered her broom up the ascending lane to the seventh floor and then around to the parking pad outside her apartment. She unlocked the door and carried the first bags of groceries inside.

"Holls? Are you back yet?"

Holly's room was quiet and empty. Rye set the shopping on the kitchen table and went outside for the remainder. As she put her broom away, a chubby, green-skinned gremlin man trotted around from the neighbour's landing. He was dressed well enough to look out of place against the second-hand, worked-in look of this neighbourhood, but his clothes were nowhere near the expensive, tailored trendiness of Flora's area.

"Hello there!" He waved a small green claw at her. "Good morning, ma'am. Do I have the pleasure of talking with Ms. Rye Woods?"

Rye frowned as she bent to pick up her last shopping bags. "Who is asking?"

He pulled out a card striped with the colours of the rainbow and offered it to her despite her not having a free hand. "Spike Spignel, ma'am. *Rainbow's End* magazine."

Magazine? The scowl she skewered him on sprang from a mixture of disbelief and dread.

"Our readers take an avid and natural interest in the lives of celebrities," Spike said. "Your relationship with Flora Withe would—"

"Fuck off."

Rye stepped past him, dropped her bags on the hall floor, and turned to shut the door. Spike threw his shoulder against it.

"Ma'am! I've got a great offer for you. If you'll—"

"If you don't get out of my doorway, I'll knock you out."

"*Rainbow's End* would like—"

Rye shoved the door and knocked the little gremlin back. She thumped the door shut and slid the bolt into place. *Fey.* Someone had seen that photograph of her and Flora and not only managed to identify Rye but had found where she lived. What else had they discovered about her?

Spike knocked. "Our readers would like to know the story of you and Flora Withe! Ma'am? If you give *Rainbow's End* an exclusive interview—"

"Fuck off! Leave me alone."

"Two thousand pieces, ma'am!"

Rye frowned. Two thousand?

"Ms. Woods? Oh. Hello, Miss. Do you know Ms. Woods?"

"Rye?" Holly said. "Yes. She's my sister."

Rye slammed the bolt back and yanked the door open. Holly stood looking down at the journalist. Rye stomped out and grabbed the gremlin's jacket.

"Listen to me," Rye said. "You leave me and my family alone."

"Rye?" Holly said.

"Go inside," Rye said. "Shut the door."

"But what—"

"Do as I say," Rye said.

"Ms. Woods," Spike Spignel said. "I enjoy face to face interviews, but this—"

"Shut up," Rye said. "You listen to me, you annoying green fuck. You go away. You do not return. You do not try to contact me or any of my family again. Do you hear? Or should I punch you another ear hole in the front of your head?"

"Really, Ms. Woods. There's no need for any unpleasantness."

Rye dragged him to the railing and lifted him. "You want to talk? Okay. Let's do it at the bottom."

"Aah!" Spike grabbed for the railing. His skin paled to an unhealthy grey-green. "Ma'am! Ms. Woods. Please!"

Rye let him drop back onto the landing. "If you don't want to go that way, use the stairs. Want me to help you down them?"

Spike backed away. "Look, Ms. Woods, *Rainbow's End* can—"

Rye reached for him. Spike scuttled away and tripped down half a flight of stairs.

Rye stomped back to her door. She saw Holly at the window. Several neighbours watched. A tall, skinny pixie youth took a smoke from his lips and raised a fist in salute to Rye.

"Slick, bud! Very slick."

Rye ignored him. She bolted the door and leaned back against it. She felt like a noose was tightening around her neck.

The phone rang.

"I'll get it," Holly shouted from the living room.

Rye strode the few paces to snatch up the handset first.

"Hello? Am I speaking to Ms. Rye Woods?" a strange female voice asked.

"Who are you?" Rye asked.

"I'm Violet Orris. I write for *The Weekly Spore* magazine. I was hoping to talk to Ms. Rye Woods about interviewing her for—"

"Go away and don't ever call me again. Do you hear?"

Rye hung up.

"Who was that?" Holly asked.

"Wrong number."

The phone rang again. Rye grabbed the cord and yanked it out of the wall. Holly stared. Rye brushed past her on her way into the living room. She pulled the shade across the window. Her wings were so defensively tight that the muscles across her chest ached.

"What's going on?" Holly said. "Who was that man?"

Rye could feel part of her mind shutting down, just like before one of her panic attacks. But she couldn't do that. She needed to think things through. It might not be as bad as she feared. That reporter had been interested in the sleaze about her and Flora, but he'd made no mention of her being a fairy.

"Rye? You're acting way too strange. Are you on something?"

"Um. It's just some stuff."

"Really? I wouldn't have guessed. I'm so used to seeing you threaten to toss guys off the tree that I can't think why I'm mentioning it."

"Look. Just give me a minute. I have to think."

"Are you about to have a heart attack or something?"

That gremlin had offered her two thousand pieces. With that, she would be able to afford an ident number for Holly from Knife the goblin. But if she talked about her and Flora, the additional exposure would be putting her in that much more danger of discovery by the government. Still, if Holly had a number, she'd be safe. Wouldn't she?

What a shitty thing to do to Flora. And the priestesses would use her confession of a homosexual affair against her when they dragged her back to Fairyland. It would be there in print with glossy photographs. Whatever other punishments they'd dish out for her having fled the country would be nothing to trying to cure her of eleven years worth of evil.

"Are you in some kind of trouble?" Holly asked.

"Crap." Rye banged the heel of her hand against her forehead.

Holly would not be safe. If the government people got around to checking out Rye's immigration status and shipping her back to Fairyland, they'd be able to smell out a fake ident number.

"Rye? What's going on? Who was that guy? Why did you freak out on the phone?"

"I have to keep you safe," Rye said.

"Safe? From what? That runty gremlin guy?"

Rye slumped on the sofa. She could imagine the next headline: Flora Fucks Illegal Alien. Nothing Rye might do could stop it. The darkness pressed in all around her. She could see no path out. She had ground to a standstill. The trap had sprung shut on her.

"Rye? I'm beginning to imagine all sorts of tragic shit."

Rye sighed and sagged. "I'm all out of ideas. I've failed you."

"I don't understand. Failed what?"

Rye felt a hundred years old and so very weary. "You can't apply for those scholarships. I'm sorry."

"*What?*" Holly glared down at Rye.

"You don't have a citizen ident number. Because you're not a citizen. I'm sorry."

"What the fuck?"

"I thought you'd be safe when you got your wings."

"Safe? What do you mean?"

"I thought you'd get your citizenship when you became an adult," Rye said. "That's how it works in Fairyland. But it doesn't work that way here. None of our relatives in Fairyland can claim you back once you get your wings, but what I didn't realise was that you don't get your citizenship here then. So, you're not really safe from deportation. I only found out the other day."

Holly set fists on her hips and scowled. "You didn't bother asking before? I wasn't important enough?"

"I thought I knew the answer. And there are some things that I find hard to do. Like talk to immigration."

"Hard? You find it hard? What about me? It doesn't matter to you that I can't get a scholarship and do what I want for the rest of my life?"

"I suppose I should have told you before."

"Fucking right you should've told me!" Holly shook her fists. "How could you let me think everything was okay? You promised me!"

"I know I did," Rye said. "And I tried. I really did."

"I don't believe this! You've ruined my life!"

"I thought you'd be safe when you got your wings."

"I don't want fucking wings! I don't want to be a fucking fairy freak! I want to be normal! I want to make something of myself. Not like you. But you've ruined all that, haven't you? I hate you!"

Holly stormed into her bedroom and slammed the door. She screamed with rage and frustration. Something heavy thumped against the wall. Her music blared into loud life. Rye slumped face down on the couch. So this was what it felt like when your world shattered around you.

Rye didn't know how long she lay there. Holly's music blasted through songs. Blank hopelessness played through Rye's head. Someone knocked on the door. Rye ignored it. She got up and walked into the kitchen. She grabbed a jug of beer from a grocery bag and dropped into a chair. Life 1, Rye 0. Okay. But the game wasn't over. She and Holly weren't in Fairyland yet. There was no evidence that anyone had identified them as fairies.

After Rye finished her beer, she frowned at Holly's bedroom door and sighed. She had to talk to her about this.

"Holly?" Rye pounded the door. "Holly? We need to talk."

"Fuck off."

Rye shoved the door open. Holly lay curled up on her bed. She hugged Mr. Bumble, a faded old stuffed toy which she'd had since she'd been a little girl. Rye's heart hurt. She lowered herself to the side of the bed and saw that Holly had been crying. When Rye leaned across to turn the music volume down, Holly didn't object. Rye stroked Holly's shoulder. Mr. Bumble's black button eye stared up at her.

"I never meant to hurt you, Holls," Rye said. "Never that. I'm sorry."

"I'm scared."

Rye brushed blue-black curls away from Holly's face. "We're not going back. I've been thinking. Nobody from immigration or the government knows about us. I'm sure of it. So, I think we can make it right."

"How?"

"Well, I talked to this woman in the Immigration Service. There are different ways they can make you a citizen."

"Like what?"

"You can be a refugee," Rye said. "Apparently that's common with fairies."

Holly sat up. "So, why don't I become a refugee now?"

"Well, it's complicated. We'd need to hire a lawyer."

"Fey. How could you afford that?"

"I'll find a way," Rye said. "I'll cook more dinners. Don't worry about that for now. But even with a lawyer doing the application and stuff, it'll take time."

"I need to send those scholarship forms in!"

Rye sighed. "I know. But you can send them in next year, can't you?"

Holly looked horrified. "Next year? Another year at that limping school? No way!"

"Maybe I've tried to protect you from this stuff for too long. Think about the alternatives. Would another year at school be worse than the rest of your life back in Fairyland?"

Holly scowled down at Mr. Bumble. "That reeks."

"Yeah. Welcome to adulthood."

Holly flashed her a resentful glare. "What are the other ways I could become a citizen? Would they be faster? And cheaper?"

"Um. What did she say? You're not old enough to get married." Rye straightened one of Mr. Bumble's antennae. "And no one but me likes you enough to want to adopt you. So, I guess you're stuck with me and with school for a year."

"I could get someone to adopt me? I could ask Daisy's mum. Or Flora! Yeah, I bet she'd adopt me."

Rye was surprised how much that felt like a stinging slap in the face. "We'll get a lawyer. Get your application in. Then you'll be safe and have your ident for next year's scholarships, okay? You don't have to be afraid of anything. Okay?"

"Can you imagine how scathing it would be if Flora adopted me?"

"Can you forget Flora and pay attention? I'm trying to tell you that we're going to be okay. But if the absolute worst happened, we could run away again. So, there's no need to fret."

"Run away? But that wouldn't solve anything, would it? We'd just be illegal aliens in some other country."

Rye shrugged. "If we had to, we'd do it. That's all I'm saying."

"This reeks." Holly frowned. "But, then, who was that guy? The one you threatened to throw over the railing?"

Crap. "Um. Just a guy."

Holly leaped off the bed and strode into the hall.

"Holly! Wait!" Rye darted into the hall to see Holly at the front door. "Don't go out!"

Holly picked the rainbow striped card off the floor. "Spike Spignel. *Rainbow's End* magazine? That's one of those trashy gossip magazines. Why would a journalist leave his card under our door?"

"Um."

"Shit!" Holly's eyes snapped wide. "They've found out that we're fairies. That's why you're all so panicked about us getting sent—"

"No! It's not that."

Holly scowled. "Then what is it? The only interesting thing about you is that you're a fairy."

Rye bit her lip and ran a hand through her hair. It failed to spark any inspiration.

"Flora," Holly said.

Rye's heart sank. "Um."

"It's because you know Flora. She's famous."

"Um. Yeah. They...they want me to tell them things about Flora. They found out somehow that we were friends. I don't understand how that would be interesting, but...but they're offering me money to do it."

Holly's face twisted with disgust. "What dregs! How could anyone think—Rye! You're not! You wouldn't do that to Flora?"

"No," Rye said. "I sent him away. They started calling, too. That's why I pulled the phone. Look, I think we would be best lying low and letting them forget us."

"You expect me to stay locked up in here all day? But shouldn't we be out doing something? Like getting a lawyer?"

"Holls, please. One day won't kill us. Will it? Please."

Holly looked unconvinced, but she slouched back into her bedroom and turned her music up. Rye pulled her bedroom door shut.

Rye sat at her desk and looked over her notes for menu plans. She found it impossible to concentrate. For all her assurances to Holly, she could not shake the feeling of a noose. She still had not told Holly the whole truth. She had not admitted that her own application for refugee status would founder because she was a wanted criminal.

❖

For the sixth time, someone pounded on the front door. Rye glared as if she could see through the intervening wall. She wanted to stomp out there and beat the shit out of whoever it was.

Shortly after the knocking stopped, Holly opened the living room door. She looked excited. "Rye? I've been thinking. You could get us ident numbers today. You can buy everything if you know the right people."

Having tried this method herself, Rye was unsurprised at the suggestion. "No. That's not the answer."

"But why not? I bet we could find someone around here or the burrowers to sell us ones."

"If you get caught with a fake ident, you can kiss your citizenship application goodbye. And those scholarship people wouldn't be very eager to give money to a girl with a criminal record."

Holly scowled. "You stomp on everything I want to do, don't you?"

"Only the stupid stuff."

Holly stormed back into her bedroom and turned her music up even louder. That and the occasional pounding on the door made Rye feel like a cornered animal cowering at the back of her cage. It didn't help her to shore up the belief that she was on top of her problems.

Chapter Eighteen

Rye fetched herself another beer. She usually didn't drink more than one a day, but this was an extraordinary morning.

Holly's music momentarily blasted louder. Her bedroom door shut again. Rye listened. The bathroom door opened and shut.

Rye swallowed some of her beer and noticed that she'd doodled Flora's name all over her notebook. If only she had really been the bogle-brownie mixed-breed person she passed herself off as rather than the fairy she was. If only she were not an illegal immigrant. If only she had been some rich, talented, famous person who knew which was Flora's favourite table at the restaurant. If only she had not kissed Flora in the park.

Rye sighed. That music was getting irritating.

Rye went into the hall to knock on Holly's door. "Holls? Can you please turn that down? It's bad enough that we're stuck in here without driving each other mad. Holls?"

Rye opened the door. The room was empty. She turned the sound volume down.

About an hour later, Rye knocked on the bathroom door. "Holls? I'm busting for a pee."

No reply.

Rye tried the door. It wasn't locked, so she pushed it open. The room was empty. Devoid of not only Holly but any steam from a shower or bath. There were no wet towels on the floor or Holly's discarded clothes draped over the towel rack.

"Crap. No. She wouldn't."

Rye darted into the hall. The front door bolt had been slid back. Rye strode outside. Of course, Holly was nowhere to be seen.

Rye knelt to mend the phone cord. She dialled the Barks' number.

No one answered. She belatedly remembered Holly telling her that they'd gone to a wedding.

Rye strode into Holly's bedroom. Holly's privacy be damned. She rummaged through the books and notes on Holly's desk. She had to have a list of her friends' phone numbers. Rye yanked the drawers open. She found a dog-eared little notebook. It contained addresses, phone numbers, and cryptic comments about Holly's friends. *Moss F. 645-239. Cute. CTWE!! MM?? Kissed!!!! First time?*

Rye dropped onto Holly's bed. First time did not refer to being kissed. Rye knew that for a fact. First time must mean sex. Holly had had sex with this boy Rye had never met? Other girls Holly's age were sexually active, but Rye had not imagined that Holly would have lost her virginity by now. She had not thought of Holly as beyond handholding and kissing. She seemed so young. She did not have her wings. Fairy women didn't go to the men until they had their wings. But this was not Fairyland.

"Fey."

At least Holly would not be in danger of an unwanted pregnancy. That could not happen until she finished her physical development, as signalled by the appearance of her wings. But what about diseases? Had Rye covered that in her inarticulate, acutely embarrassed discussion about sex? Had Holly been listening?

"No point worrying about this now. I've got to find her. We can worry about sex later."

Rye phoned Moss's number. His mother told her that he was not home. He'd gone out early this morning. She did not know when he might be back. No, she had not seen Holly Woods.

Rye returned Holly's notebook to the drawer. Mr. Bumble watched her from the bed. Rye sat and picked him up.

"I bought you for her at a second-hand shop. She loved you. She wouldn't let you out of her sight for years. You had to sleep with us every night. She cried when she couldn't find you. She told you everything. Does she still tell you things? No? Me neither."

Rye sighed and smoothed one of Mr. Bumble's bent wings.

"Where did we go wrong, Mr. B? How did I make a complete mess of my life? All I ever tried to do was make things right. I tried so hard. I couldn't give her everything I wanted to. I thought I'd given her what she needed. But it turns out I didn't even manage to keep her safe."

Rye set Mr. Bumble on Holly's pillow.

"I can fix it, can't I? I have to."

Rye sagged back onto Holly's bed and stared up at the ceiling. A patch of fungus grew up there.

"Flora. I loved her so much. I still do. More than anything in Infinity." Rye threaded her hands into her hair and tugged. "Not more than Holly. Different. Do you understand, Mr. B? I never felt so good about myself as when I was with Flora. I was happy when I made her happy. It killed me to see her cry. Being with her on those Fifth Day mornings was like stepping into a different world. A happy one."

Rye frowned.

"I'm proud of Holly. And I love her to death. I'd do anything for her. But Flora..."

Rye sighed and turned her head to look at Mr. Bumble.

"Am I ever going to find someone else remotely like her? Something died in me in that gallery when I watched her walk out with that Frond."

The phone rang.

Rye leaped off the bed and dashed into the hall to snatch up the phone. "Hello?"

"Hello, ma'am. I'm trying to get in touch with Ms. Rye Woods," a strange female voice said.

"And who the fuck would you be?"

Pause. "I'm Constable Maple, ma'am, from the Hollowberry Police Station. Would you be, or know the whereabouts of, Ms. Rye Woods?"

Rye could feel her eyes widen with shock. Police?

"Hello?" Constable Maple said. "Ma'am? Are you still there?"

"Um." Rye swallowed with difficulty. "Yeah."

"We found this contact number for Miss Holly Woods. I really need to find Rye Woods because—"

"Holly? Oh, shit. Is she okay? Has anything happened to her?"

"You are Ms. Rye Woods?"

"Yes! Yes, I'm Rye. Holly's sister. Please. What has happened?"

"Holly is currently being held in the Youth Section at Hollowberry Police Station."

"Held?"

"She was a passenger in a carpet which was involved in a traffic incident. She—"

"A crash? She's hurt?"

"No, ma'am," Constable Maple said. "Your sister was in the back. She was unharmed. However, she is intoxicated and some of the occupants of the carpet were found in possession of certain restricted substances."

Rye sagged against the wall with a hand to her head. Drunk. Drugs. Fuck. She would kill Holly for this.

"She was using drugs?" Rye asked.

"Miss Woods did not have any restricted substances about her person," Constable Maple said. "Though her proximity to others so in possession will require her to undergo a course about drug abuse. This will all be explained to you at the station, ma'am. We need you to come to pick up Holly."

"Yeah, of course."

Rye set the handset down. Holly drunk and in a carpet full of idiots who were doing drugs! What the fuck was she thinking? And now she was at a police station. Rye's chest tightened. She drew a restricted breath. They would take all sorts of details. Her species? If Holly was drunk, would she tell the usual story or would she blurt out the truth? And ident number. The police would want that.

"Crap."

Rye's hands shook as she put her jacket on. Her body moved reluctantly as if some back part of her brain was sending secret, panicked instructions to her limbs not to go anywhere near the police.

She climbed on her broom and flew off down the street. She remained in the low, slow lane. She tried talking to herself in an effort to keep calm. Slow, even breathing. She wiped sweaty palms on her thighs.

The kauri tree had Municipal Police engraved across the front and highlighted in bright orange lights. She, Rye Woods, illegal alien, had to walk in there, amongst all those police, and get her sister back. Rye could hear her own breathing. Shallow and fast. Her primitive survival instincts tried to elbow aside her rational self. The organism that was Rye craved safety. Every fibre of her being wanted to turn around and flee.

A pair of police pixies came out the door. Rye flinched. They walked past without giving her a glance. Rye's heart hammered so hard that it might break out of her chest.

"Holly," Rye whispered.

She took a deep breath and strode down the narrowing tunnel of her vision to the door.

A sprite woman in a police uniform stood behind a large desk. Doors with hand pad locks were the only way out of the foyer apart from the main doors. Posters on the walls recommended ways to deter burglary, shoplifting, and carpet theft.

"Can I help you, ma'am?" the spite asked.

"Um." Rye clenched her fists tight enough to dig her short fingernails into her palms. "Um. I got a call. About...about my sister. Holly Woods. I've come to take her home."

"Is she being held, ma'am? Is that what you mean?"

"Um. Yeah. Youth Section."

"Okay, ma'am. Let me just check."

Rye chewed her lip and sweated while the sprite tapped something beneath the level of the desk. The main doors opened. Rye started. A couple of brownies came to stand behind her. She forced her hands to unclench. Stay calm.

"Here we are," the sprite policewoman said. "Holly Woods. Ma'am? Are you feeling okay? Perhaps you'd like to sit?"

"Um. No, thanks. I'm fine. I have to take Holly home. Where is she?"

The sprite's antennae twitched. "I've notified one of the officers in the Youth Section. He'll be here shortly, ma'am."

"Oh. Right. Thanks."

Rye stepped aside and let the brownies talk to the woman at the desk. She sweated profusely. The veins in her neck throbbed uncomfortably. But she could conquer this. For Holly.

One of the locked doors opened. A tall bogle policeman stepped out. "Ms. Woods? I'm Sergeant Rivers, ma'am. If you'd like to come this way."

He held the door open for her. Rye did not want to go any deeper inside the station. Not past locked doors. But she had no choice. Holly needed her.

"Holly isn't in very much trouble, ma'am," he said.

"She...she's a good kid."

"I'm sure she is. We see this sort of event all too frequently. A group of teenagers together."

He said more, but Rye found it hard to concentrate. She walked past desks at which uniformed people sat. Some glanced at her. Her wing muscles hurt. She was feeling light-headed. Her breathing would not slow down.

"Here, ma'am." Sergeant Rivers pointed to a chair. "If you'll take a seat. We just need a few details from you."

"I thought—" She could feel her brain shutting down. "Holly. I...I came to take...to take her home."

"Ma'am? Are you feeling all right? Please sit. I'll fetch you some water."

"No. I...I want Holly."

"Of course," Sergeant Rivers said. "She's not under arrest. We're only holding her because she's intoxicated. But there are some details we need about her, ma'am. Her full address, citizen ident number, date of birth—"

His other words slipped into sounds without meaning. Rye tried hard to concentrate, but thinking was so hard.

"Ma'am? Why don't you sit down? Should I ask the apothecary to come here? You're really not looking so good." Sergeant Rivers put a hand on Rye's shoulder.

Rye hit him. Her mind blanked.

Chapter Nineteen

Ms. Woods? Are you back with us at last?"

Rye peeled open her eyes. She lay on her side. A young gremlin woman peered down at her.

"How are you feeling?" the gremlin asked.

Rye didn't feel anything. Neither surprise, nor curiosity, nor much of her body.

"We'll soon have you up and about again." The gremlin wore a nurse's green tunic almost the same shade as her skin. She fiddled with something near the end of the bed.

Rye noted the rails on the side of the bed, the empty cleanliness of the room, and the antiseptic smell. This must be an infirmary. When she tried to take stock of herself, she discovered stiffness. Every muscle ached and protested at her slightest move. What, in the name of the Almighty King and Queen of the Fey, had she done? The brown chitinous cast on her right arm jogged no memories of how she had broken it. When she rolled onto her back, her right wing bud screamed with pain. Rye gasped and awkwardly rolled back onto her side.

A tall, lithe banshee woman wearing a doctor's red tunic entered. Very attractive. Though not a match for Flora. "Good afternoon, Ms. Woods. I'm Doctor Trefoil. How are you feeling?"

"Um. Confused."

The doctor catalogued Rye's broken arm, snapped wing supports, and miscellaneous contusions.

"Is that why I feel so stiff?" Rye asked.

"You reacted badly to the standard antidote to the police stinger."

"What?"

Rye listened with incredulity as the doctor explained, in not always straightforward language, that she had been brought into the infirmary four days ago from a police station. The police had stuck her in the back of the thigh with the stinger they used to immobilise violent perpetrators. Something in her fairy metabolism had reacted adversely with the antidote that the doctors had administered to reverse the stinger. That had sent her into some weird fever and left her unconscious for those four days.

"Police station?" Rye said. "Why was I at a police station?"

"I'm afraid you'll have to ask the police that."

Rye cooperated passively with the doctor's examination. Police station? Fey. What had she done?

After the doctor left, Rye lay frowning at the tips of her fingers protruding from her cast. What had happened? What could she remember doing last? That annoying gremlin reporter? No. She'd argued with Holly.

Rye went cold.

"No," she whispered. Not Holly. Anything but that. Don't let me have hurt her.

Rye squeezed her eyes shut and saw her mother lying dead at her feet.

"No!"

Rye shoved herself upright. Her muscles shrieked protest. She awkwardly jerked the sheet aside one-handed. The railings on the side of the bed made it difficult and uncomfortable to climb out. Her feet hit the floor and sent a jolt all through her body. Rye gasped and grabbed the railing. Fever? It felt like they'd put her through a blender for several days.

The door opened. The gremlin nurse came in.

"Ms. Woods! You shouldn't be out of bed."

As the nurse gently but firmly herded Rye back to bed, Rye saw an orange-uniformed policeman at the window in the top half of the door. Rye felt like her heart stopped.

"What did I do?" Rye asked. "Did I hurt Holly? I have to know."

"My job is to take care of you while you're here," the nurse said. "Now, let's get you under this sheet. Please lie back."

"I have to know."

"Perhaps you'd better ask the policeman. Now, let me check your temperature." The nurse stuck something on the side of Rye's neck.

"Can you ask him to come in. Please? It's important."

Shortly after the nurse strode out, the policeman entered. His presence triggered a familiar jolt of fear.

"Yes, ma'am? The nurse said you wanted to say something." He held a pencil and notebook. "I should remind you that you're still under arrest."

Something hard and large and cold dropped through the bottom of Rye's stomach. "Arrest? What...what for?"

"Assaulting a police officer. Resisting arrest. And damage to government property."

Rye's breath caught in her throat. It took her several long moments to get it back. "Did I hurt anyone else?"

The policeman wrote in his notebook. "I believe you hit several officers in the station, ma'am."

"Anyone else? My...my sister. Is she okay?"

"Your sister, ma'am? I'm afraid I don't know nothing about anyone else."

Rye lay chewing her lip. If she'd hurt Holly, surely they would have charged her with that, too.

Much later, though how much Rye couldn't tell because there was no clock in the room, the door opened. A male leprechaun and a female sylph walked in. Both wore dark suits. The sylph exchanged a quiet word with the policeman. That stopped him from following the suits into the room. Rye's wings tried to tighten defensively against her back. Her broken one hurt. Rye greeted the unidentified pair with a wince.

"Ms. Rye Woods?" the leprechaun said.

"Um. Yes, sir, I am."

He showed her his mobile. The screen display identified him as a Senior Officer of the Special Investigations Bureau. Rye's life felt like it began draining out of her toes.

"I'm Senior Special Officer Evening," he said. "This is Special Officer Peach."

Rye glanced at the sylph's mobile. The sylph then pressed a couple of buttons.

"We'll be making a recording of this conversation, ma'am," Evening said.

Rye looked between them. Implacable. Professional. She guessed what was coming before Evening spoke.

"Would you prefer to be called Rye Woods," he said, "or Righteous?"

Rye had difficulty swallowing.

"You are the fairy female, Righteous, who is the bonded servant of the Vengeance Valley temple in southern Fairyland," Evening said, "and who left Fairyland eleven and a half years ago without a travel permit, are you not, ma'am?"

"Um," Rye said.

"I'm sorry, ma'am, I didn't catch your answer," Evening said.

"What...what is this about?" Rye said.

"The government of Fairyland, through their ambassador, has filed a request for repatriation of one Righteous and her sister, Holy Word. Who are both Fairyland nationals."

Rye's gaze jerked up to him. They'd got Holly, too.

"The information we have about you and your younger sister, known, I believe, as Holly Woods, fits that supplied by the Fairyland authorities," Evening said. "Do you have any comment, ma'am?"

"I...I want to be a refugee," Rye said. "Both of us. Me and my sister. Refugees."

"Your residence status is the subject of this investigation, ma'am," he said. "Now that the doctor has given clearance, we'll be moving you to a more suitable facility while we conduct our enquiries."

❖

The nurse who helped Rye dress bristled disapproval of Rye's removal from the infirmary. Special Officer Peach looked utterly impervious. When the nurse finished with the lace on Rye's shoe, Peach stepped forward and snapped a handcuff around Rye's left wrist. It joined to the Special Officer's right wrist.

Outside the infirmary room, Senior Special Officer Evening waited with a policeman. The latter found himself curtly dismissed. Patients, visitors, and infirmary staff stared as Rye and her escort made their way out to a waiting carpet.

Rye's broken wing made it uncomfortable to sit in the back of the carpet. She stared out the windows, but had little idea where they were going. The carpet finally slowed and halted at a guarded gate. A security fence and a dense tangled hedge of thorny blackberry surrounded a squat totara tree stump.

A blue-uniformed imp opened a thick door in the base of the stump. Rye took a last look at the sky before Peach tugged her inside.

They made her strip and searched her before giving her a loose, bright yellow overall. It had inmate printed across front and back in large black letters. Rye struggled to get it on. Peach stood impassively watching.

They took her fingerprints, inventoried her possessions, and made her sign a lot of forms left-handed.

"Is my sister here?" Rye asked. "Holly Woods. Did they bring her here, too?"

The guard shrugged and scooped her papers into a file. "I can't disclose information about any other inmates."

"She's my sister. My kid sister. I'm the only family she has."

"All in order?" Evening said.

The guard nodded. "Yes, sir."

Peach and Evening departed without another word. The female imp and a half-goblin female guard herded Rye toward a barred door. They escorted her down a grim, empty corridor. She had to stand a certain distance from the next barred door before the guard unlocked it.

"What is this place?" Rye asked.

"They didn't tell you?" the guard said. "Scrub Street Detention Centre. Through here."

Rye turned into another corridor. This one contained many doors that all looked the same with hand pad locks and dark picture screens. The female guard activated one of the doors and swung it open. Rye paused in the doorway. She faced a tiny room with a cot, a stool, a toilet that projected from the back wall, and a tiny table. No window.

"In you go," the guard said.

"How long am I going to be here?" Rye asked.

"I can't tell you that."

Rye glanced around at all the other doors. "I've got to know about my sister. Is she here? Holly Woods. She's just a kid."

"A kid? She won't be here if she's a juvenile. In you go."

Rye shuffled forward. The door clanged shut behind her. She heard the whir of a lock being activated.

Rye slumped on the cot. Detention centre. Prison. Next stop Fairyland.

❖

Rye dozed fitfully. She roused every time she rolled over and pressed her broken wing against the cot or the wall. Her thoughts were as uncomfortable as her sleep.

She had never had much in the way of possessions to lose. What really mattered was Holly. And Flora. Now that she would never see Flora again, Rye realised that some part of her had never given up hope that they would get back together. Perhaps after Holly had grown up and moved beyond Rye's care. Perhaps one day Rye might have been able to offer Flora something. Not much, probably, but something. If only love could have been measured in a tangible way, maybe then Rye could've proved herself. Surely no one could love Flora more than she did?

Did Flora ever think about her? Would she ever learn that Rye had been sent back? Would she feel anything?

The morning after Rye had cooked Flora's dinner for her posh arty friends had probably been one of Rye's happiest. She and Flora had to be careful not to betray themselves with Holly around, but having the two women she loved together like that had been magic. Holly and Flora did have a lot in common. Holly had never spoken of Flora except with admiration, respect, and enthusiasm. Flora liked Holly, too. Rye could hardly ask for more from relations between her sister and her lover. If only it could always have been like that.

She had once read that the only things you regret are the things you don't do. She hadn't agreed, until now.

Rye did so very deeply regret not overcoming her fears and getting Holly's immigration sorted out properly. She would have given anything for the chance to tell the kid how proud she was of her, and how much she loved her. And how sorry she was that, in the end, she had failed her.

Rye wished she could wind back time to that art gallery. Instead of thinking about throwing herself at Flora's feet, she would've done it for real. Begged Flora to let them see each other. How trivial all her worries and fretting seemed now. They had loved each other. Surely they could have worked it out?

Rye would regret to her last breath that her final glimpse of Flora had been that second time, in the gallery, when Flora walked away.

Chapter Twenty

The door beeped. Rye waited for the breakfast tray to appear. Instead, she heard the whir of the lock. The door swung outward. A blue-uniformed pixie woman beckoned to Rye.

"Out you come, Woods."

Rye wandered out into the corridor. Voices and people and a large space were momentarily strange and threatening. Another female guard waited on the other side of the door.

"This way," the guard said.

Rye followed. The other guard walked behind. They took her through several barred doorways and along corridors that all looked the same except for the number of doors in them. At one point, Rye glimpsed a room in which several women in bright yellow inmate overalls moved and talked. The guards marched her past. Finally, the guard opened a door with a window set in the upper part.

Rye stepped into a medium-sized room with a table in the middle. Two men stood near the table. A paunchy middle-aged limoniad, with black streaks in the typical earth brown hair of a meadow nymph, wore an expensive-looking suit. The other man was a young sylph, who also wore an expensive suit rather than the loose, flowing clothes generally favoured by his species. More government agents come to question her. High-powered ones by the look of them. Rye's heart, which she didn't think could sink any further, dropped at the same time the female guard thunked the door shut behind her. The back of the guard's head was clearly visible through the barred window.

"Ms. Woods?" the limoniad said.

"Um. Yeah."

"Won't you join us? And take a seat?"

Rye didn't have a choice. She wandered to the table. Before she sat, the nymph offered his hand. It did not contain his mobile showing his credentials. Rye awkwardly shook his hand with her left. His skin was smooth, his nails immaculately manicured, and he wore three chunky gold rings.

"My name is Basil Summerbank," he said. "This is my associate, Ash Vervain. I'm pleased to make your acquaintance, Ms. Woods."

"Um. Yeah."

When they had all seated themselves, Mr. Summerbank retrieved a gold pen from inside his jacket. Rye noticed the thin pile of papers on the table in front of him. Young Mr. Vervain sat poised to make notes on a thick pad of blue paper.

"My associate and I are attorneys," Mr. Summerbank said. "If you choose to accept our services, Ms. Woods, we shall represent you for as long as you require."

"You're lawyers? You're on my side?"

"Yes. If you'd like. If not, we can arrange for the representative of your choice to attend you."

Rye had to look away for a moment. Caught unawares, the rush of relief threatened to spill out of her as tears.

"Ms. Woods? Are you feeling unwell?"

"Um. No. I'm fine. Thanks." Rye ran her good hand across her face. "Um. I didn't expect that you'd be—Yeah. I'd really like some help. But…um, I don't have much money. To pay you."

"We have been engaged on your behalf by Ms. Flora Withe."

He said more, but Rye wasn't really listening. Flora hadn't forgotten her. Flora had absolutely no reason to do this, yet she'd thrown Rye a lifeline. The only one Rye was likely to get.

"Ms. Woods? If you're not feeling well enough to continue, we can return later," Mr. Summerbank said. "Have you been seen by an apothecary or doctor since you left the infirmary?"

Rye tried to pull herself back together. "Um. No. I haven't seen anyone. Except you. You're the first."

"Uh huh." Mr. Summerbank made a note with his gold pen. "I think we can arrange to get you checked up. Now, Ms. Woods, are you aware of the proceedings being moved against you?"

"Um. That agent guy said that Fairyland wants us extradited. Me and Holly."

"Yes. A formal request for repatriation has—"

"Mr. Summerbank, where is Holly? What's happening to her? No one will tell me anything. Holly is my sister. My kid sister. She's a minor. Sixteen years old. Look, can you help her? Instead of me. She has to stay here. They can't send her back. You've got to do something. Please."

"Miss Holly Woods is also subject to a repatriation request." Mr. Summerbank pulled a sheet of paper from his pile and slid it across to Rye. "She's a very pleasant young woman. Vervain here has initiated the process of filing an application for refugee status for her."

Rye glanced incredulously between the two men and the form in front of her. "Already? You've talked to her?"

"Yes. I interviewed Miss Woods a few days ago, in the company of Ms. Withe."

Rye stared at him. "She's okay?"

"I think it's fair to say that your sister is not unaffected by the current state of affairs. But you need not concern yourself unduly, Ms. Woods. Holly's case looks very strong. She has some excellent references from her school. There is every indication she will be a valuable and law-abiding citizen."

Rye ran a hand through her hair. She couldn't quite believe she was hearing so much good news.

"Her brush with the police won't have any detrimental impact on her case," Mr. Summerbank said.

Rye scowled as Mr. Summerbank told her about Holly being drunk in a carpet full of kids drinking booze and smoking dreamweed. Rye wanted to give the kid a shake. If she ever got her hands on her again—

"Perhaps you'd like to read that through," Mr. Summerbank said. "If you agree with the application, we'll need your signature as Holly's legal guardian."

"Oh. Right." Rye bent her frown down on the paper. "This will get her citizenship?"

"If approved, yes."

Mr. Summerbank offered Rye his pen. She had never held a gold one before. She felt awkward trying to write her name with her left hand. The resulting scrawl looked like the handiwork of an illiterate child.

"We'll get that lodged immediately," he said.

"How long will it take? Until she's safe?"

"That's hard to say. We'll file for priority consideration in light of the repatriation request."

Rye nodded. "She has a good chance, you say?"

"That would be my assessment. There is another option that we have in Holly's case."

"Yeah?"

"I was asked to broach this matter with you by Ms. Withe. She has made the offer to adopt Holly, if other avenues fail, and only with your approval."

Rye felt like someone had punched her in the stomach. "Adopt her?"

"Adoption by a citizen would confer that status on Holly."

Rye ran a hand over her face. Flora adopt Holly? Sign over the responsibility for Holly to someone else? It would be the ultimate acknowledgement that Rye hadn't been good enough to look after her. Holly had raved over the idea of being adopted by Flora and enjoying the lifestyle that Flora's money could buy. Flora could give her everything Rye could not, even safety. That hurt.

"Ms. Withe was most adamant that this would be a last resort and only with your complete agreement," he said. "As I can't see any possible reason why such an application, with your consent, would fail, this guarantees that, one way or another, Holly will evade extradition."

Rye tugged at her hair as she frowned at the scarred table top. Holly would be safe. That was the crucial fact here. For once, Rye had to forget her pride. There was too much at stake. This wasn't Flora trying to take the kid from her. This was Flora making sure Holly would have the chance that Rye had worked so hard for: a life free to do what Holly wanted. This wasn't Flora slapping Rye in the face with a thick wad of money, it was a stunningly generous offer.

"She...she would do that?" Rye said. "For Holly?"

"I have known Ms. Withe and her family for a very long time," Mr. Summerbank said. "Her offer is sincere."

Rye frowned down at her lap and tried to blink back tears. She wasn't wholly successful. She roughly wiped her eyes. It was as if a grinding weight had been lifted. Holly would be safe.

"Ms. Woods?"

Rye sniffed. "Um. Yeah. Look, I...I don't know what to say. I can't believe she's doing this. Yes. Of course, I'll sign anything I have to for Holls."

"I have the requisite paperwork here. It will be used only if it proves necessary. But it would probably be best if we had it all ready to go should we need to. Are you comfortable with that?"

"Yes. What do I have to sign?"

Rye felt a strange jolt when she saw Flora's handwriting on the form. Rye was never going to be able to repay her for this.

"Where is Holly now?" Rye asked. "Not in somewhere like this?"

"She's staying with Ms. Withe. After your arrest and removal to the infirmary, Holly called Ms. Withe from the police station. Vervain here attended Ms. Withe on that occasion. The police agreed to allow Holly to be released into Ms. Withe's custody. When the repatriation papers were filed against Holly, Ms. Withe stood as Holly's guarantor and posted the necessary bond to keep Holly from being sent to a juvenile detention facility for the duration of the proceedings."

Rye scowled down at her lap. Tears dripped from behind her fingers to spot her yellow overalls. During that blank period, she had left Holly in police custody. She had let her down even more badly than she had imagined. Rye had shattered her life and Holly's. Flora had picked up the pieces. Rye didn't think she could feel her failure any more keenly.

"Ms. Woods?" Mr. Vervain set a packet of tissues on the table near Rye.

She sniffed and grabbed a tissue. "Thanks."

"Perhaps now we should turn to your case, Ms. Woods," Mr. Summerbank said.

Rye blew her nose and listened numbly as Mr. Summerbank detailed the charges against her.

"However, these are not our highest priority," he said. "The government, Ms. Woods, is staying those actions against you pending the result of the repatriation request."

"What does that mean?" Rye asked.

"It means that those charges won't be pressed in the event that the courts grant the Fairyland government's request for repatriation," Mr. Summerbank said. "Our government has chosen not to hinder that action by instituting criminal proceedings against you which might result in a delay to a possible extradition. So, we need to concentrate our efforts initially in defending the repatriation request. I assume, Ms. Woods, that that is the course of action you would like us to pursue?"

"Yeah. I don't want to go back. I'll...I'll do time in jail here. But I don't want to go back to Fairyland. Please."

Mr. Summerbank nodded and consulted one of his papers.

"I have the formal request here," he said, "and you're welcome to read it. But I can reduce the basis of their application down to three points. One, you are a citizen of Fairyland who has never received permission to travel beyond the borders of that country. Nor have you ever received naturalisation or other permission to legally reside elsewhere. Is any or all of that correct, Ms. Woods?"

Rye frowned down at her lap. "Yeah. It's all true."

"Have you ever applied for residence or citizenship?" Mr. Vervain asked.

"No."

"Is there any reason that you didn't?" Mr. Summerbank asked.

"Um." Rye ran her hand through her hair. "I didn't think I would get it. And I didn't think Holly would need it. I thought she'd become a citizen when she got her wings and became an adult."

"Do you have any particular grounds for believing that you would be refused residence or refugee status?" Mr. Summerbank said.

"Um." Rye bit her lip. Yes, there was a very good reason, but even now she couldn't admit it. "I'm...I'm just a labourer. I never had any education when I grew up. I'm not the sort of person any country would want."

Mr. Summerbank picked a page from his pile and slid it across the table to her. "This is a copy of a statement from a Mr. Reed Bulrush, the head teacher in the economics department of the Hollowberry Municipal School. He has endorsed your aptitude and diligence in attending night classes over several years. Which also demonstrates a commendable and desirable drive for self-improvement and acquirement of skills useful to the broader community. And I have an affidavit here sworn by a Mr. Radish Nuttal to the effect that you are a conscientious, honest, and diligent worker."

Rye frowned at him.

"We took these as background evidence to use in support of Holly's application," Mr. Summerbank said. "We can use both, of course, in your own case. And if there are others likely to furnish you with character references, that would help. Ms. Withe has offered herself."

On prompting, Rye suggested the owner of Pansy's Fried Sandwiches, but flatly refused to let the lawyers approach anyone from the construction company. Working alongside the likes of Knot Knapweed, with his connections to Lichen Street, would not be to her advantage.

Under questioning, Rye conceded that she had never had a bank account, credit card, or paid income tax. On the other hand, she had never once had recourse to a single piece of welfare aid from any government agency.

"Let's move on to the second point in the repatriation request," Mr. Summerbank said. "That you kidnapped your sister, whom they name as Holy Word."

"I did. I didn't give her a choice."

Rye explained how she had run away from the temple and gone back to the commune farm specifically to take Holly with her. She omitted all reference to her mother. Both lawyers asked her questions about the escape and what had led to it. Rye could not tell them about Chastity or her punishments. Instead, she mentioned the unpleasant living conditions at the temple and how becoming a bond servant had meant she'd lost the right to own anything. In answer to their questions, she admitted the humiliating truth that she had legally become a non-person, and as such she would not have been allowed to apply to leave the temple, let alone the country.

"In effect, then," Mr. Summerbank said, "what you are describing is a form of slavery. Well, Ms. Woods, this is an important factor. Every civilised country regards this practice with abhorrence. If we can establish that an extradition would return you to slavery, this will be a potent argument in our favour."

"Um. Right."

"Now, the third and final point is that you have been convicted of the murder of your mother," Mr. Summerbank said. "And you are wanted back to serve your sentence."

Rye's gaze snapped up to him. She went cold.

"The trial appears to have been held in your absence," Mr. Summerbank said. "Which is not a legitimate procedure in this country, though it is within fairy law. You were found guilty."

Rye couldn't breathe. Her good hand clenched into a tight fist.

"Ms. Woods, do you understand?"

"Um." Rye swallowed with difficulty. She could see her mother dead in the mud. "Um. Yeah. I...I did it."

The lawyers started asking her questions. Rye rose and walked away. She stood close to the wall with her back to them. Her chest tightened and her heart raced with the first stages of the onset of her panicked flight reaction. Rye pressed a hand against the wall. She tried to dig her fingers into the grey paint as she struggled to keep herself under control. Murder. Yes, she must have done it. Right in front of Holly.

She had run back to the women's compound to get Holly. Her mother had seen her. Penance's face twisted with fear and hatred and she snatched up a heavy stick and lashed out. She shrieked and shouted at Rye. Calling her evil and wishing she had never been born. Saying how she wished Rye had died rather than bring shame on them all. How she regretted that she hadn't known what she had given birth to because she would have left Rye out for the cold and animals to take like they did the deformed babies. Her neck had been corded and her words so wild that she sprayed them out with spittle. She hit Rye hard and fast about the head and arms. Beating out years of disgust and self-loathing. Wanting to hurt, bruise, and break. Holly had started crying behind their mother, reacting to her frenzy.

Then Penance lay dead with cold mud oozing around her. A silent, slow trickle of blood crept from the corner of her mouth. So very red. The stick dropped from Rye's hands. Holly's wails were joined by women's shouts and cries. Rye picked Holly up and ran. Ran because her life depended on it.

"Ms. Woods?" Mr. Summerbank said.

"I did it. I killed her."

When Rye returned to the seat, Vervain produced a paper cup of water for her. Her hands trembled as she took a sip. "They're...they're going to get me back for this, aren't they?"

"But you have never had an opportunity to defend the charge, have you? In person or by proxy?"

"No, sir."

"We will stress that a conviction *in absentia* is not a recognised practice in this country," Mr. Summerbank said.

"But me being a murderer will mess up any refugee application, won't it?" Rye said. "Immigration won't want me, will they?"

"As I said, we'll stress the irregularity of the procedure," Mr. Summerbank said.

Rye heard in his evasions the truth she feared. A life for a life. That's the way it was going to work. Her mother was going to get her wish in the end.

"One important facet in asking the court to refuse the repatriation application is to establish that you would suffer harm were you to be returned." Mr. Summerbank squared the slender pile of papers on the table in front of him. "The slavery issue is very much in our favour. We can also make a strong case, I believe, out of the international reputation that Fairyland has for their treatment of certain minorities. This has been documented by internationally recognised humanitarian agencies. Did you personally suffer in any way because you are a homosexual, Ms. Woods?"

Rye glared at him. Her wings and chest muscles snapped taut.

"If we could present definite details about any harm you believe you would suffer on your return," Mr. Summerbank said. "And any occasions where you have suffered because of your sexual—"

"No," Rye said.

Both men frowned at her.

"Ms. Woods, if—"

"No!" Rye slammed the paper cup down so hard that it crumpled and sprayed water over the table. "I don't want you to say anything about that. I won't admit it. Not in front of them."

"Ms. Woods, this is obviously an uncomfortable matter for you," Mr. Summerbank said. "But the reason you're reluctant to broach this in the presence of representatives of the Fairyland government is precisely—"

"No," Rye said. "Not that. You don't understand."

"Perhaps if you—"

"No."

The lawyers exchanged a look. Vervain began gathering the papers.

"We have quite a lot to work with for now," Mr. Summerbank said. "Perhaps you'd like to think if there's anything else that might assist us, Ms. Woods. We'll return tomorrow."

Rye awkwardly shook hands with them both with her left hand.

"Do you have any messages you'd like conveyed to your sister or Ms. Withe?" Mr. Summerbank said.

"Um. Yeah. Please. Could you tell Holly that—" Rye frowned. What could she say? Sorry that I failed you? I'm glad you've got someone else to take care of you? "Can you tell Holly that she's not to worry. About me or anything."

"I certainly shall," Mr. Summerbank said.

"Um. Can you tell Flora...Can you tell her thanks? Thanks for everything."

❖

Rye lay on her cot. The lights shone with unwavering brightness, though she felt like her life had burned so low that it was flickering on the point of extinction. There was very little of Rye Woods left to snuff. The murder conviction was going to be her undoing. Another blank period. Another self-inflicted disaster.

If, as looked likely, the fairies were going to get her back, she would rather have a clean death by the noose for her mother's murder than have the priestesses scourge her in their attempt to "cure" her and "save" her from the "evil" inside. Quicker and far, far less painful.

Mr. Summerbank didn't understand what she was facing. They would kill her in the end, so the method was the only thing left to decide. She knew what the whip felt like. And the clubs. As far as the priestesses knew, Rye had last indulged in the perversion of sex with another woman over a dozen years ago. They might think she'd been saved, that the evil had been successfully scourged from her the last time they'd done it to her before she escaped. Rye would not let them know that she was still a vessel containing evil. She didn't think she could bear the pain of another cure again, and especially not one that had to drive out twelve years worth of evil. They'd kill her far too slowly that way. She had to keep quiet about her sex life. Admit nothing.

❖

The guards came for her the next afternoon. Mr. Summerbank and Mr. Vervain waited in the interview room.

After greetings, Mr. Summerbank slid an envelope across the

table. It was simply addressed to "Rye" in Flora's handwriting. Rye opened out the single sheet.

> *Rye—*
>
> *You are constantly in my thoughts. And those of Holly. She's with me. Safe, but missing you. We both are. I will continue to do everything I possibly can to ensure that Holly remains in this country. I know this is what you want. Much as I like Holly, I am acting for you, Rye. There is nothing I will not do to help you. If you'll let me. I have only ever wanted to help you and make you happy. I had hoped that we would have a lifetime together to get to know each other and learn how best to please and enjoy each other. I realise that I made mistakes. I have given them a great deal of thought. I hope I've learned. I would give anything for another chance.*
>
> *The one constant through all that has happened, and is happening, is my love for you. I cannot pretend to understand all the choices you make, but I do know that you have strong reasons for what you do. I beg that you don't forget those who love you when you make your decisions.*
>
> *All my love,*
> *Flora.*

Rye put her hand over her face to cover her pain. This did not make what must come any easier.

Miserable, Rye listened without much interest as the lawyers explained that the hearing had been scheduled with indecent haste for just a few days time. They'd apply for a postponement to allow them a fair time to prepare her case. Rye numbly agreed with whatever they suggested, except when they broached the matter of her homosexuality.

"Ms. Woods, we have compiled a wealth of evidence about civil rights abuses perpetrated in Fairyland against homosexuals," Vervain said. "Using your personal experiences—"

"No," Rye said.

"It would help us establish a strong argument against your return to Fairyland," Mr. Summerbank said. "In these cases—"

"No," Rye said. "I don't want it mentioned. At all."

"We won't do anything against your wishes, Ms. Woods, of course," Mr. Summerbank said, "but I would strongly urge you to reconsider. In my opinion, it would be very much in your best interests."

Rye glanced at the letter. Had the lawyers discussed this with Flora? Was that what was behind that second paragraph? No. Flora knew Rye's past experiences in Fairyland complicated her open acceptance of her sexual identity. Rye hoped Flora would understand that her refusal to make a case out of her homosexuality was not a denial of Flora—of them. It was deadly pragmatic, though Flora had no way of appreciating that.

After Vervain packed away his papers into his case, he asked for Flora's letter. He looked apologetic.

"We're not allowed to give anything to the inmates." He offered her a pen. "Would you like to write something in return?"

Rye could not write left-handed. She folded Flora's letter and handed it to him. If this hearing went as she expected, would they allow her to see Holly and Flora one last time? Awkward and diffident as Rye was at expressing her feelings in person, that had to be easier than writing it down or dictating them.

Chapter Twenty-One

The guards came for Rye some time after breakfast but before the lunch tray. They herded her into a strange room. They locked a chain around her waist with shackles and manacles attached. The guard snapped the shackles around her ankles and one of the manacles around her good wrist. The remaining manacle, which would not fit around her cast, swung against her front when she shuffled out to a waiting transporter carpet. Another yellow-clad, chained prisoner sat in the back. The female half-goblin sneered at Rye, spat on the floor, and nibbled her claws.

When the guards unlocked the rear of the carpet, the carpet was parked in some underground vault. Rye followed the other prisoner through a tunnel. Guards separated her from the other prisoner and led her to a small room where Mr. Summerbank waited. He looked impressive in an official flowing green tunic.

"I'm afraid our application for a postponement was turned down earlier this morning," he said.

Rye knew she should be more concerned. But she felt numb, as if she accepted the inevitability of the decision to come and the futility of trying to avert it. She tried to concentrate when Mr. Summerbank quickly described the inside of the hearing room and what would happen.

"Do you have any questions?" Mr. Summerbank asked.

Rye shook her head.

Mr. Summerbank nodded and strode to the door. He lifted his hand to tap, but paused. "Ms. Woods, if you change your mind about using your probable treatment in Fairyland as a homosexual, we—"

"No."

He nodded. "Then we'll do our best without that."

The guard let him out.

Rye waited. She frowned down at the chains. Would they put them on her to take her back to Fairyland?

A green-uniformed pixie opened the door. He read from a clipboard. "Rye Woods, also known as Righteous the Fairy?"

Rye followed him out the door and up a short flight of steps. The doorway opened into a large room with highly polished walls. Mr. Summerbank, Vervain, and a pixie woman sat at a desk facing the big, heavily carved desk under a green canopy. A green-clad old limoniad female sat under the canopy. She must be the adjudicator.

A touch on Rye's elbow urged her forward. She awkwardly climbed up a few shallow steps to a chair surrounded by a waist-high railing on three sides. It looked like they wanted to put her on show and keep her boxed in and isolated.

"Your Sagacity." The green uniformed man with the clipboard bowed to the adjudicator. "The Scrub Street Detention Centre has delivered to this hearing the person of Rye Woods, also known as Righteous the Fairy. Detainee YD-44689."

The adjudicator nodded at him and cast a swift glance at Rye. Rye stiffly nodded a bow.

The guard unlocked her manacle and gestured for her to sit.

From her seat, Rye looked across the front of the desk of her lawyers. Barely two paces separated them from the other desk. At that far desk sat the representatives of the Fairyland government. A sylph man stood and began speaking. Rye's attention moved past him. The next man was a fairy with his wings unfolded but closed. The tips softly tapped against each other as he followed the sylph lawyer's opening remarks to the adjudicator. He was relaxed but concentrating. Rye had not seen wings since her escape from Fairyland. They triggered instincts that had lain dormant, a different world of unspoken language that had been missing around her.

Rye pushed her attention past the fairy man to the woman beside him. She saw wing tips and a brown robe of a priestess. Rye's wings tried to tighten defensively. Her broken one stabbed a sharp pain into her back. The priestess turned her head to stare back at Rye with an expression both bleak and unforgiving. Her wings opened a little and quivered. Rye shrank into the chair. She grabbed the wooden railing in front of her and clenched tight to anchor herself against the surging desire to flee in terror. She had to remain in control of herself. That priestess could not hurt her in this room.

Rye closed her eyes. She heard Mr. Summerbank talking, but tried to ignore him. She needed to slow her breathing down to a calmer level. That blank period in a police station had brought her here, and the blank period with her mother was likely to determine the outcome of this hearing. Another blank period would be tantamount to pulling the noose around her own neck.

The sylph lawyer for the Fairyland government started talking about the murder of Penance, a matriarch of the Birdwood Valley Commune Farm Number Two.

Rye saw her mother dead at her feet. The urge to flee for her life had driven the younger Rye to snatch up Holly and run. The Rye in the hearing room trembled as her self-control frayed.

"Rye Woods," Mr. Summerbank said, "was not present at this trial. She was not afforded the opportunity to defend this charge in person or by proxy. I submit, Your Sagacity, that a trial which proceeds without the presence or knowledge of the defendant cannot be regarded as just in any sense of the word. I therefore submit that it would be unjust and contrary to the moral and intellectual basis of our own legal system to grant this so-called conviction the same weight as an outcome of a trial by peers. Accordingly, I ask that this point be struck from the repatriation application."

"Madam Adjudicator." The Fairyland lawyer stood. "The judicial system of Fairyland is not on trial here. I contend that it is beyond the authority of this hearing to pass judgement on the validity of the laws, and the means of enforcing and enacting those laws, of a sovereign nation."

Rye tried to ignore the words. She could do nothing about them. That was Mr. Summerbank's job. The only thing she could do to help herself was concentrate on her breathing, hold onto the railing, and wrestle her fear down where it would not overwhelm her into stupid action. She had to stay calm. Sweat dripped on her lap with the effort. The words beat against her.

"A convicted murderess," the sylph lawyer said, "also wanted on charges of kidnapping a minor."

Rye could imagine herself standing, turning, pushing past the guard and bursting out the door.

"It would be unconscionable to send my client back to a life of slavery," Mr. Summerbank said.

"With all due respect to my learned colleague," the sylph lawyer said, "his language is more emotive than accurate. The term bond servant is used to describe an individual who has been taken in by a temple and provided with not only the necessities of life, but also counselling. We're talking about troubled individuals who have no other place to go. In an act of charity and caring, the temples take in these people and attempt to give them a sense of purpose through the development of a richer spiritual life and practical work schemes. This is not slavery, Your Sagacity, it is a generous act of compassion and rehabilitation."

That slick bastard was twisting and warping everything. She wanted to hit him hard. Make him hurt. Feel a little bit of her pain. The priestess looked past him to Rye. Rye could almost hear the crack of the whip.

When the sylph lawyer started to summarise the reasons why Rye should be sent back to Fairyland, he vilified her as a violent recidivist criminal whom no decent society would want to let loose amongst law-abiding, tax-paying citizens.

Rye's arm muscles ached with the continued effort of gripping the railing.

"Kidnapped a minor," the sylph said.

Rye squeezed her eyes shut.

"Murdered her own mother," he said.

Rye gritted her teeth.

"Fled to evade justice," he said.

She had scooped up Holly and run for her life, despite knowing what they'd do if they caught her. A dozen years would not lessen that. They were not going through all this trouble to get her back to be lenient. They were going to kill her. Rye's body tensed beyond her control. She had to take two turns to get out to the parking lot. Her thinking slowed and narrowed. She stood up.

"Rye!" Flora called.

Rye's head snapped around. She saw Holly and Flora sitting together behind a railing that divided off the back third of the room. Rye took a ragged breath. Holly was here, but she was going to be safe from anything these bastards wanted to do to her.

"Ms. Woods, you must resume your seat."

Rye blinked at Mr. Summerbank and sucked in a deep breath. She was in court.

"Ms. Woods," Mr. Summerbank said.

"Um. Sorry."

"There are to be no interruptions from the gallery," the adjudicator said. "Any further disturbances will result in the removal of the offending parties."

Rye sat down and ran her hand through her hair. Holly had heard it all. All that stuff about what a terrible person Rye was and what she'd done to their mother. When Rye turned a fearful look on Holly, her gaze snagged on Flora. She looked pale and sad, just like last time in the gallery when Rye had said nothing and let her walk away.

Mr. Summerbank resumed talking, trying to chip away at the lies the sylph had said about Rye. Not all of it was lies. That was the problem.

Rye looked at the adjudicator. Well-groomed and powerful, that woman was going to decide Rye's fate. She read little hope in that granitic expression. She turned back to Flora. This was probably the last time they would see each other. She flicked her gaze to the priestess. One way or another, they were going to kill her when they got her back. Rye knew it without a shadow of a doubt.

"Does your client have nothing to say, Mr. Summerbank?" the adjudicator said.

Flora looked tense and on the brink of tears as she watched Rye. The time had passed when Rye could have gone to throw herself at Flora's feet. What an absolute idiot she'd been.

"Your Sagacity," Mr. Summerbank said, "Ms. Woods has expressed the wish not to—"

"They're going to torture me to death," Rye said.

"Ms. Woods? Do you wish to make a statement to this hearing?" the adjudicator said.

"Yes, ma'am," Rye said. "If you send me back, they're going to kill me by beating and whipping me."

Rye glanced briefly at the priestess before returning her stare to Flora with Holly beside her. "Because I'm gay."

Flora bit her lip.

"My client would be liable to suffer persecution because of her sexual orientation." Mr. Summerbank grabbed a sheaf of papers that Vervain held up for him.

"I'm gay." Rye felt strangely calm as she returned Flora's stare. "They didn't cure me. It didn't work. In fact, I'm worse than I ever was. I've never loved any woman like I do now. So, when I go back, they're going to try to save me by scourging this evil from me."

"Might I submit this evidence," Mr. Summerbank said, "gathered by creditable international humanitarian organizations detailing the abuse of—"

"After they made me watch them scourging Chastity," Rye said to Flora, "I ran away from the temple. But they caught me and took me back. They said they would beat the evil out of me. Maybe it was in the blood that runs from the cuts. I was never sure how it worked. But they didn't do it. Not at first."

Rye could feel the panic hovering again, pressing, fed by the memories. She kept her attention fixed on Flora, her calm in the centre of the storm.

"They had to punish me for running away first," Rye said. "They tied me to a table with rope around my wrists and ankles. I couldn't move. Two priestesses grabbed my wings and pulled them open. This other priestess brought in a club. A big, heavy, rounded wooden club. I thought she was going to hit me with it. But they didn't. They put it under the top section of my wing support and pressed down either side until my wing support snapped. Then they moved the club down to the next section."

Flora put her hand over her mouth.

"They broke every section," Rye said. "I screamed a lot. And wanted to faint. But I didn't. Not until they cut me loose and carried me out. But they weren't finished with me. You see, they made sure that the broken sections of my wings didn't set straight. They're bent and weak. My wings won't support my weight. It's so I could never use my wings in another escape attempt. But when I did run, I used my legs. And that worked fine."

"Are you saying, Ms. Woods," the adjudicator asked, "that you fear this form of physical torture should you be returned to Fairyland?"

"No, ma'am," Rye said. "It'll probably be much worse."

"Your Sagacity!" The sylph stood. "This is all highly emotive and unsubstantiated."

Rye glanced at the frowning priestess before returning her attention to Flora.

"When I'd healed," Rye said, "I was fit to be cured of liking women. Because that was evil. An offence against the gods. I was never sure why. It felt right to me. Nothing has ever felt more right than loving the most wonderful woman in Infinity."

Flora looked like she shed a tear.

"But the priestesses didn't see it that way," Rye said. "Their duty was to save me. So they tied me standing up between two posts at the front of the temple. They read these prayers and got everyone chanting a song while they whipped me. Praying for me, you see. While the whip cut into my back to force the evil out. It wasn't an ordinary whip. Not one long thong. This had six or seven short strands. About this long. They cut through my wing membranes. I could feel blood running down my legs. And saw it on my feet."

Rye could see tears running down Flora's cheeks.

"I pretended that it worked," Rye said. "Lied. I had to. Because I couldn't go through it all again. I was too scared and hurt too much. I didn't think I could take it again. So, I told them that I saw how terrible it was, what I'd done with Chastity in the robing room. And how I was perverting the gods' creation by denying my womanhood and not having children. I said everything they wanted to hear."

Rye stared at the priestess. "When I could walk, they took me to a men's compound."

The memories surged again and pushed her closer to panic. Rye gripped the railing and fixed her gaze back on Flora.

"They put me in a room," Rye said, "like they do girls who have just got their wings. To wait for a man. Or men. I was cured, you see, so I was ready to breed and fulfil my purpose in creation. Only I didn't want to. Not at all. But I knew if I ran, they'd make me suffer again. And if I refused, they'd know I wasn't cured. And they'd scourge me again."

Rye swallowed with difficulty.

"This guy came in. A big guy. Really big. I suppose they picked him specially, so that I couldn't hurt him. Like I did those others. He—"

Rye scowled and blinked back tears. "He—Shit."

Flora had a hand over her face still and the other on the railing in front of her as if reaching out to Rye.

"Ms. Woods?" Mr. Summerbank said.

"I had no choice," Rye said. "I had to let him. I couldn't stand the whip again. I was too scared. It hurt so much. I thought they'd kill me if they did it again."

Rye lowered her head and clamped her hand over her face in a vain effort to stop the tears.

"Your Sagacity," the sylph lawyer said. "This uncorroborated fabrication can hardly be admissible as evidence."

"I ran away over the hills," Rye said. "I wanted to take my chances with all the evil people than stay there. They'll punish me again for that, like they did before when I tried to run. And I'm still gay. In fact, I know that I'm never going to be cured of that. Even if they don't hang me for mother or running away, they'll kill me trying to save me. Because it won't work. No matter what they do or how many times they whip me."

Rye blinked through the tears to see Flora.

"I love you," Rye said. "No one is ever going to beat that out of me. You're in me. Always will be. I should've tried harder. I'm sorry."

Chapter Twenty-Two

Rye stepped into the cell. The guard thunked the door shut behind her. She dropped onto the side of the cot. Mr. Summerbank said she had another three or four days in here to wait the adjudicator's decision.

After Rye had finished her statement to the hearing, Mr. Summerbank had excitedly offered a pile of papers for submission. The Fairyland lawyer had put in a lot of objections. Rye hadn't paid much attention to the legal arguments. Flora had looked so upset. When they took Rye out of the hearing room, Flora had stood and blown her a kiss. With the manacle on one wrist and her other arm in a cast and sling, Rye couldn't blow one back.

Well, she'd sealed her fate now. The priestesses weren't going to let that confession slip by unnoticed. Rye knew she was going to suffer for it, but it had been her last chance to get Flora to understand. Rye could not let the opportunity pass her by like she had last time. She owed Flora that much. She owed it to herself. That would not be another regret she carried to her last breath.

Holly now knew about her and Flora, but that would hardly have registered as a surprise after hearing that Rye had killed their mother. What would Holly think of her for that? Would the kid hate her? Rye couldn't even explain herself, because she couldn't remember.

Rye had come so close to another bout of self-destruction when her panic slipped beyond her control. That Fairyland lawyer had characterised her as violent, uneducated, troubled, and below average intelligence. Perhaps he was right. She couldn't control herself properly. It might be a mental problem. Would she be able to get it fixed so that she would never again have to worry about blacking-out and hurting herself or anyone else? Those therapists could work wonders, couldn't they? However much she might hate the thought of raking over her past with a complete stranger, she had done harder things, hadn't she? And they hadn't killed her. Admitting that she was a head-case to get it sorted out wouldn't be nearly as bad as continuing on as she was and possibly killing someone else. She needed to get herself straightened out. Not that she was likely to get access to any counselling in Fairyland. Perhaps they'd try to beat that out of her, too.

Rye stood up to pace.

She should have known that Flora would attend the hearing. Flora had been with her every step of the way, if unseen and at several paces removed. Absent but not forgotten. Apart but still tethered. If they did end up sending Rye back to Fairyland, there was no one better to look after Holly. Perhaps Flora might be able to persuade Holly that Rye was not the evil person the Fairyland lawyer painted her as.

Rye had missed lunch being out at the hearing, so she was surprised when she heard someone at the door. It couldn't be dinner time already?

The lock whirred. The door swung open.

"Out you come, Woods," the guard said.

"What's wrong?"

"Visitor. Your lawyer."

Rye frowned as she stepped out and fell in behind the guard. It had only been a matter of hours since the hearing. Surely he had not heard the result yet? Or had the Fairyland government's case proved so devastating that the adjudicator had needed no time to make up her mind?

Rye waited as the guard pressed her palm to the lock on the interview room door. She braced herself for the bad news. She hadn't expected this decision to go in her favour, had she? Not after that blow about her mother's murder. They'd got her there. And even if Mr. Summerbank defeated the extradition, Rye still had an armload of serious criminal charges to face. After she did any jail time she earned for assaulting that policeman, her conviction would ensure a speedy deportation the moment she was released. Fairyland was going to get her back anyway.

The guard swung the door open and nodded at Rye to go in. Rye stepped into the room and stopped. Mr. Summerbank stood near the far end of the table. Instead of young Mr. Vervain, the person beside him was Flora.

The door thunked shut behind Rye. Flora started around the table. Rye jolted into motion. She met Flora halfway and awkwardly pulled her into a tight one-armed embrace. Flora's arms looped around Rye's neck. Warm. Nice smelling. Flora. *Love*. An aching, broken part of Rye healed.

"Oh, Elm," Flora said.

Rye hugged Flora as if she might meld them into one, as if she never wanted to let go ever again. She wished she didn't have one arm in a sling. She wanted to feel Flora with all of herself. Flora embraced her just as hard. Rye could feel Flora's breath, and kiss, on the side of her neck. Rye closed her eyes so that the whole of Infinity became her and Flora with no prison walls around them.

"I love you," Rye said.

"I know. I heard. Oh, Rye, don't leave me. Not again."

Rye reluctantly opened her eyes. She lifted a hand to the side of Flora's head to get Flora to look at her. Flora's eyes looked liquid bright.

"The only thing I wanted was a chance to talk to you," Rye said. "I love Holly. I'd like you to tell her that for me. But Holly will grow up and would've left me to live her own life. You should have been my present and future. I've had a lot of time to think about things. Calmly. With no distractions. Babe, I was wrong. I was an idiot. I should've tried harder to make things work. I should've put my stupid pride aside. I should've let you help me. I should've—"

Flora put her fingers on Rye's mouth. "It wasn't just your fault. We both made mistakes."

Rye kissed Flora's fingers and gently pulled them down. "I left you. It was my stupid decision. I was wrong. That's what I wanted to tell you. I should have looked harder for a way to make it work. There usually is one. But I ran out on you and hurt you. I'll always regret that. I'm sorry. I hope...I hope you'll be able to forgive me one day. You see—"

"Rye—"

"I know that I'd never be able to give you everything. Or even much. Not like...not like I would if I were rich. And—"

"Rye!"

"And I'm just me. Not a rich and famous person. Not someone your parents and friends would approve of. But—"

"Rye." Flora put her hands on either side of Rye's face. "There are only two of us in this relationship. Not all those others! If I love you and want to be with you, why do you care about anyone else?"

"Not rich or famous or much of anything," Rye continued doggedly. "But the richest, most famous, fanciest, most successful woman in the world couldn't love you more than I do."

Flora smiled even as tears leaked from her eyes. "Oh, you adorable wooden-head! That is what is important to me. Worth more than anything. It's what no one else has ever given me. That is what I need. That is what has been missing from my life, what I've been looking for."

"Yeah?"

"Yes!" Flora clutched the back of Rye's neck as if she might shake her. "All that other stuff: money, other people's opinions, how different we are in lots of ways. We can work through it. Together. I'm sure of it. I know it. We can do it. If we want to. You and me."

"Yeah?"

"Yes," Flora said. "Oh, yes. Because we've got what's important. We love each other. You could work a hundred jobs for a hundred years, but you wouldn't earn enough to buy me that. No one could. But you give it to me."

Rye reached up to gently wipe one of Flora's tears away from near the side of her mouth. "I'll give you anything you want."

"You do. That's my point, lover. But I think we seriously need to work on your self-esteem. Like working out what you would really like to be doing. If you want to start a catering business. Get yourself the education you want. Maybe when you start feeling better about yourself, you'll stop putting yourself down with these illogical comparisons you obsess about."

Rye frowned.

"This is not me trying to buy you," Flora said quickly. "If you wanted to stay a builder's labourer for the rest of your life, I would love you. But I'd like you to love yourself, too. You hate your job—jobs. But you love cooking. You're the only person I've ever heard hum in a kitchen. And you're fantastic at it. And, for reasons that elude me utterly, you get a bounce out of making omelettes! Didn't you feel a sense of satisfaction at cooking for my dinner party? And Letty's?"

"You weren't there."

Flora frowned. "I couldn't do it. I'm not strong like you. I couldn't have acted like nothing had happened. Not with you so close."

Rye didn't know what to say, so she kissed Flora. Flora managed a smile.

"We can make us work," Flora said. "I know it."

"Are you sure you'd not prefer...prefer someone who—" Rye scowled. "That Frond person."

"Frond? Frond Lovage? What has she got to do with anything? Oh! How can you be so smart and so dense at the same time? Lover, I didn't get buds for her. Nor any of the others I've ever dated. Only you, Rye Woods."

Flora guided Rye's good hand up to her hair to feel one of the knotty lumps. "You are my budmate."

Rye frowned. She drew her hand down by stroking Flora's hair and caressing her cheek. Part of Rye was confused, part dazed, part elated. Flora loved her. Still. And wanted to make it work. Infinity wasn't such a bad place.

Over Flora's shoulder, Rye glimpsed Mr. Summerbank at the table looking through some papers. She dropped back to reality with a hard bang. She was holding Flora, but they were inside the detention centre, not Flora's apartment or even the municipal park. All this talk of love and a future together was happening inside four grey walls.

"Fey," Rye said.

"What's wrong?"

"Life is shit. And I've dropped us in it pretty deep, haven't I?"

"It might not be as bad as you think. Mr. Summerbank said that your statement had a powerful effect. He needs to take a detailed written account from you, but he's cautiously confident that the adjudicator will find in your favour."

Rye shrugged. "I'm sorry. For doing this. To you. To us. To Holly. I'll never be able to repay you for—"

Flora put her hand over Rye's lips. "You were doing so well. No backsliding."

Rye reluctantly grinned.

"I can imagine this place isn't very conducive to positive thinking," Flora said. "But Holly is safe and you will be too, soon."

Rye shook her head. "No. I've messed up good and proper."

"Mr. Summerbank says he feels you have a very good chance of beating the repatriation. He's the expert. Try not to let yourself get too gloomy."

"It's not just that. Even if they don't send be back, I—Fey. Babe, I did something really stupid. Um. I blanked out again and beat up a policeman. They're going to put me in prison for that. Then throw me out of the country afterward. I'm sorry."

"I know about those charges. We can fight them, too."

"But I did it!" Rye couldn't meet Flora's gaze. "I bring all this on myself. I don't know why. Or how. I don't even remember what I do. Maybe...maybe it's best that they lock me up. Then I couldn't hurt you. I couldn't bear that."

"I don't think you would."

Rye shook her head. "I wouldn't want to. I would rather hurt myself than harm you. But I don't know what I'm doing. It nearly killed me when I thought I'd harmed Holly, and that's what got me arrested. Maybe...maybe there is something wrong with my brain. Something doesn't work right in me, babe. What I do isn't normal. I've been thinking that I probably need someone to help me sort it out. Therapy. A shrink."

Flora stroked Rye's hair. "Far stronger than me. I am utterly in awe of you sometimes. Yes, my love, I think you need help with that. And I've never loved you more than right now."

Rye tentatively glanced up. "Yeah? Even though I'm...I'm some violent freak? A head-case?"

"You're not a freak. I'm no expert, but I don't think we have to delve too deeply to see where things went a little astray for you." Flora slipped her arms around Rye's waist to give her a reassuring squeeze. "I'm sure someone can help you. We can start the ball rolling straight away."

"You think I can get counselling in prison?"

"It may not come to that, with extenuating circumstances and a first time offence. I've been assured that it's not as bleak as it may appear."

"But it's going to kill any chance of getting my citizenship through refugee status," Rye said. "That's what they said at immigration. About a criminal record."

"We can talk with Mr. Summerbank about it," Flora said. "But I was hoping you wouldn't need to apply as a refugee."

Rye frowned. "Babe, they're not just going to let me stay."

"They will if you marry me."

Rye blinked. "What?"

"Marry me. Why do you look so shocked?"

"Marry you?"

"Of course. We love each other. We both want to spend the rest of our lives together. We're determined to make our relationship work. Is that not what marriage is all about?"

"But—" Rye frowned and shook her head.

"But, what? Are you about to say something stupid?"

Rye didn't know what she was going to say. Marry Flora? Rye frowned down at the second button of Flora's blouse without a single erotic thought in her head. Without any thought in her head.

"Stay with me. Be with me. Always. Crazy in love. My budmate."

"You...you'd do that for me?"

Flora looked incredulous. "Do what? You make it sound like self-sacrifice. This is what I want. To be honest, since I'm guessing it would be hard to frighten you any more at this point, it's what I've wanted since the first weeks of our affair. This is not a quickie wedding to beat immigration. We have plenty of evidence of that. Some supplied by a certain magazine."

"You want to marry me? Despite—"

"I wouldn't let you get away from me even if they extradite you to Fairyland. I'd follow. I'd find a way. Barefoot, if necessary. On the other hand, you being married to a United Forestlands citizen will throw a rather substantial stick in the works of that proceeding."

Rye shook her head. Nothing seemed quite real. Too good to be true.

"Lover," Flora said, "I want to be with you and have your babies and—"

"Babies?"

Flora smiled. "Perhaps I'm getting a little ahead of myself. Oh, Rye, you're my budmate. Trust the buds. It's the oldest dryad saying."

"One of these days, you're going to have to explain this bud thing properly. I'm feeling like there's still a lot I'm missing."

"I promise." Flora looped her arms around Rye's neck and looked into Rye's eyes from close range. "Well? Will you?"

Rye felt another of those utterly calm moments brought on by an unexpected certainty. "Yes. Yes, I want to marry you."

Flora beamed and kissed her.

Rye might have liked to continue their embrace, but she heard Mr. Summerbank stifle a cough. She crashed back to an ugly reality that had everything to do with extraditions and prisons rather than loving embraces and lifetimes together for happy couples.

"I hope you don't mind a long engagement," Rye said.

"Actually, I wasn't planning on very long." Flora reached into the front of her blouse as she turned away. "Uncle Basil, would you mind?"

"Of course, Flora." Mr. Summerbank stood and slid a green form from a folder.

Rye frowned. "Babe, if they send me back to—"

"Hold out your hand."

Flora looped her thin gold neck chain over her head. She unhooked the chain and let the pendant slide into Rye's palm. Only it wasn't a pendant. They were two matching gold rings.

"I couldn't bring my purse in here," Flora said. "Do you like them? I had to guess your size. A friend designed and made them. They're probably a bit too arty farty for you. We can choose different ones later if you hate them."

Rye was too astonished with the wider implication to form much of an opinion about rings.

Mr. Summerbank tapped on the far door and asked the guard to step inside.

"Witnesses," Flora said. "We need two."

"Now?" Rye said. "We're going to get married right now?"

"Yes," Flora said.

"But...but don't we need to—"

"Mr. Summerbank has the licence. I applied for it a few days ago. Just in case. He's registered as a celebrant." Flora's smile faltered. "Am I being too pushy again?"

"A bit. A lot. Yeah."

Rye turned to see Mr. Summerbank asking the female guard to step inside.

"I suppose this is something you're just going to have to get used to," Flora said.

Rye stared at her. Flora smiled and put a hand on the side of Rye's face.

"I love you," Flora said. "I promise I'll work on my pushiness. Okay?"

Mr. Summerbank halted near them and smiled. "Are we ready?"

"Don't work too hard on it," Rye said to Flora. "I think I need it sometimes."

Flora smiled broadly as she slipped her hand into Rye's. It was a great way to start a wedding ceremony, even one conducted in an interview room at the Scrub Street Detention Centre.

Chapter Twenty-Three

Rye fingered the ring on her thumb. She had done that a lot in the last three days. It was the only tangible evidence she had that she had not dreamed about marrying Flora. This was a wedding ring with some weird engraving twining around it. And too big for her proper finger. But it was the ring that Flora had pushed onto her finger when Mr. Summerbank married them.

Married. To Flora. Surely that was a dream?

Although, had it been a dream, Rye would not have spent their wedding night, and the two following ones, alone in a cell. Her imagination would also have dispensed with broken wing and arm. Both would hamper consummating their marriage.

The door lock whirred and the door swung open.

"Out you come, Woods," the guard said.

Rye obediently stepped outside. "What is it?"

"Your lawyer."

Rye hoped that this meant her lawyer and Flora. She had expected Flora to visit her. Surely, now that they were married, they'd be allowed to see each other?

The guard turned left at the end of the corridor instead of right.

"Aren't we going the wrong way?" Rye said.

"Nope. Trust me, Woods, I've worked here fifteen years. I know my way around."

The unprecedented burst of loquacity surprised Rye.

They herded her into a room where Mr. Vervain, the young lawyer, waited.

"Good afternoon, Mrs. Woods," he said.

"Um. Hello. Yeah, I guess I am."

"Allow me to offer my congratulations," he said.

"Um. Thanks. What is this about? You need to take more photographs of my wings and back?"

"No, Mrs. Woods. I'm here to facilitate your release."

Rye blinked. "Release?"

"Yes. The repatriation request was declined. I have a copy of the full text of the adjudicator's response and reasoning for you."

Rye thanked him automatically. She couldn't quite believe what she was hearing. "Is this because I'm married to Flora?"

"No, ma'am. Although, that did complicate the case for the applicants. The adjudicator drew heavily on the suffering you expected should you be returned. It was your evidence, Mrs. Woods, which determined the case."

Rye put her hand to her chest because she needed to feel something, to make sure she wasn't dreaming.

"Now," Vervain said, "this brings us to the criminal charges against you."

"Oh. Right." This wasn't a dream after all. "What happens?"

"We'll need to build a defence," he said. "First, though, would you like to be released on bail?"

"I get a choice? Does anyone ever say no?"

He smiled. "Your wife has asked me to ask you if you have any problems with her posting the bail for you."

Rye grinned. "No. I don't have a problem with that."

"I'm relieved to hear it. I had no relish for passing on the message Mrs. Withe asked me to convey in the event you declined."

Rye smiled and signed the forms he offered her. She was very tempted to ask how much the bail was, but resisted. She had promised Flora that she would work on her problem with money. Now was a good time to start. And it wasn't as though she was going to run away and cause Flora to forfeit the bond. She had run away from her problems for the last time.

The guard took her through to another room where they brought out a bag containing her possessions. She had to sign for them before struggling to dress in her own clothes. The guard helped her.

Vervain waited for her on the other side of the last barred doorway. He and a guard accompanied Rye to a sturdy door. It opened to the outside. She stepped out and looked up. Sky. Sunlight.

"This way, Mrs. Woods," Vervain said.

He indicated a guard post beside a gate. As she walked toward it, Rye saw a taxi carpet on the other side. And Flora. Rye smiled and walked faster. The guard passed them through. Rye trotted down the steps and walked into Flora's embrace.

Flora was laughing and crying at the same time. Rye just wanted to hold her.

Flora broke off to offer her thanks and her hand to Mr. Vervain. Rye assured him that she would remember to report in to the police tomorrow.

Finally, Flora and Rye climbed into the back of the taxi. Flora instructed the driver to fly them to Whiterow Gardens.

"I could've come in my carpet," Flora said. "Except, I want to touch you and concentrate on you."

"Thank you for bailing me out."

Flora looked expectant. Rye guessed she was waiting for some comment about the amount of money, and for Rye to say how she could never pay it back. Instead, Rye bent to kiss her long and deeply. Flora's arms slipped up around Rye.

"Mmm," Flora said. "I've never kissed a married woman before."

"Me neither. I think I could get used to it."

Flora smiled. "You don't mind? No regrets, now that you've had time to think about it?"

"I love you. More than anything."

Flora's hands became a little more exploratory as if she, too, needed the reassurance of touch to convince her that this was real. "Elm, I've missed you."

"Mind the wing, babe. Fey, you are a dream."

Flora smiled and pulled Rye's head down for another long, hot kiss. "You taste nice. But you need a shower."

"Or a bath. I'd need help. With this arm."

"I think it must be my wifely duty to scrub your back. And other bits."

The driver coughed.

Rye sharply glanced at him and her cheeks warmed with a blush. Flora put a hand to her mouth but failed to stifle giggles.

Rye tried to settle as comfortably as she could between accommodating her broken wing and wanting to be in constant contact with Flora. She clasped Flora's hand as if she would never let it go. Flora snuggled against her. Rye rested her cheek against Flora's hair and smelled that faint trace of pine sap. Oddly, that small touch finally convinced her that she really was with Flora and not still back in her cell dreaming. Rye reverently pressed a gentle kiss to one of the knotty buds in Flora's hair. Just when everything seemed right, she realised something was missing.

"Where's Holls?" Rye asked.

"Waiting for you at home," Flora said. "I asked her if she wanted to come, but she said she'd rather wait."

Rye frowned. "Fey. She must hate me a lot."

"Hate you?" Flora straightened to study Rye's face. "Why?"

"Because of…um…what she heard about me. At the hearing."

Flora stroked Rye's jaw with the back of her fingers. "I have a confession to make. I outed you to Holly before the hearing. It was unavoidable with her living with me and the discussions we had with the lawyers. Now, I'd hate to be one of those wives who says 'I told you so', but I did tell you that Holly had probably guessed about you. About us. And I was right. It was neither news nor shocking. She thinks it's scathing that we're a couple. Or were. Which reminds me."

Flora released Rye so that she could rummage in her purse.

"I didn't mean about being gay," Rye said. "Well, I suppose I did. But not mainly."

Flora pulled her ring out of her purse and offered it to Rye. Rye accepted it with a frown.

"I haven't been wearing it." Flora held her hand up. "I think you have to be the one to tell Holly that we're married."

"Oh. Right."

Rye awkwardly pushed the ring on Flora's finger. Flora finished settling it into place and kissed Rye.

"So, what else are you fretting about?" Flora said.

"Um." Rye scowled down at their joined hands. "Mother."

"Oh. Lover, I don't think—"

"I did it. Right in front of Holls when she was a little kid. I think I hit mother with a stick. It must have been. I remember dropping it. I suppose I should've told you before we got married."

"Was this one of those times when you went blank?"

Rye frowned at the patched knees of her pants. "The first, I think.

I can remember what happened before it and afterward. I can't recall actually doing it. But I must have. I'm sorry."

Flora was quiet for a long time. Each moment was an agony for Rye. Rye could understand if Flora wanted to distance herself from a killer.

"Holly hasn't said anything to me about this." Flora tightened her clasp on Rye's hand. "Darling, I think it's a miracle that you didn't kill more people on your way out of Fairyland. I don't blame you for this. It doesn't make me love you less. It can't be easy for you to carry around. Which is why I think it would be so good for you to talk to a professional about your past. And get some things sorted out. To get some resolution for your sake. We can find you a therapist as soon as you feel up to it."

Rye nodded. Her fingers closed more tightly on Flora's hand. "Yeah. I need to. Before I do anything else."

"I'm guessing that this is something you're going to find tremendously difficult." Flora stroked Rye's cheek. "But you're about the strongest person I know. And I'll be with you every step of the way. Neither of us imagined this was going to be like one of those stories where the heroines get married and live happily ever after. Did we? We know we have issues to work out. Both of us. But we're going to do it, aren't we? Together."

"Yeah."

"Kiss me."

"You're wonderful."

"You're not so bad yourself."

Rye and Flora were still cuddled close when the taxi pulled up on the penthouse parking pad at Whiterow Gardens.

Flora gave Rye a reassuring smile before opening the door. Rye felt strange walking into Flora's apartment. The last time she had been here, she had broken off their relationship and run away. Oddly, she could hear the jarring beat of Holly's crash music.

"Holly!" Flora shouted. "We're home."

Rye followed Flora around the corridor. Holly came bounding to meet them. Rye felt a spurt of unease. Would the kid reject her? Hate her?

Holly threw her arms around Rye and hugged her far too enthusiastically for Rye's broken wing. Rye grunted but bore the discomfort. She felt perilously close to tears. She gave Holly a quick kiss on the cheek. Holly astounded Rye when she reciprocated.

"You've looked better," Holly said. "And you reek!"

"Yeah. I haven't had a shower for a while."

"We thought you were going to die," Holly said. "When wc saw you in the infirmary. They said it was some weird reaction to something they pumped in you."

"You visited me?"

"Of course. Me and Flora. Brought you flowers, too. Except they wouldn't let them in the room, because they weren't sure what your freaky system was doing. We had to put on these gown things, like sheets, before we could go in and see you."

"No one told me that you'd been."

"Those grunts beat the shit out of you, didn't they?"

"Language," Rye said. "And don't call the police grunts."

"Time inside hasn't changed you at all, has it?"

"I was in a detention centre," Rye said. "Not prison. And you shouldn't have that music up so loud. Flora isn't used to annoying teenagers blasting—"

"Flora doesn't mind," Holly said. "Do you?"

"Flora is going to make tea," Flora said. "Why don't you two go and sit in the lounge? I think you have things to say to each other."

Rye cast her a dark look. Flora smiled sweetly and strolled away to the kitchen door.

When Rye perched on one of the sofas, Holly slumped beside her.

"How are you doing, Holls?" Rye said. "I was worried about you."

Holly shrugged. "Flora has been scathing. She said that lawyer would get you out. Are you going to be a refugee, too? And, hey, Rye, Flora talked with the people who run the scholarships and some of them let me put in a late application! It would've been nice to have been able to tell you that I've got one when you came home."

Rye frowned. "You applied? Already? You've got your ident number?"

Holly nodded.

"You're...you're a citizen?" Rye said.

"Yeah. Came through yesterday. I'm all legal. The lawyers rushed it all through and breathed down people's necks."

Rye beamed and awkwardly reached to give Holly a one-armed hug. She blinked back tears.

"You pleased?" Holly said.

"This is the best news I've had in a long time."

"But you knew that Flora had offered to adopt me, didn't you? Just in case they wanted to chuck me back to the fairy freaks."

"Yes, I know she did. But I'm glad she didn't have to. For her sake."

Holly stuck her tongue out.

Rye grinned. The idea of the size of the lawyer's bill tugged at the edges of her thinking. Rye tried to ignore it. She and Flora would work something out.

"Um." Holly suddenly took a strong interest in picking at a thread in her pants' leg. "If you're bounced about me being a refugee and you getting out of the slammer, I guess now would be a good time for me to...um. About getting drunk. I guess it was pretty stupid."

"Oh, yes. We need to talk about that."

"Look, before you get knotted, I know it was stupid. I just said so, didn't I?"

"Drinking and drugs? What, in the name of the Almighty King and Queen of the Fey, did you think you—"

"Rye! I've admitted my idiocy. Okay? What more do you want? I realise I fucked up."

"Language!"

"Sorry. Look, I was only trying to help."

"By getting yourself arrested?" Rye said.

"No! Fey. I don't know why I bother trying."

Holly stood. Rye grabbed her wrist and tugged her back down.

"Okay," Rye said. "You talk. I'll listen. Just make it good."

Holly glowered. "I thought I was helping. I thought those burrower kids would be able to sell me an ident number. They gave me a drink. One thing led to another—" She shrugged. "I didn't expect to end up with the grunts. Or to get you into so much trouble. I'm...I'm sorry. Okay?"

Rye had a hundred things she wanted to say, the first being that everything was not okay. But Holly had apologised. She said she realised that she had made mistakes. Would there be much point ramming it down her throat?

"Did you have a hangover?" Rye asked.

Holly looked up, surprised. "Yeah. It was deathly."

Rye smiled and patted Holly's leg. "We all do stupid things. The idea is not to do the same stupid thing twice. Okay?"

"Okay."

Flora entered with a tray. She set it down on the coffee table closest to Rye and Holly. Holly wriggled forward to pour the tea.

"Have you told her?" Flora asked.

"Um," Rye said. "We were talking about Holly."

"Told me what?" Holly said.

Rye looked imploringly at Flora. Flora picked up a cup of tea and raised her eyebrow at Rye. Rye frowned down at her hand in her lap, the hand with the ring on it.

"Is it good?" Holly said. "Hey! Did you hear about one of my scholarships? Is that it?"

"Um," Rye said. "No. Um. Holls. You know that—"

"Here." Holly handed Rye a cup of tea.

"Oh. Thanks." One-handed, Rye didn't quite know what to do with it. She balanced the saucer on her thigh. "Um. Thing is, Holls. It's...um. Well, it's sort of...um."

"Wow," Holly said. "This must be really important. You haven't been this incoherent since you told me about sex."

Rye blushed. She glanced up to see Flora imperfectly hiding a smile behind her cup.

"It's sort of along those lines," Rye said.

"You're giving me sex education in instalments?" Holly said.

Flora choked out a chuckle. Rye glared up at her. Flora bit her lip but her shoulders shook.

"The thing is," Rye said. "Um...you know that...well, Flora said that you know that...um, that I'm gay."

"Yeah, so?" Holly slumped with a disgusted look. "Is that it? The big news?"

Rye frowned and shifted. She nearly tipped tea all over herself, so she reached across to set the cup and saucer on the table. "The thing is—"

"Holy shit!" Holly grabbed Rye's good wrist. "Rye! You didn't! You did! That's a wedding ring. Oh, that is so utterly, utterly scathing! I never thought you'd do it in a zillion years!"

Rye watched, stupefied, as Holly leaped to her feet to envelop Flora in a hug.

"You're not displeased, then?" Flora asked.

"This is the best thing ever!" Holly said. "Wow. That means we're sisters-in-law, doesn't it? My mind is melting."

Flora smiled down at Rye.

"That means we'll be living here, not going back to our cruddy apartment," Holly said. "Astronomical! Can I keep that room beside the bathroom? And use the pool whenever I like? I can't believe it. My life just got great! Can I invite Daisy over? She'll gnaw her leg off with envy!"

Rye sat stunned.

"Can I see your ring?" Holly peered at Flora's hand. "This is too scathing. Does Rye's match?"

"They're not exact copies," Flora said. "They're complementary. Slightly different patterns which make a harmonious whole when you put them together."

"You picked them," Holly said. "When did you do the deed? This morning?"

"Um. We got married three days ago," Rye said. "In the detention centre."

"I'm her prison bride," Flora said. "That'll be something fun to tell the grandchildren. And my mother."

Rye scowled. Flora smiled and sat down beside Rye. She clasped Rye's good hand between hers.

"I bet you asked Rye," Holly said.

"Does it matter?" Flora said.

"You know, I've never seen you hold hands before," Holly said. "But it was so utterly obvious that you were gone on each other."

"You're...um. You're okay with it, then?" Rye said.

Holly rolled her eyes. "No, Rye, I am not okay with it. There are not two letters in the whole alphabet to describe how scathing I think it is that you and Flora are married."

Flora mouthed "I told you so" at Rye. Rye couldn't help grinning. She lifted her hand to kiss the back of Flora's fingers.

"That's my cue to leave," Holly said. "I'll be in my room with my music on. Won't see or hear a thing, guys."

Rye blushed hotly as she watched Holly stroll out through the side door. Flora laughed.

"Elm, I adore you," Flora said. "We have a few things to work out, you and I, but I know we're going to make it. And life with you is not going to be dull."

Rye didn't feel like she was standing on firm ground yet. But there were two things she was certain of. "I love you. There's nowhere I'd rather be than with you."

Flora wriggled closer. Rye glanced at the doorway, just to make sure they were alone, before she kissed Flora.

About the Author

L-J Baker lives in New Zealand. She is happily wed in a civil union. Her educational background is in the physical sciences. This is ideal preparation for writing fantasy, because she strongly subscribes to the theory that, to be able to convincingly portray a new world, you need to have a few clues how the real one works. Most of *Broken Wings* was written while she had a cat appropriately named Troll sprawled in her lap.

You can find more information about L-J and her fiction, including her published and forthcoming short stories, novels, and e-books, on her webpage:

http://homepages.ihug.co.nz/~wordchutney/index.html

Books Available From Bold Strokes Books

Sleep of Reason by Rose Beecham. Nothing is at it seems when Detective Jude Devine finds herself caught up in a small-town soap opera. And her rocky relationship with forensic pathologist Dr. Mercy Westmoreland just got a lot harder. (1-933110-53-8)

Passion's Bright Fury by Radclyffe. When a trauma surgeon and a filmmaker become reluctant allies on the battleground between life and death, passion strikes without warning. (1-933110-54-6)

Broken Wings by L-J Baker. When Rye Woods, a fairy, meets the beautiful dryad Flora Withe, her libido, as squashed and hidden as her wings, reawakens along with her heart. (1-933110-55-4)

Combust the Sun by Andrews & Austin. A Richfield and Rivers mystery set in L.A. Murder among the stars. (1-933110-52-X)

Of Drag Kings and the Wheel of Fate by Susan Smith. A blind date in a drag club leads to an unlikely romance. (1-933110-51-1)

Tristaine Rises by Cate Culpepper. Brenna, Jesstin, and the Amazons of Tristaine face their greatest challenge for survival. (1-933110-50-3)

Too Close to Touch by Georgia Beers. Kylie O'Brien believes in true love and is willing to wait for it. It doesn't matter one damn bit that Gretchen, her new and off-limits boss, has a voice as rich and smooth as melted chocolate. It absolutely doesn't. (1-933110-47-3)

The 100th Generation by Justine Saracen. Ancient curses, modern day villains, and a most intriguing woman who keeps appearing when least expected lead Archeologist Valerie Foret on the adventure of her life. (1-933110-48-1)

Battle for Tristaine by Cate Culpepper. While Brenna struggles to find her place in the clan and the love between her and Jess grows, Tristaine is threatened with destruction. Second in the Tristaine series. (1-933110-49-X)

The Traitor and the Chalice by Jane Fletcher. Without allies to help them, Tevi and Jemeryl will have to risk all in the race to uncover the traitor and retrieve the chalice. The Lyremouth Chronicles Book Two. (1-933110-43-0)

Promising Hearts by Radclyffe. Dr. Vance Phelps lost everything in the War Between the States and arrives in New Hope, Montana with no hope of happiness and no desire for anything except forgetting—until she meets Mae, a frontier madam. (1-933110-44-9)

Carly's Sound by Ali Vali. Poppy Valente and Julia Johnson form a bond of friendship that lays the foundation for something more, until Poppy's past comes back to haunt her—literally. A poignant romance about love and renewal. (1-933110-45-7)

Unexpected Sparks by Gina L. Dartt. Falling in love is complicated enough without adding murder to the mix. Kate Shannon's growing feelings for much younger Nikki Harris are challenging enough without the mystery of a fatal fire that Kate can't ignore. (1-933110-46-5)

Whitewater Rendezvous by Kim Baldwin. Two women on a wilderness kayak adventure—Chaz Herrick, a laid-back outdoorswoman, and Megan Maxwell, a workaholic news executive—discover that true love may be nothing at all like they imagined. (1-933110-38-4)

Erotic Interludes 3: Lessons in Love ed. by Radclyffe and Stacia Seaman. Sign on for a class in love…the best lesbian erotica writers take us to "school." (1-933110-39-2)

Punk Like Me by JD Glass. Twenty-one year old Nina writes lyrics and plays guitar in the rock band, Adam's Rib, and she doesn't always play by the rules. And, oh yeah—she has a way with the girls. (1-933110-40-6)

Coffee Sonata by Gun Brooke. Four women whose lives unexpectedly intersect in a small town by the sea share one thing in common—they all have secrets. (1-933110-41-4)

The Clinic: Tristaine Book One by Cate Culpepper. Brenna, a prison medic, finds herself deeply conflicted by her growing feelings for her patient, Jesstin, a wild and rebellious warrior reputed to be descended from ancient Amazons. (1-933110-42-2)

Forever Found by JLee Meyer. Can time, tragedy, and shattered trust destroy a love that seemed destined? When chance reunites two childhood friends separated by tragedy, the past resurfaces to determine the shape of their future. (1-933110-37-6)

Sword of the Guardian by Merry Shannon. Princess Shasta's bold new bodyguard has a secret that could change both of their lives. He is actually a *she*. A passionate romance filled with courtly intrigue, chivalry, and devotion. (1-933110-36-8)

Wild Abandon by Ronica Black. From their first tumultuous meeting, Dr. Chandler Brogan and Officer Sarah Monroe are drawn together by their common obsessions—sex, speed, and danger. (1-933110-35-X)

Turn Back Time by Radclyffe. Pearce Rifkin and Wynter Thompson have nothing in common but a shared passion for surgery. They clash at every opportunity, especially when matters of the heart are suddenly at stake. (1-933110-34-1)

Chance by Grace Lennox. At twenty-six, Chance Delaney decides her life isn't working so she swaps it for a different one. What follows is the sexy, funny, touching story of two women who, in finding themselves, also find one another. (1-933110-31-7)

The Exile and the Sorcerer by Jane Fletcher. First in the Lyremouth Chronicles. Tevi, wounded and adrift, arrives in the courtyard of a shy young sorcerer. Together they face monsters, magic, and the challenge of loving despite their differences. (1-933110-32-5)

A Matter of Trust by Radclyffe. JT Sloan is a cybersleuth who doesn't like attachments. Michael Lassiter is leaving her husband, and she needs Sloan's expertise to safeguard her company. It should just be business—but it turns into much more. (1-933110-33-3)

Sweet Creek by Lee Lynch. A celebration of the enduring nature of love, friendship, and community in the quirky, heart-warming lesbian community of Waterfall Falls. (1-933110-29-5)

The Devil Inside by Ali Vali. Derby Cain Casey, head of a New Orleans crime organization, runs the family business with guts and grit, and no one crosses her. No one, that is, until Emma Verde claims her heart and turns her world upside down. (1-933110-30-9)

Grave Silence by Rose Beecham. Detective Jude Devine's investigation of a series of ritual murders is complicated by her torrid affair with the golden girl of Southwestern forensic pathology, Dr. Mercy Westmoreland. (1-933110-25-2)

Honor Reclaimed by Radclyffe. In the aftermath of 9/11, Secret Service Agent Cameron Roberts and Blair Powell close ranks with a trusted few to find the would-be assassins who nearly claimed Blair's life. (1-933110-18-X)

Honor Bound by Radclyffe. Secret Service Agent Cameron Roberts and Blair Powell face political intrigue, a clandestine threat to Blair's safety, and the seemingly irreconcilable personal differences that force them ever farther apart. (1-933110-20-1)

Protector of the Realm: Supreme Constellations Book One by Gun Brooke. A space adventure filled with suspense and a daring intergalactic romance featuring Commodore Rae Jacelon and a stunning, but decidedly lethal, Kellen O'Dal. (1-933110-26-0)

Innocent Hearts by Radclyffe. In a wild and unforgiving land, two women learn about love, passion, and the wonders of the heart. (1-933110-21-X)

The Temple at Landfall by Jane Fletcher. An imprinter, one of Celaeno's most revered servants of the Goddess, is also a prisoner to the faith—until a Ranger frees her by claiming her heart. The Celaeno series. (1-933110-27-9)

Force of Nature by Kim Baldwin. From tornados to forest fires, the forces of nature conspire to bring Gable McCoy and Erin Richards close to danger, and closer to each other. (1-933110-23-6)

In Too Deep by Ronica Black. Undercover homicide cop Erin McKenzie tracks a femme fatale who just might be a real killer…with love and danger hot on her heels. (1-933110-17-1)

Erotic Interludes 2: Stolen Moments by Stacia Seaman and Radclyffe, eds. Love on the run, in the office, in the shadows…Fast, furious, and almost too hot to handle. (1-933110-16-3)

Course of Action by Gun Brooke. Actress Carolyn Black desperately wants the starring role in an upcoming film produced by Annelie Peterson. Just how far will she go for the dream part of a lifetime? (1-933110-22-8)

Rangers at Roadsend by Jane Fletcher. Sergeant Chip Coppelli has learned to spot trouble coming, and that is exactly what she sees in her new recruit, Katryn Nagata. The Celaeno series. (1-933110-28-7)

Justice Served by Radclyffe. Lieutenant Rebecca Frye and her lover, Dr. Catherine Rawlings, embark on a deadly game of hide-and-seek with an underworld kingpin who traffics in human souls. (1-933110-15-5)

Distant Shores, Silent Thunder by Radclyffe. Doctor Tory King—and the women who love her—is forced to examine the boundaries of love, friendship, and the ties that transcend time. (1-933110-08-2)

Hunter's Pursuit by Kim Baldwin. A raging blizzard, a mountain hideaway, and a killer-for-hire set a scene for disaster—or desire—when Katarzyna Demetrious rescues a beautiful stranger. (1-933110-09-0)

The Walls of Westernfort by Jane Fletcher. All Temple Guard Natasha Ionadis wants is to serve the Goddess—until she falls in love with one of the rebels she is sworn to destroy. The Celaeno series. (1-933110-24-4)

Erotic Interludes: ***Change of Pace*** by Radclyffe. Twenty-five hot-wired encounters guaranteed to spark more than just your imagination. Erotica as you've always dreamed of it. (1-933110-07-4)

Honor Guards by Radclyffe. In a wild flight for their lives, the president's daughter and those who are sworn to protect her wage a desperate struggle for survival. (1-933110-01-5)

Fated Love by Radclyffe. Amidst the chaos and drama of a busy emergency room, two women must contend not only with the fragile nature of life, but also with the irresistible forces of fate. (1-933110-05-8)

Justice in the Shadows by Radclyffe. In a shadow world of secrets and lies, Detective Sergeant Rebecca Frye and her lover, Dr. Catherine Rawlings, join forces in the elusive search for justice.(1-933110-03-1)

shadowland by Radclyffe. In a world on the far edge of desire, two women are drawn together by power, passion, and dark pleasures. An erotic romance. (1-933110-11-2)

Love's Masquerade by Radclyffe. Plunged into the indistinguishable realms of fiction, fantasy, and hidden desires, Auden Frost is forced to question all she believes about the nature of love. (1-933110-14-7)

Love & Honor by Radclyffe. The president's daughter and her lover are faced with difficult choices as they battle a tangled web of Washington intrigue for...love and honor. (1-933110-10-4)

Beyond the Breakwater by Radclyffe. One Provincetown summer three women learn the true meaning of love, friendship, and family. (1-933110-06-6)

Tomorrow's Promise by Radclyffe. One timeless summer, two very different women discover the power of passion to heal and the promise of hope that only love can bestow. (1-933110-12-0)

Love's Tender Warriors by Radclyffe. Two women who have accepted loneliness as a way of life learn that love is worth fighting for and a battle they cannot afford to lose. (1-933110-02-3)

Love's Melody Lost by Radclyffe. A secretive artist with a haunted past and a young woman escaping a life that has proved to be a lie find their destinies entwined. (1-933110-00-7)

Safe Harbor by Radclyffe. A mysterious newcomer, a reclusive doctor, and a troubled gay teenager learn about love, friendship, and trust during one tumultuous summer in Provincetown. (1-933110-13-9)

Above All, Honor by Radclyffe. Secret Service Agent Cameron Roberts fights her desire for the one woman she can't have—Blair Powell, the daughter of the president of the United States. (1-933110-04-X)